MW00447031

MARGARET GUMM
AND
THE SONG OF SOLOMON

BY

DEREK ANDERSON

Margaret Gumm and the Song of Solomon
© 2016 Derek C. Anderson
Cover design and artwork by Tommy Anderson

All Rights Reserved. This book or any portion thereof may not be reproduced or used in any matter without prior written permission of the publisher, except as provided by the United States of America copyright law.

To JMA III

For showing me how to imagine great things

CHAPTER ONE – THE DAY OF THE DOMINION

Every fortune hunter and adventurer in the past fifty years would tell you that Gaston Gumm was the most important man they'd ever met in their lives. "The Great Explorer" they called him, and every one of them had a story. A *Gaston Gumm story*. Some incredible act he did, whether it was saving a single life or an entire town, discovering something amazing or stopping someone evil and deadly. To them, the small, chubby man with a square nose and knobby knees was as famous as any movie star and as important as a President or Prime Minister. But to the rest of the world, Gaston Gumm was nobody. Just the way Gumm liked it.

His admirers believed he could do amazing things that other men simply could not, but Gumm never hesitated to tell them they were "full of beans" and that he was no different than anyone else. "Greatness," Gumm always said, "is born from insignificance, so control the little matters, and leave the big ones to fate. This is the key to everything. Master this and you'll master the world." It was the last thing he told his two brightest students, Wilbert Johnson and his wife Laura, before he died.

Laura Johnson was never reckless when it came to shopping; she was fastidious to a fault, coupon clipping, watching for sales and bargains. But she found herself on one May afternoon dancing and singing through the aisles of a grocery store, loading her cart with every type of junk food imaginable. She took a bag of Cheetos from a shelf, stared it down, and kissed it.

"Simmy," she whispered to the bag. "We've won. I don't have to hide anymore. I can show you everything!"

She gave the bag of Cheetos a strong hug until it burst with a – –POP! — sending cheese puffs flying in every direction. It seemed to awaken Laura from her trance and she noticed other shoppers staring at her. She grinned, dropped the Cheetos bag back on the shelf, and hurried past them.

Cheetos were the favorite snack of Laura's youngest daughter, Simone, who was just like her mother: energetic, spunky, and forever happy to be alive. Laura hadn't seen Simone in weeks and missed her.

An old family photo was out of Laura's purse and into her hands before she realized it. There was Simone, front and center, with her big silly grin, missing her two front teeth. Aiden, her eldest, was looking moody as ever, as was Flair, wearing a scowl along with her button-up sundress. Laura grinned. Flair, a tomboy back then, threw the biggest tantrum when they insisted she wear that dress. Now, Flair had dozens of dresses and knew every fashion designer in the world. Children and how they change.

There was frantic rapping on the front window and Laura turned. Her husband was outside, beckoning her, looking nervous, never a good thing. Laura left her cart and rushed outside to the parking lot. Wilbert took her by the arm, steering her towards the passenger side of a gray sedan.

"They found us," Wilbert said. "They're here in Canterbury Springs."

Laura looked stunned. "But how? And I don't have—" Laura stammered. "Wilby, I left my gloves at Mom's."

"It's too late now," Wilbert said. "Just get in!"

Both doors slammed shut. Wilbert's foot smashed on the gas pedal and the sedan leapt the curb, speeding off down the street.

For the next hour, the couple rode in silence, never taking their eyes off of their rearview mirrors. No one was following them. The highway had been empty for miles. Finally, Wilbert and Laura stared at each other, sighed in relief, and Wilbert's foot eased off the gas pedal. They were safe.

"Contact Art and Summer," Laura said. "They need to know about this."

"What about Nick and Lydia?" Wilbert asked, and his voice carried a hint of anger.

"I'm not sure what to tell them," Laura said. "We don't know enough."

"You don't? Well, I do."

"No, Wilby, we're not making the mistake everyone else makes. We'll get back to Granny's and…"

CRUUNNCCH!!!

Out of nowhere, something massive struck the sedan. The world spun and there was an explosion of noise: screeching wheels, crunching metal, shattering glass, and then silence.

Wilbert stirred, blinking his eyes. It took him a moment to realize he had blacked out. But for how long? Seconds or minutes? He wasn't sure. He stared through his spider-webbed windshield at the smoking, dented hood of a black SUV. To his right, Laura brushed glass from her blonde hair into a deflated airbag in her lap.

His mind was swimming in an ocean of confusion. He was trying to refocus, trying to remember. *Where had they been? What was happening?*

That's right. *They* were coming. *The Goon Squad.*

Call Art and Summer, Wilbert's mind thought, but his hands weren't reacting fast enough. He fumbled for his cell phone when…*What was that? Doors slamming? No, no, not now…Laura doesn't have her gloves…. But maybe it's not them…Maybe this is only a car accident.*

The car jerked violently; a wrenching sound followed. Through the shattered glass, Wilbert saw two monstrous men tearing barehanded through the sedan as if it were plastic. The passenger door was ripped from its hinges and flung like a Frisbee by a behemoth with swollen arms thicker than a man's body. A red and black tattoo reading MUSCLEHEAD stretched down his left arm. The brute yanked Laura from the car, throwing her through the air like a toy doll. She landed with a thud near the back of the SUV.

The other man, tall, skinny, with ridiculous arms that hung past his knees leapt onto the hood of the car. A stiff breeze swept his long trench coat behind him as he tipped his squashed fedora hat to Wilbert. His skin was yellow, matching his teeth.

"At last," the skinny man cackled, and he promptly punched a hole through the roof of the sedan. "The elusive Wilbert Johnson!" He peeled open the jagged edges, reaching inside for Wilbert.

With a yelp, the long-armed Goon yanked his hand back through the hole, but was unable to avoid what was coming. A long, metal rod charged with electricity burst through, striking the skinny man in the chest. His spindly frame flew from the car and crashed to the concrete.

"Lanky!" Musclehead said, sneering and turning towards his comrade. "Need some help?"

"Shut up!" Lanky growled, rolling onto his back.

Wilbert stumbled out of the car, rushing to get to Lanky before Lanky could stand. With a push of a button, his electrified metal rod stretched into a six-foot long bo staff. Lanky drew a bo staff of his own, quickly deflecting Wilbert's attack, but another swift strike caught the Goon in the stomach. Lanky's body shuddered as it was electrified.

Lanky recovered quickly, twisted his staff, and razor sharp blades jutted out from both ends. Wilbert had to backpedal as Lanky sprang to his feet and went on the offensive. He knew Lanky was no slouch when it came to fighting. Not only did he possess superhuman strength, he was good with that bladed staff and could easily take his head off if he wasn't careful.

But Wilbert was blessed with uncanny speed. Blocking a barrage of blows from Lanky, his electrified staff connected with a hard roundhouse flush on the brute's jaw. Lanky spun on the spot and collapsed, down for the count.

Wilbert turned around, searching the highway. It was empty, except for a white SUV that just pulled up. Wilbert's blood went cold.

"Laura! Get up! Get out of here!" Wilbert yelled.

"Can't," she shouted back. "My leg's broken."

Musclehead stepped forward, towering over Wilbert, sneering. He grabbed the damaged SUV's hood, ripping it easily from the vehicle and crumpling it into a long metal club as if it were paper. Wilbert's breathing quickened; he glanced at the second SUV for a moment before turning his attention to Musclehead.

"There's a little road construction today, Wilbert," Musclehead laughed, pointing down the road with his crude weapon. "Road's blocked off ten miles in both directions, courtesy of me. It's just you, your wife, and us. So give it back," the muscular brute said, pounding the club into his free hand. "There's more on the way."

"A lotta Goons for two people," Wilbert replied.

"Oh, there's more than Goons coming," Musclehead said. "Tell me where it is, maybe *he'll* go easy on you."

Wilbert took in Musclehead's words as his eyes again darted towards the white SUV.

Musclehead smiled. "He don't get out much, Wilbert. But he made this special trip, just for you two."

"I guess I should be honored," Wilbert said.

"Ya really should hand it over. Ya got kids, go and tend to them," then with a smirk, "unless you want us to."

The remark got to Wilbert and he launched at the Goon. Musclehead was ready. He tore the smashed SUV's front wheel from the axle and deflected Wilbert's attacks, using the tire's rubber as a shield from the electricity.

Musclehead's defense was effortless, blocking each of Wilbert's blows with ease. After just dealing with Lanky, Wilbert felt fatigue setting in.

"Wilbert, you're getting' slow," Musclehead laughed. "Give it up, you wasn't keepin' it from us anyway. You got two daughters, don't cha? Ya want this to get personal?"

Wilbert didn't answer, he charged. Dropping to his knees, he avoided a swipe from Musclehead's metal club and kneecapped the Goon with the bo staff. Musclehead howled in pain as electricity surged through him. With Musclehead's defenses down, Wilbert struck with swift, viscous blows to each side of his ribcage. The giant collapsed, trembling.

"Slowing down?" Wilbert said in a cool voice before slamming the staff into Musclehead's chest, sending another painful shock of electricity through him. "I'm disappointed. You know better than to threaten my kids, Musclehead. This won't be pleasant..." And as he raised his staff over his head...

"Wilby! Look out!"

Wilbert turned at Laura's warning. The third stranger was across the road, a stocky man wearing a metallic green three-piece suit, with scuffed leather patches covering his elbows and knees. His hands were large, powerful, wrapped in white tape just over the knuckles, much like a boxer before the gloves go on. But the strangest thing he wore was a form-fitting black and green mask covering his entire head.

Wilbert grimaced. "Mr. Quick. I see they saved the best for last."

The masked man nodded to him. "Kind of you to say so, Wilbert," he replied. His voice was coarse, bitter, and full of hatred.

"It's been years."

"Has it?" Mr. Quick said, a slight hint of amusement. "Time is all a blur to me."

The two men paced a wide circle, staring down one another: Wilbert holding his bo staff at the ready, Mr. Quick stretching and shaking his arms to loosen them. Musclehead and Lanky had recovered from their beating, but they stood back and observed, like spectators watching a long anticipated face-off.

"No more wasted time, Wilbert," Mr. Quick said. "To business, then?"

They assumed fighting stances. Wilbert separated his staff into two batons. Mr. Quick retrieved a black and green bo staff of his own from underneath his jacket, spinning it nimbly between his fingers. Then, without a word, they launched at each other.

It was a battle to behold. Both men were swift, powerful, and agile; they dodged and ducked, predicting each other's moves like old sparring partners. Mr. Quick was living up to his name, and Wilbert was meeting the challenge. However, something unusual was happening with Mr. Quick's green suit. It seemed to swallow Wilbert's electric attacks, brightening each time it did.

Wilbert, stunned at this development, dodged a hailstorm of punches before one connected on his chin.

Mr. Quick's suit was glowing a brilliant, blazing green as Wilbert stumbled backward from the blow. To his dismay, Mr. Quick seemed to be getting faster. He barely deflected another onslaught, needing to shield his eyes from the steadily brightening suit. Mr. Quick flew at him again and Wilbert could do nothing to stop the four hammer shots to his jaw. He was flattened; his batons knocked away before he realized it.

Wilbert stood, wobbly and weaponless, and felt a roundhouse kick smash into his chest, knocking the wind out of him. He slumped to the ground like a lifeless doll. Lanky leapt into the air, pumping his fists.

"Told you, Musclehead!" Lanky whooped, pointing a hand in Musclehead's face. "I told you! Pay up!"

"Was there any doubt?" Mr. Quick said, turning towards them. Musclehead grumbled, slapping Lanky's hand with a wad of crumpled money.

The passenger door of the second SUV closed. Another man approached, examining Wilbert with curiosity. Unlike the Goons, this man looked mostly normal; a middle-aged businessman with dark brown hair, wearing a stylish sports coat and Oxford suede shoes. But he had one extraordinary item: the silver glove on his left hand, shining in the setting sun. His face looked pleasant, but something about his slow pace was menacing.

This was Mochtier Mackleford.

He stood in front of Wilbert, sighing with satisfaction. "At long last," Mackleford said, his voice traced with a hint of age and power. "The infamous Wilbert Johnson."

Wilbert didn't look up. "Mackleford. What brings you to Florida?"

Mackleford nodded to Lanky, who grabbed Wilbert and propped his back against the sedan, forcing him to face Mackleford.

"Wilbert," Mackleford said, "let's not waste the little time you and your wife have. Incidentally, an amazing performance against Mr. Quick. How old are you exactly?"

"Forty-five. How old are *you*, Mackleford?" Wilbert said.

Mackleford bristled at Wilbert's question for a moment, but then smiled benignly. "Twenty years ago, you would've been the ideal candidate for my program. The Squad said you were good. I didn't believe them until now."

"So how did you find us?" Wilbert asked.

Mackleford knelt, examining Wilbert's wounds, almost like a concerned father. "Should've been obvious," he replied.

Wilbert sighed. "It's always the same people stabbing us in the back."

"Saboteurs," Mackleford said, nodding. "We both suffer the same problems."

"Some of us don't understand the problems."

"And some of us are so blind, they can't see the truth," Mackleford said. "Wilbert, you're an intelligent man. Why fight us? What are you afraid of?"

"Men like you," Wilbert said, "killing and claiming it's for the best." He spat a wad of blood from his mouth and looked Mackleford in the eye. "You're a mad man, Mackleford, not the savior of mankind. Just make it quick, will you?"

"I'll determine how quick it will be," Mackleford said, tugging at his silver glove. "Let's begin with the million-dollar question. Where is it?"

There was a brief moment of silence that was broken by Wilbert's laughter. He was beside himself, cackling aloud. Even Mackleford seemed to be amused.

"Mochtier, you really need to work on your interrogation skills," Wilbert chortled.

"Well, it's just that Gaston and I both believed in getting to the point. Offer the easiest solution first. Who knows? In situations like yours, people tend to be more agreeable."

"Not today," Wilbert said, wiping tears from his eyes.

"Well," Mackleford paused, staring at the horizon with a disappointed gaze, then: "Perhaps *Laura* knows." And he removed his silver glove.

Underneath the glove, Mackleford's hand was scrawny and ghastly white. Spotted, looking diseased. A thin layer of slick, sticky ooze covered it, causing it to shine as bright as the glove.

Wilbert fell silent, the last echoes of his laughter fading into the distance. He had heard of this weapon of Mackleford's, *the White Hand*, but he had never seen it. The White Hand had killed many of Wilbert's colleagues over the years, and now here he was, with Laura, both of them injured and defenseless.

"Bring her here, Musclehead," Mackleford said softly.

Musclehead grabbed Laura's shirt collar, dragging her. "Not so tough without those gloves, are you Laura?"

"Wouldn't be talking if I had them, would you Musclehead?" Laura replied.

"Why don't you just leave Laura out of it?" Wilbert said, trying to remove Mr. Quick's boot from his chest. "You've been trying to find me for years, Mackleford. Here I am! You have *me*!"

Musclehead dropped Laura against the sedan, feet away from Wilbert. "Correction: I have you both," Mackleford said. "Once I get what's mine, I'll be finished with you both."

"And if you want it," Wilbert said, his tone deadly and serious, "you won't touch her."

Mackleford turned to Laura. "Laura Johnson," he said respectfully. "You're legendary within the Dominion, my dear. They fear you, you know?"

"You should too," Laura said, appearing unconcerned with the White Hand. "Go ahead and kill me, Mackleford. The Guild will only grow stronger."

Mackleford's look was contemptuous. "The Guild?" he laughed. "You two represent the last of what *was* the Guild. Gumm and Wilson are both dead, their daughters are worthless, the rest of your friends are scattered and hiding. Wilbert, shall I destroy them all, beginning with your wife, or will you return my property?"

"Don't tell him, Wilby," Laura said. "Nothing! Don't worry about me!"

Mackleford looked from Laura to Wilbert, no longer smiling. In a definite tone of finality, he asked again, "Where is it, Mr. Johnson?"

Without hesitation, Wilbert replied, "I'll die before I tell you."

"No, you won't," Mackleford whispered. "But she will." And with that, the White Hand grasped Laura's throat.

Laura's eyes popped open in amazement as she gasped. Her entire body seized. She was turning pale like the hand that clutched her throat, and her skin was becoming scaly and scabbed. Her entire body trembled in throes of immense pain, but her eyes locked onto her husband's, who was reaching for his wife, staring in agony. And with a final gasp, her eyes closed.

Mackleford released Laura. "And so falls the Legend." Her lifeless body crumpled to the ground.

Wilbert wept, staring at his wife's ashen, withered face in horror, while Musclehead and Lanky watched on in stunned silence.

"Another Journeymen dies needlessly," Mackleford said, looking distressed. "She could have lived, but you chose her death. I'm curious, what did her death gain you today?"

"SHUT UP! JUST KILL ME ALREADY!"

"Kill you?" Mackleford said calmly. "Only you know where *it* is. Killing *you* doesn't help me."

"Murderer..." Wilbert muttered, tears flowing. "Nothing but a filthy murderer. Well, you'll never have it, so you can kill me too! It's the best you're gonna get!"

Mackleford's quiet demeanor had finally collapsed. Rage filled his eyes, and the White Hand flashed like a striking serpent, seizing Wilbert's throat. Musclehead and Lanky jumped backwards, astonished.

But Wilbert didn't fight back. He stared into Mackleford's enraged face as his skin turned pale gray. But as he began choking and trembling, Mackleford released him.

"No, not yet, Wilbert," Mackleford exhaled. He immediately slid his silver glove back over the White Hand. "You don't get off that easy."

Wilbert's skin was ashen and had begun to flake away from his face, drifting down the road by a light breeze. His entire body began shivering as though he was freezing.

"A-Aiden…will d-do…" Wilbert stammered, and his voice cut off in his throat, as if something had suddenly muted it.

Mackleford stood, breathing heavily and wiping beads of sweat from his face. The ordeal appeared to have taken something out of him. He turned to Mr. Quick.

"Aiden?" he rasped.

"His son," Mr. Quick replied.

Mackleford massaged the glove around his hand, shaking his head. "Aiden will do nothing but learn what suffering truly means. Him and the rest of your family. I will make certain of it."

And Mackleford left, towing his three cohorts behind him, leaving a struggling Wilbert crawling towards Laura's body.

Several hours later, a young, sandy-haired man wearing an old army tunic jacket stood outside a twenty-story apartment building, staring into Brooklyn New York's evening sky. He hated everything about the job ahead of him. It had only just happened and the details were still sketchy, but two things were certain: Wilbert had survived, but Laura…

Laura. She had taught him everything he knew. More than a mentor and a friend, she was almost like a mother to him. His throat tightened as he practiced the words in his mind.

"Your father was a great leader, and your mom was the best fighter I ever knew…"

He rubbed his eyes, fighting the emotions he would deal with later. Right now, he was focused on the next move. Relocation. Tonight. A few hideouts came to mind, just a matter of picking one. He could hear Art Middleman's voice now…"No crazy stunts, kid, just deliver the news…."

But he knew better. Those Johnson kids were in danger. Wilbert never wanted his children in hiding, but that dream was over. Mackleford was coming and it was impossible to guess how much time they had. Sometimes the Dominion acted immediately; sometimes they waited. He needed to act now.

Finally, there was a flash of red light he'd been expecting. Turning, he saw a teenage girl, five-foot tall with waist-length blonde hair, glowing red like a Christmas light. Her purple and pink outfit perfectly matched her exquisite leather gloves, which had large red crystals centered in the palms. She removed the crystals, shoving them into her jacket pocket and her red glow faded at once.

"Rock, paper, scissors?" the young man said, holding out his fist, donned in an equally designed blue and gold glove. The girl rolled her eyes, shaking her head. "C'mon Lyric, I'm no good at this."

"Why do I have to do *everything*?" the girl complained. "I found out what happened to Laura and Wilbert and I had to race around all night telling everyone. Pull your own weight for a change."

"This requires a lady's touch," he said in a flattering tone. "I suck at feelings and emotions. But you...?"

"Don't try and butter my bread, Carson, you ain't that cute."

"I don't know how to tell these guys their parents are dead, especially since they don't know anything about anything?"

"Wilbert isn't dead," she said bluntly, "so you start off by telling them that. And what do you mean, they don't know anything about anything?"

"They have no idea what Wilbert and Laura do. I'm serious," Carson said off of Lyric's stunned expression. "They think their parents are missionaries or something."

"Wilbert and Laura were covering their whole lives? With their own kids? Why?"

"No clue."

Lyric stared straight ahead, temporarily at a loss for words. "That's crazy. They're our leaders. But how did they? My dad couldn't have hidden all this from me."

Carson shrugged. "Wilbert had his reasons. This life ain't for everybody."

"By the way," Lyric said, "I know you and Laura were close. I'm sorry."

Carson nodded gravely. "Yeah, well, once they hijacked Mackleford, you knew things would get ugly quick."

"Mackleford hasn't shown his face in years, so whatever they stole from him must be really important." Lyric looked expectantly at Carson. "What exactly did they steal?"

"Something secretive," Carson said. "The old timers won't tell me. But if you ask me, it's one of those sentimental relics Gumm collected."

"Mackleford's been in hiding for years and finally comes out in the open just to find this thing," Lyric said. "I doubt he did it for sentimental reasons."

"Yeah, maybe." Carson stared back to the building. "Well, I told your dad we'd do this, so let's get moving. We gotta get these guys somewhere safe."

"Total disagreement there," Lyric said. "Leave them alone. Let them live their lives," Lyric said. "I mean, what if the Dominion can't find them?"

"Wilbert was the best. If they can find him, they'll find his kids."

"Depends on how you think they found Wilbert to start with," Lyric muttered.

Carson glared at Lyric. "Look, don't start spreading rumors…"

"Come on Carson, everybody's thinking it!"

"Look, unless you have really good evidence—" Carson broke off whatever he was going to say, looking annoyed. "Just forget it. What floor?"

Lyric stared at the building, pointing upward. "Eleventh. Apartment 1135. That's it there, the one with the yellow railing." She pulled a slender silver pistol from her waist, fitted it with a small red crystal, and aimed towards the yellow railing. Carson intervened, pushing the pistol's barrel towards the ground.

"Are you nuts?" Carson snapped. "We can't go in like that!"

Lyric frowned as Carson stepped towards the building's front door. "But you said over the phone the elevator was broken."

Carson grabbed the handle on the door and opened it for Lyric. "We're walking."

"Why do they have to live on the eleventh floor?" Lyric groaned, lurching ahead.

They ascended the stairs in silence, barely making a sound. Carson slipped a shining white crystal into a small slot on the back of his left glove and a field of white light surrounded him. As they rounded the stairwell at the fifth floor, Carson grabbed Lyric's arm.

"Where's your *white*?"

"Right here." Lyric pulled a chain out from underneath her shirt; attached to it, a slender white crystal. "I never take it off. I don't even remember what it's like not to have it on."

"Lyric, you know better than that," Carson said. "You're gonna get *star-sick*. Gumm said if your body's gets used to it, it won't work anymore."

"It works fine!" Lyric said, rolling her eyes. "Besides, my dad said Gaston Gumm made up stuff like that to keep people from doing their own research and no one ever questioned him."

"So, Gumm made it up, huh?" Carson said, amused. "You sound like Mackleford's newest recruit. Trying out for the Goon Squad?"

"Shut it!" Lyric said. "Just because I don't believe everything Gaston Gumm used to tell people? I'm not saying he was wrong to tell people that, just don't believe everything you hear."

Carson let the argument end there. He was listening to something else.

"You hear that?" he said ominously.

The young blonde perked her ears, turning left and right. "Nope. Nothing. What is it?"

"And *that's* why you take that white down," Carson reprimanded. "Someone's coming. Someone big."

He craned his neck over the railing of the empty stairwell, listening. "Two *someones*," he said, and then—"Dammit! Goons! They're right outside the building."

"Where?"

"Coming up that side," Carson said, pointing behind them.

If Lyric couldn't hear them, she could definitely feel their presence because the building began to tremble violently. Carson shoved two red crystals into his leather gloves, and his white glow turned red. Lyric did likewise, just as the building was plunged into total darkness.

"Go get the kids!" Carson shouted. "I'll hold them off."

Lyric continued up the stairs as Carson opened the door to the fifth floor, entering a dim hallway, which was brightened by his red glow and filled with people balancing themselves against the walls.

"Is it an earthquake?" a child's voice said.

"What happened to the lights?" called an elderly woman.

"What's going on?" other voices cried out.

But the voices fell silent as an enormous shape moved in front of the large window at the far end of the hallway, seemed to take notice of Carson's glowing body, and walked towards him. The residents of the fifth floor screamed and scurried back inside their apartments, slamming their doors. Carson was alone, watching the giant shape approach.

Carson shook off his nerves and cracked his neck. "Lyric! Hurry!" he screamed out and started up the hall.

Lyric, six floors above, was struggling to read the apartment numbers, passing her hand over the small brass plates on the doors, using her red aura to see. After several minutes of looking she concluded...

"Crap, there's no 1135. Hey, Carson! We've got the wrong build...*ugghh*!"

Something heavy and sticky slammed into Lyric, throwing her up the hallway about twenty feet. Wincing in pain, she turned and saw the dark outline of the thing that hit her clinging to the ceiling, about the size of a large dog with long pincers and crab-like legs. And there wasn't just one of them.

"Grunners," Lyric whispered to herself. She should have smelled the Goons' nightmarish crustacean-like pets before they got there, she thought, as she heard their legs scuttling towards her.

Slowly, a scent of ocean water filled her nostrils. Grunner slime. *Now* she smelled it, but why not before? Lyric's face was numb from the blow and she felt slow and sluggish, as if she had suddenly put on twenty pounds.

She lifted her arm, and the glow from the red crystal illuminated the dozen or so grunners in front of her. There was a bright flash of light; energy from the red crystal inside Lyric's leather glove blasted forth like cannon fire, scattering the pack of grunners.

It wasn't a strong blast, but it gave Lyric enough time to get to her feet. She ran back for the stairs and collided into someone enormous. Taking no time to identify him, she immediately attacked, firing a barrage of red bolts from her crystals.

But as big as the man was, he was also quick, leaping and spinning away from Lyric's frantic attack. She heard the eerie sound of the grunners scuttling on the floor, getting closer; she only had seconds before the beasts rounded the corner and made mincemeat out of her.

The man leapt in the air, swinging a massive fist at Lyric, who sprang backwards as his punch splintered the wood floor. Lyric finally got a good look at him and knew him immediately.

The enormous hands tipped her off, looking like they belonged to someone three times his size. He was hunched like a gorilla, scars crisscrossing his fat, ugly face. His name was Melvin Hessman, but Lyric knew him by another name.

"Man-Child!" she snarled. "How did you get out of Morocco?"

"Lyric Middleman! A nice surprise!" He spoke with an affluent tone that didn't match his appearance. "Must be important cargo for the Guild if you're out and about after tonight's events. Wouldn't be the Johnson children, would it?"

Lyric tried to somersault over his head, but Man-Child swiped her out of the air with one of his oversized hands. Lyric struggled, unable to escape, her arms pinned to her sides.

"Now tell me where they are," Man-Child said, "or I'll make you wish you had. I'm fine either way you wish to play this game."

The smell of seawater was thick; the beasts were close. Snapping, snarling. An apartment door opened. The inhabitant took one look at Man-Child, screamed and slammed the door.

Man-Child chuckled until he looked down the hall behind him, seeing a wild-haired man bathed in a deep red aura running up the hall.

Carson's gloved hands ignited and Man-Child was flattened in a hailstorm of red blasts. He released Lyric, rolling on the ground in pain. He got to his feet and scampered down the hallway, crashing through a window with his grunners trailing behind.

Carson helped Lyric to her feet before racing towards the smashed window, looking outside the street below. Man-Child was gone.

"What about the other one?" Lyric said, checking a bleeding cut on her elbow.

"No one major," Carson said, pocketing his red and white crystals. "Looked like a newbie."

Lyric was puzzled. "Man-Child and a rookie Goon? Why would they only send them?"

"Because," Carson sighed, clearly upset, "the Dominion don't know where the Johnson kids are any more than we do. I bet they pinned it down to Brooklyn and are canvassing the whole city. Wilbert never wanted anyone to find them, remember?"

"Well, if they aren't here, exactly where are the Johnson kids then?"

Halfway across Brooklyn, three hours later, in a quiet, ordinary apartment building, a phone rang in 200A.

A gangly young man fell off the couch at the first ring, clutching in his right hand an adventure novel he had been reading.

He reached for his cell phone. "H-h-lo?"

"Aiden. It's Danny. I don't know how to say this…"

CHAPTER TWO – THE INVITATION

Seven months had passed since the Johnson family was changed forever.

They once were an ordinary family from Brooklyn, New York and even though Laura and Wilbert were missionaries with Survival International, life was pretty simple. Laura was a grocery store manager, Wilbert worked a variety of odd jobs, and Aiden, Flair, and Simone, were normal, mostly well-behaved kids. Home was a cozy four-bedroom apartment. Aiden was the oddball of the family, if one could call an adventurous daredevil and child prodigy all rolled into one an oddball. Aiden was the type of kid who would climb a broken fire escape because it was there, and by the time he turned twenty years old, he was already the youngest research instructor working under Professor Daniel Lee at Rittmoor University in Queens. For Aiden, his days were easy, peaceful, and carefree.

But on one of those days, his mother never came home.

Aiden knew something had broken in the world the day his mother died. That same morning, rumors circulated throughout Brooklyn about a series of break-ins, with eyewitnesses reporting "large, monster-like men" at various scenes. If that wasn't odd enough, the week following his mother's death, Aiden had been plagued not only with grief, but also by strange memories.

But were they *memories*? They certainly involved him, although Aiden couldn't recall these events ever happening. Talking to people he'd never met, being places he'd never been, all during different periods in his life, from toddler to teenager. These memories interrupted his day at random times: in the middle of lectures, while eating, or talking to his girlfriend on the phone. It was like living with constant *déjà vu*, and as much as Aiden wanted to dismiss these memories, he couldn't.

One recurring memory was especially vivid and had come to Aiden whenever he made arrangements for his mother's funeral. He was a child, sitting on the floor of his living room, back against the wall, reading a letter. Every detail of this letter was vibrant, down to the feel of the notebook paper. He could even remember the date, which told him he was eleven-years-old at the time.

May 10, 2002

Dearest Granny;

All is well darling. I am only receiving your last communication this past weekend (today is Monday) and Wilby and I have narrowly escaped, arriving back in C.S. The grief we feel at hearing of Gus' death is immeasurable. I know he'd been ill, but one's heart can never be prepared. Wilby's been recovering from some nasty injuries and hasn't spoken to anyone since the day we found out, not even to me, although I think he called Nick once because he still has that Warriors of Patagonia novel he borrowed from Aiden. Wilby loved your father with all his heart. We are going to spend the summer in East Town so we will be there for the funeral.

Here are my updates as promised...my campaign against the Dominion at their new campus was successful. They grow more vile every year. It lifted our spirits in this difficult time that your father's efforts weren't in vain. I shut down their operations, perhaps temporarily, but it's a start. We still haven't heard from Ashton and Summer on the whereabouts of the Martinezes. Lydia fears the worst, which is expected by most of us, but I am hopeful. Summer has agreed to watch over Sonya in the meantime. Lydia also told me you think only one person can take your father's place. She wouldn't tell me who, but I know who you're talking about Granny. I disagree. Wilby and I will be taking up your father's list where he left off. I know you will try and talk us out of it, but this is our call.

Life is harder on the outside than it was in East Town. I think I understand your concerns, especially when thinking about the Martinezes, that it's not easy to remain out here. But Wilby has a plan for the Dominion, and I don't see...

The letter always stopped there and Aiden couldn't recall if there was more. It seemed too real to be unreal, floating on the edge of his mind, like a daydream that had just happened. The people in the letter certainly were real. The Martinezes, Nick, Lydia, Ashton, Summer; he had heard these names before from his parents. So this letter was real, but like his other strange memories, he had no true recollection of it.

Two parts of the letter kept Aiden up at night, the first being the novel. *Lionel Vann and the Warriors of Patagonia* was the first book in the Lionel Vann series that Aiden had collected since he was nine. He owned all seventeen first print originals that featured foldout detailed maps and sketches of curios and relics. He was very proud of his Vann collection, but they were children's adventure novels, fantastic, even ridiculous. Why would his mother bother mentioning the book in this letter, and why had his father needed to borrow it?

The second part of the letter that disturbed Aiden was this group his mother had mentioned, the group she had shut down, whom she called *vile*. The group his father had a plan against. *The Dominion*. He didn't understand who this group was, but something about the name gave him the chills.

Even without the puzzling memories, it had been Aiden's worst week ever. His favorite cabbie retired, forcing him onto those grimy, crowded subways, which he hated. His laptop computer crashed, meaning he had to use the university computer lab, which he equally hated. When curiosity drove him into the storage closet to find his Lionel Vann collection, he discovered several books were missing. And finally on Sunday, he buried his mother.

Aiden and Simone noticed the Survival International missionaries seemed frightened at the funeral, glancing over their shoulders as if expecting someone dreadful to turn up. One man named Ashton Stillwell, who had introduced himself to Aiden as a fellow missionary and old schoolmate of his mother's, jumped ten feet in the air when Aiden asked if he could pass Simone's jacket. They barely spoke to the Johnsons, only speaking in whispering huddles while secretly looking in their direction.

During the funeral service, the preacher was eulogizing about the unique gift of life, and at that moment, another recurring vision flooded into Aiden's mind. He was in a dark room, and with him, a scary, dark-skinned man covered in tattoos. It was the fourth time Aiden had this particular memory, but this time, Aiden noticed something else. The tattooed man was speaking to someone, a man standing in shadows…

"See, there they go again," Simone said, waking Aiden out of the daydream. She was staring at the missionaries seated in the pews to their right. They flinched when Aiden looked in their direction and turned in their seats, facing the preacher.

Flair, however, noticed nothing strange about the missionaries. In fact, she didn't seem that upset about her mother's death. During the wake, she was chatting with anyone who'd listen about some company that had just bought her favorite clothing labels. Everyone, including Simone, was annoyed at Flair's casual attitude, but Aiden understood.

Whenever difficulty arose in Flair's life, she escaped into her favorite hobby: fashion. Flair wasn't as close to her mother like Aiden or Simone, but in Aiden's opinion, she had taken her death the hardest, drowning herself in fashion magazines, fashion television shows, and fashion websites. So when Aiden mentioned the Survival International members' behavior…

"So what? We lost both parents, they're worried," Flair said, shrugging. "Anyway, *Mailani* has this insane new line of boots that I have to get…" Aiden opened his mouth to say something but declined.

The truth was they hadn't lost *both* parents. Wilbert was alive, but couldn't speak and needed constant care. Dr. Haskins, the family physician, said there was nothing the hospital could do for Wilbert and kept him at home. Aiden didn't understand how his father wasn't better off at a fully staffed hospital, but he also didn't understand how some virus could do what happened to his parents. Having his father at home brought a little comfort, but often it felt like he wasn't even there.

As time passed, the strange memories of the letter and the tattooed man disappeared as suddenly as they had arrived. Aiden hadn't stopped to consider how or why this had happened because he suddenly found himself with a far more challenging concern: taking care of his two sisters.

"You need to take me to cheerleading practice NOW!" Simone yelled.

"You need to sit down and shut up NOW!" Aiden yelled back.

"Will you just walk her to the train station, clown boy?" Flair snapped.

"I'm gonna be late, Aiden!" Simone nagged.

"Flair, take her," Aiden said. "I've got sixteen essays to grade by tomorrow."

"You're cooking dinner then!" Flair said.

"You really want to eat my cooking?" Aiden asked.

"Yuk! I know I don't," Simone said. "I'll just take my chance with the crooks."

"You want your sister mugged, idiot?" Flair shouted.

"You're an idiot!"

Aiden hated his new job.

To make matters worse was his girlfriend, Candace, restless as a five-year-old and always needing attention. She assaulted his cell phone with messages around the clock, hassling Aiden for dates and visits, and questioning him about the tiniest details of his day.

One December afternoon, not for the first time, Aiden ignored the buzzing phone in his pocket. Exhausted from a full day of lecturing and grading papers, he crashed into a subway seat and slid his father's old flat cap over his eyes, hoping to catch a nap on his way home. His cell phone, however, wouldn't stop buzzing. He pulled it from his jacket, checking the display. Sure enough…*Candy Bear*. He rolled his eyes and answered, figuring if he didn't, he wouldn't hear the end of it.

"Hey, sweets—"

A shabby young man dropped into the seat across from Aiden, smiling. He wore a grungy military jacket, dirty frayed jeans, and the strangest gloves Aiden had ever seen. He also smelled like he hadn't washed in days. Aiden looked around, seeing the dozens of other empty seats on the train this guy could have selected and rolled his eyes. *Here we go*, he thought, another punk who had nothing better to do except annoy people who wanted peace and quiet.

"Train's filthy," the young man said. "Beats walking though." Aiden suddenly found himself glad Candace had called.

"Yeah, I got your text, but you know how the last few days before Christmas break are," Aiden said, staring at the young man. "You get a lot of *annoying* interruptions."

The subway train slowed as it reached a station. Right away, Aiden's call disconnected, but he smiled and nodded as if he was listening to the most fascinating story in the world. The train moved along with Aiden's intruder still there.

"Your call dropped already," the young man said, smiling. "Always does right here."

Aiden knew his charade was up, but still looked at his phone in shock and held it in the air, praying to regain a signal so he could call Candace. Or anyone.

The pest chuckled. Annoyed, Aiden stuffed his phone back in his pocket and pulled his briefcase closer to him.

"You're Aiden Johnson, aren't ya?"

"I am," Aiden said defensively. "You are?"

A blue and yellow leather glove had grabbed Aiden's hand before he realized it. "Glad to meet you finally! Took me a while to hunt you down."

Aiden yanked his hand back, looking warily at the young man. "You stalking me or something, pal?"

"Relax, Aiden," he laughed. "I'm taking Professor Lee's class next term. You're his research assistant, right?"

"You puttin' me on?" Aiden answered, eyeing his disheveled clothes. "You go to Rittmoor?"

The young man smiled. "Don't let my elegant wardrobe fool you. I just have an unusual job."

"Yeah, good for you, but my office hours are twelve to three. It's way after three and this ain't no office."

"Sure know how to charm new students," the pest quipped.

Aiden smirked at the sarcasm. "Yeah, I can be a charmer. What'd you need? A syllabus?" Aiden opened his laptop case, handing him a sheet of paper.

The young man stared at the syllabus thoughtfully. "My mentor says *history* can teach us a lot, but *historians* these days don't teach us nothing. All they do is talk about the past."

"Shocking," Aiden said. "Historians talking about the past. Why, you'd think they were *historians* or something."

"But what good is *talk*, Aiden? The first historians didn't just talk about life, they *lived*. They explored, they discovered, they made history themselves. They were pioneers."

Aiden felt himself growing impressed with the intruder. "Fair point. What's your name, pal?"

"Carson Dillinger," he replied with a grin. "No relation to John."

Aiden's eyebrows knitted into a frown. "Albuquerque, New Mexico," he said in a confident voice and chuckled when Carson showed confusion. "Your accent. Southwest U.S., not quite a Texas twang, so you grew up a little further west. Your hands are a dead giveaway, though. All calloused and weather beaten from desert heat. How's that?"

Carson laughed. "Not bad. Santé Fe."

"Close enough," Aiden said. "Your eyes look old too. Means you keep late hours. Won't work with my class, Carson. I start at eight-thirty a.m. sharp."

"You can read people?" Carson said. "Heard you were some kind of genius."

"Just a trick my old man taught me. But, yeah, the original historians didn't sit around in offices. They were out there in the thick of things. Probably sounds exciting to a guy like you."

"But not to you?"

The subway car squealed to a stop, the doors clunked open, and Aiden grabbed his briefcase, straightened his father's flat cap and stood.

"You're like my parents. They were missionaries, heroes solving the world's problems, until seven months ago when they contracted some disease nobody's heard of and nobody can cure. Now my family's lost a mother and has a father who's barely alive."

Aiden pulled out a business card, tossing it on Carson's lap.

"You see Mr. Dillinger, sometimes it's better to take care of your loved ones instead of flying all over the world, playing historian and hero. There's my number, office hours are twelve to three, in my *actual* office on campus. Have a good one."

The crowded subway platform swallowed Aiden in seconds. Carson stared at the floor as the subway train rolled off. He hadn't expected the conversation to go the way it did, but it confirmed some important details. At the next station stop, a young blonde stepped aboard and fell into the seat next to Carson, wearing a purple and pink scarf and knit cap that matched her gloves.

"How'd it go?" Lyric Middleman asked.

"Terrible," Carson said, shaking his head. "He thinks his parents were the victims of a virus, just like the cover story says."

Lyric looked puzzled. "Well they're not gonna be Journeymen, so how is that terrible?"

"They're helpless, Lyric," Carson sighed. "Mackleford will catch up with them eventually. Your dad's wrong about this. They should be underground, especially if everything we've heard about Aiden is true."

"Mackleford's helpless too," Lyric said. "And I think it's awesome they don't know. Sometimes, I wish I didn't. Look at our lives. Look at Sonya's life, she's even worse. But them? They're just—*living*."

Carson glimpsed at the people crowded on the subway as the train pulled off.

"If you think that's living, you're nuts."

The living room of apartment 200A was deserted, quiet except for an old television showing a black and white version of "Miracle on 34th Street". The room was cluttered with unfolded laundry on the couch, empty pizza boxes, a coffee table piled with ungraded term papers, and a half decorated Christmas tree leaning sadly against a box of ornaments.

BUMP BUMP BUMP

Thudding sounded throughout the apartment, and within seconds, a pair of feet pattered down the hallway, its owner bursting into the room at the end.

The barefoot child had curly brown hair, a tanned complexion with chubby, dimpled cheeks, and striking, brown eyes. She was scowling at an older, paler version of herself: a teenage girl with a fresh, pretty face and eyes and hair of amber. She was lying on a bed with a notebook computer open, browsing the Internet, music earphones inserted, oblivious to the world.

"Flair!" Simone Johnson shouted, her curly locks bouncing. "HEL-LO-OHHHHH! It's your turn!"

Flair Johnson looked up, not at Simone, but rather at a message she just received on her computer. She giggled and typed a reply.

Simone's scowl turned into a sneer. "I've got something for you, *Ms. FacePlace!*" she murmured. Simone nimbly mounted the dresser quickly without making a sound. Measuring the distance with her eyes, Simone launched herself towards Flair, who was bopping to her music, unaware.

WHOMP!

"SIMOOONE!" Flair bellowed as Simone planted an elbow in her back. "WHAT'S THE DEAL?"

"The deal is we've been on break for three days and you're—"

Flair swung a kick at Simone but missed, and her momentum carried her off the bed. She crashed to the floor and roared: "Get out! OUT!"

Simone escaped into the hallway, throwing her hands into the air dramatically. "Fine! I guess I'm the only one who loves Daddy!" she shouted as Flair's door was slammed and locked.

It wasn't that Simone minded checking on her father, but Flair never did. Ever. Simone wondered when Aiden took her to cheerleading practice if Flair ever realized they'd even left. One day, Simone thought to herself, she'd prop up a trap against her father's door to see if it was tripped while she was gone.

She entered her father's bedroom, lit only by a small flat screen television also showing "Miracle on 34th Street". A frail man in a narrow hospital bed shakily removed an oxygen mask from his face, lowering a metal cane he had used to bang on the wall. His wrinkled arm stretched towards his youngest daughter, as she spoke at lightning speed.

"Hi Daddy. Did you need something? I'm sorry, but Flair just locks her brain up in that stupid computer. I don't know why you got her that thing, because as soon as you did, she forgot about all the rest of us."

Simone turned on a light, illuminating Wilbert's features. He looked like a man hanging onto life by the barest of threads. The skin on his face sagged around his eyes and cheeks and his once thick, curly hair looked thin and brittle.

She moved towards a dresser topped with dozens of pictures. "I wish you could tell me stories about these pictures, Daddy," she sighed.

Lately, Wilbert had been requesting various pictures from the dresser. He'd point at a photo and Simone would follow his finger the best she could until she brought him the right one. Wilbert usually kept the picture with him for days until he banged on the wall for another.

As expected, Simone waited quietly for her father, and after a moment, Wilbert's long, shaky finger aimed at the host of photos: old buildings, classic automobiles, and people she had never paid attention to before her father's illness. Simone's eyes fell on a picture of her parents on their wedding day.

"This one? You haven't looked at this one in a long time." Simone picked up the photo, staring at it longingly. Her mother was elegant, dressed in a flowing white dress abounding with frills and a pretty, glittering tiara atop her blonde hair. But the most pleasant thing to Simone was that spunk in Laura's eyes that only she and her mother recognized. Simone took after her father in appearance, but as far as personality, she was her mother's twin.

"You miss Mom, don't you?" Simone said. "So do..." Looking up from the photo, she saw Wilbert's hand still pointing at the dresser.

Simone turned back to the spot where she had removed the wedding picture, seeing another photo. It looked like a Rockwell painting: the town square of a village, fog lamps lining a cobblestone road with shops, backed by snow-capped hills and cherry trees.

"I don't think I've ever gotten this one for you before. You remember this place, right? East Town, where you and Mom grew up? You always said we would go with you one day, but we never did. Are you trying to tell me something?"

Simone handed the photo over, looking anxious. Wilbert stared at it, and Simone stared at him. It was so quiet, Simone could faintly hear the music coming from Flair's room. Simone was about to turn and leave when suddenly Wilbert lunged over the side of his bed.

"Daddy!" Simone shouted. "What are you doing? You don't need to move, I can get it!" Wilbert, half-on, half-off the bed, had barely moved in months, but now fought his daughter's assistance with surprising strength, reaching for something under his nightstand.

Simone was on the bed, grabbing his shoulders, pulling and screaming for help. "Flair! FLAAAIR! Why did you get her that stupid computer? I can get it, Daddy, just...stop!"

After much pulling and tugging, Simone finally brought Wilbert back onto the bed. His face glistened with sweat, his skeletal chest heaved up and down, and in his hand was a long envelope with fancy black lettering. It fell from his hands into his daughter's, as he grabbed for the hissing oxygen mask.

For several moments, Simone's mouth hung open. She didn't know what to do. Should she get Flair?

"Forget Flair," she said. "She doesn't help." She drew a large breath and stated importantly, "I'll take a look at this."

She glanced at her father to see if he approved or not and thought she saw a hint of a smile on his face. Without a moment's hesitation, Simone opened the envelope with confidence, withdrew a piece of paper, and read. She read it three times, and when she finally looked back at her father, he was staring at her quite seriously. Simone felt her heart thumping in her chest as she backed away from the bed, clutching the envelope, not taking her eyes off her father.

She shouted loud enough to wake the dead. "FLAIR! FLAIR! COME HERE!"

There was snowfall on Aiden's long walk home from the subway station. His phone was still buzzing in his pocket, and he knew it was Candace, but he didn't answer, as his mind was on the weirdo from the train. Despite the random encounter, the meeting felt rehearsed. But then, Aiden heard his father's voice saying, "There's your brain working overtime again, son."

After all, this was New York City, and weirdos were a fact of life, although this one felt different: smooth, intelligent, charming. Maybe he was trying to talk Aiden into something or set him up for a scam. Aiden was regretting giving his business card. His father had warned him about giving his name and number to complete strangers.

But then again, Aiden thought, his father was always paranoid. Too much solving the world's problems to understand life in the city. Carson Dillinger was probably just some loser who'd followed him from campus. He loosened his tie as he climbed the stairs of his apartment building.

He wasn't prepared for what awaited him.

Simone had a knack for dramatizing even the smallest of issues, but if something important happened, she became a human buzz saw. When Aiden opened the door, the buzz saw erupted.

Simone was yammering, babbling, almost screaming at Aiden, who could only make out bits and pieces: something about their father, East Town, someone named Margaret Gumm and a *reading*. It was like having a conversation with a swarm of bees.

It wasn't until Aiden saw Flair on the sofa biting her lip that he became concerned. Normally, whenever Flair did that, it meant one of her favorite pop stars had been arrested. Family matters rarely bothered her. So her look was enough to make Aiden grab Simone from behind and muzzle her with his hand so he could get some answers.

"What's wrong? Is Pops okay?" Aiden asked, holding Simone firm.

"Dad's fine. He's not the problem." Flair held up the letter. "This is."

Aiden released Simone, taking the letter. Simone started up again. "I can't wait to go! I'm so excited!"

Aiden scanned the letter. It was an invitation, typed with an old style typewriter on thin, flimsy paper:

```
             MARGARET GUMM READS!
           OUR 41ST ANNUAL READING
           FROM HER BOOK OF WISDOM

    Greetings fellow Towners!

    Join us for the annual Reading of the
    Grand Book from our own illustrious
    Margaret Gumm! We meet together once
    again, family and friends, old and new, to
    celebrate our history and our great love
    for our very own East Town.

    We look forward to your arrival. As rooms
    at the Cranberry Inn tend to fill up
    quickly, be sure to make your reservations
    today.

    Date:  Jan. 1, 2016
    Site:  The House of Gumm, 1255 Melanie Ave,
    East Town

                   AGENDA

          Welcome - 10:45 AM
      Lunch in the Garden - 11 AM to 1 PM
    Margaret's Tour of The House - 1 PM to
                   2:30 PM
      The Reading - 2:30 PM to 3:30 PM
        Closing - 3:30 PM to 4:00 PM
```

Aiden was slightly amused; he didn't expect this. As he and his sisters had never visited East Town themselves, he'd forgotten about the annual trip his parents took to their hometown. He placed the invitation back inside the envelope, shaking his head.

"I'm sure Pops understands he can't make it this year. Getting him out there would be too much for him. And besides—"

"Excuse me, Aiden," Simone blurted out, "but he wants *us* to go."

Aiden paused, looking back and forth at his two sisters before laughing.

"*Us*? C'mon Simmy, they never wanted us to go before. Why now?"

"Because they never said goodbye to East Town and all their friends. That's what they would have wanted." Simone crossed her arms, facing Aiden. Aiden knew she wouldn't back down without a fight.

"Simone," Aiden sighed, "this invitation is clearly meant for Mom and Pops. Look." He tapped the words *Greeting Fellow Towners!* on the invitation. "We're not *Towners*. Besides, we don't have enough money for tickets."

A dejected Flair passed a second envelope to Aiden.

"What?" Aiden said, looking puzzled. His confusion turned into astonishment when he opened the envelope and removed three train tickets. "Who gave you these?"

"Daddy did," Simone said. "Three tickets, one for me, you, and Flair. He wants us to go Aiden, and we're going."

Aiden looked at Flair, his expression halfway between helpless and furious.

"Speak up, *sunshine*. Don't tell me you wanna go?"

Flair looked as upset as Aiden did. "Hey, I'm with you. But—"

"It's what Mom would have wanted!" Simone chirped. "She always wanted us to go, but Daddy always said no!"

"Maybe that's true, but I have to work. My job's putting food on the table. Sorry."

Simone walked up to Aiden, jabbing her finger into his chest. "You said Professor Lee would let you off for any family matters."

"With pay," Flair groaned.

"And you haven't taken any time off, not one day! And we don't have school for the next three weeks."

"And it's okay to send Dad to St. James Memorial," Flair continued. "Simone already asked Dr. Haskins."

Aiden's mouth went dry, staring back and forth between his two sisters, before finally rounding on the youngest.

"What does she mean you already asked Dr. Haskins?" Aiden snarled.

"I already asked Dr. Haskins," Simone replied coolly. "He said having Daddy for the holidays would be fine, might even make him feel better. You aren't a doctor, are you, Aiden? Because I think a doctor would know best."

Aiden stared at Simone, speechless. He turned back to Flair out of sheer desperation.

"So you just stood by and watched Simone make arrangements? Wait…let me guess…cell phone and FacePlace?"

"Look, clown," Flair said, "by the time I finished reading the invitation and looking at the tickets, Simmy was already on the phone. What was I supposed to do, knock the phone out of her hands? "

"Yes," Aiden shouted, "knocking the phone out of her hands would've been much better than this!"

"You know how Simmy gets," Flair said, rolling her eyes.

Simone stood between her brother and sister, defiant. Aiden took a deep, calming breath and sat on the couch.

"Simmy, we've had this talk half a million times. You can't make decisions like this. That's my job."

"And we all know how that goes," Flair muttered.

"I didn't make any decision," Simone said. "Daddy did. He gave me the invitation and the tickets. What do you think he wants us to do?"

"Maybe I should ask him."

"Maybe you should!" Simone countered.

Aiden walked down the hall towards the bedrooms. Simone chased him, grabbing his arm.

"Don't you—you better not!" Simone squealed, dangling from Aiden's arm as he dragged her down the hall. "He wants us to go Aiden! You better not talk him out of it!"

"That's exactly what I'm going to do because Pops doesn't know what he's doing. He thinks the world works like that where you can just get up and go whenever you want, but it doesn't."

"You're so mean!" Simone shouted. "Just because *you* never did anything, you don't want *us* to do anything!" And she fell to the floor, covered her face and began crying.

"What?" Aiden stopped, staring at his sister. "C'mon, that's a buncha…Simmy, I'm not like that."

"Yes, you are," Simone whimpered.

Aiden hated to admit it, but there was a bit of truth behind Simone's words. He had spent his whole life in New York, feeling isolated and trapped, as his parents had never taken them anywhere. Making matters worse for Aiden was being a history lover, fascinated with many famous places all across around the world, but being unable to visit any of them. It was torture. The only time they had ever left New York was so his grandparents in Florida could see Simone after she was born. He had always secretly resented that. But with each sob and sniffle from his sister, Aiden felt himself surrendering.

"Okay okay okay," Aiden moaned. "We'll *go*. All right? I won't try to talk him out of anything. Now, can I please talk to Pops for a second?"

Simone sprang off the floor, face dry as a bone, yelled "WOOHOO!" and sprinted to her room, euphoric and triumphant. Aiden narrowed his eyes. He'd been had.

Aiden walked into the doorway of his father's room, looking at his frail father propped with pillows in the hospital bed, his head drooping to one side.

The relationship Aiden once had with his father had deteriorated a while ago, maybe ten years. Aiden wasn't sure. They had been civil before the tragedy struck back in May, but that was about it. The friendship they had, how they could talk together for hours, that was long gone. Aiden couldn't help but remember those better days each time he came into the bedroom. He wished he could return to those moments, but whenever he'd talk, his frustrations would come out.

"I guess we're going to East Town," Aiden said. Wilbert's eyes were locked on his son, his chest rising and falling steadily. "I guess this was something you felt we couldn't do before, but I guess we'll go now that Mom's not here."

Aiden stopped himself, taking a breath. He didn't want to lay into his father. He needed to measure his words.

"Simmy's over the moon about it," Aiden continued. "Flair's not too excited. I think maybe she's hiding it, because she's always wanted to go. I used to want to go too. But…well, there was always something. Some *reason*."

Wilbert shifted slightly in the bed. His hand reached for his oxygen mask, removing it.

"East Town always sounded like I great place to be a kid," Aiden said. "Always wanted to be a kid there. I guess Simmy will enjoy it. Guess that's why I'm doing it, because it's not about me. That's the difference between me and you, y'know Pops? I always missed out. 'Aiden's made eighth-grade scholar of the year, where's mom and dad?' 'Oh, they're out feeding the hungry people of Cambodia. Couldn't be bothered.' 'Aiden was invited to meet the mayor, where's mom and dad?' 'Oh, couldn't make it, tsunami in India.'"

Aiden noticed his father was trembling. It would have been easy to pity him, but he didn't. "So, I won't let them down, Pops. Because they deserve better than that."

And Aiden left the room, ignoring Wilbert's hand reaching out to him.

The following morning, Professor Lee dropped by to deliver some essays for grading and Simone got to him before Aiden did. Aiden had laid in bed all night, working out a plan to make Lee reconsider his promise of giving Aiden time off. But he overslept, and after talking to Simone, Professor Lee gave Aiden an additional week off for good measure. Dr. Haskins also proved to be inconveniently helpful, deciding to pick Wilbert up a day earlier than expected so the kids could focus on their trip. He was due any moment.

As for his sisters, Flair was agonizing over how many suitcases she needed, setting her DVR, and if East Town had good wireless coverage. Simone was beside herself with glee, dancing through the living room, singing, or rather *screeching*, all the songs she had downloaded for the trip, which finally drove Aiden out of the apartment and into the cold, snowy afternoon.

He sat at the bottom of the steps of their apartment building, trying to understand the timing of this trip. *Why now?* Maybe Simone was right, and their father wanted them to say goodbye to East Town, but wouldn't this have been a better trip for the entire family? He thought it would be depressing visiting places his parents used to enjoy without them.

Aiden spotted the lights of an ambulance coming up the street, led by a dark town car and followed by Dr. Haskins' old Pontiac. He went back inside to let his sisters know.

"Heads up guys," Aiden said, dusting snow from his shoulders as he re-entered the apartment. "Dr. Haskins is here."

Simone froze in the middle of her dancing, stared at her brother and sister momentarily before sprinting down the hallway. Aiden knew she wanted one last moment with their father before they left him for three weeks.

Fifteen minutes later, the Johnsons' apartment was filled with nurses and paramedics. Dr. Haskins, a grandfatherly man with a bushy mustache and beard, walked up to Flair, who stared outside at the ambulance.

"Flair, your father will be fine," Dr. Haskins said. "Our intensive care is the best in New York. Everyone at the hospital loved your parents. He'll have the best bed, the best food. He'll have a team of nurses fighting each other to look in on him."

"Yeah," Flair said, "but he won't have us."

"I know," Dr. Haskins said kindly. "But Dr. Chu, Dr. Rome and I are all taking shifts with him. Your parents' humanitarian efforts, the things they fought for, the enormous contributions they made, not just to the hospital, but also—" He cut off. "Well, we're all in their debt. Wilbert couldn't be in better hands."

Dr. Haskins patted Flair on the shoulder before walking over to speak to a nurse as the paramedics wheeled Wilbert's hospital bed into the living room. Aiden walked over to his father's side.

"Well Pops, you win again. Thanks for the trip, and, uh…" He cast his eyes to the ceiling, thinking, wanting to say something 'fatherly' about watching over his sisters. "And I'll hold down the fort while you're gone."

Wilbert reached out and gripped his son's hand, surprising Aiden. The look on Wilbert's face told Aiden this was a serious moment. Aiden squeezed back, meeting his father's eyes and nodding. But as he pulled away, he felt something in his father's hand.

It was a small black envelope. Wilbert pressed it into Aiden's hand and looked towards his daughters, who were talking with the nurses. Wilbert shook his head slightly and his eyes rolled back to Aiden. Aiden figured the meaning. Whatever was inside this envelope, his father didn't want the girls to know about it.

Wilbert's face was grim, almost frightened. *What was this all about?* He stared at his son until Aiden nodded, showing he understood. Wilbert then closed his eyes and gave the envelope to his son.

There was little left to do but watch Haskins' staff load Wilbert into the ambulance. The children watched from the front window overlooking the street, Simone's eyes glimmering with tears and Flair looking pitiful. Aiden watched Dr. Haskins instructing the paramedics, lost in thoughts of the late night talks he used to have with his father, not hearing the front door open, nor realizing Simone went to give her father one last hug until he saw her outside.

"I'll get her," Flair sighed. "You wanna start dinner?"

"Why is this so important?" Aiden looked at the picture on the invitation sitting on the coffee table, the smiling old woman clutching her book. "I don't get it. They never wanted us to go before."

"It's an East Town thing," Flair said. "Listen to Old Mother Hubbard read from her book, spread some Christmas cheer, and come home. Sixteen days of old school holiday fun. It's like Simmy said, they didn't say goodbye, so we're just standing in."

Flair closed the door as Aiden dropped onto the couch and opened the black envelope, sliding a dozen coins of various shapes and sizes into his hand. Aiden recognized them at once—his father's lucky coins, collected over the years, gifts from the unfortunate souls he had helped during his missionary work. But something else was inside the envelope: a note, written in unfamiliar handwriting.

From the top of the stairs, look carefully.
The cornerstone is where you'll find the key.

Aiden frowned. It was a riddle.

Aiden and his father used to play riddle games when he was younger, with Wilbert writing the riddle and Aiden trying to guess its answer. But this was different. This wasn't his father's handwriting, and the way he gave Aiden the envelope…this was something else.

The coins had no great monetary value; they were worthless mementos from his father's travels. Why would he want to keep these a secret from Flair and Simone? And what was this riddle about? *Stairs? The cornerstone? A key?* Aiden felt a headache coming as Simone returned from the outside and sat next to him on the couch, wiping her cheeks.

"What's that?" she asked.

"Pieces for Professor Lee," Aiden lied quickly, throwing the coins back in the envelope and standing. "I'm going to the library and finish up some work."

"Flair said you were making dinner."

"Simmy, you're not helpless," Aiden said. "You're eleven. What if I ended up like Mom and Pops? You gotta learn to take care of yourself."

Simone stared quietly at her shoes as Aiden grabbed his jacket. He felt guilty, but he needed to research those coins.

"Okay, maybe when I get back," Aiden sighed as he grabbed the front doorknob. "I should only be an hour or so, okay?"

Four hours later, Aiden sat stumped in the New York Public Library. Spread over the table before him were the coins and dozens of books on coins he had been sifting through. He had successfully identified all but two of them: a half-dollar sized silver piece with the head of a pig and the letters "H-O-G", and a heavy copper coin displaying a strange "P" on one side and a man's face on the other.

The face on the coin looked familiar, but Aiden couldn't locate anything on him, and now exhausted, he stared at the mountain of library books he had pulled from the shelves with a growing headache. It would take an hour to put them all back where they belonged, and Mrs. Reed had been a stickler for library rules since forever. He glanced up, scanning the library desk, and to his delight found it empty. Mrs. Reed must've been in the restroom. He scooped the coins up as quickly as he could and made a beeline for the exit.

CHAPTER THREE – FROM NEW YORK TO EAST TOWN

"No indeed, Laura's death was shameful," Mochtier Mackleford said, seated behind a large mahogany desk in a darkened room. A desk lamp cast light upon a formal place setting and a steaming hot meal Mackleford was enjoying. "A true tragedy, as there are no winners with death. But the Johnsons chose their path."

Across the desk sat a young man, who despite wearing thin frameless glasses, collared shirt and a sweater vest, came across as tough and brawny. He was scribbling several math equations in a spiral notebook.

"Something I don't understand, Mochtier," the young man said, still focused on his work. "You crippled Johnson, eliminated his wife, but didn't find out where they hid the Song."

"Yes, I know that Ellis."

Ellis Vicartan looked up from his notebook, staring into Mackleford's passive face. "Are there others who know its location?"

"I don't think so," Mackleford said, dabbing his mouth with a napkin. "Wilbert would have guarded that secret beyond everything. I doubt he even told his wife."

"Well then," Ellis said, looking confused, "it appears they've won. The Song is gone and you've disabled the only man who knew its location. Musclehead and Lanky said you lost control."

Mackleford raised an eyebrow and shook his head, mildly amused.

"Ellis, do you know me to be a man of outrageous emotion? Try and understand. This move was necessary to bring their final plans to light. *Lost control?* Have a little faith, son." He said those last words with a hint of disappointment and Ellis looked disheartened.

"I'm sorry, Mochtier. These last few months have been difficult."

"Don't apologize, please," Mackleford said, waving his fork in the air. "Wilbert knew what he was doing when he stole my property, and I suspect during the time he had it, he used it well. Things have been bad these few months, but I warned you to expect it after the theft. You weren't around when the Journeymen were strong. Things were difficult then, but look at us now."

Ellis nodded. "What is this about their final plans?"

"Wilbert won't allow failure just because he is disabled and defeated," Mackleford said. "There is one final play, a 'Hail Mary' as it were. When that fails, we shall regain the Song and the Journeymen will be finished. And it is crucial that the Journeymen are finished so that everything else falls into place."

"Of course you have a plan, Mochtier. I should have known."

"And *your* time to lead this organization is coming soon, Ellis," Mackleford said, reaching down and retrieving a bottle of dark red wine from a desk drawer and two wine glasses. "Understand your opposition. Know their strengths and weaknesses, their habits, their determination, even in obvious defeat."

Mackleford poured a glass, offering Ellis, who declined. He returned the spare glass and bottle to the desk. "The Journeymen have always been fearless, like my old partner, Gus. Wilbert is admirable if for nothing else, for his fearlessness. There is something to be said for that."

Ellis snorted.

"There's nothing wrong in respecting your adversary," Mackleford said in admonishment, and Ellis bowed his head respectfully. "However, don't mistake my generous tone. Wilbert Johnson is a fool; foolish to believe in Gus, foolish to oppose me. A short-sighted, overly emotional dupe."

"Emotional, crafty, and determined. This Hail Mary will be highly unpredictable."

"Indeed it will," Mackleford paused, taking a long sip of wine. "Journeymen are gathering in East Town soon and I know how important that is for them. We will need to be there to see what develops. This is the Dominion's time; our ambitions are nearly complete. We must put a permanent end to the Journeymen to move forward."

"I'll have Musclehead prepare."

Mackleford shook his head. "Not the Squad, Ellis. I'll only require six members of the Black Masks to accompany me. Tell Mr. Quick."

Vicartan stopped writing and sat the notebook down, removing his glasses. "Are you concerned about the Squad, Mochtier? I assure you our loyalty to the Dominion is—"

"Now you're being overly emotional," Mackleford interrupted. "Loyalty isn't my concern, Ellis. You're needed elsewhere. Have you found a suitable candidate?"

"I have," Ellis said, the coldness returning to his voice.

Mackleford smiled, leaning back in his chair. "Arrange a meeting please. And Ellis, I know this bothers you, but you are carrying out the most important leg of our current agenda. The Journeymen are more of a personal pain of mine."

The sixteenth of December arrived before Aiden and Flair knew it, but for Simone, it seemed to take forever. When the day had finally come, her excitement was evident during the cab ride to Penn Station in Manhattan.

"What do you think it's like out there?" she chattered. "Will there be enough time to see everything? Oh my God, it's soooooo pretty out there! Have you seen the pictures? I'll bet it's prettier than Dad's pictures! I hope it's a lot of kids my age! I read all about East Town online and I found Margaret Gumm! Her dad was this awesome explorer and…"

When the cabbie stopped at Penn Station, he was so eager to rid himself of Simone, he almost forgot his fare. He gave Aiden a sympathetic pat on the shoulder as he collected his pay and Aiden wondered if he would survive the next three weeks.

Aiden and Simone had packed reasonably light and wound their way easily through packed Penn Station, crammed with holiday travelers. Flair, however, looked miserable, struggling with four large bags and a suitcase on wheels. Aiden had warned her they would each pull their own weight, so Flair stumbled along in silence, but she still shot dirty looks at her siblings as they sped through the station.

"Simmy, where are you going?" Aiden yelled.

"The train, of course!" Simone shouted back, disappearing through the crowd. Aiden turned, looking back for Flair, and spotted her getting jostled, shouldered about, and falling further behind.

"Wow, you guys suck!" Flair screamed. "Slow down!"

"We gotta keep up with Simmy!" Aiden bellowed. They were yelling over the crowd of travelers who were giving them dirty looks. "We can't wait for you, sunshine! I warned you!"

"But I need this stuff," Flair yelled back. "What if I told you to go on vacation without your briefcase and laptop?"

"Ok, but I'm not crying about my briefcase and laptop, am I? And if I had—*Do you have a problem?*" he barked at a woman who had been glaring at Aiden, but then slunk away. "And if I had to carry a million bags to bring my briefcase and laptop, I would have left them at home. Simmy! Hold on!"

A portly attendant was examining Simone's ticket as Aiden arrived at a booth window.

"West Gate, track thirty-four. Tell Orosco you want East Town. Only two trains go that way, Lake Shore's better, but they'll get you on the next one."

"Thanks so much, oh, and Merry Christmas!" and Simone was off again, zigzagging towards a large staircase. Aiden was exhausted just watching her.

Sonya Martinez had a difficult job to do, but one she had performed hundreds of times: blend in and watch her target, without being spotted herself. She had her eye on Aiden, following him through the crowded terminal.

"I don't think he's noticed that," Sonya said quietly. "He's still chasing his little sister."

Sonya wasn't a typical teenager, but she looked the part, wearing blue jeans, black-rimmed glasses, tattered sneakers, a hooded sweater, with earphones plugged in. Everything fit, except for an exquisite pair of red, white and blue leather gloves Sonya was trying to remove, which was proving impossible.

"No. I can't see. Wait hold on a second...are these gloves glued on all of the sudden? What? Hey, look, I ain't Lyric, alright? I took 'em out already. What? Okay, let me check."

Sonya glanced around the area, eyeing two men wearing tan colored suits with their backs to her, watching Flair.

"Yeah, they're still there. They tailing the older daughter, probably won't move until she's downstairs."

Sonya finally got the first glove off, exhaling in relief, flexing her fingers.

"I swear Art makes these things to shrink. What? Search me, who knows they're up to? We got it covered, don't worry. But look, okay, when they get there, you're telling them everything, right? No, we trust you'll do it the right way. I won't…don't worry, I'll watch them, and make sure they get there, but you're gonna do all the talking. Yes ma'am. Okay. Over and out."

Aiden reached the large staircase screaming, "Simone! Stop!" as he headed down. Sonya flipped her hood over her head and followed.

One hour later, Aiden was sitting across the aisle from his sisters on an Amtrak, reading a pamphlet about East Town while Flair and Simone enjoyed coffee and pumpkin pie. Although she had a miserable time in the train station, Flair was talking excitedly about spending the holidays in East Town.

"I can't believe we're finally going," Flair said. "I always figured I'd have to wait until I was a grown-up and go by myself."

"Same here," Simone said, removing her winter hat, shaking her flattened curls back to life. "What about you Aiden? You're grown up, you've never gone."

"Because I *am* a grown-up, doofus. I have a job." He turned the pamphlet over, looking at a hotel advertisement on the back. "Guess we'll stay at the Cranberry Inn. It's the biggest hotel in the town."

"How many people live in East Town anyway?" Flair asked, finishing off her coffee with a long gulp.

"Says here population *1971*," Aiden said. "I hope they have indoor plumbing."

Simone giggled, stuffing pie into her mouth.

"Wow, check this out," Aiden said, his attitude perking up. "The Cranberry Inn, at seven stories, is East Town's tallest building. Established in 1912, used to be a cranberry sauce factory until owner Marley Middleman started keeping visitors for extra money. The seventh floor was damaged by a fire in 1944 and hasn't reopened since.. Interesting."

"Look, can you save the history lessons for your stupid students?" Flair sneered. "That's not our type of fun, is it Simmy?"

Aiden's hearty tone faded at Flair's remark. "Well, just make sure you two have lots of your type of fun. This is all for *Little Miss Impatient* anyway."

Simone dropped her head, staring awkwardly at her pie plate. Flair's empty coffee cup narrowly missed Aiden's head, bouncing off the window.

"Seriously, Aiden?" Flair said, glowering at him. Aiden shook his head and looked back to the pamphlet.

The Johnsons were silent for the next hour. Simone kept glancing at Aiden, clearly itching to say something, while Flair had her eyes closed, apparently asleep. Finally, Aiden said: "Okay, out with it Simmy."

"Okay," Simone burst out, "two things. First. Can we find where Grandma and Grandpa Maidenfair and Papa and Mama Johnson lived?"

"Nope," Aiden said. "Second?"

"Whaddaya mean *nope*?" Simone shot back. "We're gonna be there for over two whole weeks and not find out anything on our family? You nuts or something?"

Aiden rolled his eyes. "I know everything I need to know about our family, but whatever, feel free. Just don't bother me. Second?"

Simone didn't argue. Getting Aiden's half-hearted blessing on anything was usually the best she could expect. "I was just wondering what *else* was in that envelope Dad gave you."

"What? Were you going through my stuff?" Aiden reached into his jacket pocket to retrieve the slip of paper with the riddle. But he paused for a moment, thinking. Though he'd been sworn to secrecy, his father's riddles had the knack of keeping Simone preoccupied and, most importantly, quiet. He didn't have to tell her about the coins…could mean hours of busy work for her, and a peaceful train ride for him.

"Here, I don't know what it means." Aiden passed the paper to Simone, but Flair snapped awake and intercepted it.

"HEY!" Simone shouted.

"From the top of the stairs, look carefully…the cornerstone is where you'll find the key," Flair read aloud. "What's this?"

"Oh!" Simone gasped. "A riddle! I love Dad's riddles!"

Flair frowned. Try as her father might to engage her in the pastime, Flair hated riddles and guessing games. "What's this supposed to be?"

"Like Simone said. Pops gave me a riddle before we left."

"What stairs is he talking about?" Flair asked.

"Maybe at Dad's old house," Simone said. "Or at a church. Or maybe the burnt-up seventh floor of that creepy old hotel! Oooooooo!" She spotted a stewardess and shouted. "Hi! More pie and coffee please!"

"Decaf for her," Aiden shouted back. "Look, I can see this going places I don't want this going. Simmy, please don't make me regret telling you."

Simone fell silent, but her mischievous eyes darted in every direction.

"So, we're supposed to find some key?" Flair asked, re-reading the riddle.

"A key" Simone muttered. "A key to what?" She was fidgeting feverishly as the stewardess returned with a pot of coffee and three plates of pumpkin pie. Aiden waited until she left before starting the conversation again.

"You know Pops," Aiden said, cramming a hunk of pie into his mouth. "Might not be an actual key. I was thinking its something symbolic or…" Aiden paused as he swallowed, but then, realizing he was getting swept up in the mystery of it all, said: "Look, Pops didn't want you guys knowing about this, and I don't need Simone on the loose looking for staircases and keys. Let's just drop it."

"Drop it?" Flair laughed. "Dad actually gave us something interesting to do on this trip—"

"Gave *me* something—" Aiden corrected.

"Key, key," Simone mumbled.

"And it beats some old lady reading a book," Flair replied.

"It sounds like trouble," Aiden said.

"Sounds cool and mysterious…" Simone said.

"Cool and mysterious?" Aiden burst out laughing. "Get this straight, East Town is neither cool nor mysterious. Small place. Small people."

The train jerked to a halt, shaking Aiden out of a deep sleep. His wristwatch showed he'd been asleep for two hours, with two hours remaining before they arrived. He groaned; a broken down train was the last thing he needed.

"What happened?" Flair said, rubbing her eyes, also annoyed at the train stoppage. Aiden and Flair looked at one another and then both looked around for…

"Simone?" they said together.

"Where'd she go?" Aiden said, standing up.

Flair peered over her seatback. "I don't know, you're the *adult*, remember?"

"Probably wandering around," Aiden said, looking down the aisles.

"Maybe she got off the train?" Flair said, worried.

"She wouldn't have gotten off the train." Aiden sneered.

"We're talking about Simone," Flair sighed. "She could be the reason the train stopped."

The moment Flair said those words, Aiden developed a headache. Simone had proven she was capable of anything, and causing a train to grind to a halt wasn't out of the question. Aiden started off down the aisle.

"Where are you going?" Flair said, looking concerned.

"To find Simmy and kill her if she's done something stupid."

"ATTENTION PASSENGERS!" the loudspeaker blared. "Our train has malfunctioned and we're expecting a five-hour delay. We apologize for this inconvenience. Stewardesses will be around with complimentary snacks and drinks."

Aiden rolled his eyes. "Great. This gift just keeps on giving, doesn't it? And where the hell have you been?"

Simone was coming up the aisle, looking insulted.

"Don't talk to me like that! I was in the bathroom."

Aiden felt a little stupid, as several passengers were now scowling at him. "Well…you shouldn't wander off without saying anything, Simmy."

"You guys were asleep!" Simone snapped. "I wasn't waking you up for that! First I gotta start doing things on my own, now I need permission to go to the bathroom?"

Aiden was about to respond, but Flair pulled him back to his seat. "Just sit down, idiot, you're making us look bad!" Simone plopped into her seat, looking on the verge of tears. "He was just worried, Simmy. The train stopped suddenly, we woke up and couldn't find you."

"It's okay," Simone said, staring at her shoes. Flair punched Aiden in the arm, mouthing "apologize" when a portly man in an Amtrak uniform approached them.

"You folks Towners too, ain't cha?"

Aiden, Flair, and Simone stared at each other, confused. "What do you mean?" Aiden said.

"My apologies," the man said, removing his hat, "but your stewardess heard you talking about the Cranberry, and I saw your bag tags from earlier. East Town, right?"

Simone brightened. "Yeah, we're going to East Town!" She was back to normal that fast.

"I'm a Towner. Justin Mimble. I'm headed back next week once my vacation starts. Anyway, we're roundin' up some folks who wouldn't mind walking to the station in Woodwind, about an hour back up the tracks. Most folks on this monkey are going to Chicago and places beyond, but Towners can catch the AM77. That'll head ya to Proctor's Landing so you can catch the shuttle."

"What shuttle?" Flair asked.

Justin Mimble smiled. "The shuttle used to be the only way into Town before this line came along. Most Towners prefer the shuttle. It's chillier, adds time on the trip, but—"

"Thanks, but no thanks." Flair interrupted, sitting back down.

"You kidding me, Flair?" Aiden said. "I'm not sitting here for five hours."

"And I'm not dragging my stuff up some train tracks in the middle of the night. It's winter!"

"Oh, we'll make sure your luggage gets to East Town," Justin said. "And the tickets'll be on the house."

"Just an hour's walk?" Aiden said, with a sideways glance to Flair.

"If that," Justin said. "Maybe forty-five minutes, not a big deal. Beats sittin' around."

Flair looked at Aiden, who nodded. There was no point in asking Simone her opinion. She already had her winter hat on and her duffle bag thrown over her shoulder.

Twenty minutes later, Aiden, his sisters and a host of travelers shivered their way along the train tracks, which sat against the foot of a tall, sloping hill and a cliff, overlooking a large valley. But even with the gorgeous view, the trek to the Woodwind station was way more miserable than Aiden imagined. Ten minutes into the hike, a strong icy wind had kicked up, and sharp flecks of ice whipped around them, stinging their faces. Even Justin Mimble, who was leading the group to the Woodwind station, seemed to be regretting the decision.

"What a fantastic idea!" Flair bellowed over the gusting wind, shielding her face with her hands. "This is way better than sitting inside of a warm train!"

Aiden heard Flair but looked over his other shoulder in the opposite direction, far up the slope of the hill. A faint popping sound had caught his attention. He stared at the dark hillside. *What's going on?* he thought. *Is it moving?* He felt the ground shudder and staring down, he noticed the snow around his feet shifting, sliding towards the cliff.

"MOVE AIDEN!"

Aiden looked ahead. Everyone else was high-tailing it up the train tracks, yards ahead of him. He looked backwards at the snow-covered hillside. It was collapsing.

Hammered by clumps of snow, Aiden found his balance and ran. Flair was flying at top speed, dodging the rushing pelts with ease, as Simone leapt one massive snowball after another. Flair avoided a shower of snow that smashed into the ground, but Aiden watched another wall of white powder engulf her. Cursing, he ran around the pile of snow and ice, only to see Flair up ahead, still running.

The snow slide came to an abrupt end, the noise and tremors subsiding. From where they just ran, Aiden saw the train tracks piled with snow at least ten feet high, with clumps of snow falling over the cliff's edge.

Justin was doing a nervous head count. "Aiden! Flair!" he wheezed. "Okay, that's twenty-one and twenty-two. Where's Simone?"

"Behind you," Aiden said, catching his breath.

Justin spun and saw Simone, hands on her knees, panting. "Okay that's everyone," he said and joined the other passengers searching the snow for their belongings. Simone clutched her bag, trembling. Flair, however, looked exhilarated.

"Haven't ran that fast in months!" She exhaled, mussing Simone's hair. "What's the matter, bro, outta shape, huh?" She slapped Aiden on his stomach. "Two hours on the treadmill every night!"

The upside to their flight from a snowy grave was it had shaved off twenty minutes of walking. Aiden's heart hadn't stopped pounding until he saw the lights of the Woodwind train station. Snow had begun to fall as they entered the station, but Aiden wasn't aware of it. His mind was on another matter: the sound he'd heard before the snow slide

He thought it sounded like a firecracker. Maybe a branch snapping under the weight of snow? No, that wasn't it. It was an unusual sound, distinct, and curiously, he could have sworn he'd heard this sound before, but wasn't sure where or when. But then Aiden shook his head. It was stupid dwelling on some random sound he'd heard before the snow slide. It could have been anything.

The Woodwind train station was empty except for Mimble's group, who were drinking hot coffee provided by the station manager. Aiden, Flair, and Simone sat amongst the passengers, excitedly discussing the night's adventure.

"Wild, wasn't it?" Flair said.

"Amazing!" Simone exclaimed. "Bet Mom and Dad never did anything like that!"

Aiden was less enthusiastic. "We could have been killed. That's nothing to get excited about. Besides, they were missionaries. This probably doesn't even hit their top ten."

He turned away, sipping his coffee, but could feel Flair's glare.

"You enjoy being a depressing, sad little bookworm, don't you?" Flair said. Aiden returned a sarcastic smile.

Twenty minutes after the small shuttle left the station, the Johnsons were quickly and easily fast asleep.

The village of East Town was nestled inside of a wide valley carpeted with a dense forest. The surrounding hills were blanketed in white from the previous night's snowstorm, which gave everything a clean, pristine look.

The shuttle train exited a tunnel and glided along a downward slope into the valley. It was early morning and the sun peeked over the rim of the valley at the far end, shining into Flair's face, waking her.

She stared out the window at a majestic view of the town. It could have been out of a storybook: a small village with tiny cottage houses lined up neatly against narrow, winding cobblestone roads, each lined with snow-covered trees. Unchanged and untouched for decades. The train took a wide circle against the snow-frosted hills, and just below, Flair could see a crescent-shaped frozen lake sitting above the town.

She shook Aiden. "Yo! Wake up. We're here!"

Aiden woke, rubbing his eyes and glancing outside the window. He stared for several seconds, speechless, before tapping Simone.

"Simmy, wake up. We made it. We're in East Town."

The shuttle eased to a stop at the East Town station. Everyone stood, stretching, yawning, and slowly, they emptied onto the platform. The passengers greeted family and friends, but the Johnsons stood together, a little confused and unsure, before entering the red brick station house.

Although it was hardly warmer inside than out, the station house was comfy. A small fireplace blazed in front of a row of glossy wooden benches that looked freshly stained. A sleepy little man stood behind a bright red coffee stand, serving cups to several passengers. Simone joined a group of people discussing one of the large posters adorning the white walls, the largest reading:

Visit the World Famous
HOUSE OF GUMM
Museum and Historical Landmark

World famous? Aiden thought. Never heard of the place until a week ago.

"So what do we do now?" Flair asked Aiden.

"Get a cab, find the Cranberry Inn," Aiden answered, looking at another poster: *GET FED AND BED AT THE CRANBERRY INN,* picturing a woman serving food to a smiling family and a man in a fuzzy nightcap fast asleep in a cozy bed.

"First thing you wanna do is crash at the hotel," Simone said. "Figures."

"I have work to do. Sorry, some of us aren't happy-go-lucky kids on a field trip. I have adult responsibilities." Aiden turned his back, glancing outside for a cab. Flair silently mimicked him, wagging a reproving finger at Simone, who snickered.

"Yeah, the Cranberry Inn!" Simone suddenly burst out, looking at the Cranberry Inn poster. "Let's go, I wanna see the seventh floor all burned up!"

"Simmy, you're crazy, I swear!" Flair laughed.

"Amen to that," Aiden agreed. "Settle down."

"I'm not crazy!" Simone said. "He said I could explore!"

"And you thought exploring meant going through places blocked off since World War Two?"

"Hola youngins! Need a cab?" a crusty voice said.

The three Johnsons jumped and turned in unison, spotting an old man in a sky blue sweater, short and pot-bellied, with a head of thinning gray hair and silver-rimmed glasses limping forward. He approached Simone, who was barely shorter than him.

"Yes, we need a cab," Aiden said. "The Cranberry Inn, please."

The old man stared at Aiden, looking puzzled.

"Y'know, I never forget a face, and yers looks familiar," he said, scratching his stubbly chin. "I know who ya look like. Wilbert Johnson. I'd say yer the spittin' image of him, yessir! You his kin or something?"

"Yes. He's my dad."

The old man straightened up, examining each of their faces as an enormous grin spread across his.

"Wilbert and Laura's kids?" And when they nodded, he slapped his thigh, laughing. "Well, that's just *right all right!* These're your sisters?"

They introduced themselves as the old man threw out his hand, shaking each theirs vigorously.

"Name's Harold Mimble," he said, grinning. "As long as yer in town, I'm at yer service!"

"Mimble!" Simone shouted, and she relayed their meeting with Justin Mimble on the train, which turned out to be Harold's son. Mimble looked slightly upset at this news.

"Cain't believe he didn't tell me th' Johnson kids were on his train! But no matter." Mimble sighed, resting his hands on his hips and shaking his head. "Never thought I'd meet ya. Well, makes sense yer here. Never said g'bye ta East Town, did they?"

Simone and Aiden's eyes met, with Simone mouthing "Told you".

Mimble removed his glasses. "My condolences of course. Your folks were wonderful people."

"*Were?* My father's *still* alive, you know," Aiden said.

Mimble looked slighted. "I know that," he said, "but it's…they were a pair, is all. Ne'er saw one without th' other. Used ta drive th' Ninth Main carriage when they started dating, everyone would just stare at 'em. A coupla lovebirds on a branch. Inseparable."

The mood had changed dramatically. Flair blinked her eyes, turning her face, and Simone was looking downcast. Mimble noticed this and brightened his voice.

"Well, let's see! On everyone's first visit to East Town, I start 'em with the Grand Tour. Ready to see the town? There's lots to see, believe me!"

CHAPTER FOUR – RESTORATION COLLEGE

Ricardo Suarez was as miserable as anyone could be.

He didn't blame his parents as some kids do. It wasn't their fault. They were hardworking, loving, and gave him everything anyone could want. Ricardo's problem was he was a nice kid, just *too* nice. Too shy; decent-looking, but not smart; good at sports, but talked funny. He didn't have one person he could call a friend and was an easy target for bullying.

As a teenager he grew into a loner, but he was never satisfied with that. Determined to have friends who understood him, he ended up finding friendship with members of a street gang, who accepted the quiet, obedient, and especially big and strong Ricardo. The rules of the streets were easy enough to understand: don't get caught, and if you do, don't snitch. He knew crime was wrong, but as long as he was loyal and followed the rules, he had friends who accepted him. He also became too familiar with courts, probation officers and juvenile hall.

To no one's surprise, including Ricardo's, he ended up in jail, doing twelve months for armed robbery. Inside prison, he joined up with another gang, and after a few fights, he eventually extended his sentence twelve more months.

He was nineteen when he returned home and was unsure of what to do with his life. He sat around the house for months, trying to stay out of trouble, but it was difficult. Jobs were limited, his reputation made most people afraid to give him a chance, and gang members were the only friends he'd ever known.

So Ricardo believed it was nothing short of divine providence when Ellis Vicartan visited him one Friday afternoon. Ellis was a teacher at a nearby college, whose mission was to "reform, re-educate, and restore" criminals back into society. The school was aptly named Restoration College.

"You'll love the people, Ricardo," Ellis said, handing him a few brochures. "The teachers are friendly. There's no formal requirements to enter the school. Just come as you are."

"I ain't got money for that," Ricardo had told him. "Barely takin' care of myself."

"You work off your tuition, it's part of the deal. You get paid for the work you do around on campus, around the community, helping the staff—"

"Look, college and hangin' around a bunch of stupid kids just ain't my thing, okay?"

Ellis removed his glasses and Ricardo suddenly felt like he was back in the prison yard, getting schooled by one of the lifers. "Look, Ricardo. R.C. ain't for high schoolers, okay? They wouldn't wanna be around a bunch of crooks anyway. It's guys like us, looking for another shot. Most of my students are older than you."

Ellis paused, waiting for a response while Ricardo examined the brochure. "R.C. does what it says," Ellis said. "I'm you ten years ago, one bad choice away from another stretch, or worse. You don't wanna go there."

Ricardo was still reading from the brochure. *Nine campuses worldwide.* He saw a picture of people in front of a dormitory, smiling and laughing.

"So I stay on campus? Sounds like prison. Three hots and a cot?"

"You're a laugh!" Ellis snorted. "We travel the world, friend. You'll see things most people never see. We get holidays, Christmas, spring break, summer. As long as you complete your credits and work, you get spending money. That sound like prison to you?"

Ricardo didn't have anything better to do or any real reason to say no, so he accepted and enrolled. His four years at Restoration were the best years of his life. He made true friendships with students who were once like him, shy and lonely and wanting acceptance. He travelled the world, studying at Restoration campuses in Greece, China, Germany, and Brazil, becoming one of Restoration's better students, and Ellis' protégé. Five months after graduating, he returned to the campus to meet with the head of Restoration for an exit interview.

Ricardo's heart swelled as he re-entered the school, looking at the walls lined with posters and plaques, smelling the polish of the main hallway's hardwood floors. Restoration College always had a bright, clean feeling and Ellis had been correct, it was nothing like a prison.

"Rico!" yelled a familiar voice. Ricardo turned and saw Ellis Vicartan at the end of the hall. He walked over and embraced his mentor and friend.

"Hey, Mr. Vicartan!"

"I ain't your teacher anymore," he corrected, giving Ricardo a playful punch in the arm. "It's just Ellis. You look great, Rico. Ready?"

Ellis removed his glasses, giving Ricardo a once-over. He was dressed in Levi's, sporting a jacket, and tie, and was so nervous, he was shaking.

"S'matter, Rico?"

"I've never met *him* before," Ricardo said. "Just don't wanna embarrass you."

Ellis glared at him. "You better not embarrass me!" he snarled, grabbing Ricardo by the collar, forcing Ricardo to snort out a laugh. Ellis always knew how to relax him.

"Look, he's a regular guy." Ellis straightened his collar back. "He'll like you. Just be cool." He patted a large thick manila folder as they stopped at an elevator. "We'll let this do most of the talking. Your transcripts of everything you ever did at R.C., and it's impressive. *Very* impressive."

A large, lavish circular office awaited them at the bottom of the elevator. It was clear to Ricardo that Restoration College was doing well for itself. The entire back wall of the office was an aquarium, replete with hundreds of fish and sea creatures. The carpet was deep purple, plush, and there were decorations from the world over. But what caught and held Ricardo's attention was the man standing next to a magnificent oak desk, facing the aquarium, playing a violin with festive exuberance.

Ellis cleared his throat. The man stopped playing and turned.

It was Mochtier Mackleford.

Dressed impeccably in a tailored suit, Mackleford set the violin on the desk, not taking his eyes off Ricardo. Ellis walked forward, handing the manila folder to Mackleford and speaking quietly. Ricardo twitched his foot back and forth, trying to master his nerves. He faintly heard himself being introduced and, in sort of a knock-kneed stumble, walked forward.

"I think you'll agree Mochtier," Ellis said proudly, "that Mr. Suarez is exceptional. Very intelligent, strong, and easy to work with."

Mackleford sat behind his desk, silently flipping through the folder, while Ellis examined the fish tank. Mackleford nodded to the empty seat opposite him, and Ricardo sat.

"Mr. Suarez?" Ricardo's heart skipped at the sound of Mackleford's voice, which was deep and distinguished. "Well done, young man, I'm impressed. You're clearly one of Restoration's better success stories." He flipped another page. "Fine marks in our most difficult courses." He flipped again, and his eyebrows rose. "Won the Fitness Championship three years in a row," he said excitedly. "Never happened before in our history. Explain."

"Mr. V-Vicartan said a fit body is the d-doorway to success," he stuttered. "You can't do well in this world if you're always sick and not a hundred percent. So I made sure I ate right, exercised, and disciplined myself, Mr. Mackleford."

"Listen, we're friends here!" Mackleford said, closing the file and smiling. "His name is Ellis, yours is Rico. I can call you Rico, right? It's what your *friends* call you, isn't it?"

"Yes, sir," he replied.

"Friends don't call each other *sir*. It's Mochtier. My old business partner used to call me Mack. Anyway Rico, this is no exit interview. You were brought to meet me because of your trustworthiness. Like your mentor and my friend Ellis; he's extraordinarily loyal. I would trust him with my life."

"So would I." Ricardo looked towards Ellis, who hadn't acknowledged the compliment, still examining the fish behind the glass.

"But he wasn't always that way. Once upon a time he was just like you. A dirty, disgusting blight upon the earth, like an ugly scar on the face of a beautiful woman. A thief, a liar, a thug who ran with gangs and peddled illegal narcotics. Worthless, despicable waste of life. But, like you, he was educated and passed all his examinations. Like you, he paid back those he had wronged tenfold. Like you, he met the qualifications of our institution and graduated with all honors and distinction.

"However, obtaining knowledge is elementary, and passing tests just proves you can learn things. But that isn't the reason you or Ellis came here, is it, Rico?"

"No sir, um, er...Mr. Mackle...um, M-Mochtier."

Mackleford continued talking, indifferent to Rico's nerves. "A famous man once said the worst of all feelings is misery. Not just sadness, but an aching, a longing for something unattainable—that's misery. And the worst misery of all, Rico? To know so much and yet control nothing. You've obtained knowledge; you are not only a finished product of Restoration's fine education, but the shining example of why this school was founded. But what are you going to do with that knowledge?"

Rico was ready for this question, and clearing his throat, he stated: "I want to decide my own fate. I want the power to decide my fate, to create a better life, not just for me, but also my fellow man. I believe in the greatness of the world and the ability of mankind to overcome their human frailties. I believe I can bring meaning to the world. I want—"

"Hold on, son," Mackleford said coolly with his head tilted to one side. "Is that what they teach you upstairs? Is that what represents education for you after four long years? Is this why we spent all of our time, money and effort? For you to walk down here and recite some lines to me? How long did it take you to memorize that?"

"Uh...I..." Rico's mind was blank, his jaw still hanging slack and open. Shaking from head to toe, he looked to Ellis, who only seemed interested in a strange yellow fish.

Mackleford suddenly burst out into hysterical laughter and Rico stared curiously. Mackleford gasped and heaved enormously, finally settling down and reaching over to a desk drawer. He retrieved a small bottle of water and drank from it.

"Forgive me, Rico, my strange sense of humor!" he panted. "I'm just giving you a hard time."

Rico finally exhaled, gasping for air as if he had run a marathon, which prompted a couple of additional hard chuckles from Mackleford.

"Of course I know what they tell you up there," Mackleford chuckled. "It's my school after all! Sometimes it's hard to organize our thoughts and articulate them, which is why we teach concepts like this by memorization. But we don't want you to just recite them, because the question isn't if you can say the right things. The heart of all things is belief. Do you *believe* what you just said?"

"Absolutely!" Rico sputtered out as fast as he could, wanting to say something that wasn't memorized. "I want to see the world as it should be, not as it is!"

"Of course you do. And who shouldn't want to see the world born anew? We weren't meant for this life, were we Rico? Look through history. What has the human race amounted to? Is man the towering giant we've romanticized? We're still creatures cowering in the dust, afraid of our own mortality, cutting each other's throats for money and power! Is that MAN?"

Mackleford slammed his hand down on the desk, emphasizing his point. Rico, inspired, stood up. "NO!" he shouted. "I mean YES! I mean…yes, that *is* man, but no, it shouldn't be!"

Mackleford smiled. Rico straightened up, feeling slightly embarrassed, and sat down as Mackleford returned to his chair, folded his hands, and continued.

"As I said Rico, I trust Ellis, and Ellis brought you here because he believes you would be a valuable addition to an organization on the cusp of greatness. We have many brothers and sisters worldwide, some you've already met. But the greatest of us, the men and women who have endeavored to make the ultimate sacrifice for our cause you haven't met, but you will.

"Humanity is shifting Rico, sadly and unfortunately, into a backwards form of thinking. We are in *de-evolution*. Instead of striding ahead, we are regressing. There is power out there, however. The true power of this planet. More powerful than harnessing the energy of a storm or splitting an atom. Those who thought they knew better hid this power from humankind for centuries. Our goal is to bring that power to every man, woman and child on Earth. But be aware. Creating a better life for us all comes with enormous responsibility. You *do* understand that?"

"Yes," Rico said confidently. "I do."

"While our cause is right and we are courageous pioneers, nevertheless there are those who don't understand this process of revolution and oppose us. It is not their fault. Change is often difficult for even the wisest of men. But we are the solution to what ails mankind. If need be, we must help them see their folly and gain understanding. Are you ready to accept this challenge, and join us?"

"Yes. I am."

Mackleford smiled. And at last, Ellis turned his attention to them, beaming like a proud father. "Rico, thank you. You've just joined a great association of men and women who want nothing more than to see mankind at its apex. World changers. Stand up, brother."

Rico rose from his seat, holding his head high. Mackleford walked over, shook his hand firmly, and hugged him. If Rico had seemed nervous before, it didn't show. Mackleford's speech seemed to inspire him. He puffed his chest out as Ellis walked over.

"Now Ellis, take our new protégé upstairs and prepare him for his new life."

Ellis led Rico back to the open elevator car, patting him on the back heartily, and Mackleford resumed his violin playing. But another interruption came in the form of a ringing phone at his desk as the elevator doors closed.

"Good afternoon, *Sonya*," Mackleford answered. "About time I heard from you."

Rico lay on his bare back, dressed only in underwear, looking like someone who was having second thoughts. He was in a white, sterile room, cold, clearly some sort of laboratory, and the table he laid on looked like any operating table he'd ever seen. He had no idea what to expect. He just tried to focus on Ellis Vicartan, his friend and mentor, and those words he had said to him: "Trust me, Rico. It's going to change your life forever."

But that was a month ago after the interview with Mr. Mackleford. It wasn't until Ellis invited him to spend his Christmas at Restoration College that Rico even remembered his commitment to Mackleford's program. He tried to relax as Mackleford walked through the white door at the far end of the lab and closed it with a loud 'clack'.

Although Mackleford's smile was warm and soothing, the contrast of his dark suit against the sterile, white room was intimidating, and his slow, echoing footsteps certainly didn't do Rico's nerves any favors. Mackleford leaned over the table, patting Rico gently on the arm.

"Hello Rico. Hope you're not nervous."

Rico took a deep breath. "A little bit. What are we about to do?"

Mackleford straightened up. "Change your life. I know I have your word, and I know you, like Ellis, are trustworthy and fearless. So it's only fair that I give you full disclosure and tell you what we're going to do before we start."

"Okay, sir."

Mackleford sat on the edge of the table. "Several decades ago, on a little island in the Indian Ocean so seldom travelled, it only showed on up on a few maps and atlases, a discovery was made. Probably the most important discovery in the history of mankind—a pool of pure liquid. Whole. Uncontaminated. Unadulterated. Clean."

Mackleford paused, perhaps for dramatic effect, Rico wasn't sure, but he certainly looked distant before continuing. "Upon drinking the liquid, everything improved. Muscles, bones, it even slowed the aging process. The man who discovered it named it Purity. Truly remarkable, nothing like it had ever been seen, before or since.

"Purity, Rico, has taught us so much, more about the human body than we could have dreamed. He spent years developing it, but he soon realized it was not without side effects. I personally took up the challenge of learning and mastering these effects, *Purification*, and the secrets of genetic manipulation. Those experiments almost killed me."

"They did?" Rico sat up with a start, his nervousness finally breaking through. "Is that what we're doing?" He eyed the exit door, some thirty feet away.

Mackleford patted Rico on the shoulder and Rico laid back onto the table. "Easy, Rico. After much work, I improved it, eliminating many of the terrible side effects. Still, it wasn't perfect. Not until now."

At that moment, a man wearing surgical scrubs, latex gloves, and a mask walked into the room, pushing a cart filled with an intimidating array of needles, fluids and surgery equipment. Rico heard Ellis's voice over and over in his head, *"Trust me, Rico…Trust me…"*

"Ready, Mackleford?" the man asked, not looking at Rico.

"Almost, Dr. Standis. I'm explaining to Rico how the process works. Anyway, with the brilliance of your mentor, Ellis, I believe we have reached fruition. You will become the first in a new class of man. You will be important Rico, important to everything we stand for and believe in."

Rico gulped. "What's it going to do to me?"

"Strengthen you. Improve you. Purify you. You will never get sick. You'll be impervious to most external damage. You won't be plagued by the weaknesses that have troubled humanity. Your body and mind will become completely adaptable to its surroundings. Heat? Cold? Nothing. Barren wastelands will be a walk in the park. Not only that, you will be perfectly strong, perfect vision, perfect hearing. I must admit Rico, I am jealous. You are going to have the power you wanted, the power to change the world. If I weren't so — if it weren't for my circumstances, I would be enjoying the same benefits you will soon experience."

Rico barely heard what Mackleford was saying. He was focused on the medical cart, so much so, that he didn't notice the doctor reaching underneath the operating table for a long black leather strap. He quickly swung the strap around Rico's legs before he realized what was happening.

"Hey! What the hell is that for?"

"Easy son. Take it easy," the doctor said in a passive voice.

"Don't tell me to take it easy! Get off me!"

Mackleford grabbed Rico's arm, slamming it to the cold metal table. Rico realized although Mackleford didn't look it, he was powerfully strong.

"The procedure is difficult," Mackleford said, his demeanor was no longer cool and calm, but manic. "These straps are necessary. Hold still!"

"Mr. Mackleford, sir, I don't want this anymore!"

"I thought he submitted to this," shouted the doctor.

"Lankershim! Clarkson!" Mackleford bellowed.

Two enormous men burst into the room, a tall brute with long, gangly arms and an enormous, gorilla-sized man with shoulders so thick and broad, you couldn't find a neck on him. Rico threw the doctor away and reached for the strap around his legs. The two brutes pounced.

Mackleford stepped away from the melee on the operating table now that the Goons were in control. He pulled a buzzing cell phone from his pocket and reviewed a message.

A smile grew across his face as he read. He turned to Rico, who was gagged, bound to the table with four leather straps, staring at Mackleford with bulging, terrified eyes. Mackleford leaned over him as he smoothed his silver glove over his hand.

"Doctor, begin the procedure immediately."

"Shouldn't I wait for Mr. Vicartan?"

"Ellis will join you shortly. I need to speak with him regarding another matter, and then I will be off campus for a few days. Provide me with updates as regularly as you can."

"They've surfaced? In East Town?" Ellis said. He was seated on a weight bench in a large gym, shirtless and drenched in sweat, looking at Mackleford as he examined his silver glove.

"As I expected they would," Mackleford said calmly.

"And you're going? To East Town?" Ellis sounded concerned. Mackleford nodded.

Ellis shook his head. "It's risky, Mochtier. Journeymen will be crawling everywhere. Take No-Neck and Lanky with you."

"Think I cannot handle the Journeymen, Ellis?" Mackleford said, agitated. "The Squad remains here, but I do need those members of the Black Masks. Have Mr. Quick arrange it, please."

Ellis stared at the floor, looking contemptuous. Mackleford started to turn and walk away when a distant cry of deep pain and anguish sounded from somewhere. Mackleford nodded, remembering.

"Oh yes, Rico has started his procedure. You should be there to oversee Dr. Standis."

CHAPTER FIVE – MIMBLE'S TOUR

The streets of East Town were easily the most festive streets the Johnsons had ever laid eyes upon, and that's saying something for a trio that grew up in New York. Aiden would later remark, "It's like living in a snow globe."

Hanging over the streets were thousands of glittering Christmas bulbs lighting the frosty morning. Every tree brimmed of tinsel and ornaments and a holiday wreath hung on every door. Children were dressed in scarves, mittens, and woolly caps, making snow forts, stacking snowballs into giant pyramids, preparing for battle.

Mimble's old cab was a soothing ride, ambling over the cobblestone streets. Mimble hummed along with the holiday songs on the radio, taking them through a guided tour of the village.

"Good thing ya got in today," Mimble remarked. "Tomorrow's when Towners show up in droves. Mightn't be able to give you th' Grand Tour."

Simone looked to the left, seeing a long line of people crammed onto the sidewalk outside of a corner store. "What's going on over there?"

"There's Darby's General. Everything you need. Darby the Fourth, we call him Four, he runs it now. His pap ran it before him, and his before him. One o' them big chains put a store on the other side o' town. Kreegers I think. Don't know, never been in there. Most of us still shop at Darby's."

Harold rounded the corner. The line stretched the entire block.

"I think I'll be going to Kreegers," Aiden said.

"Suit ya'self. Long lines at Darby's ain't so bad. Always see someone ya ain't seen in a good while to catch up on th' latest."

Aiden looked at his sisters who were admiring a large stone and brick church on the opposite side of the street where a man in a gray sweater swept the church driveway with a push broom. Mimble pulled to the curb and reached across Aiden to roll down the passenger window.

"Here's First Street Church," Mimble said cheerfully. "That's Reverend Jack Lafayette. Used to be mayor a ways back…Mornin' Reverend Jack!"

The Reverend walked over and peered inside.

"Mornin' Harold! Songbooks are in, just in time for tonight." The Reverend was tall, skinny man with stark white hair, although his face was very young. "Who do we have here? Visiting for the holidays, folks?"

"These ain't just *any* visitors, Jack. Take a closer look," Harold said, nodding to Aiden. "Who's he look like?"

Aiden felt himself reddening.

"Well, good mornin' t' me," Lafayette whispered. "You're Wilbert's son, ain't cha?"

Introductions were made, and Simone screamed in Aiden's ear when Lafayette told them he had married their parents. Aiden thought to himself she was lucky a pastor was here.

"M' first marriage," Lafayette reminisced. "I was a nervous wreck, but your parents just took over the whole thing, like no one else was even there, r'member Harold? Wrote their own vows and ev'rything."

Minutes later, they said goodbye, with the Reverend reminding them church service started promptly at nine. Aiden and Simone grumbled. Their parents had been off and on churchgoers and never forced their children to attend, but Flair endured their eye rolling and promised they would be there on Sunday.

The cab gamboled along the snow-lined roads, and Harold introduced the Johnsons to what seemed to be every citizen in East Town. They met Mimble's wife Anna, who was preparing a shopping list for Darby's, Elsa Majors, East Town's oldest resident, and more children than Aiden ever wanted to know. Mimble purposely doubled over his route, claiming he had forgotten to show them something, but Aiden suspected this was to give the snowball throwers a shot at the cab.

The cab shuddered as it climbed Theodore Avenue, a long, steep road set against the woods. Harold stopped the cab, pointing out a small narrow path carved out through a grove of trees.

"There's the path to Weingarten Lake, probably saw it on your way in. Ice-skating and fireworks every evenin', and the East Town band will be out there playing 'til mornin'. It's the best part of it all! *Silent Night* and ev'rything, puts the whole valley to sleep. A couple of the band members are…well, speak of th' devil! Just as I'm sayin' it, here they are!"

A man and a woman holding instrument cases approached, staring into the cab. The man was tall with a trimmed head of gray hair and a stiff posture, wearing a sour look on his face; Aiden figured he didn't want to be bothered, but felt inclined since he was spotted. The woman had large, expressive brown eyes and fading good looks, like a former beauty queen just outside of her prime. Once they saw the children, they froze, and the man said something quickly to the woman. It reminded Aiden of his students when a pop quiz was announced.

"Nicolas and Lydia Gannares. Your parents' best friends," Mimble announced. "Nick, Lydia, look who's here!"

"Hello kids," Mr. Gannares said, improving his acidic look slightly. "I'd recognize you anywhere. Laura always sent family photos. How are you enjoying East Town?"

"It's pretty cool so far," Simone said, hanging out of the window and talking. The Gannareses were polite but didn't seem genuine to Aiden. Their body language suggested they wanted to end the conversation without being rude. Lydia kept hitching up her instrument case, and Nick checked his watch every thirty seconds. After minutes of boring chitchat, Aiden decided to have some fun.

"Argentina, right?" Aiden declared, and Nick raised an eyebrow to Aiden. "Distinctive accent, I picked up on it last year from one of my students. Yeah, you've been in the country a while, but you haven't lost it. And you may dress conservatively, but your body language suggests you're far from it. You have the eyes of a worldly man. You've seen a lot in your life, Mr. Gannares, and not all good."

"Well, how about that?" Harold laughed, albeit nervously. "Aiden knows ya bett'r 'n I do!"

"Very good, Aiden," Nick said. He didn't meet Aiden's eyes, but was no longer checking his watch, rather glancing up and down the street, as if looking for someone. "Seems like your father has taught you his old parlor tricks," he said as his eyes finally landed on Aiden.

Wow, if looks could kill, Aiden thought. Nick's jaw was rigid, his eyes cold and cruel. "Go on, Aiden, entertain us. What *else* did your father teach you?"

"Ah…uh…" Aiden stammered, then turned to Lydia. "Well, Mrs. Gannares, you…"

But Lydia's bright brown eyes flashed a threatening look that made Aiden change his mind mid-sentence. "You, uh, play the saxophone. Probably a big fan of bands and, uh, stuff," he finished awkwardly.

Harold seemed to sense the tension. "Welp, guess we'll get a move on," he said, pulling at the stick shift. "You two have practice and we've got a tour to finish!"

Harold pulled off down the street as Aiden stared into his rear view mirror.

"Think I made them mad?" Aiden said, watching the Gannareses cross the road. "What's their story, Harold?"

"Your parents' best friends," Harold shrugged. "No one took the news harder than Nick and Lydia."

After twenty more minutes of visiting Mimble's favorite haunts and speeding away from snowball-wielding children, they stopped at an enormous white building, adorned with decorations, which Aiden recognized from the brochure.

"At last, the Cranberry Inn," Aiden sighed. "Thought we'd never get here."

"Ain't she beautiful?" Harold said. "Largest building in Town. Already filling up with folks coming in for the Reading."

"A lot of people come back for that?" Flair asked.

"Yessir! No self-respectin' Towner would miss it!"

"We're gonna check-in and get settled," Aiden said, unbuckling his seatbelt. "Thanks for the tour."

Harold smiled, grabbing Aiden's seatbelt and fastening it again. "Tour ain't over yet. You ain't seen half of nothin', but don't worry, you'll get settled in just right." He winked and the cab drove off. Aiden looked at his sisters again, who seemed to be enjoying themselves.

An hour later, however, even Simone looked bored, and the warm air blowing from the cab's heater had Flair nodding off. Harold had covered every one of East Town's thirty-four streets, showing them everything from the bell tower to the local diner to East Town High School. Finally, he stopped the cab outside a narrow two-story brick house and announced: "Here we are!"

"Here we are, where?" Flair yawned.

"Must be Margaret Gumm's place," Aiden said. "It's the only place we haven't seen."

"Margie's house?" Harold laughed. "Heck no! No, this is your *parents'* place."

The Johnsons' faces went blank.

"My parents' what?" Simone gasped.

"My parents don't have a house here," Flair said, frowning.

"'Course they do!" Harold laughed. "Where'd'ya think they stayed when they came into Town? The Cranberry?"

Aiden looked at Simone, who was gazing at the house. Flair was shaking her head, bewildered. Their parents actually owned a home in this town? Could it be true?

"It's yer grandpa's house actually. Used ta pick yer dad up from this very spot when I drove the school bus."

Simone exploded like a tiny bomb.

"OH-MY-GOD-ARE-YOU-SERIOUS-MY-DAD-LIVED-HERE-THIS-IS-WHERE-HE-GREW-UP-THIS-HOUSE-RIGHT-HERE?"

Harold hooted with laughter. "Sure did, little squirrel."

"I have GOT to see it!" she screamed, and as Aiden opened his mouth to speak, "AIDEN I DON'T CARE!"

The cab door burst open and Simone flew up the front walk, examining the house from every angle. Harold shook his head, smiling.

"Quite a little spark. She's Laura all over again."

Flair went after Simone, trying to calm her, but Aiden hadn't moved. He was still staring at the house, his eyes fixed on an upstairs window.

Another memory had come to him, his first in months. He was a young boy, maybe seven, staring at that same upstairs window, fearing what awaited him up there.

"Going in, son?" he heard a voice say. It wasn't Harold's voice, but when he turned and looked, there was only Harold. The memory had faded.

"No key," Aiden muttered. "How are we supposed to get in?"

"Aiden, you're in East Town," Mimble laughed. "No one locks doors around here 'cept Margie, but she has reason to. Let's get your bags."

Simone, hearing the remark about East Town homes being unlocked, raced through the front door at top speed. Aiden and Harold entered shortly afterwards, lugging suitcases.

"Dag-blass-it!" Harold said, checking his watch. "All this time touring you folks, forgot I have some runs to make. Be back in a coupla hours to finish up. That should give you enough time to unpack."

Aiden had his wallet out. "What do we owe you, Mimble?"

Harold smiled. "Seeing you kids in Town is all the payment I need." And he closed the door behind him.

The home looked cozy and inviting. A modest living room with a hearthrug laying in front of a brick fireplace, framed by a sofa on one side, two end tables, and an easy chair.

"It's cute," Flair commented. "Charming."

"It's small and it's cold," Aiden retorted. "Dusty and dirty, look at this place. The hotel would have been warmer and better and ...OW!"

Flair scored a solid punch on the back of Aiden's head, knocking off his flat cap.

"What's that for?" Aiden said, grabbing his cap from the floor.

"For being a butthead! Simmy's counting on you."

Aiden tried to hit her back, but Flair dodged, pelting him in the face with multiple slaps until he covered his head, surrendering. He'd never beaten Flair in a slap fight; Aiden was fast, but Flair was faster and always determined to win. He was certain she had been secretly training to be a prizefighter.

Simone rumbled down the stairs. "It's AMAZING!" she shouted. "Oh my God, there are pictures of Mom and Dad everywhere! And Aiden...AIDEN! You've got to check *this* out!"

Simone flew up the stairs again. Flair, glaring at Aiden, jerked her head towards the steps and followed her. Once again Aiden felt fearful, and he followed uncertainly, falling behind Flair with each step.

Upstairs were four rooms, two at the far end, one in front of Aiden, and one to his left. Entering the first door, he found a small office, with a desk and a bookshelf behind it. Aiden sat in the desk chair and a strange feeling overcame him. He had been here before.

"AIDEN...IN HERE!" Flair called.

Aiden entered the bedroom at the end of the hallway. His mouth fell open.

It was a toddler's bedroom, complete with sports car bed, a large toy chest, and a rocking chair. A layer of dust covered everything, completely untouched for ages.

Simone shook a toy truck in Aiden's face. "Look, Aiden! It was yours!"

The childlike writing across the blue truck was as clear as day.

PROPERTY OF AIDEN J

CHAPTER SIX – THE HOUSE OF GUMM

Flair sat at the brick fireplace, poker in hand, stoking the remains of a once crackling fire whose dying embers gave the living room a warm, orange glow. Simone was curled upon the large hearthrug, snoring loudly as Aiden, on the sofa, reviewed a photo album against the flickering shadows.

So, his parents had a home in East Town, and at some point he must have lived here. Questions flooded his mind. Why hadn't they told him he lived in East Town? Why were they renting an apartment in Brooklyn when they had their own house? And most importantly, why didn't *he* remember living here? Aiden was kicking himself for thinking Flair and Simone were right, but now he wanted to learn as much as he could about their parents' lives in East Town.

"I don't get it," Aiden said. "I thought they just visited this place. How come they never said anything?"

"Who knows?" Flair said. "Mom and Dad were crazy. Probably coming here living some double life instead of going on missionary trips."

"Mom and Pops weren't crazy, just secretive…I think." Aiden was at a loss.

"Whatever it is," Flair whispered, making sure Simone was still sleeping, "this is the worst trip ever. Avalanches, a boring two-hour tour, and look…"

She held her cell phone in Aiden's face.

"No data service. Nothing from FacePlace. This town sucks. I just wanna leave."

At that moment, Harold Mimble entered, stamping his feet and dusting snow from his shoulders. "Sorry, took a bit longer than expected. Elsa and Anna bought up half of Darby's."

"What did they buy?" Flair asked.

"Ingredients for th' Christmas pies they make for every Towner household. Which reminds me. Your choices are apple, pumpkin, pecan, or Towner pie. It's sort of a strawberry rhubarb tart, but it's delicious!"

"They don't have to make us anything," Aiden said. "We're not Towners."

"Wilbert and Laura's kids not get a Christmas pie? Foolishness!"

Simone stirred on the floor, then sprang to life like a charged up toy.

"Mr. Mimble, you're back! Are we finishing your tour?"

"Yep, little squirrel! Just one stop remains, saved the best for last! The crown jewel of East Town, and there's someone who'll be pleased as punch to see ya!"

Minutes later, the cab hummed along the streets of East Town, its passengers enjoying the scenery: homes, trees, even the sidewalks were decorated with lights, tinsel, and ornaments. Snow had begun to fall, which mingled perfectly with the Christmas music on the radio.

"You guys love really Christmas, don't you?" Flair said.

"We do. A lot of us never left East Town," Harold proclaimed with pride. "Born, raised, and we'll pass on, right here in Town. Folks like your parents come back, tell us how th' world ain't like where they grew up. They say little things don't matter out there. But we love th' little things, feel they're the best part o' life. Folks come back for the lights, decorations, snowball fights, Elsa's stories, Anna's pies, and Margie's Reading. We remind 'em sometimes the best things in life ain't always the biggest."

The little things. Aiden could hear his mother's voice echoing those exact words. She always told Aiden to pay attention to the little things. East Town was simple and quiet compared to New York City and the chaos he dealt with every day. He slowly nodded.

"So that's why everyone comes back," Aiden said.

"Yessir!" Mimble replied. "For a slice of Towner pie and a slice of Towner life. Once a year, ya recharge them batt'ries and go back into the world."

"How long does the Reading take?" Aiden asked.

"An hour, maybe. Don't disparage it, son. Lotta wisdom in that lady…whole family actually. Wouldn't be East Town without the Gumms, they're everything to us. Thought of renaming the town Gummville, but Mr. Gumm wouldn't hear of it. Angry enough when they made the House of Gumm a state landmark. He built it from the ground up, been standing over sixty years now. Beautiful home, world famous! And look, there she is!"

The cab turned the corner on Twelfth St. and Melanie Ave. Sitting behind a large front garden was a colossal two-story home surrounded by a fancy rod-metal fence adorned with intricate designs.

The House of Gumm was gorgeous. The property expanded the entire block, and despite its enormous size, the house itself looked like a quaint cottage out of a storybook. It had slush-and-brush exterior walls and a large slanted roof, with wooden awnings over each window trimmed green and blue. Every window emitted a soft, golden glow from within and white smoke puffed out of the brick chimney.

Simone's eyes were large as saucers.

"Oh man," Simone breathed in awe, "that's the prettiest house I've ever seen!" She grinned at her brother. She could tell he was impressed.

Aiden took it all in. He was impressed, but something else was on his mind. Another memory. A vivid vision of this house blossomed in his mind: an old woman with salt and pepper curls serving a tray of cookies to children on this same front porch before him. A young girl with long, wavy auburn hair sat with him on a porch swing, sharing cookies and laughing. She leapt off the swing and gave Aiden a kiss on the cheek…

"Aiden…let's go! Quit being rude!" Flair pulled Aiden's jacket sleeve, interrupting his daydream while Simone and Harold stood at the front gate admiring the giant house.

A tiny woman with neat gray curls tucked under a felt hat exited the house, wearing a red-checkered dress and overcoat, with a matching handbag. Simone recognized her at once.

"It's *her*," Simone whispered excitedly as Aiden approached. "It's Margaret Gumm!"

They walked up a winding footpath as the little woman closed the door behind her. She turned and jumped, startled at the sight of people, and her handbag flew from her hand, smacking Aiden in the face. He grimaced, holding his mouth and bent over, retrieving the handbag from the ground.

"Oh my, I'm so sorry, dear! The House is closed for the day. Visiting hours are from nine until…"

She paused, taking her handbag from Aiden and gaping at him with disbelieving eyes.

"Even for Wilbert and Laura's kids?" Harold said, grinning.

The woman covered her mouth and squealed: "I don't believe it!" She threw her arms around Aiden, bumping him in the mouth with her head, tears welling in her eyes.

A tear almost dropped from Aiden's eye as he rubbed his jaw. He patted her on the shoulder, unsure of what to say. She released him and pulled back, getting a good look at him.

"Aiden Johnson," she muttered, wiping her cheeks and staring at him. "And the girls too! Oh my, Aiden, you certainly have grown up since I last saw you. Oh, Harold, he looks like Wilbert at that age, doesn't he?"

"Yep! Been sayin' it since they arrived. Spitting image of Wilbert!"

"When?" Margaret said. "When did they arrive? Oh, who cares? Come in, you all must come in!"

Margaret threw the double doors open, revealing a room that Aiden, Flair, and Simone weren't prepared for.

It was a cavernous auditorium, filled to the ceiling with fantastic works of art and ancient artifacts. The Johnson children froze at the doorway, staring in every direction at portraits, statues, tapestries, and rows and rows of glass cases housing important looking relics. Aiden entered first, feeling like he was in a museum rather than someone's living room. Simone bolted ahead, eyes popping, and Flair reached out, grabbing the scruff of her sweater.

"Slow down, kiddo," Flair said. "This stuff looks extraordinarily expensive."

Aiden, the history lover that he was, forgot anyone else was in the room, mumbling to himself: "Sixteenth century…that's a relic from the Crimean War…from the House of Luxembourg? Unreal!"

Margaret was halfway across the large room when she turned, realizing her guests weren't following her and were gawking at the room of ancient treasures.

"Oh my, excuse my poor manners!" She stepped in front of the Johnsons, gave a ceremonial bow, exclaiming: "Flair, Simone, Aiden…Welcome to the House of Gumm! You are standing in the Grand Room, and this," she said with pride, "is our Grand Gallery! A favorite attraction for many who visit East Town."

The Grand Gallery nearly encompassed the entire Grand Room, with only a small living room off to the side in front of an impressive marble fireplace. There was a maze-like walkway cutting through and around the Grand Gallery's displays. The lack of guardrails made Aiden nervous as he saw Simone's face teeming with excitement.

"Where did all this stuff come from?" Aiden said.

"My father, Gaston Gumm, the Great Explorer! He was a serious collector of all things ancient. It's okay," she said to Flair, who was still restraining Simone. "Please, look around."

Simone tore away from Flair and darted into the maze of antiques. Aiden approached a bronze statue, certain it was only a replica of a Renaissance era satyr, but it looked aged and worn. He pushed it with the edge of his foot, feeling its weight, and turned to Margaret, dumbfounded.

"This…this is…it isn't, is it?"

"The Fountain of Neptune's stolen satyr?" Margaret said, smiling. "My father believed so. The man he acquired it from didn't deal in fakes."

Simone ran up, grabbing Aiden's arm. "Come here bro, you gotta see this!"

"Ok, but don't touch anything," Aiden said as Simone pulled him towards the back of the Gallery. "Some of this stuff is unbelievably ancient."

"You ain't seen half o' nothin' yet," Harold laughed. "Wait 'til you get to…"

"Harold!" Margaret snapped. "Now don't ruin my fun! I'm quite sure you've had your tour already. This is mine. Besides, shouldn't you be going? It's nearly six."

Harold checked his watch. "Jimmy Crack Corn, I'm late! See you folks later!"

Harold waved goodbye and dashed off as the Johnsons scattered into the maze, bombarding Margaret with question after question, which she was more than happy to answer.

"Miss Gumm, what's this thing?" Simone stood in front of an exquisite wooden artifact, an intertwined dragon and elephant.

"Oh my, call me Granny, sweetie," Margaret said, approaching Simone. "It's a Japanese hallstand, five hundred years old, made by a Samurai warrior as a gift to his parents before he journeyed on a long campaign. Coats and hats were hung on the dragon's arms, tail, or the elephant's tusks, and shoes would go in this drawer below."

"Five hundred years," Simone gasped. "That's old! A warrior made this? But it's so beautiful! Wasn't he a good warrior, Granny?"

Margaret chuckled. "Yes, Simone. Samurai were not only great warriors, but they were fascinated by poetry, literature, and art. This particular warrior apparently had a fondness for wooden sculptures."

Aiden had left the maze and was standing before the marble fireplace, reading an inscription upon it:

WISDOM—THE GREATEST OF ALL GIFTS

Flair, meanwhile, was staring at a beautiful white rug with blue, gold and silver sequins encased in a glass frame, hanging against the far wall of the Grand Room.

"What's this one, Granny?" Flair shouted. "Looks like a giant fancy tablecloth."

"A traditional Moroccan wedding rug," Margaret said. "Early fourteenth century, one of the oldest in existence. Customarily, this item was hand woven together by the bride and her mother in the week before her wedding, a time of immense bonding between them."

"Hmm. Mother and daughter," Flair said in a flat tone. "How cute." She turned away, studying a suit of armor behind her.

Margaret stared after Flair, sighing and looking heartbroken. She searched around for Aiden and saw him standing before the fireplace, staring at a row of photos on the mantle. She approached him carefully.

"And what's all this over here, Ms. Gumm?" Aiden said.

Flair and Simone stopped what they were doing at once. From the sound of Aiden's voice, they knew he was irritable and possibly angry. They followed Margaret into the living room, standing behind their brother.

In his hands, Aiden held a picture in a small black frame: a photograph of two couples standing in front of the House of Gumm. A young boy and girl held hands between them, and a much younger Margaret stood behind the children, smiling.

"Well, those are your parents, of course," Margaret said, taking the picture from him. "And their friends, Lydia and Nicolas Gannares."

"Oh yeah, we met them earlier," Simone exclaimed, standing on tiptoe behind Margaret and pointing at the photo. "Who are those kids?"

"That's your brother, Simone, and that's Gloria, the Gannares' daughter."

It was the same girl from Aiden's daydream, the girl from the swing who had kissed him on the cheek.

"Gloria?" Aiden murmured.

"You don't remember Gloria, do you?" Margaret said wistfully. "And you two were so close."

Flair took the picture from Margaret and Simone moved next to her to get a better look. Flair wiped the dust from her mother's face.

"She looks so young," Flair sighed.

Simone smiled as Flair passed the picture to her. "She looks like you, Flair, and I bet that's you in there," she said, tapping her mother's pregnant belly on the photo.

"Yes, Laura was pregnant when your parents left," Margaret said. "This was the last time I saw you Aiden. You were such a troublemaker, but if I baked cookies, you made sure every child got one. Especially Gloria."

Flair handed the picture to Aiden, who didn't look at it, but placed it back on the mantle and rounded on Margaret.

"Why did my parents leave?"

"I'm sorry? W-why did your parents leave?"

Aiden's teaching experience told him that Margaret was buying time. She wasn't caught off guard by the question; she had been expecting it and possibly dreading it.

"Yes," Aiden said, articulating every word. "Why. Did. They. Leave?"

"Well, uh, people leave, you know," Margaret gulped. "East Town isn't going to be home forever." The answer sounded rehearsed.

"C'mon Margaret, you're not dumb. They have a *home* here, don't they? So why? You seem to know them well enough, and right now I don't feel like I know my parents at all. They never told us anything about East Town except they were raised here and came back to hear you read a book, which always sounded crazy, but whatever. The Reading and old friends, but there's more to it, isn't there?"

Margaret looked back at the mantle as though she were considering something.

"They just left one day, about a month after this photo was taken. They came over, kissed my sister Vera and I goodbye. No explanation, that's all there was to it."

Margaret patted him on the arm.

"If your parents never told you about East Town, then you have questions of course. But I don't know what to say. Only they would know their reasons."

"And what do *they* know?" He pointed at the Gannares' in the photo.

Margaret fidgeted, looking fearful. This time she was caught off guard. "They? Not the best folks to discuss your parents, at least not now. They still haven't gotten over Laura's death. Give it some time, Aiden."

Margaret was thrilled to switch gears when Simone asked to see the rest of the house. Flair looked equally happy to change subjects, so Margaret led them up the wide staircase to the second floor.

The upstairs didn't have the magnificence of the Grand Gallery below, but it was still incredible. An enormous gourmet kitchen met them at the top of the stairs, which Margaret explained was built when her mother fell ill and couldn't travel the stairs anymore. They walked along wide hallways, adorned with suits of armor and fancy pottery, through the twelve humongous bedrooms, each as large as the Johnsons' apartment and decorated with the grandeur of a palace. Margaret had prepared the rooms for several houseguests that came in for the holidays, expecting her sisters before the end of the week, and a few other notable East Town families.

"And they stay all here?" Simone said. "That sounds cool!"

"Yes. The Finnes, the Martinezes, my friend Ms. Weingarten," Margaret said with pride. "Great people, and all grew up right here in East Town."

They left the last bedroom, heading down a spiral staircase that ended in a large sitting room adjacent to the Grand Gallery. The Tea Room, as Margaret called it, was crammed with small tables adorned with frilly tablecloths and doilies, comfortable leather sofas, and a low hanging chandelier that Aiden avoided as he wound through the room. And just past the tables were two large, double glass doors covered with mist.

"What's through there?" Aiden asked.

Margaret grinned, walking over to the glass doors. It was the first question of Aiden's she seemed excited to answer.

"The highlight of the tour, Aiden. The reason the House of Gumm is such a wonderful place to visit. Watch your step—"

KNOCK KNOCK KNOCK KNOCK KNOCK

Knocking echoed through the Grand Gallery, making Margaret jump. "Oh my," she said, "more unexpected visitors?" She bustled around the corner, tottering through the Grand Room, leaving Aiden, Flair, and Simone behind. The knocking turned into banging as Margaret reached the front door and opened it.

A young woman with waist-length auburn hair was balancing a tower of brown paper grocery bags in her arms, nearly falling over when Margaret opened the door.

"Granny, so glad you didn't leave!" the woman puffed. "I got the shopping done and you should've seen the crowd at Darby's! Everyone's showing up early this year, just like Mr. Mimble said they would."

"Oh my, dear, look who's here?"

The woman plowed past Margaret and dumped the bags on the living room sofa.

"Just catching my breath Granny, I'll take these up to the kitchen in a minute," she said. "And sorry, Four was out of corn syrup, and I just couldn't go to Kreegers, even though Four said he didn't care. I just can't see myself ever shopping at Kreegers, can..."

She turned around. Standing there, facing her, was Aiden.

"...You?"

Her face was as pretty as it had been in his daydream, Aiden thought. Her eyes were sparkling, she had perfect complexion and her reddish-auburn hair was flawlessly styled. Gloria Gannares was in a word: stunning.

"Gloria?" Aiden said automatically.

"Yes?" She stared at him curiously for a moment, and then— "Aiden Johnson." She turned to the girls. "And Flair and Simone. Well, it's about time you three visited our little village!" She laughed and her smile had Aiden in a trance, so that when she held out her hand, he had to forcibly wake himself to accept it. "Gloria Gannares, my parents told me you were in town. Wow, Aiden, you're more handsome than your pictures."

Aiden felt blood rushing into his face. "Haha, uh, thanks…" he stammered, suddenly feeling warm.

Margaret was overjoyed. "Oh my, seeing you two back together again, it's been so long!"

Gloria, cheeks flushing, rolled her eyes at Margaret. Flair and Simone wiped away pretend tears.

"Isn't it touching?" Simone whispered to Flair.

"Granny, stop," Gloria said. "You're gonna scare Aiden away."

"*Puh-lease!*" Simone laughed. "Aiden's not going *anywhere* now! Is he Flair?"

"Oh no, Simmy! We'll be moving to East Town permanently now that Aiden's met Gloria!"

The sisters giggled, Gloria turned an even deeper shade of red, and Aiden's eye twitched. For once, he had no comeback.

"Yeah, you're Johnsons alright, always playing *matchmaker!*" Gloria said smiling, and she turned to Aiden, hands on her hips. "Well Aiden, we haven't seen each other since we were kids, but shall we start our wedding plans?"

Everyone laughed, including Aiden. He was glad Gloria had a sense of humor, but his mind was shifting towards something else as he glared at his sisters: payback.

"Isn't this splendid?" Margaret exclaimed, bouncing in place and clenching her hands together. "This will be the best holidays in ages! We have so much to talk about. I'll make a pot of ginger tea. Or do you prefer coffee, Aiden?"

"Oh no you don't, Granny," Gloria said. "It's almost seven. I'm putting these groceries away and we're going caroling. You haven't been out all week." Gloria turned to the Johnsons. "You're coming caroling too, right?"

The Johnsons stared at one another, looking uncertain. Flair finally spoke up.

"Wait, so when you say caroling, you mean singing, right? Walking around singing Christmas songs? You don't really do that around here. Do you?"

Fifteen minutes later, caps, gloves, and scarves had been excavated from a large closet and Aiden, Flair, Simone, Gloria and Margaret stepped into the frosty night. The East Town streets were flooded with people; many grouped together singing Christmas carols, while others walked amongst the throng, greeting one another.

Margaret chatted with Flair and Simone about the history of the streets in East Town, but Aiden was too distracted to listen in. He thought Gloria kept staring at him, but she always seemed to turn away just at the right moment, so he wasn't sure if she'd been looking at him, or one of her many passing admirers. One thing was certain: Gloria was popular. Young men were practically lining up just to say hello, some to receive a hug from her. One teenager even offered her a red rose, clearly having a crush on her. And then there was Brett Morris.

You couldn't miss Brett Morris in a crowd if you tried. He was as handsome as he was humongous, standing six-foot-five, with broad, brawny shoulders as wide as a doorframe. He strode impressively across the street towards the group, kissing Gloria on the cheek and hugging Margaret. Noticeably the only person this frigid evening without winter clothing, Brett wore a baseball jersey that displayed his thick, muscular arms.

"Where's your jacket, you silly goose?" Gloria gasped. "It's freezing out here!"

Brett smiled. "Don't need one," he said in a deep, booming voice. "Just up from winter baseball. Arizona is in a heat wave. This cold air feels great!"

"Don't play with me, Mr. Morris. I going inside Granny's to get you a jacket." She pulled off her mittens, rubbed his arms with her hands and gasped again. "You've got to be kidding me, Brett! Your arms are icicles!"

"Glo, do I look like I need a mother?" he said with a smile. "I'm a big boy now."

"Whatever, tough guy!" Gloria laughed. "Hey, this is Wilbert and Laura's son, Aiden, and those," she pointed towards a hot chocolate stand, "are his sisters, Flair and Simone. Brett's our resident superhero. He's going to the Major Leagues one day."

Brett shook Aiden's hand. "The elusive Johnsons…from Brooklyn, right? Been through there once. Tryout for the Mets. East Town's a lot different, ain't it?"

Aiden and Brett had a very brief discussion about New York City and baseball, which ended once Aiden admitted he'd never visited Yankee Stadium once in his life.

"Oh…" Brett said, looking confused, "well, you should check them out when you get a chance. They're kinda good!" He chuckled loudly, Gloria laughed heartily, on the verge of losing her breath, while Aiden wondered what was so funny.

"Hey Gloria, tomorrow, the lake, you and me, okay?" Brett gave Gloria another kiss on the cheek, shook Aiden's hand warily, and rejoined his family on their front lawn.

"Ooo, nice!" Flair said, returning with a cup of cocoa and staring in Brett's direction. "This place isn't so bad after all."

"Shut up!" Aiden snarled.

"Oh crap! Did I say that out loud?" Flair said, blushing.

Meeting Brett Morris seemed to suck the warm feeling of meeting Gloria out of Aiden. Suddenly, even with layers of warm clothing, he was downright freezing. An icy wind blew through the valley, encouraging everyone towards the hot cocoa stands. Gloria bought everyone a round of cocoa, which was sweet and tasty and warmed Aiden to the bones.

But the cold night was nothing compared to the frosty reception the Johnsons received from Gloria's parents, who, along with Harold Mimble, had joined them to form a group of carolers. Not only did the Gannareses barely speak to Aiden or his sisters, they hardly even made eye contact.

Neither Flair nor Simone noticed anything. They were having entirely too much fun as they set off down Twelfth Street, watching families gather on their front lawns and huddle under mounds of blankets, drinking cocoa and eating pie. Harold led the group in their first carol, belting out the first lines of *God Rest Ye Merry Gentlemen* in a rich, baritone voice. Everyone joined in.

Everyone, that is, except Aiden, Flair, and Simone. They hummed and fudged the verses, having no clue what they were singing. Gloria walked behind Flair and Simone, handing them each a songbook.

"Where's mine?" Aiden asked with a sly frown.

"*Et tu,* Aiden? Pathetic." Gloria grinned, passing Aiden a songbook.

"Sorry, I'm a city boy. I didn't grow up in Santa's Village like you."

Gloria smirked. "Hardy har. Love it, don't you? Just like your parents. Every year, all they said was East Town was too small, too backwards. But every year, back they came."

"Yeah, well, my parents were insane."

"Don't be so snarky, Aiden. You're going to move here one day. Just watch."

"Are you kidding?" Aiden laughed. "I don't know how I'm gonna stay awake for the next three weeks."

Gloria shook her head. "Mark my words. There's never a dull moment in East Town."

"Really?" Aiden said. "My parents never talked much about this place."

"They must have," Gloria said, staring at her own boots. "How else did you remember me after all this time?"

"Some people you never forget," Aiden said smoothly. Gloria reddened, fighting a smile.

"Your parents always promised they'd bring you back," she said, "but I gave up hope. It's not the same without them here. How is your dad doing?"

"He's…the same," Aiden muttered uncomfortably. "And speaking of fathers, I think yours hates me. It's like he's hoping a reindeer drops out of the sky and hoof-kicks me in the face."

Gloria laughed. "It's hard for them. Our parents were best friends."

"Everyone keeps saying that, but I can't remember my parents mentioning them."

Harold hobbled towards them, rapping on his songbook. "Hey! We talkin' or singin'?"

The song switched to "Walking in a Winter Wonderland", and Gloria led the way with a cheerful rendering, with Aiden, Flair and Simone fumbling through their books to keep up.

They passed house upon house, singing to young couples with children, elderly people in Santa suits, and a group of kids in elf costumes who performed a dance routine to their rendition of *Have A Holly Jolly Christmas*. There were people everywhere: eating pie, drinking cocoa and coffee, singing, laughing and enjoying one another's company. The Johnsons had never experienced anything like this. They had been to church events, big parades, and Christmas festivals before, but this was different. There was a feeling of genuine love radiating through East Town like a warm fire.

Margaret suggested that their guests pick the next song, and Aiden chose *Santa Claus is Comin' to Town*, the only Christmas song he knew. As he started to sing, Nick Gannares had tugged Gloria's sweater sleeve, easing her towards the rear of the group as the song began. He didn't look happy.

"Just what do you think you're doing?" Nick said in a volume only he and Gloria could hear. "We've already discussed this."

"I ran into them at Granny's, Dad. I didn't know they'd be there."

"You know what's at stake, Gloria," Nick said. "I don't need any problems from you."

"You think *I'm* the problem, Dad?" Gloria said, smiling, but clearly furious.

"We don't know enough. Just stay away from the Johnsons, especially Aiden."

"This is how you honor your best friends?" Gloria snarled. "Guess I'm not surprised!"

"This isn't about honoring—" Nick's voice rose suddenly. He looked around, but no one heard him with Simone screeching at the top of her lungs. He pulled his daughter closer. "It's about protecting my family," he finished.

"Oh, *now* you want to protect the family? Well, how about this Dad? I'm an adult. I make my own choices. Just like you did."

Gloria yanked away from Nick and walked ahead. Their brief argument went unnoticed as the carols continued to switch at a rapid pace. A few bars of *Good King Wenceslas* then it was on to *Jingle Bells*, which Flair and Simone sang louder than anyone.

They were blocks away from the House of Gumm as they finished singing, and Margaret and Gloria led everyone up the wooded pathway that ended at the crescent-shaped lake overlooking the town. Nick and Lydia excused themselves, joining a group of people unpacking musical instruments near a small bandstand. Aiden, feeling frozen solid, broke away from the group, spying another hot cocoa stand.

Weingarten Lake was crowded and cheerful. Snowballs flew everywhere, couples retreated into the woods for romantic walks, and skaters laced their blades, preparing to hit the ice. Aiden was sipping cocoa and looking for his sisters when a snowball whizzed past his ear. He spun and saw Gloria kneeling, smiling mischievously while lacing a pair of ice skates for Simone, who was laughing hysterically.

The band struck up, playing *We Wish You A Merry Christmas* and Aiden turned towards the bandstand. The Gannares' were front and center, Nick with his trumpet, Lydia with her saxophone, and both staring daggers at Aiden.

Why did they hate him? Maybe they weren't great friends with his parents as everyone said. Aiden pondered this as he turned back to Simone, and this time he didn't miss it: Gloria gazing avidly at him. Her face glowed as their eyes locked and she smiled.

And even though Aiden could have sworn that Nick and Lydia never took their icy stares off of him all evening, he had a nice, warm feeling that no hot cocoa could ever produce.

CHAPTER SEVEN – WILBERT'S RIDDLE

Gloria had been right about East Town: there never was a dull moment for the Johnsons. Each morning, the bell tower woke the village at six A.M., and by seven, Aiden, Flair, and Simone went to have breakfast with Margaret at the BLD., a restaurant whose initials (Flair correctly guessed) stood for *Breakfast, Lunch, and Dinner*. Bo "Big Tank" Russo, owner of the BLD, was a former high school classmate of their parents, and upon meeting Aiden and his sisters, their meals became instantly on the house.

"Towners eat free on their birthday, so I owe ya quite a few," Big Tank growled after Aiden tried for fifteen minutes to force his credit card on him. "Now put it away already!"

Most Towners ate breakfast at the BLD, so the Johnsons met almost everyone during those early morning hours. Cecil Badmore and Jasper Jones were former mayors of East Town and Harold Mimble's childhood friends. Simone discovered they belonged to a club called "The Majors", which consisted solely of former East Town mayors, and they had a private room at the BLD. They met two members of the Middleman family, Diana and her daughter Echo, owners of the Cranberry Inn. Lance, Larry and Robbie Darby, triplet sons of Darby's General owner Jack the Fourth, arrived in two large campers full of their wives, sons and daughters. They also met three of Margaret's sisters, Vera, Nellie, and Jane, with the remaining three expected to show up sometime after Christmas. And Ashton Stillwell, who Aiden remembered from his mother's funeral, was just as jumpy now as he was then.

Flair and Simone made many friends as the days progressed, Simone because of her outgoing, talkative nature, and people loved Flair's flamboyant looks and rich Brooklyn accent. Flair had been invited to several Christmas parties before the first morning was done, and the younger boys were hoping that Simone would return for the Weingarten Lake Summer Camp. Much like Gloria, the Johnson sisters were a hit with boys, who seemed to follow them everywhere like obedient puppy dogs. That is, whenever Aiden wasn't nearby, which to his sisters' delight was more often than not.

Aiden was determined to get papers graded, but soon discovered this task was nearly impossible. Once Towners caught wind of the Johnsons' arrival, the doorbell never stopped ringing at the narrow house on Carolina Avenue. After four unproductive hours on that first afternoon, Aiden decided to take a break and visit the House of Gumm.

He'd actually been anxious to return to the House of Gumm because many visitors had remarked that morning that seeing the "Grand Garden" would be the highlight of their holiday. Thinking the Grand Gallery was easily the most unforgettable thing he'd seen, Aiden wanted to take another look at Margaret's front garden, as it had been dark last night.

He arrived at the House of Gumm, staring mystified through the wrought iron gate. The garden was certainly "grand" in size, artfully crafted, with little walkways cutting in and around sculpted shrubs. But it was a laughable comparison to an enormous room packed with priceless artifacts. Oh well, he thought, shaking his head. Must be those *little things* again.

Although the House had plenty of visitors, no one bothered Aiden in the living room, and he was able to work in peace. From that day onward, Aiden went to the House of Gumm after breakfast to grade papers, taking more than a few breaks to wander through the Grand Gallery.

Flair and Simone, however, teased Aiden about what they said was "the real reason" he visited the House of Gumm daily, which had nothing to do with the Grand Gallery or grading papers. Gloria was at the House of Gumm so often she practically lived there. She arrived early each morning to help Margaret with chores, and as more visitors arrived into town, the House became extremely busy. Soon, Aiden felt it was only right to offer his assistance to Gloria, seeing how he was there anyway.

"Look at you, no papers graded again," Gloria said one afternoon as Aiden collected his briefcase. "All you did was fold laundry and wash dishes with me. I'm just taking up your time."

Aiden stared into her eyes as Gloria squeezed his arm apologetically. He suddenly lost command of the English language.

"Oh, uh, nothing, ah, it's, always can grade, don't mind—"
Why was it so hot? Did Margaret turn up the heat?

Throughout the week, Aiden's briefcase of ungraded papers became abandoned and forgotten. Each day, he'd arrive at the House, toss his briefcase onto the sofa, and immediately head upstairs to the kitchen with Gloria. He carried luggage, folded laundry, served tea in the Tea Room, and even joined one of Cecil Badmore and Jasper Jones's epic Monopoly battles, which took three hours and ended with an accusation of stealing money. He also took over dusting duties from Gloria so she could prepare lunch for Margaret and her many guests.

Once morning chores were completed and guests comfortable, afternoons were spent visiting *The Ninth Main*, the town square that stood along East Town's two main roads, Ninth Street and Main Street. Aiden and Gloria did the shopping for the visitors at the House of Gumm as well as buying their own Christmas gifts. Although only knowing her for a few days, Aiden considered getting Gloria something, but then remembering Candace, thought better of it.

On their fourth day in East Town, Flair and Simone arrived at the House of Gumm for a shopping trip with Gloria, surprising an apron-donned Aiden, armed with towels and a can of furniture polish, dusting the living room table.

"What in the world, Aiden?" Flair yelled, startling Aiden, who nearly crashed into the table. "You pig! You don't even clean your own house!"

Simone fell down laughing, while Flair shook her head sympathetically, muttering "wimp" under her breath. At that moment, Gloria came out of the Tea Room holding a large coffee pot and mugs.

"Perfect, you're here. I'm taking this up and then we can go." She looked at Aiden, wrinkled her nose with a mousy smile, and trotted upstairs. Aiden held his head high, adjusted his apron and continued dusting.

Hours later, Aiden's hands and arms were saddled with shopping bags as he, Gloria, and his sisters returned to the House of Gumm. The sun was setting; nearly time for another night of caroling and fellowship at Weingarten Lake, which Aiden hated to admit he enjoyed.

"You have to visit Brooklyn, Gloria," Flair said with insistence. "Aiden's a war horse with you around. Cleaning, shopping, being nice. I don't even recognize this guy. Look at him, carrying bags! Betcha never sweated this much in your life, have you, bro?"

Gloria laughed, blushing. "He's wonderful. I've never had so much help at Granny's. He's a good boy." She pinched him gently on the cheek.

"Yes," Aiden smiled, "I'm always glad to lend a helping hand. Flair, however, is a stranger to good deeds so you'll have to forgive her. Notice the only time she came by the House was when you invited her shopping."

Overloaded with bags, Aiden couldn't stop the punch Flair delivered to the back of his shoulder. Gloria and Simone laughed.

"Be nice," Gloria said, "or I'll make you put on skates tonight."

"Yeah, right," Aiden snorted. "You've got a better chance making me eat a whole plate of Towner Pie, which is terrible by the way."

Gloria's face suddenly brightened, as if an idea had just struck her.

Two hours later, the villagers crowded the lakeside, but there were no skaters and no band. Everyone was gathered around wooden tables and chairs that stretched across the clearing. The people seated at the tables wore oversized bibs, all smiling, laughing and joking. All except one.

A grouchy Aiden sat next to Harold Mimble, who elbowed him rudely, making space for himself at the table.

"Move yer arms, Johnson," Harold said. "I'm winning it all this year! Let's go! Where's m' first plate?"

Behind the scene hung a long banner tied between two large trees: "The 29th Annual *Towner vs. Out-of-Towner* Pie Eating Contest". Aiden glared at his sisters and Gloria, who were taking pictures on their camera phones, laughing hysterically.

"This is the *before* shot," Flair said. "We'll get the *after* picture when you're done. Come on, *Wimpy*, smile!"

"And when you're done," Gloria laughed, her eyes filled with tears, "we'll work off that Towner Pie with a couple of laps around the ice!" An enormous plate of Towner Pie was dropped right in front of Aiden, and he stared at it, feeling sick to his stomach.

Just past one a.m., Simone came downstairs, snug in her robe and pajamas, looking to finish the Christmas cookies Margaret had given them. She stopped at the bottom of the steps; Aiden sat on the sofa in front of a roaring fire, reading a Lionel Vann novel.

"What are you doing up?"

"Found one of my missing books in Dad's study, hadn't read it in a while," Aiden yawned.

"Those Vann books are crazy," Simone shouted as she entered the kitchen.

"I used to act this whole book out in our living room," Aiden said wistfully. "Mom used to lose it every time she'd come home and catch me locking Flair up in a cabinet. Got me in a lot of trouble."

Simone returned with a plate of cookies and sat on the sofa next to Aiden. "Do you remember living in this house?"

Although the fireplace was blazing, Aiden felt a chill come over him. "Sorta. I remember *being* here but not necessarily *living* here, y'know? I remember playing in the kitchen with that toy truck. I remember people visiting us, but not necessarily the people themselves, if that makes sense."

Simone had a whole cookie stuffed in her mouth. "That's weird."

"I had this dream last night, I was sitting on the stairs, waiting for Pops to come home, but when he did, he was upset and scared. He did something to the fireplace, and then grabbed me off the stairs and ran back out."

Simone nearly choked as she hurriedly swallowed, setting the plate of cookies down. "Stairs?"

"Yeah, those stairs there," he said pointing, "and I—"

"No-no-no," Simone said, "the staircase! Remember Dad's riddle? From the top of the stairs, look carefully, and blah-blah-blah, don't forget the key?"

The riddle! Aiden had discovered so much since arriving in East Town, he'd forgotten all about that riddle. He and Simone stared at each other for a moment, and then tore up the staircase together, jostling one another to reach the top first, which Simone did ahead of her brother.

At the top of the stairs, their heads swiveled everywhere for several moments before going to work. They moved objects, tapped the walls, lifted rugs from the floor, but found nothing. Simone stared down the stairs and into the living room below. She frowned, squinted, covered one eye with her hand, and then squinted again, until finally, she smiled.

"Pops just had to make this a riddle, didn't he?" Aiden said, lifting a portrait of Weingarten Lake. "I don't see anything."

"I do. Look." Simone was pointing down the stairs towards the living room.

"What? Where?" Aiden said.

Simone was still squinting, but moving her arm in a peculiar way. "See it? You have to stand here and look. The staircase, the carpet, the fireplace, they're shaped like a giant key."

Aiden knelt behind Simone, watching her arm and finger move as if tracing something large and invisible. As he looked on, *yes*, he saw it too. The red trim around the stone fireplace, the pattern on the scarlet hearthrug, the red and gray carpet that extended up the staircase blended perfectly together and formed the jagged outline of a skeleton key.

"I see it, Simmy," Aiden whispered. "And there's the cornerstone."

The stone on the bottom left corner of the fireplace was larger than the others. Aiden slowly walked down the stairs, Simone at his heels, approaching the cornerstone. He knelt on the hearthrug and leaned in, examining it.

Aiden rapped the stone with his knuckles and heard an empty, hollow sound. He wiggled it until it came free and stood up, shaking slightly.

"Okay Simmy," Aiden announced, "move back. I'm gonna try and smash it open."

Simone ran back to the staircase and plugged her ears with her fingers. Aiden lifted the cornerstone and slammed it on the stone front of the fireplace, and with a dull *CRACK* it snapped in half.

Aiden and Simone huddled over the broken pieces, seeing a bundle of brown cloth within. Aiden picked it up, scrutinizing it by the orange glow of the fire. The cloth was rough like denim, and Aiden slowly unraveled it, feeling his pulse quicken.

"Come on, faster! Open it!" Simone squealed.

"Shhh!" Aiden snapped. "This takes time. We don't know what's inside. Sudden movement could damage it."

He finally unfolded the last layer of cloth and stared. It was a key, metal, about a foot long. *"The cornerstone's where you'll find the key..."* he murmured.

Simone reached for the key. "Ooo! I get it first! I told you how to find it! Lemme see Aiden!" Her hands clawed and grabbed, but Aiden kept her at an arms distance.

"Shut up, Simmy, I need to think!" He shoved her to the couch, threw the brown cloth in her face and turned the key over in his hands. It was solid and heavy. Old, but not ancient. Aiden bounced it from one hand to the other. The handiwork was crude, yet efficient.

"Bitted key," he mumbled. "Made of iron. Level tumbler, or a double...probably."

"What do you think?" Simone giggled. "Treasure chest, right? I was right, wasn't I?"

"My guess, this key is less than fifty years old," Aiden said. "It's not scratched up, so it's rarely used. Doesn't go to any treasure chest I've heard of. I wonder what it goes to."

Simone suddenly dove to the floor, grabbing something from within the broken brick. Aiden spun around as she stood up, holding a scrap of paper.

"Look Aiden, another one! What's it mean? I have no idea."

Aiden grabbed the paper, reading six words in the same unknown handwriting as before:

All Men Dream, But Not Equally

"I've heard that," Simone said. "Dad used to say that."

"Right, it's a quote from..." Aiden stared into the fire, grabbing his head. "Shoot, where have I read this?"

"But what is it?" Simone said, still grabbing at the key. "Another riddle? Why can't Dad just tell us what it's about?"

Aiden, head swimming, dropped the key on the sofa, and Simone pounced upon it.

"It goes to something big," Simone said, spinning the key around in her hands. "Like a secret door, or maybe it starts up a machine, like a giant car. Or what about a treasure chest?"

Aiden couldn't concentrate with Simone throwing out theories, but he wasn't entirely dismissive. "Y'know, normally I'd punch you for saying all this stupid crap," he replied, "but Pops visited some strange places. Maybe he found something that he didn't want anyone else to know about."

"Like treasure!" Simone insisted. "C'mon, let's ask Flair! I'll bet she agrees with me!" She ran for the stairs, but Aiden snared her by her robe.

"Hold up. Let's find out what it is first. Remember, Pops didn't even want you guys knowing about it, and you know Flair, she'll be updating it online two minutes after we tell her."

They sat quietly on the couch staring into the fire. Simone was trembling with an eagerness that Aiden knew all too well. She was imagining hunting East Town after dark looking for treasure chests and mysterious doors. Aiden's first thought was to join her, as he felt this sudden trip to East Town and the secrets hidden from them for seventeen years was somehow connected to what happened to his parents.

"Think we could live in East Town?" Simone asked.

Although Aiden had been thinking it yesterday, he still stared at Simone in disbelief. "Are you joking?"

"Even if we brought Dad?"

"Not a chance."

"I saw you at the lake, Aiden," Simone said, smirking. "What if you and Gloria…"

"What?" Aiden said, a bit touchy. "What if me and Gloria *what*? First of all, I'm dating Candace, and second of all, we just met. It doesn't work that way, kiddo."

"No one likes *Candy Bear* except you. Even mom hated her. Gloria is cool and way prettier too. I like her eyes."

Aiden was momentarily lost in thought. *Yeah*, he thought to himself, *I like those eyes too.* He snapped back to reality.

"Those eyes are for someone else anyway, so drop it."

"I don't think Flair would like it here," Simone said. "Gloria said we needed to get our groceries by tonight because nothing's open tomorrow."

"Why? What's so special about tomorrow?"

"Everything's closed on Sundays." Simone said. "You know Flair ain't going for that."

"Pathetic. See, that's why we couldn't live here. This town never grew up."

Aiden and Simone went to bed after another hour of speculating about the mysterious key. Simone stayed with her treasure chest theory, whereas Aiden felt it was probably once functional, but now was symbolic at this point. However they both agreed that their father wanted Aiden to find the key's secret, which he promised to do before they returned home.

They woke at seven the next morning with Flair reminding them of their promise to make the nine o'clock church service. It was cold and dark outside as they left the house, and the last remnants of a passing snowstorm fluttered over them as they trekked down Carolina Avenue, accompanied by what seemed like the whole town.

A three-hour church service wasn't what the Johnsons expected, as they were used to quick one-hour sessions. There was lots of handshaking, hellos, and hugs before the service began, followed by speeches from various people, praising the East Town Choir for organizing the week's activities. There were updates from every small group, club, lodge, or organization in East Town. There was singing and small dramatic plays. And just when Aiden thought it was over, Reverend Lafayette stood to deliver his sermon.

"It's been almost three hours and this guy is finally getting up to give the sermon?" Aiden grumbled to a snoring Flair. "You'll pay for this."

"Quiet down," she yawned, "you might learn something." She rolled her head back to the side and resumed her nap.

Lafayette spoke about "principalities and powers" and "the rulers of darkness", explaining that all good people are called to fight against them. It reminded Aiden of his parents' constant appeal to care for the world. He also could have sworn Lafayette stared at him the entire sermon, as if it were meant for him. Then again, Aiden thought, it always felt like that at church.

The congregation flooded onto First Street once the service ended. Aiden watched Lafayette and his wife see the parishioners off while Simone went back inside to wake Flair. Three hours had not improved the weather, as low, dark clouds gathered in the distance, and a brittle wind coursed through the valley. He felt a tap on his shoulder and turned to meet Gloria.

"Made it after all, city boy?"

"Of course," Aiden said. "I had to see what kind of preacher has the whole town skipping Sundays."

"And the survey says?" Gloria said.

"I thought I was gonna die in there," Aiden said. "Where I'm from you sing, you preach, you drop a few bones in the plate, and you're done. You guys like to pour it on, don't you?"

"We happen to like church, and our Sunday routine."

"And boring visitors to death," Aiden retorted.

Gloria smiled, looking slightly annoyed. "Must be hard being a jerk twenty-four seven."

"Only when I don't get any sleep," Aiden yawned, "so this morning, I'm struggling."

"Aha! Thought you were a bored visitor? Sounds like you had fun last night. Small town charm starting to rub off?"

"No, not really. Last night was painful. I can't ice skate, I hate Towner pie, and I'm not a very good singer."

"You're being kind, Aiden," Gloria laughed. "You're pretty terrible."

Aiden opened his mouth to respond as Gloria's eyes sparkled at his, a sly smirk playing on her lips, waiting for his smart-aleck reply. But words failed Aiden whenever Gloria stared at him that way. It was a feeling he hated and loved. The silence made Gloria's cheeks flush.

"Hey bro," Flair yawned, walking up with Simone. "I'm walking Simmy down the road. Some kid's been flirting with her and wants to show her a cavern. She's dying to see it for some stupid reason."

Flair's statement didn't embarrass Simone at all. "Yeah, he told me that sometimes there's a lot of cool stuff down there. You know, like *secret* stuff?" She stood behind Flair, nodding her head and winking at Aiden, who knew this meant she wanted to do some digging into the Cornerstone Key and their father's riddle.

"What's this Casanova's name?" Aiden asked.

"It's Jason if you must know," Flair said, rolling her eyes. "Relax watchdog, go have some fun for a change. That is, if you can, with *everything* closed!" And Flair and Simone left to meet a group of boys, Flair murmuring under her breath, "can't believe *everything* is closed."

"That's right," Aiden said, remembering, "no BLD, no Ninth Main. What else is there to do on Sundays beside insult visitors and go to church?"

Gloria smiled. "A lot. You're a history guy, right? Let's go see Miss History herself."

CHAPTER EIGHT – "THERE'S NO MONSTERS IN EAST TOWN!"

Gloria embarked on her own "Grand Tour", showing Aiden her favorite childhood haunts: pizza parlors, arcades, and playgrounds. If Aiden had grown up in East Town, he thought these would have been his favorite places too. It was a strange feeling walking and laughing with Gloria, for although they hadn't seen each other since they were very young, Aiden felt like they were two old friends. He couldn't quite put his finger on the connection, and whenever he tried, Candace came to mind and drove the thoughts out of his head.

An hour later, Aiden and Gloria entered the small living room of a narrow two-story home that was crammed with people. Brett Morris was inside, wearing a pristine blue suit that barely contained his broad shoulders and chest, standing amongst a group of boys holding bats and baseballs for autographs, and teenage girls swooning and staring at him.

A young boy Aiden recognized as one of Simone's admirers gazed in delight at his autographed baseball. He turned to leave and met Aiden's eye, the smile faded, and he scampered out the front door.

"Glo," Brett's voiced boomed through the room when he spotted Gloria. He walked up and gave Gloria a strong hug, and seeing Aiden, winked at him. "What happened at the lake last night, Glo? Thought we had a date."

Gloria reddened and pushed Brett away to talk privately. Aiden stood alone, feeling a bit awkward, watching teenage girls glare at Gloria until finally she returned and Brett resumed signing baseballs.

"So, *Glo*," Aiden said, in his deepest voice, "you broke your date to feed me crappy pie? You shouldn't have."

"Stop it," Gloria said, frowning at Aiden's imitation of Brett. "It's not like that. Brett happens to be teammates with an old family friend from Argentina. He's just keeping me in the loop about a situation I've been following. That's all. It wasn't a date."

"Sure, it wasn't," Aiden said. "Anyway, whose house is this?"

"It's Elsa's," croaked a voice from behind. Cecil Badmore entered the living room, followed by Jasper Jones. "She's the oldest Towner," Cecil said. "Almost a hundred. You met her yet?"

"Oh yeah, the lady that makes the pies with Harold's wife?"

"Yep, and I'm here for mine," said a voice at the doorway. Jasper Jones entered behind Cecil, working their way through the crowd. "Don't care for Towner Pie, she'd better have my sweet p'tater."

"It's pumpkin pie, you idiot," Cecil said.

"Pumpk'n pie and sweet p'tater are the same!" Jasper snapped. "They look the same an' taste the same!"

"But they're not the same, are they?" Cecil said. "Because one's made of sweet potatoes and one's made of pumpkin, so how can they be the same?"

"I jus' told ya, dumbbell! Didn't ya listen? Looks the same, tastes the same!"

They bickered while heading down a narrow hallway. Gloria laughed to herself, but then turned on Aiden, checking him over, and straightening his collar and tie. She was so close; Aiden could smell her cherry-scented perfume. The lump in his throat returned.

"Can I tell her Towner pie sucks too?" he asked.

"You better NOT!" Gloria said, slapping Aiden's arm and adjusting his tie extra tight, "or you'll answer to me! Now listen, Elsa's a sweetheart, but she likes to tell wild stories. Don't say anything mean…if you can help yourself." She pinched his cheek gently. "Okay, city boy?"

Aiden smiled and nodded, putty in her hands.

Aiden and Gloria walked down a long hallway, seeing Jasper returning with a large pie in his hands, telling Cecil "Told ya so!" They entered a large room filled with people and towering stacks of pies, and there in the midst was Elsa Majors. Tall, thin, elegant, and if she was almost a hundred, it didn't show. Her stark white hair was long and flowing, and she looked vibrant and energetic, like a woman just entering her prime. She sat on the edge of a daybed, regaling her visitors with tales of East Town lore.

"…And that was the last time we saw Winnie. The following week was terrible. It was after sundown, he told us not to go past Knox Park, where the old chicken farms used to be. He was fire chief then, said there were barrels full of chemicals down there, explosives, and they had to move them. Took 'em behind the Cranberry, far enough from the homes, he reckoned. Next thing, two of the men started brawling, one barrel knocked into another and there was an explosion! Saw the smoke clear back on Dakota Drive. I wanted to help, but my husband wouldn't hear of it. He ran off fast with Hank Johnson and the Martinez boys and the fire burned all night. Firemen came from Athena and Proctors to help. They put it down next morning, and when we all saw it, it was terrible. Whole top of the Cranberry, burnt to cinders. They fixed it up best they could, but the seventh floor, well we lost a lot of good men. No one has been up there since."

The old woman paused for dramatic effect and the room fell eerily still. But Aiden, eager to hear more, broke the silence.

"Why not?"

Everyone jumped and turned towards the door. Elsa looked angry.

"Who's that butting in?" she snapped.

The visitors all looked at Aiden, who also turned around in mock puzzlement, pretending to search for the culprit.

"It's Aiden Johnson, Elsa," Gloria said, pushing him forward. "You remember? Wilbert and Laura's son."

"Yes, we've met," Elsa said. "Full of questions like Wilbert, ain't cha? Anyway, I was coming to '*why not.*'" She was flustered as she tried to regain the mood. "He said it wasn't no ordinary fire. He said those dead men up on the seventh floor became ghouls, doomed to walk the earth as monsters. When someone went to the seventh floor, it woke them. No one dared go up there."

A whimper rose up from the crowd and everyone turned, seeing a little girl hiding behind her mother's long dress, clutching it tightly.

"It's okay sweetie," the girl's mother said. "It's only a story. There aren't any ghouls. Elsa, tell her. She's frightened."

The crowd chuckled, patting the child on the shoulder as Elsa beckoned the girl forward.

"Just a story missy, just a story," Elsa said. "He told it to keep little smart busybodies from snooping around. Funny thing is, people always say they hear things walking around up there on the seventh floor of the Cranberry. Bah! He always knew folks around here were too superstitious. Why, I remember…"

"I'm sorry, I came in late. Who is this *he* that you keep talking about?"

Elsa scowled at Aiden. "Who else? Gaston Gumm!"

Five minutes later, after Gloria apologized for Aiden's third interruption, Elsa shooed the pair of them out the front door and all the way to the sidewalk. On their way to find Flair and Simone, they passed by the Cranberry Inn. Aiden stared at the dark, mirrored windows of the seventh floor, each displaying a holiday wreath.

"Was that story true? The chemical explosion and fire?"

Gloria frowned at Aiden. "What makes you ask?"

"I don't know," Aiden said, "doesn't sound right. Chemicals on the ground floor destroy the top floor, but none of the other floors in between. Makes no sense."

"I told you Elsa is batty," Gloria said. "I've been hearing those stories for years. Who knows what happened?"

They bumped into Flair and Simone walking down Second Street. Simone ran up to Aiden, telling him about their excursion through the underground cavern near Second Street Creek, which Flair felt was a complete waste of time. But Aiden shot Simone an inquiring look, and picking up on it, Simone shook her head, meaning she'd discovered nothing about the key.

Sunday night was another evening full of carols and cocoa, and strangely, everything seemed more festive. Maybe it was the fully decorated tree that Harold Mimble had delivered to the Johnsons that afternoon, or perhaps it was the red and green jumpsuit that Gloria wore, complete with Santa hat. Whatever it was, Aiden felt closer to East Town than he had at any point since arriving nearly a week ago.

Amongst a throng of carolers, Aiden and Gloria approached the House of Gumm, arm-in-arm, laughing, drinking cocoa, unaware that Flair and Simone were hanging far back, watching them closely. Gloria stopped in front of the House, gorgeously decorated in green and white lights.

"So," Gloria said with a wry smile, "who is this Candace I keep hearing about?"

Aiden's heart thumped and his mouth went slightly dry as he opened it to speak.

"Oh, well..."

But Aiden never got a chance to answer the question. A high-pitched, blood-curdling scream cut through the cold air like a knife.

The caroling came to a halt, and all at once, the evening fell silent. A little girl stood in the middle of Melanie Avenue, right in front of the House of Gumm. She was frozen like a statue, pointing at some bushes across the way.

The crowd ran up to her, some amused, others looking a bit nervous. Aiden walked behind them, seeing Gloria already in the middle of the throng.

"What is it?" asked several anxious voices. "What did she see?"

Through gaps in the crowd, Aiden saw the same girl who had hidden behind her mother's dress at Elsa's house. Gloria was trying to calm her.

"Relax," Gloria said in a reassuring voice. "A shadow or something."

"I know what I saw!"

Reverend Lafayette cut his way through the crowd, followed by a pair of anxious adults.

"Yep. It's Claudia all right, Roberto," Lafayette said. "I'd know that scream anywhere."

"Daddy!" The child ran into her father's arms. "I saw something! They don't believe me, but I'm not lying!"

Her father knelt down, hugging his daughter. "What was it, honey?"

"Something…ugly," her voice cracked. "They were monsters."

A murmur of "monsters" rumbled through the amassing crowd, with some staring nervously at the bushes Claudia had indicated.

"Monsters? There's no monsters in East Town!" Harold Mimble shouted from behind.

"I SAW THEM!" Claudia cried. "They were right over there!"

"There are NO monsters in East Town, little girl!" Harold repeated, stepping forward and shaking his finger at Claudia. "Now, you stop that foolishness!"

"Okay, Harold, relax," Reverend Lafayette said, laying a hand on Harold's shoulder. "She saw something strange, let's not argue. Roberto, I'll give you a lift back to Cranberry."

Gloria looked worried as she rose from her knees and walked back to Aiden, who was wearing a smirk on his face.

"What's that look for?" she said, scowling and snatching off her Santa hat. "It's not funny."

"You have monsters running around in East Town?" Aiden grinned. "And I thought this place was paradise. Suddenly I feel the urge to lock my door tonight."

Gloria wasn't amused. She watched Claudia enter a car with Reverend Lafayette and her father, still protesting. "Knock it off. It was Elsa's story about the Cranberry, remember? Monsters, ghouls, and all that jazz. Poor kid. In the dark, with these flashing lights…maybe she *thought* she saw something." She said the last part without much conviction and Aiden eyed her curiously.

"Whatever it was, it sure broke up this party," Flair said. Aiden looked around, and sure enough, the streets were completely empty, except for the four of them.

"Tonight's fireworks at Weingarten Lake," Gloria said, somewhat distracted. "Everyone heads to the lake early for the good spots. I'm heading home. You guys know your way?"

"To the lake?" Aiden laughed. "Sure, we've only been up there all week."

Gloria stuffed her hands in her pockets and walked up Twelfth St. alone without another word. Flair nudged Aiden in the ribs and nodded at Gloria.

"Knock it off," Aiden said. "It's not cute."

"You're letting her walk home alone?" Flair said. "Where's your game at, bro? You know you wanna walk her home. Just go."

But amid Flair's joking, Simone was staring at the same bushes. "We should go check on Granny Gumm," she said.

"Why?" Aiden asked. "Can she vanquish the angry monsters?"

"Because I want to. *Look!* There she is!"

Simone bolted towards the House of Gumm. She was fifty feet from the front gate before she skidded to a halt, and Aiden and Flair saw why.

Margaret was tottering across the road and behind her were Claudia's monsters: three of them, each only as tall as Simone. Wearing blue jeans, jackets, and boots, they might have been mistaken for children themselves, except for their oversized heads, hunched backs, bulging eyes, elongated arms and pale skin. They all turned and looked at Simone, making ugly grunting noises.

Simone drew a deep breath, prepared to let loose with a surefire ear-splitting scream, but Margaret stopped her.

"Simone!" she hissed. "No! Don't scream. Screams hurt them."

Aiden and Flair approached Simone, both in open-mouthed astonishment, each grabbing one of her shoulders, as if to pull her away, but they didn't.

"Margaret..." Aiden began, but he found himself speechless after that. He stared at the three twisted, deformed child-like people in front of him, unable to form another word.

"Please," Margaret said, looking stony. "It's all right. I'll explain if you would be so kind as to follow me. In...inside the house."

Minutes later, Margaret entered the Tea Room trembling, moving hastily, reminding Aiden of her nervousness during their conversation about his parents. The deformed children followed behind her, and Aiden observed them with a feeling deep in his gut that said he knew them. One had long stringy hair down his back, the tallest one wore a brown bucket hat that partially hid his eyes, and the shortest had a chubby, round face.

Margaret wound her way around the tables and the Deformed followed, tugging her arms, urging her towards the misted glass doors. Flair watched their behavior.

"Granny, what's going on?" Flair said.

"Just a moment, Flair," Margaret said. "I need to gather my thoughts." She shooed the deformed children away from her as one of them had took her by the wrist with his spindly fingers. Simone sat at one of the tea tables, not taking her eyes off the Deformed.

Margaret took a stepstool from a small cabinet at her knees and climbed on it, opening another cabinet above a corner tea table and retrieving a crumpled paper bag.

"What's in that bag?" Simone asked.

Margaret reached her hand inside the bag, showing Simone peppermint candies. "They like peppermint. I give them peppermint to calm them whenever they're frightened."

"Frightened of what?" Aiden asked.

Margaret stared at Aiden, but didn't answer. Instead, she handed the bag to the Deformed, who pounced upon it greedily, gobbling up peppermint candies with loud slurps. She retrieved a second item from the cabinet, an old, black burlap satchel. The

Deformed reacted with alarm, surrounding her, grunting and squeaking, and trying to take the satchel from her.

"And what's in *that* bag?" Aiden said. Margaret glanced at Aiden, held the bag away from the Deformed, and stepped down off the stool.

"Granny?" Simone whispered. "What are they?"

"People, Simone. Just like you and I, but...different."

"Whatever they are, they're ugly," Flair said.

"Wait! How about *my* questions?" Aiden shouted. "Why these things frightened and what's in that old satchel?"

"They are not *things,* Aiden," Margaret admonished, "they're *people*, and please stop shouting!" She sounded slightly choked. "Flair, they may not be pleasant looking, but they didn't choose to be like this."

"Yeah, well, "Aiden said, "this is too weird for me. Okay Simmy, Flair, let's go."

"NO!" Margaret's voice echoed throughout the house, and the Deformed snorted at her. "I'm sorry, I'm sorry," she apologized to them before turning to Aiden. "You cannot leave, not until I explain. Please, sit. It's time you knew everything."

"*Everything*?" Simone said. "Everything like what?"

Margaret looked at the black satchel and took a deep breath. "Like what really happened to your parents."

At once, the Tea Room fell silent. The Johnsons stared at Margaret, puzzled, even the Deformed stopped eating their peppermints noisily, watching Margaret with interest.

"Finally, some truth," Aiden said.

"You suspected?" Margaret said.

"Of course I suspected!" Aiden snapped. "Nothing in this town adds up."

"*What really happened?* " Simone repeated, dumbstruck. "But Dr. Haskins said Mom and Dad caught a virus on their missionary trip to South America. Right?"

Margaret sat on a chair next to Simone. "No, dear. Your parents weren't missionaries. They never were in South America. They went to Paris to find my father's old assistant, Jonas Wilson. On their return trip, they stopped in Canterbury Springs to see your grandparents, and...and they were attacked."

Silence gripped the room once again. Margaret looked guilty, as though her statement was sinful. Aiden felt shaky. His mind was trying to grasp what Margaret had said when Flair responded.

"*Attacked?* How? What do you mean *attacked?* By who?"

Margaret took Flair's hand, patting it gently. "His name is Mochtier Mackleford…"

But Flair snatched her hand away, her eyes ablaze. "And who the hell is Mochtier Mackleford and why did he attack my parents?" she shouted.

"Please, Flair," Margaret said sharply, watching the Deformed cover their ears, spitting candy and howling with anger. "I'll explain. Please, calm down."

Flair paced behind Aiden, her fists clenched, glaring at Margaret. She looked vicious: her face flushed, nostrils flared, and teeth bared. The sudden change stunned Aiden, who had never seen his sister like this.

"Mr. Mackleford," Margaret said, "was my father's closest friend from childhood, and they…"

"Wait a minute, from *childhood?*" Aiden said, rising out of his chair so fast, it scooted backwards and fell over. "So this guy's a hundred? You're telling me some hundred-year-old dude did that to my dad?"

"Let me explain," Margaret insisted, looking flustered. "Please."

Aiden picked up his chair and re-took his seat, while Flair stopped pacing and stood behind him. All three Johnsons were fixated on Margaret.

"My father and Mr. Mackleford were friends, different men from different worlds, but they always had one thing in common: they loved exploration. They became amateur explorers as adults. Thick as thieves, they were. You see, back then, the Macklefords and the Gumms were all one family. After every adventure, our fathers would return to East Town with their relics and discoveries and relive for us their thrilling and dangerous quests. But after a while, only my father told the stories. Mr. Mackleford had changed.

"Once I turned eighteen, my father confided in me about some of their more nefarious deeds, but in particular about something they found. A liquid called Purity. Mr. Mackleford was an amateur scientist and he became obsessed with it. He said it would change humanity, change the world, but my father believed it was too dangerous and insisted they keep it a secret. If people knew what Purity could do, he said, it would be devastating.

"They argued over it for months, but in the end, they agreed if they could help people with Purity, they would. Their agreement might have lasted, everything might have been different, but during one voyage, they received news that Mr. Mackleford's father was dying. They returned, but it was too late. Both of them were devastated. Their long friendship was fractured.

"Many years later, Mr. Mackleford called my father. He said they had failed humanity by not revealing what they had found. Said he'd pushed on with Purity, experimenting on himself. He said he was eager to show my father what he had missed out on…"

Margaret paused, swallowing hard. "My father said Mr. Mackleford sounded disturbed. He wanted to help him, but when he met him, it was my father who was disturbed by what he saw." And with much difficulty, she whispered, "Mr. Mackleford had not aged a day since they last saw each other in fifteen years."

Simone gasped. Flair covered her mouth with her hands. Aiden rolled his eyes, looking unimpressed.

"You could give Elsa a run for her money. But what does that story, these three freaks or any of this have to do with my parents and what really happened?"

"Because they came to me tonight," Margaret said, nodding to the Deformed. "Their affliction is from Purity and it gives them the ability to sense him."

"Sense who?" Aiden asked.

The Deformed suddenly scrambled from their chairs, knocking the small tables aside, and with a unified effort, seized Margaret and ushered her towards the misted glass doors.

"What's going on?" Simone stood up, frightened.

Margaret was being shoved along by the Deformed, turning her head every which way and then, without as much as a sound, the house was plunged into total darkness.

"Great! Now what?" Aiden said, stumbling through the Tea Room. He couldn't see anything, only hearing grunts and squeaks from the Deformed.

"Flair! Where are you?" Simone cried.

"Over here, Simmy. Stay there. I'm coming."

"Did the power go out?" Simone asked.

"Obviously, genius!" Aiden snapped. "Margaret, where's your switch box?"

Then, somewhere in the darkness, came the unmistakable crash of shattering glass. Fear had broken over Simone.

"Help, Aiden!" she squealed, terrified. "I'm scared! What was that?"

"OW!" Aiden said as Simone collided into him. "That was my foot!"

"Shhhh! Not you dummy," Flair whispered. "The breaking glass—"

"Someone's breaking in?" Simone cried, sounding on the verge of tears.

"Wouldn't we have heard the alarm?" Aiden said.

"The alarm's for the front door, not the windows," Margaret replied.

"Well, that's smart!" Aiden said. "Who only puts an alarm on the front..."

THE ALARM BLARED!

It was deafening. The Deformed fell to their knees, covering their ears and howling in agony. The Grand Room and the Tea Room were bathed in a flashing strobe light. Aiden couldn't think straight. He covered his ears, reaching for Simone, who was running towards the spiral staircase.

"Simmy! Stay still!"

Aiden looked into the Grand Room, seeing six towering black shapes fanning out across the room, followed closely by a tall figure wearing a long winter coat striding in their midst.

"Someone's here!" Flair shouted, also watching the seven dark silhouettes advancing closer with each flash of the red strobe light.

"NO! YOU WON'T HAVE THEM!"

"Margaret?" Flair said, "What—"

"UPSTAIRS CHILDREN! RUN! NOW!"

Margaret grabbed Flair's arm, pulling her away from the Grand Room entrance, but it was too late. The alarm silenced and the lights came on.

Six men dressed in black from head to toe stood in front of Aiden, filling the Tea Room ceiling to floor. Black masks covered their heads entirely, and the outline of a soulless human face was stitched in white on each mask: vacant eyes, lips bearing no smile. With their blank white eyes staring down upon them, they were without a doubt the scariest things Aiden had ever seen.

He somehow managed to blurt out, "Simmy, Flair! MOVE!"

The nearest masked man brandished a silky white whip. Aiden turned, stumbling around the tea tables towards the spiral staircase.

With a swish and a snap, the white whip wrapped Aiden's ankles together. He tripped and smashed through a table, and at once was yanked backwards towards the large brute.

Aiden was flipped over and hoisted off the ground by a silver glove. The man in the winter coat had him by the throat, raising him above his head. Aiden kicked his legs pitifully in midair.

"You!" Mochtier Mackleford said. "The son of Wilbert."

"LET GO OF MY BROTHER!"

Simone, no longer cowering, was running at top speed towards Mackleford. She plowed a shoulder into him, but bounced off as if she were a fly, landing in the center of the Black Masks. They reached down to grab her.

"MR. MACKLEFORD!"

Everyone turned. Margaret was at the spiral staircase, the black burlap sack discarded, holding a red crystal in each hand. She aimed them at Mackleford and they brightened.

Mackleford dropped Aiden to the floor, laughing. "Little Margie Gumm. Oh, but I see no aura surrounding you, so those crystals don't have much power left, do they?"

The red crystals flickered. Margaret had a pained look on her face, as if she was trying to exert some strength or power from the red crystals.

"Didn't think so," Mackleford said, nodding to one of his minions.

The white whip lashed out again, snaring Margaret by the arm. Her crystals fell to the floor as the brute yanked on the whip, flinging the old woman out of the Tea Room and into the Grand Gallery. A loud—CLANG!—signaled that she crashed into a suit of armor. Simone screamed and ran after her.

Aiden, unsure and surrounded, crawled backwards across the floor. "There's no fight in him at all," Mackleford chuckled to his cronies. "No more deaths, eh, Johnson? Quite right, it's better this way. How your father should have made it."

Mackleford grabbed Aiden by the collar and hoisted him up. They were nose to nose.

"Now, do yourselves a favor," he whispered. "You know what I want. You know where it is. Bring me the Song, Johnson. And no Journeymen please, or else you and your sisters will suffer the same fate as your parents."

Mackleford threw Aiden to the floor and left the Tea Room, taking the masked men with him.

It was all happening too fast; Aiden couldn't comprehend. He felt pinned to the ground as he tried to move, watching the intruders leave. But then Mackleford stopped in the center of the Grand Room, seeing Simone tend to Margaret in the smashed suit of armor.

"No," Mackleford whispered. "This isn't enough. These Johnsons are too stubborn. Another example is in order. Perhaps unlike your father, you will be convinced."

"GET OFF ME! AIDEN! HELP!"

Mackleford had reached down and snatched up Simone, who struggled uselessly. He passed her to one of the Black Masks as he removed his silver glove. Underneath — a stark white, decrepit hand.

"SIMMY! NO!"

"SHE SHALL BE RESTORED!" Mackleford shouted above Simone's screams as he and his Black Masks marched towards the front door. "JUST BRING ME WHAT IS MINE!"

Aiden's stomach lurched; he finally found his feet just as the front door slammed behind Mackleford and his cronies.

The streets were empty, but the residents of Melanie Avenue were peering out of their windows as Aiden burst through the front door, trampling mercilessly over the front garden's flowers and banging through the gate. He saw Simone in the middle of the street, crumpled over on her side. He approached her and almost screamed.

Simone's face was blotched and contorted. Her nose, twisted; her skin, pale and ashen. It took Aiden a moment to absorb what he was seeing. He spun around in every direction. The streets, empty. Their attackers, gone.

Aiden scooped his sister up, knees shaking, and carried her to the house.

"Aiden..." Simone said weakly. Her whole body was trembling. "I feel cold."

Flair and Margaret met Aiden at the door, Flair helping Margaret, whose left leg was bleeding. They looked at Simone and horror fell over them.

"Simmy?" Flair gasped. "What happened?" She turned to Margaret. "What's wrong with Simone?"

"We, we need the hospital," Aiden said. "Call 9-1-1."

"No."

Aiden and Flair turned, looking at Margaret in disbelief.

"What do you mean *no*?" Aiden said. "Look at her!"

"It's not that. We should—" Margaret stammered.

"We should drive her there?" Aiden said.

"No, we can't…" Margaret said. "They cannot help us."

"What are— *Out of our way, you stupid woman!*" Flair snapped, shoving her aside, leaving her hobbling on one leg. Flair pulled her cell phone and began to dial when:

"They'll dissect your sister like a lab rat!" Margaret shouted through a face full of tears.

Flair froze in the middle of dialing, her fingers still poised over the phone, looking appalled.

"It's Purity!" Margaret whimpered. "Simone's been Purified! There's nothing any doctor can do! This is beyond any disease they've seen!"

The last of Margaret's strength left her, and she slumped to the floor, sobbing. "Doctors, they don't know how to cure Purified people. All they do is experiment on them," and her voice cracked, "until they are finished with them, and then they throw them away…"

Aiden entered the Grand Room, Flair at his heels. He laid Simone gently on the same sofa where Gloria had set the groceries on their first night in East Town, watching Simone tremble all over, exhaling frosty breath.

Margaret hadn't moved from the doorway. She was covering her mouth, crying softly.

"Simmy," Aiden shook her. "Can you hear me?"

But Simone had already passed out.

CHAPTER NINE – THE OBLONG ROOM

It had been twenty minutes since the attack. Simone was still unconscious, and Aiden, Flair, Margaret, and the Deformed huddled around her on the sofa in a silent watch. At times it appeared Simone had stopped breathing, but Aiden only needed to see the frosty mist escaping her nose and lips to know she was fine. Margaret covered Simone with a blanket, and every so often her body shivered so hard, it gave them a start.

"What about the police?" Flair finally spoke, looking hopefully at Margaret.

But Aiden answered before Margaret could. "The police will just take her to the hospital." Margaret nodded her head.

"Well, *someone* needs to do *something*!" Flair shouted, glaring at Aiden.

"Get the look off your face, Flair!" Aiden said.

"Ever since Mom died and Dad got sick," Flair barked, "all we heard was, *I'm the adult, adult responsibilities, adult this, adult that…*" Flair stood up, getting right into Aiden's face, screaming. "Where the hell were you when Simone needed you?"

Aiden felt like something had just taken a chunk out of his stomach, and even though he wanted to lash back at his sister, he couldn't. Flair was right. He had failed to protect Simone.

"No fighting," Margaret said. "It won't help Simone." She took Flair by the hand and directed her back to Simone's side, placing Simone's hand into hers. It seemed to calm Flair.

"That's how my Mom looked," Flair said, turning to Margaret. "This is what happened to my parents, isn't it?"

Margaret nodded. "Did you see his hand? The Hand of Purity. The White Hand. If he touches you with it, this happens. I first saw it when he attacked three children of some visitors to East Town."

She glanced sadly over to the Deformed, who were hovering in the shadows of the Grand Gallery. Aiden looked at them and his temper rose suddenly.

"Why didn't you tell us what happened to my parents?"

"I did, Aiden…just before it all happened, remember?"

"Are you joking, Margaret?" Aiden said. "We've been here for a week! I asked you about my parents from day one!"

"Your father never wanted you to know," she said, staring at Aiden, haunted and terrified. "He wanted you spared from this. I didn't know what to do."

Margaret's pitiful look made Aiden change tact. "The guy who did this to Simmy, you called him *Mackleford*. Who is he? A son? Grandson?"

"Grandson?" Margaret said, puzzled. "I don't understand."

"The guy that attacked Simone, who is he?"

"I already told you, Aiden. My father's friend, Mochtier…"

"This isn't a game, Margaret."

"I never said it was!" Margaret shouted. "That was *him*, the same man who explored the world side by side with my father. I told you he stopped *aging*. Aren't you listening? Mr. Mackleford is over *one-hundred years old!*"

The Deformed squeaked and protested at Margaret and Aiden felt just as angry. Margaret's answers weren't making sense, but then he looked at Simone.

What else could explain what happened to his mother and father? Why did they look like that? And now his sister? One minute, Simone was healthy, the next she was half dead, disfigured, and ice cold. Flair was right, Simone looked just like his mother lying in that casket seven months ago. For some inexplicable reason, Aiden's mind went to that name he remembered from long ago — the Dominion. Margaret broke his concentration as she spoke.

"It's the White Hand," Margaret muttered. "That's how Mackleford does it. That's what happened to your parents and these poor souls." Her eyes were tear-filled. "And now Simone. But it will not happen again. Not again."

Sniffling, Margaret stood and limped with conviction toward the Tea Room. Aiden tucked the blankets snugly around Simone and stood to follow Margaret. But the moment he did, the Deformed surrounded him, raising their arms in protest.

Flair ran after Margaret as Aiden argued with the Deformed all the way to the Tea Room. When he arrived, Flair was standing before the misted glass doors, which were wide open.

"Bro," she breathed, "take a look at this."

Aiden fended off the Deformed as he and Flair passed beyond the misted glass doors into an enormous room beyond anything they had ever seen before.

It was a spectacular living garden. Here was the "Grand Garden" Aiden had heard about, and grand didn't begin to describe it. Circling the room were seven stone pillars twelve feet thick, stretching over three stories high. Plants, flowers, trees, shrubs, bushes of every shape, size and color abounded.

"Stellar," Flair whispered as she ascended a magnificent stone staircase that led to three raised terraces above the floor, each decked with sculptures and amazing plant life. She wandered along the second terrace, looking down below to a gorgeous view of the Garden.

Aiden wandered through the Garden, dumbfounded, unaware of where Flair and Margaret had gone. A spiraling stream of water circling one of the pillars entranced him as it splashed into a large wading pool at its bottom. As he turned to see what else the room had to offer, he spotted Margaret sitting on a bench in the center of the Garden, her eyes closed, her face placid, as if she were meditating.

"What is this place?" Aiden said, approaching her.

"My refuge. My place of concentration and quiet. I need both right now."

It did indeed look like a place to lose oneself; the tranquility of the room invited deep thought. Aiden walked across a large stone patio the size of a basketball court, where dozens of folded tables and chairs were stacked. Part of the preparations for the Reading, Aiden remembered.

"Please Aiden, that window, above and to your right. Be a dear and crack it for me, let in a little breeze."

Aiden looked up, seeing the small window. He found a crank on the wall just below and wound it. The window opened an inch. A brief gust of air blew through the garden and small wind chimes sang out from above.

Aiden walked back to Margaret, who was still seated, brow furrowed and eyes shut tight. Before Aiden could speak, her hand rose, protesting for another moment of silence, when:

"AIDEN!"

It was Simone. Aiden looked above to the second terrace and caught Flair's eye and the two of them raced from the Grand Garden into the living room, arriving at the couch together. Simone was sitting up, pale-faced and ashen, surrounded by the Deformed.

"Simmy!" Flair sighed, looking relieved to see Simone awake. "Are you okay?"

"They're saying we have to protect the garden," Simone said weakly. "I can hear them."

"Who?" Aiden said.

Her finger shakily pointed at the Deformed.

Aiden's face blanched. It took him a moment to take in what Simone had said, then: "You can *understand* them?"

"Yeah, they're saying the garden has all the secrets, whatever he wants must be in the garden. What garden are they talking about?" Simone frowned, looking at her ashen skin. "And what happened to me? I feel weird."

"I'm gonna fix it Simmy," Aiden said, "don't worry. I'm getting Margaret. Wait here."

Aiden and Flair turned towards the Garden Room when suddenly there was a loud THUMP. Simone had tumbled off the sofa and crashed to the floor. Aiden and Flair turned, watching their sister rolling on the carpet.

"I…I can't walk," Simone said, squeezing her legs. "My legs won't work. What's the matter with me, Aiden?" Her eyes filled with tears.

Aiden ran back and scooped up Simone. "I don't know Simmy, but I'll take care of it."

"B-b-but what happened to me?"

"I don't know, Simmy….shhh. Don't cry; it'll be okay." But Aiden didn't know what to say and could only hug Simone as she cried into his shoulder.

Aiden carried his sister towards the Tea Room with Flair at his heels. The Deformed advanced into the Grand Gallery, grunting and squeaking in low tones.

"Okay," Simone sniffled, "That's a good idea. Thank you."

"What did they say?" Flair asked, looking back at them.

"They're standing guard, in case Mackleford comes back."

The Deformed balled their long fingers into fists and assuming fighting stances. The shortest one with the chubby face turned around, giving them a backwards wave.

When Simone entered the Grand Garden, for the first time Aiden or Flair could remember, she was at a loss for words. She mouthed like a fish out of water, breathing frosty breath in Aiden's face.

"What is this place, Aiden?"

"Margaret, Simone can understand your three amigos," Aiden said, resting Simone next to Margaret on the bench. "They said whatever Mackleford's after is in here."

"Simone can understand…" Margaret began, astonished, but recovered. "But…no, whatever Mackleford is after, this *Song*, it isn't here. He's broken into the House of Gumm years ago. He's already taken whatever he wanted because he hasn't returned. Artwork and treasure mean nothing to him. Aiden, Mr. Mackleford wants power, and there is nothing of value here except—"

She looked at an end table next to the bench, upon it, an old, leather bound journal. She picked it up.

"—*my book*."

"What book?" Aiden said. "That's *the* book? The one you read from?"

"Yes." Margaret clutched the little book to her chest protectively. "But it was here when Mackleford came last; it's always been here."

"That's not it, then," Aiden said, looking around. "Something else, maybe something hidden in the Garden. Who built it?"

"I built it," Margaret said.

All three Johnsons stared at Margaret with skeptical frowns.

"Don't look at me like that!" she replied. "I was a perfectly capable woman once! I cultivated these plants, carved all these pieces by hand, and designed everything except for the seven pillars and the pools. I even designed the layout of the terraces…"

"Wait," Aiden said. "The pillars? *Seven* pillars?"

"Yes," Margaret said. "Why?"

Aiden spun where he stood, counting each the pillars under his breath. "One, two, three, four, five, six, seven. I'm such an idiot! That's it, Simmy. That's the *key* to the key!"

"It is?" Simone said. "But how do you know?"

Flair grabbed Aiden's shoulder, frowning. "The *what* to the *who*? What are you talking about?"

"Remember Simmy," Aiden said, ignoring Flair, "Remember I'd heard that phrase before but didn't remember where it came from? Now I remember. *All men dream, but not equally. Those who dream by night in the dusty recesses of their minds wake in the day to find that it was vanity. But the dreamers of the day are dangerous men, for they may act their dreams with open eyes, to make it possible."*

Aiden ran up to the first pillar, inspecting it.

"Pops wanted us to find this," he shouted, pointing at the pillar. "There *is* something in the Garden."

"Uh, hello," Flair shouted back, "what's this about?"

"My father used to say that all the time," Margaret said.

"Ours too!" Simone said excitedly.

"It's from T.E. Lawrence's book, *The Seven Pillars of Wisdom.*" Aiden said.

"*Seven Pillars?*" Margaret repeated, now gazing at the pillars. "But my father said it was a warning about men like Mackleford."

"Can someone tell me what's going on?" Flair asked.

"Maybe it was," Aiden said, still ignoring Flair, returning to Margaret and pulling the large iron key from his jacket pocket. "Have you seen this before?"

"And what is *that*?" Flair asked, throwing her hands in the air and stamping her boot in outrage. "Will someone please…"

Margaret gasped loudly, cutting through Flair's outburst. "A Cornerstone Key! Oh my goodness, yes, my father made a whole host of these. He used them to hide things that needed hiding. Where did you get it?"

"Simone and I found this last night." He turned to Flair. "From the top of the stairs."

"Oh, so *that's* the key?" Flair said, glaring at Aiden. "When were you gonna tell me?"

Aiden smiled. "When you needed to know, which wasn't until now."

"Whatever moron, what does it mean?"

"It means Pops wanted us to find something, and I'll bet Mackleford wants the same thing."

Aiden scanned each of the enormous pillars seated in their large wading pools. Then he ran towards the pillar at the far end of the Garden Room where he had opened the window, seeing a large platform topping the pillar that wasn't on the others.

"Hey, wait a sec," Flair said, watching Aiden step on the rim of the wading pool.

"Shush!" Aiden shushed. "I'm thinking."

The wading pool was larger than the others, and the spiraling water flowed much slower. Aiden jumped in, the water splashing up over his waist.

"Did you take your cell phone out of your pocket, dummy?" Flair shouted.

He didn't. Aiden slammed his flat cap into the water, glaring at Flair, who smirked and shrugged. Yanking out the wet cell phone, he replaced it with the key and began climbing the pillar.

Aiden felt like a kid again, scaling the side of the pillar as if it were a chain-link fence. But as he looked down upon the majestic Grand Garden, he saw Simone sitting on the bench, ashen and pale, staring up at him. This wasn't any make-believe Lionel Vann adventure.

He reached the top and stood, immediately seeing a metal plate with a large keyhole on the crest of the pillar. Unable to contain his excitement, Aiden dropped to his knees and with a great exhale, inserted the Cornerstone Key and turned it.

A violent shudder almost sent Aiden over the side, but he balanced himself. It took him a second to realize the pillar was rotating. Aiden crawled on his knees towards the edge, watching the wading pool spin like a large turntable. The water drained out of the pool, revealing a narrow staircase at the base of the pillar, beyond which was the entrance to a dark passage.

"Oh wow!" Flair said.

"Sweet!" Simone yelped.

"Incredible!" Margaret gasped.

"Flair, what's she excited about?" Aiden said, watching Simone rocking back and forth, trying to get up. "I can't see anything from up here."

"It's a staircase, bro. At the bottom of the pillar, heading down."

"Simone, sit still! Flair, make sure she doesn't fall on the floor again. Margaret, what's downstairs?"

"I'm sorry Aiden," Margaret's voice echoed. "I've never seen this before in my entire life. I have no idea what's down there."

"Great," Aiden said, peering over the edge of the platform. "So how are we supposed to know what's in there?"

Although no one answered, they all knew and stared from the passageway below to Aiden on top of the pillar. Aiden sighed, retrieved the Cornerstone Key and descended the side of the pillar.

Simone stared after him, moaning, "Oooh, Aiden, I want to go too!"

"Simmy, not trying to be mean, but no. We don't know what's down there. Let me check it out and I'll tell you if it's safe."

"I'm coming too," Flair said, standing up.

"No you don't, sunshine," Aiden said, smirking. "You'll ruin your fancy boots. Just stay put and watch Simmy."

Flair bristled, watching her brother descend the staircase into the black tunnel.

"I hope something eats him," she grumbled.

Aiden descended into a dark corridor covered in dead bugs and cobwebs, the only light coming from the staircase behind him. He felt excitement and curiosity flooding his senses like a raging river. *What was at the end of this tunnel?* He couldn't imagine what he would find, but whatever it was, he knew it must be extremely important.

Inching through the dark, his head bumped into a low hanging light bulb. He found a chain, pulled it, and the light popped on. The corridor narrowed, and continued along a slight decline, with another thirty feet of visibility. At the edge of the darkness, Aiden found another hanging light bulb. He turned it on and saw the corridor widened ahead.

The thumping in Aiden's chest increased with each step he took. Another light bulb met him. Aiden pulled the chain, revealing a man's face directly in front of him.

He cursed and fell backwards, not taking his eyes off the man. He steeled himself for an attack but realized the intruder wasn't moving. His face was waxy and still, and Aiden getting a better look realized it wasn't a man at all, but a mannequin.

Aiden breathed a sigh of relief but frowned. *What was a mannequin doing down here?* It was strangely dressed like a desert explorer, wearing a turban and loose nylon clothing. Aiden moved past the mannequin as dim motion lights from above illuminated a large, oblong room. Positioned around front end of the room were more mannequins wearing various international uniforms, and at the far end of the room was a large wooden desk.

"Okay," Aiden said to himself. "This is a little weird."

He walked in slowly, approaching the desk while keeping an eye on the mannequins, which in the dim lighting looked like a creepy panel of judges watching Aiden perform some sort of test.

As he passed the middle of the room, without warning, a gust of air breezed past him. About ten feet ahead of Aiden, two large panels of thick glass rocketed in from both sides of the room, slamming together and blocking him from the desk.

Aiden tapped on the glass. It was four inches thick. Impenetrable.

"GOOD DAY TO YOU!" a voice boomed.

Aiden jumped and turned around. He looked at the mannequins, expecting to find one talking to him.

"I SAID GOOD DAY TO YOU!"

The voice was everywhere, and Aiden turned every which way, seeing nothing. Finally looking up, he spotted a loudspeaker hanging from the ceiling.

"Good…good day to you too. Who is this? I'm armed!" He felt stupid but he grabbed the key and brandished it like a weapon.

"THIS IS A VOICE RESPONSE UNIT. DO YOU KNOW MY NAME?"

Aiden thought for a moment. "I'm gonna take a wild guess…Gaston Gumm."

"You are correct." The voice had softened. "And for your sake, I hope you are a friend. I created this test to protect the valuable and dangerous information that you seek, for you would not be here if you didn't seek them."

Aiden heard a — *schufft!* — sound behind him and turned. Another pane of glass had sealed the entrance behind him.

"Okay," Aiden said, trying to stay calm, "that's not cool."

"The following questions were designed to prove your allegiance. Should you not pass these security checks, you will not be able to leave this room. Well, not *alive* anyway."

"Excuse me?"

Gumm's voice continued. "However, if you do pass, it means you are a trusted ally, not an enemy of the Journeymen's Guild, and certainly not a friend of Mochtier Mackleford and his Dominion. Shall we begin?"

Something went — *clink!* — behind Aiden, and turning, he saw a six-foot long silver spear extend from the side of the Egyptian explorer mannequin, aiming straight at him. The other mannequins followed suit and Aiden found himself surrounded by fifteen armed and deadly mannequins.

"Hey! Whoa whoa whoa! Mr. Gumm?"

"You will only have two minutes to answer the questions correctly," Gumm's voice said gravely, and then with a hearty lilt of encouragement, "Good luck!"

The mannequins moved forward, rolling slowly along small metal rails that Aiden had just noticed.

"You gotta be kidding me!"

"ARE YOU MALE OR FEMALE?" Gumm's voice thundered, echoing off the walls.

"Male!" Aiden shouted back, and a whirring noise sounded all around him.

"NEXT QUESTION! WHO IS YOUR MOTHER?"

"Laura Maidenfair Johnson."

There was a slight pause, and Aiden again heard the whirring sound. The machine was changing up its questions based on his answers. There was a loud buzz, and then:

"NEXT QUESTION. WHAT CITY WERE YOU BORN?"

"New York City."

"WRONG ANSWER!"

A Neanderthal mannequin hurtled at breakneck speed along the track toward Aiden, who narrowly avoided the spear. The mannequin began flying back and forth along its track as Aiden stared at the loudspeaker.

"What do you mean 'wrong answer'?" Aiden shouted. "I *was* born in New York City!"

"WRONG ANSWER! WHAT CITY WERE YOU BORN?"

Another mannequin dressed in Samurai armor fired out, sending Aiden diving for safety and rolling away from the Neanderthal.

"Wait, no, East Town!" he shouted. "I was born in East Town!"

"Correct!" Gumm's voice sang with delight, and the whirring noise continued overhead. Aiden watched the mannequins zing back and forth, looking for a safe place to stand if more launched out, but there wasn't as much as a foot of floor not crisscrossed with metal rails.

"NEXT QUESTION: WHERE DID YOUR FATHER DISCOVER THE CITY OF THE CAESARS?"

"The City of the *what*?" Aiden shouted out. "How am I supposed to know?"

"WRONG ANSWER!"

A third mannequin, a Sherpa, exploded forth and Aiden once again dove for his life.

"Where did your father…" Gumm's voice insisted.

"I DON'T KNOW!"

Mannequin four. Dressed in the outfit of a Russian Bolshevik. Aiden grabbed it as it zipped by, thinking he might be safer riding on one of these things. But as he touched it, an electric shock ran through him, knocking him to the ground. His brain swam deliriously as the Neanderthal and samurai bore down on him.

"HOW AM I SUPPOSED TO KNOW?" Aiden said, missing the mannequins by inches. "I'VE NEVER BEEN THERE!"

"WRONG ANSWER!"

The Egyptian explorer mannequin rushed out from its position. Aiden barrel rolled, dodging the explorer, the samurai, and the Bolshevik before face planting into the glass.

"Where did your father locate the City of the Caesars?"

Aiden rubbed his pained face, thinking quickly. He knew he had less than a minute.

"Wait a sec, I've heard of this place," he huffed. "It was in Lionel Vann and the Land of the Giants. Um, um, *Gigantes…cuidad…*It's in South America!"

"More specifically please," Gumm's voice said politely.

Aiden sidestepped the Bolshevik, shouting, "Come on, old man! *BRAZIL!*"

"Correct!"

Aiden only had a second to consider what Gumm had said: his father located the City of the Caesars? It was a legendary city, it didn't really exist, did it? Another whirring and buzz was followed by:

"NEXT QUESTION: HOW DID YOU OBTAIN THE CORNERSTONE KEY?"

"My father, Wilbert Johnson, a riddle, found it, my fireplace at my house in East Town!" Aiden blurted it out so fast. Would it make sense to the machine?

No *"WRONG ANSWER"* response came, but the mannequins hadn't stopped, and Aiden was too afraid to say anything else. If one more of those things shot out...

The whirring sound ended without the loud buzz. The mannequins halted in their tracks, their spears retracted, and then they slowly rolled back to their original positions against the wall. Aiden collapsed to his knees, clutching his chest.

"Aiden Johnson," Gumm's voice sounded full of pride, "I am so happy you have found this room and endeavored to join us. I asked questions only you would know and only you could answer. Only someone whom I supremely trust could access this location."

"Yeah, and only someone supremely insane would even want to."

Gumm's voice continued. "You must forgive an eccentric old man, but I believe in catching people unawares and off guard. The element of surprise is our best weapon against those who practice evil. Their underestimation is often their undoing. Never forget that."

"Sure, pal," Aiden said, still holding his hammering heart.

"But, you must have important business ahead," Gumm said. "My one and only admonition before you set out. Protect what you learn. The knowledge we've discovered, as you may have already seen, is lethal and dangerous in the wrong hands.

"Finally, should you ever need to access this room again, instead of enduring my question and answer session, once the glass doors close, simply say the phrase *'Gaston Gumm, a journey has begun'*, and you shall be admitted. If you forget, well," he chuckled, "I'm sure you won't forget. Welcome to the Journeymen's Guild!"

The giant glass panels that sealed off the large mahogany desk slid opened, and atop the desk, Aiden saw a keyhole that was the perfect size for the Cornerstone Key. Aiden approached the desk, inserted the key and turned it.

With a loud—*CLUNK!*—the desktop slid back and dropped over the side. Something from within the desk was vibrating, shaking the entire floor. Aiden stood back as a magnificent panoramic map of the Earth arose from within the desk. Models of famous landmarks were marked with flags: The Empire State Building, the Colosseum, the Pyramids of Giza, the Taj Mahal; even the House of Gumm was given prominence.

Aiden couldn't help but be impressed with the craftsmanship of the map; even the topography looked realistic. He leaned over to touch a model of Mount Fuji and it tipped over. Something moved out of the corner of his eye and he turned: the samurai mannequin, rolling along its railway towards the desk. It didn't wield a spear or a weapon of any kind; nevertheless, Aiden leapt to the other side of the desk and ducked. The mannequin reached the end of the track and a hatch on its chest fell open. Aiden stood up, looking perplexed.

Inside the mannequin's hatch was a long golden blade with a jade handle. Aiden grabbed it, feeling its weight in his hand.

"Over six hundred years old," Aiden mumbled to himself. He returned the blade to the mannequin and went back to the map, standing over Great Britain. "Okay, what's behind Stonehenge?"

The model of Stonehenge slid to the right as he touched it. The samurai rolled back into place as a Royal Palace guard moved forward. Its chest opened, revealing an ordinary brass teacup.

Just below Great Britain, Aiden noticed France and the Eiffel Tower, already tipped over.

"Pops," he breathed, standing the miniscule monument up.

A French policeman approached towards the desk. When it reached the end of its track, a hatch on its chest fell open, and Aiden peered inside.

Empty.

"Damn. We better not have to go to Paris."

CHAPTER TEN – THE SECRET OF THE CRANBERRY INN

One of Flair's favorite things about living in a big city was the lack of gardens and nature. The thrill she felt after entering the Grand Garden had quickly faded, and the entire time Aiden was underneath the pillar, she felt tickling sensations on her skin as if something was crawling on her. However, Simone refused to leave until Aiden surfaced, so Flair kept her mind off her squeamishness by trying to get Simone to use her legs, which simply wouldn't work. Simone couldn't feel anything below her waist, although she was able to wiggle her big toe on her left foot, which gave Flair a little hope.

"I don't get it," Flair said. "If those little guys can walk, why can't Simmy?"

"Every Purity infection is different," Margaret said, bowing her head. "Simone might experience things we haven't seen before. Aiden was right. This is entirely my fault. I should have said something. You should have been on your guard."

"It's okay, Granny," Simone said, patting Margaret on the arm. "It's not your fault. But I don't understand why he did this to me."

"He's a despicable man, sweetheart," Margaret said, scowling. "He was once good, but his father's death pushed him over the edge. He became an unstable man. That's when he began his Purity experiments."

"What is Purity?" Flair asked. "Where did it come from?"

"They found it, my father, Mr. Mackleford, and a team of their top pupils. They came upon a tiny island in the Indian Ocean teeming with incredible plant life and large, powerful insects. They had never seen anything like it. A lab was set up at Mr. Mackleford's insistence and they studied the environment for months. Finally, one afternoon, Mr. Mackleford discovered inside a deep, underground cave, a pool of pure, white liquid that nourished the whole island."

"And then what?" Simone asked.

"Well, they drank it," Margaret said simply, then off Flair and Simone's stunned expressions, "but remember, these men were reckless adventurers. Wasn't the first or last time they had done something foolhardy. Anyway, it changed them my father said.

Purity played havoc with their minds; they became depraved, vicious men. Only after a terrible incident did my father realize its danger. He stopped drinking it, but he was hard-pressed to convince the others, one of the reasons he stopped taking pupils across the world with him. Only he and Jonas traveled together until your parents came along."

"You said my parents went to Paris to find Jonas," Flair said. "What were they looking for?"

"I wish I knew. They never told me."

"What about Jonas?" Simone asked. "Can we talk to him?"

Margaret stared at a potted plant next to her, stroking the leaves, looking confused. "We don't talk anymore. Jonas and I were close at one point, too close for my father's comfort, and, well I stopped it, thinking it was for the best. Jonas wouldn't accept my call if I was the last woman on earth. He hasn't spoken to any of us since my father died. I'm not even certain your parents found him."

Margaret stood, looking around the Garden sadly. "Once, Jonas and I could fix anything. Before I ended our relationship, we were quite a team. We'd plan our best strategies against Mackleford right here in this Garden. You'll think me strange, but it always felt like the Garden was part of our team. Something with the pillars I think; after all, my father built them, and one never knows with him. Anyway, I was once capable and wise. But old age has robbed me of that. I'm no good to anyone anymore."

And she looked at Simone, who was still playing with the flakes of skin on her arms. "You're still wise, Granny. You'll help me," Simone whispered, frosty air leaking from her mouth. "But I can't believe he's over a hundred years old."

"It's Purity. Purity strengthens the body and slows aging. Mr. Mackleford experimented on himself and became addicted. It consumed him, body, mind, and soul."

A chorus of grunts and squeaks arose, the Deformed had re-entered the Garden, walking towards Simone, pointing at her and grunting at each other. Simone pointed at one who seemed to be arguing with the other two, raising his hands up and squealing in protest.

"He thinks I can be healed."

"Healed?" Margaret said. "No, it is impossible."

"But Mackleford said if we get what he wants, Simone would be *restored*," Flair said, turning to Margaret. "I heard him."

"It's been over fifty years, no cure has ever been found. Believe me, we've tried everything."

"Yeah, that's what those two are telling him," Simone said, pointing at the Deformed, "but he thinks I still have time. He says it's not too late for me."

"Did he say how?" shouted a voice from behind. Aiden was climbing out of the wading pool, shaking mud from his shoes. "Oh, by the way Margaret, your dad was a lunatic."

"I've heard that plenty, believe me, Aiden. What did you find down there?"

"Besides a splitting headache and near death?" Aiden grumbled. "We need to talk to Jonas Wilson."

Margaret looked mortified. "Why?"

"Well it's like this…" and Aiden told them, amid interrupting gasps, about Gumm's question and answer session, the fifteen spear-wielding mannequins, the giant map inside the desk, the Eiffel Tower tipped over, and the empty hatch in the French policeman.

"So we have to go to Paris?" Flair asked, sounding somewhat excited.

"We're not going to Paris," Aiden said. "Whatever Pops took outta that funhouse before he went to Paris to find Jonas Wilson, I'm betting that's what Mackleford wants. Wilson either has it or knows where it is. So let's call him up."

Margaret, Flair, and Simone looked at one another. Aiden frowned.

"What's wrong?"

"Ex-boyfriend?" Aiden shouted, springing up from the Grand Room sofa minutes later. "That's ridiculous! What are they? Teenagers?"

Flair yanked Aiden back to the sofa by his sleeve. "Be quiet! I brought you in here so Margaret wouldn't be embarrassed," she said angrily. "He doesn't take her calls and nobody's seen him since Gumm died. Why do you think Dad flew to Paris?"

"So what are we supposed to do now?"

"Do what Dad did," Flair said. "Go to Paris and find Wilson."

Aiden stared at Flair as if she couldn't be serious. "Are you insane?"

"Are you? Look at Simmy! We're not leaving her like that!"

"Right, look at Simmy. We're not getting into an airport, much less into France with Simmy looking like that! Margaret just needs to get this Jonas Wilson guy on the phone. I'll go talk to her."

"I already told you he won't answer her calls," Flair said in a hushed voice. "Maybe Simmy should stay here and…"

"I'm not letting Simmy out of my sight, not after what happened to her."

"Okay, then we'll bring her along." And now Flair was standing. "After all, if this Jonas guy can help…"

"We don't know that he can. You just said no one's seen him in years."

"But we don't know that he *can't*. Look, we can't take her to the hospital, we can't go to the police, and we've got a week to figure this out. Right now he's all we've got."

Aiden felt stuck. His instincts told him going to Paris would be making a bad situation worse, but what choice did he have? He turned around, seeing a teary faced Margaret standing behind him. It appeared she had been eavesdropping.

"Aiden," she sniffled, "I'll cover everything, travel, hotel, food, whatever the cost! It's my fault this happened. I should have warned you!" Aiden stared from Margaret's pathetic, regretful eyes to Flair's determined ones.

Oh well. He always wanted to see Notre Dame.

The Johnsons remained in the Garden Room as Margaret's houseguests returned from the lake, laughing and still singing carols. Hearing mirthful sounds echoing throughout the House of Gumm made Aiden feel sick to his stomach. One by one, the guests tucked in for the evening and the Johnsons returned to Carolina Avenue, with Aiden carrying Simone under a thick comforter.

Two hours later, after Aiden and Flair were packed and ready, Margaret entered through the front door, rolling a wheelchair and a gray lace shawl, both of which belonged to Reverend Lafayette's mother.

"No questions asked," she said, watching Simone maneuver in the wheelchair. "Probably thought it was for me." She handed the shawl to Simone, looking guilt-ridden. "The symptoms of Purity won't go over well with many. You'll want to avoid unnecessary attention."

Simone stared at the lace shawl, looking dejected, but accepted it from Margaret.

"I know dear," Margaret said, patting her on the shoulder, "but the staring and whispering will be worse." She turned to Aiden. "The shuttle leaves for Proctor's Landing in forty-five minutes. You'll meet Marcus Nefflin, my father's old pilot. He's a Journeyman, knows every trick in the book. He's going to arrange everything, passports and all, then fly you to Paris. He may even know how to track down Jonas.

"You'll also need something else before you leave," Margaret said with a serious look. "Something that will help you immensely. We'll need to make a stop at the Cranberry."

Aiden and Flair loaded their suitcases into Margaret's car, but Margaret said she didn't want to draw attention to what they were doing, so the four of them walked to the Cranberry Inn. East Town was ghostly quiet except for the band, whose mournful, sleepy rendition of *What Child Is This?* whispered across the valley. Margaret's tiny feet zipped through the snowy streets. She was practically at a run to keep up with Aiden's long strides.

Flair was pulling up the rear, wheeling the shawl-covered Simone, her teeth chattering. All the cozy warmth of East Town had evaporated into that cold voice still ringing in her ears: *"She shall be restored!"*

Simone noticed they were lagging further and further behind Aiden and Margaret, and peeked under the shawl, seeing a distant look in Flair's eyes.

"Why are you stopping?"

Hearing Simone's voice, Aiden and Margaret turned around, breaking Flair's vacant stare.

"Oh," she said, looking slightly embarrassed. "It's just, well Mom…I mean our parents, this whole time, I thought I knew her, but she, I mean *they*…they were really out there, fighting these…Dominion guys."

"Okay, can't you think about this somewhere that's a lot warmer?" Simone said.

Aiden and Margaret, both catching what Flair had said, walked back towards them. Margaret smiled warmly, patting Flair's shoulder. "They were gifted leaders. They carried my father's spirit after he died, kept his values alive. Outside of them, well, the rest of us have been replaced by the younger Journeymen."

"Hello? Adults?" Simone said. "Freezing, sick kid over here!"

"Your father," Aiden said, ignoring Simone, "mentioned *the Journeymen's Guild* in his little torture chamber underneath the pillar. Who are they?"

"Those of us who oppose the Dominion," Margaret said. "You know what a journeyman is of course. No longer an apprentice, but not quite a master. It was my father's way of saying none of us, regardless of skill or importance, had mastered anything. We're all still walking our own individual journeys."

"Why do we have to talk about this in the middle of the freakin' street?" Simone said, fidgeting under the shawl.

Aiden, finally acknowledging Simone, grabbed the wheelchair and walked on. "And the younger Journeymen replaced you?"

"Guess we're in the way now," Margaret grumbled. "Too old to face the Dominion, but they still need us occasionally, sometimes to ask a question, mostly to ask for money."

Aiden wanted to reply but didn't. He was tempted to find out more about this group, but at that moment, decided he didn't want to know. Once Simone was safe, he wanted to forget East Town ever existed.

The enormous Cranberry Inn came into view, its seven floors bedecked with Christmas lights of every imaginable color. The quartet entered the quiet lobby, pitch dark except for the twinkling blue and white lights of a tall Christmas tree near the elevator. A janitor slept beside it in a chair, his feet propped atop a mop bucket.

"Who are we coming here to see?" Aiden asked.

"Oh my, Aiden," Margaret whispered, "no one at this ungodly hour. We're here to get weapons."

"Weapons?"

"Shhhh! Not so loud." Margaret hurried them past the sleeping janitor into the elevator.

There were six buttons on the elevator panel, and Margaret pressed both the "1" and "6" and held them down. Nothing happened, but Margaret held her fingers firmly on the buttons.

"Why are you pressing both buttons?" Flair asked.

"One and six equal seven, Flair. That's how we get to the seventh floor." She explained it as though this was obvious, but the Johnsons frowned at one another.

"Wait, I thought the seventh floor was all burned up," Simone said.

"Oh my, it was. But not by any ordinary fire."

"So what's up there?" Aiden said.

"I just told you," Margaret said, slightly annoyed. "Weapons."

The two buttons lit bright blue and the elevator chugged slowly up. The numbers on the elevator panel ticked off as they passed each floor, *2...3...4...5.* The elevator rolled past the sixth floor, rattling and groaning, as if it were forcing itself through a cramped opening. The elevator cab shook to a halt, and the doors opened.

It was near pitch black on the seventh floor and Aiden noticed an odd, earthy smell filling the hallway. Margaret held a flashlight, clicking it on and casting its beam onto a blackened carpet. She left the elevator, walking with her arms stretched out along the wall to their right, shining the light against it, looking for something.

"Oh my," Margaret muttered, "this is always so difficult, now where is...Aha! Here!"

Flair could make it out in the flickering circle of light on the wall: a small bump underneath the fading wallpaper. Margaret pressed the bump and with a quiet—*whoosh!*—a panel slid open on the opposite wall.

Aiden followed her through the doorway and onto a dirt floor. His jaw fell open in amazement as he heard Simone's cry of *"Oooooo!"* behind him. The room was illuminated by several crystal formations: fiery red, glowing green and bright white. Margaret went to work immediately, grabbing tongs and two pouches, one of black burlap and the other of brown leather, from a shelf. She plucked crystals from the various red and white formations, dropping them into the black pouch.

"My father discovered these. He called them Crystal Stars. He never told me where he found them, but he showed me how they worked."

"And they're weapons?" Aiden asked.

"Oh my, yes. Yes indeed," Margaret spoke, handling the crystals with extreme care. "Powerful weapons. Dangerous. They hold the energy of the world."

"I don't get it," Aiden said. "What does that mean, the energy of the world?"

"I don't understand it either, Aiden, just another one of the many secrets my father and Mackleford uncovered. Purity was one, and these are another." She held up a white crystal, eyeing it carefully before dropping it in the burlap. "Thankfully Mackleford doesn't know we have these. They're one of the few things in the world that are effective against his Goon Squad. So please be careful you don't lose any of these. Not a one."

Margaret held a white crystal in her hands. All at once, a bright field of white light surrounded her. Aiden reached out, passing his fingers through the light. It felt warm.

"Good, you can see the *aura*. That means it is working. If you are holding a crystal and there is no aura, it'll be as useful as a box of jellybeans against the Dominion, as you may have noticed earlier.

"The whites boost your normal abilities, the five senses. You'll see clearer and farther, it improves your sense of touch, and you'll hear better than ever. Some Journeymen say it even gives you a sixth sense."

Returning the white crystal to the black pouch, she grabbed a red crystal, and a bright red aura surrounded her. "With reds you can charge up and redirect your own energy, but it takes tremendous focus to do it."

"Charge up and redirect energy?" Aiden said quizzically. "What do you mean?"

"I'll show you. Move back, Flair." Flair stood against the wall as Margaret pointed one of the crystals at the floor. Her red aura swelled, growing steadily brighter, and suddenly three loud, successive bolts of red ignited from her hands, stirring up a cloud of dust that made everyone cough. When the cloud settled, Flair was standing next to Margaret, eyeing the crystals.

"Whoa," Flair said, wiping her face. "That's pretty nice."

"Oh my, I hope no one heard that. But these charged attacks will help you defend yourselves against those terrible Goons. Red crystals can also create shields, although I'm not very good at it." Margaret touched the red crystals together, and a small red disk appeared. It flickered and almost faded entirely. "Here Aiden, you try."

She slapped the crystals into Aiden's hands, and the red aura surrounded him, as near as Aiden could tell, down to his shoes. He stared at Flair and she looked blurry.

"Focus, Aiden. You'll need complete focus to use these."

Aiden shook his head, blinking. He wasn't sure what he was supposed to be focusing on, but this was hard. His brain felt like it was doing cartwheels as the aura began to flicker.

"Good, good. Now aim and release—"

Aiden lifted his hand to aim at the dirt floor away from everyone but stumbled. The aura had faded, the room was spinning, and he felt a sick feeling in this stomach. He dropped the crystals on the floor.

"Good grief, Margaret," he coughed, balancing against the wall. "Is this safe?"

"You need time to get used to it. Crystals are hard to master, not everyone can use them, but your mother," she said, smiling at Flair, "was extraordinary. The Dominion feared her."

Aiden saw a slight smile break across Flair's face as Margaret moved over to a large column of green crystals. "Now, let's see if we have any takers here," she said, aiming the tongs into the center of the column. "The greens are very tricky, must find just the right color. Oh my, an excellent one!"

From within the green column, Margaret extracted a bright light green crystal, setting it carefully in the leather satchel.

"Greens create tremors once they touch earth, concrete, anything inorganic, which is why you must keep them in this leather pouch at all times. One green would knock a man off of his feet. Two could cause a very violent earthquake."

Flair swallowed hard. "Can you use three greens?"

"Don't toy with that idea, Flair," Margaret said sharply. "Two should be enough."

Something caught Aiden's eye in a corner of the room, a spark of blue gleaming out from underneath the dirt. He turned and walked to the corner, away from Margaret and the crystal formations.

A blue crystal was buried slightly in the dirt floor. He reached to pick it up, but remembering the sick feeling he had in his stomach from the red crystal, decided otherwise.

The blue crystal wasn't shining as bright as the others, and even though he didn't touch it, he felt dizzy. The room was drifting out of focus.

"Aiden. You don't belong over there. Come on back this way."

Aiden froze. It was a man's voice.

But there were no other men in the room. Aiden's heart hammered as he turned around, but there was only Margaret showing the green crystals to Flair and Simone.

"Can I hold one, Granny?" Simone asked.

Aiden turned back to the corner where the blue crystal rested, but it was gone. It had been another memory. Immediately, Aiden felt re-acquainted with the dark walls and the sharp smell of stale dirt. He had been in this room before, perhaps several times.

"I'm afraid not, dear. Crystals hurt those in your condition. A few Purified can use crystals effectively, but for most it just causes pain. I'd caution you against touching any of these until you're cured."

"Margaret," Aiden said, "what do the blue crystals do?"

Margaret looked alarmed. "A blue? You saw a blue? Where?" She raised her voice so loud, she was almost shouting. Aiden stood back, pointing towards the corner apprehensively, where there was obviously no crystal.

"Well, I think I might've been here before, and saw one and…"

Margaret pushed past Aiden, dropping to her knees and digging in the corner.

"Where was it exactly?" she said, throwing dirt in every direction.

Aiden pointed towards the spot. Margaret looked frantic, digging deep into the ground. After a minute, she rose up, panting and sweating, but with an expression of relief.

Flair helped Margaret to her feet and dusted her knees. "So, what do the blue ones do?"

"I wish I knew," Margaret huffed. "I've never seen one myself, only heard stories about them. Journeymen don't use them, only Mackleford and his Dominion agents know how. All I know is people have died, so if you encounter a blue crystal, there's no time to talk. Just be ready to run."

CHAPTER ELEVEN – WELCOME TO THE GOON SQUAD

Voices.

They sounded a million miles away in Rico's ears. He tried moving, but every muscle was rigid; he couldn't open his eyes, he couldn't feel a thing. He could only hear voices, which were growing louder, clearer. There were two men, one young, one old. He couldn't tell who they were or where they were, but he no longer had to strain to hear them, they were quite close.

"Stage five is complete, stage six is pending," the younger voice said. "We have some irregularities occurring that we didn't expect."

"Irregularities are always expected," an older, distinguished voice said. "Purification always gives us something new and different. What are we looking at?"

"At stage four, the human body generally rejects Purity, fights the new format, which is why we have deformities. But this is amazing. His body has accepted the change, and not only his body, but his mind is also in complete agreement with the Purity gene."

"Excellent. This was our hope. We have Ellis's new enhancements to thank for it."

"You know, Mochtier, I never question you, but why didn't you tell this young man what you were doing to him? Why didn't you let him volunteer? I'm not against human experiments, but the patient should know everything."

"Well, Standis, you asked the question, but you've already given the answer. We wanted to test the effectiveness of the enhancements that Ellis made to Purity, hoping that body, mind, and soul accepts the changes, *feels* they are good. Before you is perfection, the best that the power of our planet can offer. What's the point of improving him if he rejects his new reality because he longs for his old life?"

"I agree, but only to a point. He should have been told. We have an obligation—"

"We've told the others, haven't we?" the older voice interrupted. "How did that work? Did they accept the terms of their outcome?"

"But they were all *deformed*," the young voice argued. "Perhaps if their results returned more like his…"

"But their results didn't, did they?" And now the older voice sounded annoyed and angry. "And knowing Purity as you know it, we cannot risk *non-acceptance* as a possibility. We know what *that* leads to. Now, doctor, you work for me, you are being well paid for your services. It would be wise to cooperate."

There was a long silence. Rico was listening hard. Did he lose them? Did they leave?

"Our next step is to find safer methods of implementation," the older voice said, "but for now, this crudeness is the best we have."

"Will he be deployed?" the young voice said. "Perhaps one more week?"

"We'll see. Anticipating the Guild's next move isn't very difficult. I'll be visiting East Town this week to deliver a message to the Johnson family. I still need my property back. Once I have it, the world is ours."

"You put your faith in unusual things," the young voice said. "Customs, creeds, this thing you seek…. Mochtier, the only thing we can trust is science…. If this…. does what you…. only take us so far…we should focus…"

The voices were fading. Rico strained to keep listening, but they were gone. Rico didn't know what they were talking about: stages and enhancements, irregularities and this Purity nonsense was going over his head. But he was relaxed, at peace and, strangely enough, although he was unable to move, he felt stronger than he had ever felt in his life

"La Ville-Lumiere! Haven't been there in thirty years," Mackleford said, speaking with an air of fondness as he munched on a crisp salad. He was seated at a small table in the cabin of a luxurious jet. Ellis Vicartan sat across from Mackleford, holding a small screwdriver, quietly working on a gleaming, golden baton. Mackleford observed his work, raising an eyebrow.

"What is that you have there?"

"Rico's Ruijen Staff," Ellis said. "Finishing it for him."

"Gold, Ellis?" Mackleford chuckled. "Well, I've seen the Ruijen models in green, black, red, silver, blue and white, but never gold. The Squad's going to get jealous."

Ellis continued to work, saying nothing.

Mackleford chuckled. "Well, Rico is a special case, I suppose. He's the first."

"Rico is unique in every sense," Ellis muttered, not looking up from the baton.

Mackleford glanced at Ellis as he finished the last of his salad. "Ah. Well as I said, it's been years since I've been in Paris. Have you seen it at night in its beauty and majesty?"

"Not at all," Ellis said bitterly, although Mackleford didn't seem to notice. He stood and paced the cabin, caught up in his own reminiscences.

"We called Paris 'Jump Point', our home away from home. We would spend months there, crackling for the next adventure. The world was an open playground to us then."

"Better times, Mochtier?" Ellis remarked.

"Not better," Mackleford said, leaning against a plush chair, "just different. Easier. There's something about early adulthood. You know what it is, Ellis? Freedom. Free to live life and learn it as it comes. Before you know any better. Because after you know better, everything changes. Gus and I had that freedom. We should have continued together in the quest for the ultimate freedom, but he made his choice, as did I."

Ellis remained focused on his task as Mackleford sat back down, looking pensive.

"And Aiden Johnson understands this freedom. There was something behind his eyes."

"Fear," Ellis said. "The Masks told Mr. Quick he was a scared child."

"No, it wasn't fear," Mackleford said, "at least not fear of that moment. Something else. He is unlike his parents." And as Mackleford spoke, he frowned, just realizing something. "Ellis, what do we have on him?"

Ellis pulled out a small electronic tablet from a bag, swiped its screen nonchalantly, brought up a file on Aiden and handed it to Mackleford.

The screen displayed photos of Aiden at various locations: standing before a podium in a lecture hall, walking into a *Media Hut* store, sitting in a library next to a tall stack of books. Below the photos was a report on Aiden.

"*Intelligent, a well-read historian,*" Mackleford said, reading. "Hmmm. *Resourceful when he needs to be. Anticipation, manipulation are his strengths. Uncanny knack of deciphering people and events.* Interesting."

Mackleford's eyes held on a picture of Aiden and a cheerful Simone walking outside of her school. He sat the tablet down as Ellis twisted the golden baton; it sounded a mechanical—*zing!*—and extended to a six-foot long bo staff.

"We have surveillance at various hotels," Ellis said. "We're awaiting their report, but it appears…"

"What disturbs me," Mackleford interrupted, "is that this boy exhibits traits of cunning and intellect—"

"Traits of cunning and intellect?" Ellis laughed. "Mochtier, that's being generous."

"—but he's unaware of the Journeymen and the Dominion," Mackleford continued.

"Because he is easily misled and distracted," Ellis scoffed.

"He was also hidden, Ellis. Try as we might, until Wilbert's incapacitation, we could not find the Johnsons like we found the others. Deliberate isolation and preparation. Aiden Johnson was being groomed."

Ellis's eyes peered over the top of his glasses, looking up from the golden staff. "Groomed? This boy is their Hail Mary?"

"*Aiden will do it,*" Mackleford mused, nodding. "Those were Wilbert's last spoken words. But how? Gumm's protégés, always so well prepared."

"Wilbert was nothing," Ellis said. "Once you allowed me to get involved, I found him within days. He wasn't a threat."

"You're determined to discredit Wilbert Johnson," Mackleford said sternly. "Why must I remind you to *respect* your adversary, Ellis?"

"And why must you revere them?" Ellis shot back. "You speak about Johnson and Gaston Gumm as though they were perfect, yet *we* have created perfection!"

Mackleford stared at Ellis, considering him carefully before answering. "Ellis, you are my greatest assistant, but Gus Gumm was my equal. We grew up together, learned from each other. We should have continued as friends, but he refused. Stubbornness."

Without warning, the cabin of the plane shook with the force of an explosion. Mackleford's fingers sunk into his chair; he had almost fallen to the floor. Ellis dropped the golden bo staff to clutch the table. They looked at each other, then out of the nearest window. Red flashes illuminated outside of the plane, followed by another violent jolt.

"Stubbornness," Mackleford grumbled, "he passed down to his Journeymen."

Rico awoke, finding himself strapped into a leather chair in a spacious room. The metal floor vibrating beneath him and the curved, paneled walls with small, circular windows told him he was in an airplane's cargo hold. As Rico unbuckled himself, a door swung open and six humongous men entered, rollicking in laughter.

"Hey! Ell was right, he's awake," boomed one of the men.

They were as ugly as they were enormous, all looking like victims of horrific accidents. They had a multitude of strange deformities: stretched out noses, squashed faces, blotched, pox-marked skin with warts, bloated arms and legs. And without questioning why, Rico felt close to them, as if they were all brothers. They walked towards him, looking fascinated.

"Wow! Would ya look at that?" said a man with a squashed face.

"Bet he ain't got what we got," said a stocky man with no neck.

"Supposed to have more," said a creepy man with a gorilla-like posture and enormous hands and feet. "Supposed to be stronger."

"Doubt it," said a tall man with disfigured arms, displaying a mass of red and black tattoos. "Look at him. Too pretty to be stronger than me."

Their booming laughter reverberated through the cargo hold.

"Wonder what his Goon name'll be?" The no-necked man stroked his chin thoughtfully.

"I like Pretty Ricky," the squashed-faced man said.

"Oooo, cold-blooded, Pug," laughed a skinny man with a long, yellow face. "What about Paleface? I like that. Why's he so pale anyway?"

"Ell says it was a tradeoff so he didn't look as ugly as you," the tattooed man laughed. The rest of the group joined in, roaring at the insult.

"What do I look like?"

Rico sensed the words before he actually heard them. He also felt himself rising out of the chair and standing up, though he wasn't aware of it physically. His body seemed to be moving faster than his mind. *An out-of-body experience,* Rico thought, *but I'm in control of it.*

"Whoa!" the largest man said. "Slow down or you'll be eatin' the floor."

Rico heeded the advice, and while slowing down, felt his mind catch up with his actions. He looked at his body. His skin was pale, almost an eggshell color. His arms were muscular and heavy. He felt cold, but not uncomfortable.

"Rico, right?" one of the men said, extending a large, calloused hand. "Yeah, it was me that pounced ya last week. Sorry, just followin' orders."

"Yes, I remember you," Rico answered, shaking his hand. The apologetic man was huge and stocky; it looked as though his head were simply propped upon his shoulders. "It's okay, you were following Mr. Mackleford's instructions. What's your name?"

The Goon looked stunned at Rico's politeness. "No-Neck," the big man responded.

Rico stared at him, as if he wasn't being serious. "No-Neck? What kind of name is that?" he asked.

"Well my *old name* is Frank Clarkson. But on the Goon Squad, my name's No-Neck."

"The Goon Squad? What's that?"

"*We're* that. Name's Musclehead." The tall, tattooed man jabbed a thumb in his chest and proceeded with introductions. "Pug, the guy with the face that looks like it was smashed in by a brick. The skinny guy is Lanky. The kid with the big hands is Man-Child. He's the youngest, thinks he's the smartest too."

"I *am* the smartest," Man-Child retorted.

"Right, that's why you got nabbed in Morocco, 'cuz you're so freakin' smart!" And laughter thundered through the cargo hold again. Man-Child looked slighted.

Another Goon stood away from the rest of them. "The guy in the corner is Fats," Musclehead said. "Fats don't talk much, but ain't no better Goon in a scuffle than him."

Fats, although shorter than the other Goons, was gargantuan, at least twice the girth of No-Neck. His wrinkled forehead hung over his eyes, hiding them from plain view, and his cheeks were swollen like he had a mouthful of food. He leaned against the far wall, looking bored and uninterested, but glanced over at Rico for a brief moment at the mention of his name, then back at his shoes.

"Why call yourselves 'Goons'?"

"Sounds like an insult, right?" No-Neck said amusedly. "That's what these other Dominion bozos call us. Goons. But it's a badge of honor. See, we're the guys Mack calls on for the big stuff, for the dirty work. The Goon Squad is feared and respected, and nobody messes with us. So when the Dominion gets worked over by the Gummy bears, we come in and restore order."

"The who? Who's the Dominion? And what's a Gummy bear?"

The Goons chuckled, except for Fats, who remained quiet, nibbling his fingernails.

"You'll find out soon enough. It'll be a surprise." Musclehead walked next to Rico, sizing him up. Rico was shorter and smaller than Musclehead, but much more toned and athletic. "So you're the *'it'* they've been waiting for. *Mr. Perfect.* No flaws. What do they say you can do?"

Rico looked at his hands, making fists, seeing his large muscles flexing underneath his smooth, alabaster skin. He felt strong and powerful, with a sense of superiority. He looked at Musclehead, thinking of an answer to his question.

"I suppose everything you can't." Rico didn't mean it to be an insult, just a statement of fact. However, he knew immediately the Goons didn't take it that way. Musclehead's mouth curled and his eyes narrowed. Pug and No-Neck took a couple of steps back as if making room for a fight. Man-Child raised an eyebrow, then folded his arms and smirked, not taking his eyes off Musclehead. Even Fats was watching this exchange.

But the moment was broken by a hard shudder of the plane, causing everyone to stumble. Musclehead walked towards a window as red flashes brightened the night sky.

"Are we being attacked?" Rico asked.

"Very observant, Paleface," Musclehead said. "Yeah, that'll be the Gummy Bears!"

"Mr. Mackleford," Man-Child said, standing next to an intercom, "shall we see to this?"

"If it isn't too much trouble, yes please!" Mackleford's voice bellowed through the speaker. "Before they blast us out of the sky! Ellis, contact Mr. Quick. He's in Berlin with Harrison. Get them into France on the double!"

The Goons exploded at this, whooping and slapping high fives. Rico watched them throwing on heavy jackets and grabbing different colored batons from the corner.

"Let's move Paleface," Musclehead said, slapping Rico on the back.

"Where are we going?" Rico replied, looking confused.

"Down there," Lanky said, tucking his fedora hat into his trench coat.

"Game time!" No-Neck said, flipping his jacket collar up before slapping hands with Pug.

"I don't understand. We're landing?"

"Landing?" Man-Child laughed, and the other Goons joined in. "Yes, Ricardo, we are landing, but not in the plane."

Musclehead banged on the cabin door. "Hey, the newbie is coming. He'll need his stick."

Seconds later, Ellis Vicartan appeared at the door, smiling at Rico.

"Hey bud!" Ellis said warmly. "Awake finally. You look fantastic!"

Rico walked over, but instead of a warm greeting for his mentor, he took the golden baton from his hand, examining it.

"What is this, Mr. Vicartan?" Rico asked, looking at the weapon

"C'mon, Rico, I told you. It's Ellis!" Ellis slapped Rico on his shoulder, and then took the staff back from him, twirling it in the air. "It's your Ruijen, pal. Made especially for you." The other Goons leaned in, looking over their shoulders, and murmuring excitedly.

Rico didn't respond, only nodding and taking the Staff back from his mentor. Ellis looked over his young protégé, noticing his cool demeanor. "How ya feeling, Rico?"

"Excellent, Ellis," Rico responded. "So this is it, right? Change my life forever? Probably need a little sun, but otherwise I've never felt better!"

Ellis chuckled. "Good," Ellis said. He indicated the golden baton. "The Ruijen Staff is tailored just for you, reacts and responds as you wish."

"Want us to teach him some tricks, Ell?" No-Neck said.

"Not yet, not till it's done," Ellis said. "Back in one piece, Rico. I'm not finished all the enhancements."

Ellis Vicartan turned and faced the others Goons, who had formed a semi-circle around him. He gave them a knowing look, like a sergeant sending his beloved troops into battle. Without a word, he pulled a royal blue baton from his belt and held it into the center. The Goons responded in kind, reaching in with their elaborate bo staffs and batons, resting them on top of Ellis'.

"Step in, Rico." Ellis nodded to a spot next to Fats. "You're one of us now." Rico looked confused at the ritual but copied them, placing his golden baton in with theirs.

"Brothers," Ellis spoke solemnly. "We are entering a world that is not prepared for us. That does not understand us. That hates us and desires to destroy us. But enter we must, for this is the age of our Dominion and we are its first soldiers. Take care of business. Take care of each other. Take care of yourself. We are all we have."

"We're all we have!" they shouted in unison. *"GOON SQUAD!"* The Goons broke the circle like a football huddle, whooping and shouting. Rico had turned to talk with Ellis, but he was already at the cabin door. He turned and looked at Rico, gave him a thumbs up, and slammed the door.

Stepping to the rear of the plane, Musclehead slammed his giant fist on the cargo door controls. Red lights flashed all around them as the door opened. Violent wind swirled through the cargo hold as the Goons stared into blackness.

Rico looked at Musclehead, puzzled. "Parachutes?"

"That's your parachute right there!" shouted Musclehead, pointing to Rico's staff. Musclehead nodded to No-Neck, who, to Rico's amazement, took three bounding steps and leapt out of the plane, shouting "GOOOOON TILL I DIIIEEEEEE!"

Pug followed him, jumping into the dark sky, screaming "GOON AND PROUD!" One by one, the Goons leapt into the darkness, all yelling some Goon-related credo, except for Fats, who simply walked to the edge and toppled out. Musclehead remained with Rico.

"Okay, keep your arms at ya side and hold onto ya stick. I'll tell ya when to turn it on."

Rico stood at the brink, uncertain. Gazing out into the black void, he felt a small hiccup in his chest. He looked at his golden device, gripped it as tight as he could, and jumped.

It was a sea of icy wind. Rico struggled to keep his arms and legs together, feeling the rushing air pulling them apart, twisting him in all directions. One second, he was looking at the sky, the next the ground, seeing red flashes of light zinging past him. He found the strength to pull his arms together, stopped spinning, and leveled off.

Even in the darkness, Rico saw the outline of the Goons who had jumped ahead of him. Fats was most prominent, his hefty frame resembled an overfed pigeon slicing through the air, while Man-Child used his massive hands to perform graceful pirouettes. Musclehead had already caught up to Lanky, No-Neck, and Pug: they were side by side, pointing to one another and examining the ground below. Musclehead looked over to Rico, opened up his left arm and glided over to him.

"Down there!" he shouted. "That's them! Careful, they've spotted us!"

Just as Musclehead finished, a red flash knocked Pug sideways and suddenly the night sky was alight with red bolts. The noise was incredible. Rico couldn't tell what was louder: the wind howling around his head or the — *CRACK!* — from the red bolts below. Musclehead shoved Rico as two bolts narrowly missed them, causing Rico to flail his arms and legs again.

Rico tried to get his arms together again, but it was impossible. He was falling faster, out of control, watching the Earth grow closer. If that wasn't enough, huge bolts of white electricity crackled all around him. Lightning seemed to be striking in every direction.

Rico saw Musclehead vigorously waving a hand at him, but he was confused, distracted by the tops of trees in the distance. He was no more than a mile up at this point.

Again, Musclehead waved, this time with his black and red baton. As Rico glanced at his own baton, another bolt of lightning struck where Musclehead had been. At last, Rico understood.

The electric bolts weren't lightning at all, but rather strange, crackling streams of energy, stretching from sky to earth, and the Goons were riding them. He pressed the button on his golden weapon and felt his arm yank.

The Ruijen Staff had amazingly created a current of energy from the moment he clicked the button. Rico felt as though he were sliding down a warm, electric rope. More red bolts whizzed past him, and he saw where they were coming from: a group of people running through a wide field, away from the streams of energy, escaping into a forest.

Fats and Man-Child landed first, extinguished their electric currents, and took off after the shadowy group. From above, Rico watched a fantastic battle as the other Goons joined their comrades. He saw bo staffs energize, heard them whip through the air, firing projectiles and electric sparks. A man in a military jacket deflected a bombardment with some sort of red barrier and fired three red bolts into Pug's face, causing Pug to somersault and crash on his back. The man looked up, seeing Rico, turned and ran.

"Crap! Seven Goons! Screw it, let's book! Lyric, don't let them catch her!"

Rico landed, clicked off his baton, and joined the chase. The ground was soft and muddy, but it didn't slow him down. He passed up Man-Child and Fats with ease, closing in on their assailants.

"After them, Ricardo!" came Man-Child's voice. "Don't let them escape!"

Suddenly it felt like Rico's legs had slipped from underneath him. He stumbled and held his balance, but then the ground threw him about fifty feet into the air. He crashed head first with a hard thud, eating a large mouthful of mud and grass.

Rico rolled over onto his back in pain, spitting dirt. He heard the chatter of his pursuits dying off in the distance as he sat upright. They had reached the forest, making their escape.

Rico looked at a hand extended over his head. He reached up and grabbed it.

"You run pretty fast," Musclehead said.

"What happened to the ground?" Rico said, his head throbbing.

Musclehead hoisted him to his feet and steadied him on the mushy ground. "Green crystals. I'll explain it to ya later." They looked around to the other Goons, who were arguing.

"It was Dillinger!" Lanky said. "I'd know his voice anywhere."

"Middleman's kid too," Pug said through his swollen jaw. "Did you hear what he said?"

"He said *don't let them catch her*," Man-Child said. "What's that mean? Who's *her*?"

"It don't matter!" Musclehead roared at them. "We got the job done." He looked into the dark sky and there was no sign of Mackleford's jet.

"Where are we?" Man-Child asked.

Musclehead looked around, surveying the area. "French countryside, 'bout hundred miles from Paris. Nice night for a jog. Should be there by tomorrow morning."

"Wait a minute," Rico said, rubbing his pained head. "We just jumped out of a plane, saved it from getting blasted from the sky, chased off these guys, but no one is picking us up? We have to *walk* a hundred miles to Paris?"

Again, booming laughter followed Rico's question, echoing across the field. Musclehead slapped Rico on the back, shaking his head. "Welcome to the Goon Squad."

CHAPTER TWELVE – FROM EAST TOWN TO PARIS

Ever since she dropped her tomboyish ways at the age of twelve, Flair had always dreamed of visiting Paris. She followed many famous Parisian designers and considered herself a fashion connoisseur, spending hours reading fashion websites and magazines and watching fashion model shows. Visiting Paris would be a pilgrimage of sorts, but she never thought she'd be going under these circumstances.

The morning sun crept over the snow-covered hills as Margaret and the Johnsons entered the train station. Soon the BLD would be brimming with Towners and the smell of pancakes and sausages, but the Johnsons would not be amongst them. Aiden's mind drifted to the House of Gumm and to Gloria. Tomorrow was Christmas Eve, and Aiden had promised to help her with the preparations for Margaret's evening dinner for over one hundred guests.

"Margaret, you'll explain to Gloria, won't you?" Aiden said, dragging their bags towards the waiting shuttle. Margaret turned to him, bewildered. "I had promised her…I…well, you'll explain everything."

Margaret nodded and patted Aiden on the hand. "I'll take care of Gloria," she said, handing Aiden the two bags of crystals. "You take care of these. Losing even one would be tragic."

"What would happen?" Flair asked.

"Crystals are dangerous," Margaret said. "Terrible things happen when they fall into the wrong hands. And besides that, there aren't many left. Crystals are how we fight the Goons. The more crystals we lose, the more we cook our own goose."

Aiden looked at Simone in the wheelchair, feeling helpless. Nothing could be done except this dubious trip to Paris to find a man they'd never met. As he dropped the crystals into the wheelchair pocket, Margaret reached into her pocket and handing Aiden her Book of Wisdom.

"Here Aiden," she said, her eyes firmly on her book. "You take this."

"Why?"

"It might help. My father took it with him often." She pushed the book into his hand.

"But we might not make it back in time for the Reading..."

Margaret smiled. "Silly, I've done the Reading for decades; I've practically memorized it."

"Really?" Aiden said, opening the book and flipping the pages. "What's on page eighteen?"

She smiled. "You win, Aiden. If you can make it back before New Years, that would be great. But just make it back."

The announcement for the shuttle's departure to Proctor's Landing had been made. Flair rolled Simone's wheelchair towards a ramp when Margaret tapped her.

"One thing, Flair. A favor." She had waited until Aiden was aboard and said, "Tell Jonas that I'm sorry about everything. He'll know what I mean."

Margaret looked so pitiful, Flair could only croak out "it's gonna be okay..." but it didn't sound very encouraging. Margaret hugged them and said goodbye and five minutes later, the shuttle eased up the tracks. Flair wheeled Simone towards a window, which Simone pressed her nose against, waving. They watched Margaret's tiny silhouette shrink into the distance until finally the train entered the tunnel, and East Town was gone.

Margaret was back at her car when she heard a squeal of rusty brakes. Harold Mimble's cab just pulled up. Margaret approached him and together, they stared at the empty tunnel.

"Where're they headed to?" Harold asked.

"After their parents, of course," Margaret sighed. "As we always knew they would, Harold. Let's go to Tank's, I'll fill you in."

The trip back to Proctor's Landing seemed to take forever. Aiden couldn't see how this Paris trip was going to work. Simone's condition made entering a foreign country a nightmare, not to mention navigating a city they didn't know to find a man they'd never met. Margaret gave Aiden a photograph so he'd know what Jonas looked like. The caption at the bottom read, "Location #2, 1961", meaning it was fifty years old. Aiden didn't believe it would be useful.

It showed four men standing before the mouth of a large cave. Margaret's father, Gaston, was short and chubby, wearing a

Cincinnati Reds cap. With his round, cheerful face and his hands in his pockets, he looked like an overgrown child having the time of his life. Kneeling on his left was Jonas Wilson, wearing a thin Fu Manchu mustache and a mane of long blonde hair. On Gumm's right was Mackleford, clean-cut and handsome, looking almost the same age as he did the other night. Margaret was right; Purity had completely stopped him from aging. Directly behind Mackleford, almost standing in his shadow was a clinical looking man with hunched shoulders, wearing a sour face as if he had eaten something rotten. Margaret said this was Boris O'Reilly, Mackleford's protégé.

Aiden had studied the picture for most of the trip to Proctor's Landing, because just like his other memories, he felt certain he had also been to this location before and that something important happened there. His train of thought had broken when they arrived at the Proctor's Landing train station.

Standing in the parking lot was Marcus Nefflin, a tough-looking middle-aged man, grizzled from his face to his clothes. Much like Brett Morris, freezing weather didn't seem to bother Nefflin as he wore a button-down short-sleeved shirt, a ragged pair of blue jeans, and a filthy army cap. He flicked a cigarette into the snow as the Johnsons approached.

"Wilbert's boy, eh?" Nefflin said. His gnarled hand gripped Aiden's, giving it a strong shake. "Hands're all soft 'n tender like a basket o' posies. What 'cha been doing in life?"

"I teach history."

"Hist'ry," Nefflin sniffed. "Figures you'd be doing some'n like that. Our kids're out there fightin' the Dominion. You three, guess Wilbert had diff'rent plans for ya."

Nefflin grabbed the shawl covering Simone's face and lifted it. He didn't seem bothered by her appearance, but rather intrigued.

"Int'restin'. How long ya been like this?"

"I dunno," Simone replied. "Overnight, I guess."

"Hrmmm, Mack wernt tryin' to kill ya then. He wants some'n."

"He wants to trade the cure for something my parents took from him," Aiden said. "But we don't know what it is or where it is."

"But Jonas might, right? I'll tell ya right quick, Jonas Wilson don't fool with us much anymore. And from what I hear, he's a hermit out there in Frenchy land, livin' by 'imself, designing kooky little houses for kooks like 'im. Lots of rumors say he's dead. Might be dead."

"Dead?" Flair said with a note of concern. "But my parents went to find him in France before they were attacked by Mackleford."

Nefflin shook his head. "Jonas was one o' the first Journeymen, darlin'. If he wants to disappear, he's gone…not even Wilbert's findin' 'im."

"But Margaret said you could."

Nefflin looked slightly uncomfortable. "Mebbe, mebbe not. I got folks I can ask, but they ain't generally agreeable. I'm gonna have to finagle and finesse."

"With all respect Mr. Nefflin," Aiden said, "we don't have time for finesse."

"Well son, I don't know how it works in hist'ry class, but out in the world, there's rules. Cain't just push a button and make Jonas Wilson drop outta the blue sky. You want my help, that's what I do. Finagle, finesse…understand? So, if you'll pardon me, I gotta finagle three passports and finesse you three into France."

Three hundred miles away, Carson Dillinger was racing down a Tennessee highway, weaving through early morning traffic, adjusting the volume on the car speakers.

"Going to find *who?*" he yelled over the roar of the motor.

Sonya Martinez's voice spoke over the speaker system. "Jonas Wilson. He's an old—"

"I know who Jonas Wilson is!" Carson said, annoyed. "Mackleford sent them to find *him*? That doesn't make sense."

"No," Sonya replied, "actually he told them the opposite. Said no Journeymen better show up. At least that's what Margaret said he said."

"*And she sent them to him?*" Carson screamed. "What's the matter with that old dingbat? Doesn't she run anything past anybody anymore?"

"Them old timers are missing screws, dude. How are they getting over there?"

"How else?" Carson said. "Nefflin."

"Neff owes the Gumms everything," Sonya said. "He's gonna do whatever Margaret tells him to do and not ask questions."

"Believe me, Margaret gave him a fat wad of cash too," Carson grumbled. "Nefflin don't do charity." He dodged around a pickup truck and accelerated.

"Has anyone tried to contact him," Sonya said, "and tell him to hold off?"

"C'mon, Sonya, Nefflin's old school. He don't keep a cell phone on him."

"This is all bad," Sonya said. "There's another development. I didn't say anything until now because I wasn't sure, plus Libby said don't jump the gun because—"

"Stop justifying, just spit it out."

"Okay, okay. Well…someone tried to kill the Johnsons."

Carson frowned, slightly stunned. "What? Mackleford needs them alive to find the thing."

"No, I don't think it was the Dominion," and Sonya paused for a second. "Okay, so, check this out, Mike and I are on the train, right? Keeping an eye on things when — *bam!*—the train malfunctions. The Johnsons got off the train and decided to walk back to Woodwind and take the shuttle to Proctor's Landing."

"You're joking?"

"I wish I were," Sonya replied. "We didn't realize that they got off, apparently Mimble's kid rounded up a few Towners on the train. Come to find out, as they were walking back, a snow slide nearly wiped everyone out."

"You're joking?" Carson repeated with frustration. "So wait, you think Mimble's kid—"

"No, no," Sonya said, "he's just polite, he isn't the type."

"You sure the snow slide wasn't accidental?"

"Whoever did it, didn't even try to hide it. There were scorch marks on the trees, Carson. Red crystal marks."

"One of us," Carson said with grim finality. "It's getting out of control, Sonya. I told you this would happen. I told you to let me and Lyric hide them!"

"Blame Wilbert, what are you getting mad at me for?" Sonya snapped back at him. "Anyway, it's spilled milk, let's move on. Where's Wilson live?"

"Outside Paris in Chartres. He changed his name and started dropping rumors that he was dead. But Nefflin knows the right people, and…dammit!" Carson stopped short, shaking his head and grimacing at the rising sun.

"What?"

"Mack thinks Jonas is dead. What's he gonna do when he finds out—one, he isn't, and two, the Johnsons are trying to get in touch with him?"

"Maybe this is a blessing in disguise. Remember, you wanted to hide them, and the one thing the old timers are good at is hiding. Neff's got cash and connections up the wahzoo, and Wilson has been *quote-unquote* dead for ten years. Maybe they got this covered."

"Sonya, no one's encountered Mackleford in the last ten years, but twice this year he makes an appearance? Whatever Wilbert stole from Mackleford, he wants it bad. We've got to get to them."

"So Mack says no Journeymen, yet you want to go help them? And you call me reckless."

"We have to do something. And I think I have a plan."

"So he can control this Purity stuff? I figured he just hurts anyone he touches."

"Yep, has total control over it. He can git'cha a little or git'cha a lot."

"How long have you been in the Guild?"

"Twenty-two years, jus' after the break in."

There was a conversation going between Flair, Simone, and Nefflin of which Aiden was only faintly aware. They were three hours into their flight, aboard a rickety 1985 Cessna single engine plane somewhere over the Atlantic Ocean. Nefflin's finesse had worked; after some quick talk and a money exchange with a man at the Proctor's Landing airport, he returned with three passports and a grin on his face. This must have been how Gaston Gumm travelled the world, Aiden thought, slipping in and out of countries through connections and payoffs.

But how Nefflin was able to slither the three of them out of the country wasn't on Aiden's mind. He had been thumbing through Margaret's book, reading over some of the wisdom she had written, and had come across a poem entitled *The Wise Old King*:

> The Wise Old King spoke words of sooth
> And nations gathered to pay heed,

To understand, to learn the truth
Of love and might, of thought and deed.
For who can know the minute's hand
And all the lies that lie therein,
The fortune of the cynic's plan
And devices that shall spoil their sin?
'Tis he who hears with breath or wind
The melody upon the air.
That ageless power once scorned by men
Forsook and lost so none can bear.
And thus the King's solution finds,
Granting me that once was hidden
The conqueror of polluted minds,
Greatness sought, no longer given.

He had been staring at it for two hours, having no idea what it meant but feeling like it spoke about the very thing they were looking for. Those words—*ageless power*... What was it Margaret said? Mackleford wanted power, not treasures and trinkets. But his parents hadn't stolen some vague or intangible power. They had taken something solid and real.

Aiden drifted to sleep, unaware of time and place, enjoying a dream. He was a boy, maybe six or seven, chasing a young girl his same age, sprinting through the terraces of a bright garden. She was inches away...frustrating him and delighting him at the same time. She was within reach; he stretched out, his fingers flitting against the edges of her auburn hair...

"Wake up, bro!" Flair's voice erupted in Aiden's ear. He snapped awake and blinked. It was dark; he was back on the plane. He grumbled at his sister, looking angry until she pointed out of the window to his left. The plane dipped through the clouds and Aiden got his first glimpse.

It was Paris. If words could only express the thoughts of Aiden's mind...

Wide and sprawling, the dark outline of the Seine River snaked around the city's monuments. The Eiffel Tower, pictures never did it justice; it stood like a beacon of life; the Invalides, the resting place of Napoleon. Notre Dame Cathedral looked mysterious and phenomenal, and off in the distance, the unmistakable golden outline of the Arc de Triomphe. Aiden held his breath, mesmerized. Wonderful, glorious history was everywhere.

The Cessna descended quickly, cutting Aiden's joy short. He had barely registered that he was in Paris when Nefflin touched down at Charles de Gaulle Airport, taxiing towards a remote hangar on its edge.

"Hold tight, Johnsons. Gotta coupla more calls to make. Ya hungry?"

They shook their heads, looking groggy. Nefflin shrugged and left, but he wasn't gone long. Aiden didn't know how he had done it, but within half-an-hour, they were shuffled off the Cessna, across the snowy airport grounds, and into a taxicab driven by a smiling black man with a rigid jaw and a head of thick gray hair. Nefflin introduced the driver as he leaned inside the cab's window and handed a business card to Flair, who was seated behind him.

"Rainier," Nefflin said, slapping the man on the shoulder. "Here's 'is number. Anything ya need. He's the best cabbie in the world."

The driver turned to them, smiling.

"Ahh, look at zem," Rainier said. " Zest like zeir folks! Zee Journeymen are growing strong again! Wheech hotel, Marcus?"

"Hotel De L'Escapade," Nefflin stated, buttoning up his jacket.

"Ahh," Rainier breathed. "Five star. Very fancy."

"An' after ya drop 'em Rainier, bring it back here, we'll have us a drink."

The Johnsons didn't care that Hotel De L'Escapade was a fancy, five-star hotel. Their exhausted bodies collapsed onto their hotel beds the moment they saw them. They woke late the next morning and it took the Johnsons well over an hour to get ready, so it was late into the afternoon when they finally exited the luxurious lobby, meeting a smiling Rainier.

"Where will it be, Johnsons?" Rainier said, swinging open his cab door for Flair.

"Business district, to the Architectural Expo before it closes," Aiden said. Nefflin had told Aiden about this assembly of architects while they waited on the tarmac. Today was the last day of the Expo and Jonas could certainly be there, if he were indeed alive.

It was a short drive from the hotel, and within minutes, Aiden was pushing Simone along a wide sidewalk, heading towards a building at the far end of the street. The late afternoon streets were flooded with people, and much like East Town, festivity was in the air. It was Christmas Eve; thousands of shoppers were rushing through the streets with packages and presents.

The Expo building was small but jam-packed with architects, specialists in the field of architecture, and visitors examining exhibits with everything from small homes to skyscrapers. Aiden took his time examining the presenters at each booth, not speaking to his sisters, who probably wouldn't have heard him due to the loud buzz of chatter.

As they entered another room, Aiden noticed a thin old man wearing a silky, green trench coat standing on a far platform alongside the model of a strange "bubbled" building. He was arguing with a lively group of hecklers surrounding his platform, which displayed a large, gaudy sign made of bronze:

DEMETRIC
INTERNATIONAL DESIGNER
VANGUARD OF ART, ARCHITECTURE, AND ACADEMIA

"Hmmph," Aiden grunted, looking from the sign to the man, "so he's alive after all." Despite the name on the sign and the garish wardrobe, there was no question who he was. He even had the same Fu Manchu mustache and mane of long hair, though it was now white and tied in a ponytail.

"That's him," Aiden whispered to Flair. "Wilson."

"A monstrosity!" yelled a man with a heavy English accent.

"Monsieur, these ees not a functional structure!" cackled a Frenchman.

"Narrow! You're so abominably narrow," the thin man screeched at them, whipping off his green trench coat with flamboyance, laying it gently on a chair. He spun back, facing his audience. "This is the future of our passion, my friends!"

"The mind is usually the first to go, eh, Demetric?"

Laughter and jeering erupted, but the slender man just smiled.

"My mind is deeper than the depths of the sea! You critics adore the fashions of the moment, following your friends and contemporaries, and limiting your minds to the curiously constrained concepts of a few notables! Whereas I, Demetric the Vanguard, continue to set trends! Behold my latest construct—*the Atlantian!*"

After a dramatic wave of his hands, the audience exploded into hysterical laughter, but it didn't seem to bother the old man. He continued arguing with his hecklers as Aiden crept forward through the crowd.

The old man soon spotted Aiden and stopped squabbling with his opponents at once. He stared curiously at his face for a moment, and then scanning the room, he saw Flair and the wheelchair in front of her, seeing a tiny face peering through the lace shawl.

His knees buckled and Aiden thought he was going to fall off the platform. Trembling head to toe, the old man turned and threw on his long green trench coat.

"He saw me, bro," Flair said, approaching behind with Simone. "He looked right at me."

The old man turned to his crowd, looking pale and ill, deliberately avoiding Aiden's eyes. "Dear friends…uh…m-my hour is finished, I must depart. Merry Christmas!" And he leapt without warning from the platform, high into the air, astounding his crowd, some of whom laughed at the stunt, and sped off towards the exit.

"He ain't gonna be *Mr. Cooperation*. C'mon." Aiden grabbed Simone's wheelchair and broke into a jog, as the old man was only yards away from the exit.

But Jonas Wilson stopped before he reached the exit. Blocking his path was a man dressed in a tan suit. Jonas grimaced turning around and working his way back through the crowd.

Another tan suit cut him off. And another. They reached inside their jackets as if to pull out weapons.

"What's going on?" Flair said to Aiden, noticing men cornering Jonas at every turn, seven in all, wearing identical tan suits. Jonas looked like a caged animal, frightened and unsure. Another man grabbed him by the shoulder and spun him around, standing eye to eye with him.

Aiden recognized him. He was the same man from the photograph, the same hunched over posture, the same sour face. Mackleford's assistant, Boris O'Reilly. He couldn't have been any older than thirty.

But Boris and Jonas were the same age in that picture, Aiden remembered, *which was over fifty years ago.*

Jonas's fearful look faded, replaced by a grin. "Boris! My God, it's only you. I was worried for a moment."

"I've finally caught up with you, Wilson," O'Reilly smirked.

"Yes, you've caught up with me, you pathetic underling. Who are your consorts? Not Dominion agents, surely."

"Just some well-trained, well paid, and very deadly associates of mine, waiting for you to do something stupid," O'Reilly said, adjusting his glasses.

"I see. So Mack no longer troubles his Goon Squad to come after me? Am I not worthy? Instead, he summons in his worthless stooge. I feel insulted. Go back and tell Mack to send his Goons if he wants to…Oh wait, silly me, I almost forgot," his voice turned somber. "You two aren't friends anymore. Poor Boris."

O'Reilly frowned, looking from side to side at the tan suits, who were now staring at Jonas, puzzled. "Think what you want, Jonas. Mochtier still calls on me, especially when it comes to tracking you down."

"No, Boris, Mack didn't send you. Maybe you want *them* to believe that, but we both know the truth. Mack only wants one thing and he wouldn't send an errand boy. If he thought I had it, he'd be here himself. Do your friends know who they're dealing with?"

O'Reilly's tan suited accomplices were now staring at one another, looking uncertain. "Boris, you simpleton," Jonas laughed, "let me explain something to you. I don't know how you found me, or why, or if Mack sent you or not. It truly doesn't matter. But you thought you would catch me unawares and off-guard. Let me assure you that ten years have not diminished my preparation one bit. So let's shake hands and part ways before someone gets hurt."

"Not one bit?" Boris sneered. "But that is it, isn't it? Between you and your little girlfriend, things are catching you unawares. You've lost your touch Jonas, and all of your old friends are paying the price, especially the Johnsons."

"What are you talking about?"

"I've been tailing you for months," O'Reilly said. "I knew about your little meeting with Wilbert and Laura in Paris before they even left the States. You've been slipping for ages now."

Jonas looked around, catching Aiden and Flair's faces. He looked a little worried.

Flair leaned over to Aiden and whispered in his ear. "What does that mean, *especially the Johnsons?*" she asked, but Aiden shushed her. He didn't want to miss anything.

O'Reilly continued mocking Jonas. "Ten years, and you have once again found yourself alone, surrounded and outnumbered. Don't you have any friends, Jonas? How you always find yourself in these fixes is beyond me."

"You say when we last met, I was alone, surrounded and outnumbered? Yet here I stand. Hmmm...I wonder why?"

Jonas unbuttoned his green coat, placing his hand inside. The tan suits replied in kind, stepping closer to Jonas. O'Reilly held his hand up, stopping them.

"Easy, gentlemen. Jonas isn't about to do anything. He used to get his hands dirty, but look at him? This broken-down wreck went into hiding for a reason. Isn't that right Jonas?"

Jonas paused, his hand still inside his coat, his eyes darting towards the exits. "The Johnson kids recruited you to find me?" he said. "Must admit I'm surprised."

O'Reilly opened his mouth, glancing around. "The Johnson children? What are you talking about?"

"Aha...so it wasn't *you* that brought them here." Jonas remarked with surprise. "That's not good."

"They're here?" O'Reilly exclaimed, glancing around. "Well, old friend, let's do everyone a favor. Button that coat back up, get the Johnsons, and let's all take a walk outside."

Jonas shook his head. "I don't think so, Boris. These ten years has made me aware of something: the unpredictable nature of life. How in one day, in one moment in time, the fate of a man that had plotted his course so carefully can be altered."

"Still like to make things ugly Jonas? Aren't you getting too old for that?"

Jonas Wilson grinned. "Never."

At once, a short baton sparking with electricity flashed from beneath Jonas' trench coat and jabbed into O'Reilly's chest. A resounding—*zzzaaappp!*—crackled and O'Reilly went airborne, flying thirty feet away, smashing antique home models.

Everyone's attention turned from viewing models buildings to watching Jonas and O'Reilly's henchmen square off. Another—*zzzapppp!*—sent a tan-suited henchman sailing through the air, bowling over a group of businessmen.

"Get him!" yelled one of the tan suits, and they charged.

But instead of defending himself, Jonas dropped to a knee, hiding completely underneath his green trench coat.

The tan suits pounced on Jonas, punching and kicking. One had a pair of brass knuckles fitted to his hands, another brandished a blackjack. They went to work on Jonas as O'Reilly pulled himself out from underneath the glass display.

"No!" cried O'Reilly. "Not against the coat!"

Aiden thought it was a strange thing to say until he looked closer at Jonas's coat. Wherever a blow had struck, it glowed bright green. The henchmen, recognizing this, stopped and backed up. Humming emanated from the coat as it glowed brighter.

"Aiden, we need to help him!" Simone said.

"No," Aiden said, staring at the glowing green coat. "I think we need to move."

"Ditto." Flair agreed.

Aiden had just wheeled Simone backwards when—
BOOOOOOMM!—a brilliant burst of green light flashed from Jonas' coat followed by a shockwave that sent people flying in every direction, the tan suits receiving the biggest brunt. Jonas rose from the epicenter, watched Aiden crawl off the floor, and headed towards the far exit.

"What was that?" Flair shouted, lying on her stomach, as papers and pamphlets rained down over them.

"On your feet, sunshine! He's getting away."

"Yeah, okay, but seriously, what *was* that?"

Aiden helped Flair stand, grabbed the handles of Simone's chair and they were off, chasing after Jonas, who was already outside. Congestion at the exit made it impossible to catch Jonas, but it did make it easier for Aiden to spot his white ponytail swishing away and ducking into a shuttle.

"There!"

They were too late to catch it by a hundred feet as the shuttle pulled off down the street. Aiden stopped in the middle of the road, staring at the shuttle's roof light.

"Chase it down," Flair said. "I'll watch Simmy."

"We don't need to. We just need Rainier."

"Well, he's not here, smart guy, and Wilson's getting away!"

"No, he isn't. *M-U-R-O-U-Q.*"

"What's that?" Flair asked.

"I saw those too, the letters on the shuttle," Simone said.

"Right," Aiden said. "But backwards. The shuttle was for a hotel. Q-U-O-R-U-M. That's where he's headed."

"Why would he stay at a hotel if he lives in Paris?" Flair said, confused.

"Because he doesn't live in Paris, he lives outside of Paris, remember? And for an old guy in town for the Expo, it makes sense for him to stay *in town* until it's over. At a hotel."

The Hotel Quorum shuttle squealed to a stop and Jonas struggled to stand. He shook and slapped his left leg to regain circulation and staggered down the aisle, tipping the driver before he exited.

He hadn't been in a scuffle in years, and would have tried making sense of why the Johnson children and O'Reilly were in Paris, but he was in severe pain. Bruised, but not broken, he needed pain medicine and a strong drink. He entered the cozy, quiet lobby of the Hotel Quorum, and the desk clerk smiled.

"Monsieur Demetric, good afternoon. How was zee Expo?"

"Terrible Jacques. Anything for a headache?"

"Jus' zee theeng," the desk clerk smirked, and reached under the desk, retrieving a long neck bottle of brown liquid. Whiskey. Jonas smiled.

"This time, I'll need real medicine," Jonas quipped. The clerk rifled through his desk drawer, at last finding a bottle of pills. Jonas read the label and shook it, hearing the rattle. He turned to the elevator but then swiveled back, grabbing the liquor bottle.

"I'll still take this though. And no visitors please, Jacques. I'm not here."

Jonas took his hotel key card from his pocket and swiped the lock to room 505. He entered a beautifully furnished hotel suite, tossing the pills and whiskey onto a small sofa as he sat down. While removing his shoes, he sniffed something in the air and his head sank.

"Your expensive Fifth Ave. perfume betrays you, my dear. Come out please."

CHAPTER THIRTEEN – THE TWO LEGENDS

Flair stepped out from the bedroom first, wheeling Simone, Aiden pulled up the rear.

Jonas sighed. "Aiden, Flair, and Simone Johnson. And I'll bet Rainier brought you, didn't he?" The Johnsons looked at each other, somewhat confused but nodded.

"Only Rainier could have gotten you here ahead of that shuttle driver and into this room. That man is good at his job." Jonas laid his green trench coat on the sofa, uncapped the bottle of pills, threw four in his mouth and swallowed. "Well, after all these years, the Johnson kids have finally surfaced. Untrained, unprepared, and not very smart."

"Not very smart?" Flair said, sounding insulted.

He rolled his eyes at Flair and grabbed a small glass from an end table. "Public places are not ideal for first-time meetings. Didn't it occur to you that you might've been followed? Blunders like that will get us all killed!"

"What are you talking about?" Aiden said

"Showing up at the expo!" Jonas barked, pouring himself a drink. "Thank God O'Reilly is still the inefficient whelp he's always been, but I swear, there are reasons why people move to foreign countries and don't return calls. I left all of this behind me when Gaston died."

"Wait, wait, wait, stop the circus, pal," Aiden said. "We're here is because Mackleford did *this* to my sister, and the way to fix that is to return something my parents stole from him. We don't know what it is, but Margaret said you can help us, so can you or not?"

"Margaret told you about *us*?" Jonas said, astonished.

"We know you don't talk anymore," Aiden replied. "Sounds reasonable and mature to me, but yeah, Margaret told us, otherwise we would've *called* and avoided the Trans-Atlantic flight."

Jonas stared at Simone quietly for a second, then took a deep breath. "Crossing the oceans for your family is admirable. You are true Johnsons. But a cure for Purity?" He shook his head.

"Mackleford has done this for years. Do his bidding, and he'll set things right. Never works out that way."

"So I have to stay like this?" Simone asked.

Jonas leaned in towards Simone and lifted the shawl.

"Hmm…" Jonas grabbed a nearby lamp and held it above Simone's face, examining. "This looks different. Mack did this to you himself? The White Hand?"

Simone nodded.

"Well, it's not as bad as most Purity victims. Mack always had a soft spot for little girls, going back to his own daughter. Might he was telling the truth." He straightened up, twirling his thin beard between his fingers. "Then again, we're talking about Mackleford. I wouldn't hold my breath. Simone, I've heard you aren't the shy type…"

"She sure isn't," Aiden and Flair said in unison.

"Well then, don't hide yourself," Jonas replied with a soft smile. "There are people worse off in this world than you."

Simone grinned and whipped the shawl away, tossing it on the sofa next to Jonas's glimmering trench coat. Her hand reached towards the coat when Jonas snatched it away.

"No," Jonas shouted, "don't touch!"

"You don't have to yell!" Simone bristled. "I just wanted to see what it felt like."

But Jonas said nothing. Grabbing the coat seemed to have caused it to glow bright green and he was holding it at arms length as if it were a bomb, smoothing the ripples on the coat like he was stroking a kitten.

"It's made of Aurorum Silk," Jonas said. "Purified people cannot touch Aurorum, it's toxic to you."

"Aurorum?" Flair said.

"Yes. From Aurora silkworms, in caverns deep beneath the Arctic," Jonas said. "One of Gus's discoveries, silk charged by the North Pole's strong magnetic fields. When disturbed, it emits a powerful electromagnetic shockwave. You saw it at the expo, yes?"

Aiden and Flair nodded, staring at the coat in amazement.

"The shockwaves alone are dangerous, but touch the silk even for a second, it would poison you, Simone. Absorb your physical energy. You could die."

Simone gulped and stared at the coat.

"Look, Mr. Wilson," Aiden began, "maybe there is a cure, maybe there isn't, but right now, we don't even know what he's looking for. So again, can you help us?"

"First, tell me everything you know."

Starting from the night Simone got the invitation, Aiden told the whole story amid constant interruptions from his sisters. Jonas stopped Aiden halfway through his frustrated experience in the oblong room to ask a question.

"Did anyone meet anybody wearing strange gloves? Leather gloves, very exquisite?"

No one said anything for a moment until Aiden burst out. "As a matter of fact, I did. Weirdo on the subway, that same day Pops gave Simone the invitation."

Jonas stood, slapped the back of his head, pulling his ponytail. "Fantastic! That *weirdo* was a Journeyman."

Aiden almost fell over. "A Journeyman?" Aiden said. "A member of the Guild?"

"Yes." Jonas heaved a heavy sigh and paced around the room. "Asked a bunch of questions about you, didn't he?"

Aiden nodded, "Yeah and stuff about history."

"Secrets are hidden within history," Jonas said. "He thinks your father told you something. This isn't the day to be Jonas Wilson."

"What do you mean?" Flair asked.

"Your parents did an outstanding job hiding you, which makes everything you just explained feel orchestrated. Strings are being pulled here. The question is by who?"

"You mean it's not Mackleford?" Flair said.

"Maybe, maybe not. Both the Guild *and* the Dominion use similar tactics."

"You mean the Journeymen wanted this to happen to Simone?" Flair gasped. "I thought they were good guys..."

"I don't mean that, Flair," Jonas said, retaking his seat on the sofa. "I mean they pull the same tricks. Half-truths or outright lies, set-ups and secrets, stringing their own members along, assignments with double meanings. Journeymen schemes are *world famous!*" Jonas laughed wheezily. "Always more than one agenda. For instance, I have no doubt the Guild has been tailing you since you left New York, but they've told Margaret to keep quiet. I just don't understand why she didn't…" but he broke off, staring at Simone with a regretful look.

"In any case," Jonas said, "it's not Gus's way. It's this *new* Guild. Be thankful Wilbert kept you from it. Why do you think I left? Can't even trust your own friends."

"And you think we're being followed by the Journeymen's Guild?" Aiden asked.

"Because Boris was there, that's my guess." Jonas stared into space, twirling his long, thin beard around his fingers. "O'Reilly was booted from the Dominion years ago, so Mack didn't send him, but he's always in the middle of things. Always knows when something big is going down. The Dominion is tight with information; the Guild on the other hand is sloppy. Word must have gotten out what you three are looking for, and if it's what I think it is, Mack will be here next. We don't have much time."

Flair cut in. "Mackleford said something about finding a *song*."

Jonas grimaced. "Yes. He's looking for the Song of Solomon."

"The Song of Solomon?" Aiden said, puzzled. "The book in the Old Testament?"

"Again, Aiden, history hides many secrets. History is written by *people*, and as you just discovered, *people* don't always tell us everything."

"Okay, so what didn't history tell us about the Song of Solomon?"

"That it was once called *Solomon's Seal*. You're familiar with the stories, aren't you?"

Aiden opened his mouth to speak, then paused. He stared at Jonas, skeptical. "*Aandaleeb?*"

Jonas nodded in agreement. "Aandaleeb."

"Aandaleeb's a myth," Aiden said. "Even if it wasn't, it would've been destroyed."

Jonas chuckled. "You certainly know your myths and legends, Aiden."

"Well *we* don't know *ours*," Flair said, "so what is it?"

"It's a ring," Aiden said. "Aandaleeb's a powerful ring, created by some great magician or God Himself depending on which version of the legend you've read."

"Oooo!" Simone gasped. "A magic ring? How cool! What does it do?"

Jonas smiled at Simone. "Command animals, command genies, in some stories it controlled the weather."

"A magic ring?" Flair scoffed. "*That's* what Mackleford's after?"

"Not quite Flair," Jonas said, and he lowered his voice, speaking mysteriously like a grandfather telling tales around a campfire. "Aandaleeb was just a ring, but its true power rested in the Seal that was set upon it. Legend says Solomon desired it, but Aandaleeb was supposedly lost in the Dead Sea. Once he became king, Solomon sent an expedition after it."

"But it turned out Aandaleeb wasn't lost at all," Aiden continued. "Solomon's sister had the ring, discovered her brother wanted it, and made up the whole lost at sea story so she could keep it for herself. But she never learned how to use it. Solomon found out and threatened to kill her, so she created a different story to make it look like the Ring was lost and then found."

"The fisherman's story," Jonas said

"Right," Aiden said. "So she gave the Ring to a fisherman, told him to prepare a meal for Solomon and place the Ring inside the fish. Solomon found the Ring, forgave his sister, and they all lived happily ever after, the end. Oh, except that part where none of that ever happened."

"Is that so?" Jonas laughed, grabbing a large suitcase next to the sofa and digging through it. "Gus always said this was my good luck charm, hasn't left my side for sixty years. My first discovery, found while exploring Mesopotamia ruins.... Where did I put...? Ha! Here it is!"

From inside the suitcase, Jonas extracted a cylindrical artifact of polished stone, preserved inside of a glass casing.

"What is that?" Aiden gasped, looking as though he had been temporarily transported back to the Grand Gallery.

"I found this in the grave of a Phoenician ruler," Jonas said, grinning at Aiden.

"Ph-Phoenician? It's gotta be twenty-two hundred years old!"

"Twenty-four I believe. Know ancient Greek, Aiden?" Jonas said, handing over the glass case.

"Of course I know ancient Greek," Aiden stated, awestruck. His hands trembled so much he was unable to read the faint Greek writing on the top of the cylinder. Finally mastering his nerves, he took a deep breath and read: *"The fisherman, desiring his own legacy, removed the Seal of Power from the Ring and fashioned his own creation. The King of Jerusalem, not to be made a fool, discovered the deception and retrieved the Seal. Unable to undo the fisherman's deed unless he destroy the Seal, he enjoyed the artistry of the item, making it his own song."*

Jonas peered at Aiden over the top of his glasses, waiting for understanding to strike, but Aiden only frowned.

"His own *song*, Aiden!" Jonas thundered. *"Solomon's Song!* The item created by the fisherman. Men have gone through great lengths, even dying, to hide its existence, which is why you've never heard of it. But you have heard its results—a small tribe becoming a powerful nation almost overnight, flushed with treasure, great temples, and a mighty army. And men and women, queens and kings, nation upon nation, coming from thousands of miles to hear the wisdom of the king."

Aiden stared at Jonas. "Wait a minute. So you're saying that this thing, this Song of Solomon that Mackleford's after is—"

"The source of King Solomon's legendary wisdom," Jonas finished. "You've heard of Herodotus?"

"Of course, but he never wrote about—"

"Oh, but he did," Jonas interrupted, nodding to the artifact. "Read the other side."

Aiden turned the glass box over, revealing more Greek engraved on the bottom of the cylinder, and gasped.

"It's HIM!" Aiden yelled as he stared at the writing. "I'd recognized his writing anywhere! Herodotus wrote this! Look Flair!"

Flair leaned in. "Who?"

"Who?" Aiden said, sounding affronted. "The father of history! The first man who traveled the world and recorded what he saw! And he didn't just write it, he lived..." And Aiden stopped short, remembering Carson Dillinger. Flair gave Aiden a "get on with it already" glare.

Seeing Flair's impatience, he recovered, reading breathlessly: *"The wisest men of Athens know neither the wisdom nor the power of the great king, whereas I alone have found it and with its greatness I could destroy their very foundations...* So Herodotus had it!" he exclaimed. "Where?"

"No idea. I don't even know what it looks like. Boris and I were too young to travel exclusively with Gus and Mack back then. They searched for three years and, as always, they found what they were looking for. Gus told me he immediately realized the Song's power and its potential in the wrong hands and determined to keep it hidden, except for he and Mack. But then…" Jonas stopped, looking pained as if remembering a bad dream.

"What?" Simone asked, on the edge of her wheelchair. "What happened?"

"Purity happened. Purity's powerful stuff, highly addictive, and Mack became obsessed with it after his father died. He used it on himself, experimenting, trying to build the perfect man, using the Song of Solomon as his aide. We didn't realize what Mack was doing until he could no longer be reasoned with. So Gus took the Song from him. Needless to say, Mack didn't appreciate that."

"What did Mackleford do?" Aiden asked.

"That's when this rift started. Gus versus Mack. That's when things got ugly."

"Ugly how?" Flair said.

"You see, we were all friends at first," Jonas said. "The exploration crowd, all of us, just adventure lovers. We had our different organizations: the Expeditioners, the Adventure Association, the Society of Explorers, and the Guild of course. All in fun, hired out mostly by fat cats looking for a thrill. We toured the world and emptied their wallets…" Jonas sighed, smiling. "Our golden age. But once Gus and Mack split, everyone picked sides. At first, the fat cats came with us. Mack liked that. He liked being the underdog, thinks he's an *everyman*. But Mack was always more resourceful than Gus, so before long, a far worse organization emerged."

"The Dominion," Aiden said.

"Yes, on the heels of Restoration College. You know all about them, I'm sure."

"No. What's Restoration College?" Flair said.

"Universities," Aiden answered, "specializing in advanced sciences and biotechnology. What's their deal?"

"They're Dominion strongholds, funded by billionaires, founded by Mackleford."

"Get outta town!" Aiden said with an uneasy laugh. "Really?"

"Nefarious organizations with nefarious purposes often operate legitimately for the public, all the while biding their time, waiting for the right moment. The Dominion is no different. There are eleven of these so-called *colleges* worldwide, where Mack recruits, trains and converts criminals into Dominion agents."

"Jeez," Aiden said, shaking his head. "And I actually thought about applying for a job."

"Your parents were their main opponents," Jonas continued. "Since the first campus opened twenty-one years ago, Restoration's growth was incredible. New campuses were springing up yearly. Shut down one, two more would replace it. After their eighth campus, Gus finally admitted to me Mack had long before stolen the Song back. Gus spent the rest of his life searching for it but failed."

"But Mom and Dad found it," Simone said. "How, when Gaston Gumm couldn't?"

"An excellent question, Simone," Jonas said. "They were close to Gus before he died, maybe the only two people he trusted. He may have given them some information about the Song, what it was, where Mackleford might have it."

"Margaret said my father came to Paris to talk to you," Aiden said. "What about?"

"Another good question, because he never showed up," Jonas said. Aiden and Flair looked surprised. "Yes, I was shocked too. Very unlike Wilbert to say one thing and do another. Thought he'd been captured. Strange behavior, but I guess he wanted all of us to remain in the dark, much like Gus."

"And then he gives us riddles and puzzles." Flair said. "Why did he send us to East Town unprepared?"

Aiden looked at Flair with remorse. "Pops didn't want you guys to know. I was supposed to keep quiet and I blew it. I shouldn't have said anything. Simmy would be okay."

"Bro, if it wasn't for me, we wouldn't have found the Cornerstone Key."

"A Cornerstone Key?" Jonas exclaimed. "You have one?"

Aiden nodded, pulling the large metal key from his belt and handing it to Jonas. "An original," Jonas said, reviewing it and handing it back to Aiden. "Take care of this. Your father trusted you with it, take that trust seriously."

"Why me?" Aiden said. "I'm no Journeyman. Maybe he wanted me to bring this to you. That room under the pillar…"

"No son, didn't you hear me? For the twenty-one years since Restoration was founded, it was your *parents* that kept them at bay. Your father clearly meant you…"

"Twenty-one years?" Aiden said, cutting Jonas off. "Wait a second. Wait…*twenty-one years ago* was when Restoration College was formed?"

"Yes, March the sixth to be exact. Why?"

"The Song of Solomon…" Aiden muttered, smacking his head as if trying to shake something loose. "Solomon's wisdom…*Solomon's*, right?"

"What are you getting at?" Jonas said, looking puzzled.

"Unbelievable," Aiden whispered. Everyone stared at him as he stared into space, seeing possibilities, seeing the truth…

Aiden stood, checking his jacket pockets for something. "Crap, I left Margaret's book at the hotel, but the last entry in the book is dated twenty-one years ago."

He was back in a trance, speaking to no one. Flair looked annoyed but pressed a finger to her lips when Jonas was about to speak.

"Margaret said old age robbed her of her *wisdom*, remember?" and Aiden stared back into their confused faces. "But that's not what happened. Mackleford robbed her of it."

Jonas's face slackened and he sat up. "What? *She* had the Song of Solomon?"

"What do you think?" Aiden said, suddenly looking illuminated. "Mackleford broke into her house years ago, attacked three kids, ransacked the place, looking for something. Margaret wrote a book of wisdom for years. Mackleford stole the Song and used it to start Restoration College. C'mon, this is kid's play."

"Wait, so Margaret knew—" Flair said.

"Nah, she never knew she had it," Aiden remarked, "otherwise she would've told us what it was. Mr. Gumm made sure she didn't know. Remember, Margaret believed *she* was wise, it was *her* wisdom, not calling her dumb or anything, y' know. Gumm didn't want her to know what it was, but he wanted her to use it. *Wisdom, the greatest of all gifts—his* gift to *her*. He put it somewhere where she could use it, but not realize it. Remember, when she was trying

to help us, Flair? What did she do? She reverted to her old habits—
went to the garden, sat on her bench, opened that far window to
hear—"

"The wind chimes," Flair said. "That's it, isn't it?"

"Yeah. The *chimes*," Aiden announced. "Mackleford switched
a copy in its place, so she never knew the difference, although
Gumm obviously did."

Jonas stared at Aiden in a peculiar way. "You're a lot like
him…"

"My father?"

"No, not your father," Jonas said, but he was interrupted as the
building shook, almost knocking everyone off their feet. There
followed a loud scratching sound coming from somewhere.

Jonas hurried to the window, and, looking below, saw three
enormous men climbing the side of the hotel, followed by a dozen
slimy creatures.

"Dear God," he whispered.

Aiden looked puzzled. "France gets earthquakes?"

"This is no earthquake," Jonas said, "It's the Goon Squad, and
they've got grunners with them! This way!"

Jonas grabbed his Aurorum Coat and threw open the bedroom
door as Flair wheeled Simone through. Aiden drifted towards the
window, his curiosity getting the better of him, but Jonas grabbed
him by the shoulder, pulling him into the bedroom. "No Aiden, here!
Help me with this dresser!"

Aiden and Jonas shut the bedroom door and slid a heavy oak
dresser in front of it, which exposed a large indentation in the wall,
covered by a wooden panel. Jonas removed the panel, revealing an
empty space behind it and a large dumbwaiter in a dark shaft.

"What's that?"

"The owner of Hotel Quorum was kind enough to allow me
this escape hatch. Not the first time I've used it." The Aurorum Coat
flickered brightly as Jonas fastened his buttons. "There's a tunnel
leading to an alley behind the hotel. Hurry!"

"That's not going to fit everyone," Flair remarked.

"I'll hold them off. We can't let Mackleford catch you three.
Simone, you first."

"Simone can't walk, Jonas!" Aiden said.

"Very well, Aiden! You first!" Jonas grabbed Aiden by the collar and directed him towards the dumbwaiter. "In you go!" he shouted, thrusting him headfirst into the cart. Aiden was upside down as the dumbwaiter disappeared down the shaft.

Inside the plummeting cart, Aiden grabbed the rope to slow his free-fall, singeing his hands in the process. He reached the bottom and tumbled out onto a hard dirt floor. As he stood upright, he saw he was in a dark, cramped tunnel with little headroom, heading off in one direction to his right.

Jonas held the black metallic baton he used earlier, staring at the door with apprehension.

"What's that for?" Flair asked.

"Twenty thousand volts is about the only thing that will stop a Goon. Do you have one?"

"No."

"Then stand back and prepare your sister!"

Glass shattered outside the bedroom door, followed by a series of deafening thuds.

"Wilson!" bellowed a raspy voice. "You here?"

The hotel room shuddered and quaked like a subway train was passing through. Pieces of ceiling crumbled down upon them and then—*WHAM!*—the battering began. It might've been a force of fifty men trying to break down the bedroom door, which was braced with every piece of furniture Jonas could stack against it.

Jonas backed the girls behind him as the bedroom door bent inwards under the pressure. "Hurry, son, hurry!" he muttered, glancing over his shoulder at the dumbwaiter shaft. The hinges had just popped off the doorframe when Jonas noticed Flair reaching into Simone's wheelchair pouch, pulling out the leather and burlap satchels.

"Those aren't—?" His face brightened as Flair opened the bag of Crystal Stars.

"I—I've never used these before. Do you know how?"

"My dear! Why didn't you tell me?"

Jonas snatched the burlap bag and reached inside, grabbing a bright red crystal. His body was instantly illuminated in red. His eyes gleamed, his Aurorum coat radiated. Another red crystal was slapped into Flair's hand and in a flash, a pulsating red aura surrounded her.

"Stellar!" Flair exclaimed. Her hair looked ablaze as she flipped it, looking into the cracked dresser mirror. "Oh, I could get used to this!"

"Not hard to use. Focus and aim. Stand next to me!"

"Flair!" Simone shouted. "The dumb-thingy is back!"

Flair saw the dumbwaiter inching into place and wheeled Simone towards it, lifted her from the wheelchair, and sat her inside.

"Hold the rope, you'll have to lower yourself down. Tell Aiden to send this right back, soon as you get down!"

"Okay. Be careful Flair."

With a loud—*CRASH!*—they were in. Flair released Simone and spun, firing a red bolt from her crystal. Lanky, tall, skinny and yellow-faced, plowed into the bedroom and was hit in the face with Flair's attack. He screamed in pain and tumbled out of sight. After his two comrades, No-Neck and Man-Child, saw what became of him, they armed themselves with bo staffs, all the while fighting the urge to laugh.

"That appeared to hurt," Man-Child said.

"Where are all these damn crystals coming from?" Lanky growled, grabbing his bo staff, preparing to charge into the room until an arm as thick as an elephant's trunk held him back.

"Send the beasts first, idiot!" No-Neck grumbled. "That's what they're for!"

Within seconds, a strong, smell of ocean water filled Flair's nostrils.

"Grunners," Jonas said. "Keep your eyes open for that dumbwaiter!"

In the dumbwaiter, Simone and the cart had been rocketing downwards until she grabbed the rope. She heard voices, bangs, shouts, and now a powerful odor of ocean water suffocated her. She coughed, lowering herself as fast as she dared.

The tiny bedroom was alive with deafening blasts and brilliant flashes of red, as a pungent odor like burnt seaweed began suffocating the air. Grunners were leaping through the gap in the door, and Flair and Jonas, their backs planted firmly against the far wall, picked them off one by one. Flair couldn't believe how easy it was to use the crystal. It was natural…energy coursed through her like a current of fire. All she needed to do was focus on her target and the energy released through the crystal.

But something else was being released, something inside of Flair that she was only now aware of. Anger. Hatred. Each crystal blast seemed to expel these emotions from her. How long had this pent up anger been building? She didn't know and didn't care; it was liberating and phenomenal, this release. Two more grunners caught blasts to their hides and flew backwards through the crumbling doorway.

The noise diminished although the slimy creatures continued squealing and writhing in pain.

"Well, well, well, Jonas Wilson," Man-Child's smarmy voice called out from behind the shattered door and pile of furniture. "And everyone thought you were dead."

"You guys can't seem to kill off crippled old men nowadays," Jonas retorted.

"You'll wish you *were* dead," Lanky said, rubbing the giant red welt on his yellow forehead. "Mack's in town."

"That you, Lankershim?" Jonas said. "I'd thought you'd be mixing with the Dominion's elite by now. Still clunking around with grunners and Goons, are you?"

"Shouldn't worry about me, punk," Lanky snarled. "Old guy like you has tons of family, right?"

Jonas's sneering expression fell away, taking on a darker, deadlier look.

"Leave my family out of this, Lankershim," Jonas said lethally.

"Now you know me better than that, Wilson," Lanky said, grinning and licking his long yellow teeth. "Don't worry, I'll be paying them a personal visit, especially your old girlfriend, just as soon as I'm done here."

It happened so fast, Flair barely caught it. The aura around Jonas brightened and swelled as he swung his arm in a giant circle and launched the crystal from his hand like cannon fire. It hit the doorway and there was a bright explosion, scattering furniture throughout the room.

Jonas, aura gone, empty-handed, stared through the haze of smoke when several black cords shot through the hole where the bedroom door once stood, snaking around Jonas. No-Neck stepped through the haze, holding the other end of his black and silver bo staff, with the thick black cords extending from its tip. Jonas's struggled, but it was useless.

"Fish in a barrel," laughed No-Neck. He walked into the bedroom, and with a flick of his staff, the Aurorum coat was ripped from Jonas's body, leaving only the sleeves draped around his arms.

The black cords retracted into the staff, but their tips still held tight to the glowing Aurorum. No-Neck didn't touch it, but he held it at eye level, considering it for a moment.

"You were always far too emotional, Wilson," No-Neck said. "Now you're gonna to die in this flea-bitten hotel room. Such a pity for such a great man. Farewell."

But before No-Neck could finish his goodbye speech to Jonas, his bo staff was blasted out of his hand. He turned and saw Flair standing on the bed, brandishing two red crystals.

Goons and grunners crowded the doorway: it was one teenager against a room full of brutes and beasts. No-Neck snickered, holding a hand to the others.

"Fellas, just a moment." He bent over, picking his staff from the floor, casual and unconcerned. "You know, Musclehead used to says there was one person out there who could do anything with any crystal, who no Goon would ever defeat. Always thought he was whistlin' Dixie 'til I met your mom."

Flair raised an eyebrow. "Oh yeah, you're Laura's kid alright," No-Neck continued. "You look like her and fight like her. Your mom's practically a living legend. Oops, sorry…now she's *only* a legend."

The Goons laughed. And Flair felt hot blood racing through her.

At the bottom of the dumbwaiter shaft, Aiden pulled Simone from the cart and turned to set her down, but realized—

"Crap, we don't have your wheelchair, do we?"

Simone reached down, looking at her leg.

"No, but Aiden, I think I broke my leg when Flair dropped me into the thingy. I don't feel it, but I heard a snap. I don't know, I think it's broken, but maybe not."

"Okay, Simmy let me take a look."

Aiden moved Simone into a sliver of light coming from the shaft. Sure enough, it was snapped at the ankle. Simone should have been in excruciating pain, but she just stared at it.

"Geez. Yeah, it's broken. When we get out of here, I'll find a way to set it."

"But the scary thing is, I don't feel anything. Isn't that scary, Aiden? It should hurt, shouldn't it?"

"It's gonna be alright Simone. Flair! I got Simone, I'm sending it back up!"

No-Neck walked towards Flair, his voice steady and pleasant. "Now, you may think you are on the right side of this war little girl, but you're wrong."

"I'm against the man who murdered my mom and hurt my dad and sister," Flair said. "Is that your side?"

No-Neck laughed again. "You've got your mother's strength, girl, I'll give you that. Let's hope you don't have her brains. Drop the crystals. Don't be like her, dead for no reason."

Flair's eyes narrowed, she felt tears of anger welling in her eyes.

"Stop talking to me about my mother." Her voice was trembling. She snarled the words like a wild beast.

"Don't be an idiot. This is obvious defeat. Your brainless mother was too blinded by Gaston Gumm to see the wisdom of living. But let me explain something to..."

It was too much, anger overtook Flair and the crystals seemed to act on their own, firing several blasts at the ugly Goon. No-Neck was ready, flipping his staff around and ducking behind Jonas's tattered coat, letting the Aurorum swallow the blasts.

The other Goons rushed in, but Flair only needed to look and aim, the rest was easy. The noise was so loud, she might have been wielding a howitzer. Lanky, Man-Child, and the grunners ducked, dodged, but eventually were mowed down by Flair's crystal blasts. Jonas crawled, crouching behind the bed, watching Flair in action as No-Neck whipped the glowing Aurorum coat overhead.

"Together Flair!" Jonas yelled, hitting the floor. "Put the crystals together. Now!"

Flair obeyed, slamming her red crystals together. A red field of energy shaped like a giant disc flashed as green waves of energy from the Aurorum Coat thundered through the room, sending everything that wasn't nailed down airborne. Flair was unaffected, not budging an inch, but the rest of the room was flattened.

Flair wasted no time as No-Neck was already on the move. He swung his staff and missed, knocking a giant hole in the wall. Flair ducked and rolled towards the dumbwaiter, firing bolts back at the great Goon while hearing the *squeak-squeak-squeak* of the pulley. No-Neck was big and massive, but he was also quick and nimble, dodging Flair's attacks.

"Flair!" Jonas shouted. "Look—"

The black cords shot out again but grasped nothing but air as Flair dove next to Jonas, who was still hiding behind the bed. No-Neck was enraged and charged again, and Flair, seizing her chance, kicked the bedframe into his legs. No-Neck tripped, falling head first across the mattress towards her.

Before she realized what she was doing, Flair clutched the crystal in her fist and delivered an almighty right cross to the toppling No-Neck. There was a spectacular flash where fist connected to face, knocking the Goon upwards, his head smashing through the ceiling and then back into the last chunk of the bedroom wall that hadn't fallen. He wobbled on his feet momentarily, and then crashed to the floor, out cold.

The walls were crumbled, furniture destroyed, Goons and grunners scattered about. The room looked like a hurricane had hit it, yet, amid the carnage and destruction, Flair was still standing, ablaze in her aura, radiating like a goddess.

Jonas was mesmerized. "Incredible…"

"Yeah, I know," Flair said. "Let's go, get up!"

"Flair, it's over for me. Now I know why your father hid you from the Dominion, to be our saviors when the time came. Go, my time is over—"

"Shut up and move!"

"No!" Jonas shouted, shoving her away. "O'Reilly is right. I'm too old. You, your brother, your sister, you're the important ones! *Go!* Let them capture me!"

No-Neck stirred under the rubble. The other Goons were coming around. Sirens sounded in the distance.

"Knock it off!" Flair said angrily. "I didn't go through all of that just to leave you here!"

She directed Jonas to the dumbwaiter, mocking him as she went along. *"Go on without me, save yourself, I'm just an old man—*whatever! Aiden!" she screamed into the dumbwaiter shaft, "Mr. Wilson is coming down!"

Jonas squeezed into the tiny cart and lowered it, watching Flair disappear above him. When he reached the bottom, Aiden pulled him out of the dumbwaiter, propping the old man against the wall.

"Hurry," Jonas wheezed. "Send it back!"

"What happened?" Aiden said. "Why didn't Flair come first?"

"She…she saved me…*us*," Jonas gasped, "all of us! Hurry Aiden!" Jonas looked up the shaft as the dumbwaiter ascended, Aiden pulling the rope with all his might.

"Flair, the dumbwaiter's coming back!" Aiden shouted. "Flair?"

But Flair didn't respond. What Aiden didn't see was No-Neck holding the remains of the giant oak dresser over his head and turning on Flair. Flair's eyes were as big as golf balls.

"The dumbwaiter's gonna be out of order, bro…" Flair's voice cracked.

"What are you talking about?"

"I'm gonna take the stairs!" she shouted.

As Flair finished speaking, she dove for her life. The heavy oak dresser crashed into and through the wall.

Down below, Aiden leapt aside as the wreckage of the dumbwaiter and the oak dresser tore down the shaft with a deafening crash, leaving a cloud of dirt and dust in the tunnel.

"Flair!" Aiden bellowed, but there was no answer. "Flair!"

"Aiden, help me up, let's move," Jonas groaned. Jonas was completely covered in dust and was looking more his age.

"What about Flair?"

"She's just fine! This way, down the tunnel!"

Aiden scooped Simone into his arms and followed Jonas.

"How is Flair *just fine*? What happened up there?"

"Those Goons are no match for your sister!" Jonas wheezed. "She's got your mother's talent. Let's worry about ourselves, getting out of here, and hopefully avoiding the police."

It was a painful walk for Aiden. The ceiling wasn't very high and he had to stoop the entire way. Jonas was hurrying him and Aiden reminded him repeatedly he was carrying Simone. The tunnel dipped and curved several times, making Aiden stumble as he tried to keep up with Jonas, who zigzagged through effortlessly. At last, the tunnel widened and sloped upwards, and to Aiden's great relief he saw a crack of light and a door.

"Thank God," Aiden said straightening up as they reached the door. "I thought my spine was going to explode."

They stepped into a dark alley. There was a lot of commotion at both ends of the alley as police cars sounded and people ran to back and forth on the main streets. But they were far enough away that they were safe from detection.

"Okay, let's wait here until things settle down so Flair can find us."

"No, we need to find Flair now!" Aiden barked. "All hell's breaking loose. What if she needs help?"

"You didn't see her, son. Believe me, she's—"

CRASH! Glass shattered from above. Everyone looked up and what they saw made their jaws drop. No-Neck was plummeting from a fifth-floor window, with Flair standing atop his hulking body, riding it down to the concrete like a surfboard.

The Goon hit with a crushing thud and Flair, beautiful and radiant, rolled off of No-Neck. As she stepped away, No-Neck caught her by her high heel boot. Flair yanked her leg free and stomped his hand with the heel. No-Neck yowled in pain, jumped up and scampered down the alley.

Aiden, Simone, and Jonas stared at her in wonder.

"Is it hot or is it just me?" Flair said, slipping off her jacket. "Everyone okay?"

"Well, I can see you're okay, warrior princess," Aiden snorted.

"Riddle me this butthole, how does it feel to have your life saved by your little sister? I can tell you from this side, the life saver side, it feels really great!"

Something inside Aiden stirred. "You didn't save me," he shot back, "but what you did do is break Simmy's leg because you threw her in the dumbwaiter like a dumb idiot."

"What are you talking about?" Flair dropped the reds inside the burlap pouch and her appearance returned to normal. She stepped next to her brother and looked over at her sister's leg, and her face fell. "Oh, oh no, oh Simone…"

"It's okay Flair," Simone said, frowning at the back of Aiden's head. "You were busy stopping Goons from killing your family."

"I had no idea, Simmy," Flair muttered through trembling lips. "I'm so sorry." Within seconds, Flair was wiping tears from her face. She shot Aiden a deadly look but said nothing. She couldn't have put two words together right now if her life depended on it.

"Listen, it's no one's fault," Jonas said. "I have some splints and bandages at my cottage in Chartres. We'll patch up there. Let's move."

They started up the alley away from the main street. A few turns down some narrow streets and they were in a quiet neighborhood, the sound of sirens fading with each step.

"These Goons, your pal O'Reilly," Aiden said, "seem to know our every step."

"I told you. It's hard to say if anywhere is truly safe. This the most Dominion activity I've seen in years, and they don't stop until they get what they want. Where are you staying?"

"At the *Hotel Esca-pay-dee*," Simone said. "Or something like that."

"L'Escapade. That's straight ahead, twenty blocks. Head straight there. The Goons are going to lay low with the police around so you should be fine. I have some arrangements to make. Collect your things, call Rainier, and meet me in Chartres at my cottage."

He handed them a business card with an address. Aiden looked puzzled.

"What arrangements?" Aiden asked.

"We're going to go underground for a while," Jonas said. "Stick together. And if you run into any trouble at L'Escapade you can't handle, head to the roof and you'll find help there. Prepare for anything. I have a feeling Mack is close."

CHAPTER FOURTEEN – THE BATTLE AT HOTEL DE L'ESCAPADE

The walk back to the hotel was cold, long and quiet. Aiden was enjoying the beauty of Paris, Flair wore an expression halfway between anger and remorse, and Simone, sensing tension, remained quiet. Aiden finally broke the silence as they passed Notre Dame Cathedral.

"Amazing. The premier example of French Gothic architecture. An important building during the French Revolution. Warring factions of cults clashed with the Monarchy and the Clergy. A lot of history in that building."

"Aiden," Simone said, seizing the opportunity to speak. "Is what Jonas said true?"

"About what?"

"Well, I remember Solomon from Sunday school. He was a king with gold mines and stuff, but I don't remember anything about a magic ring."

"Not every story about Solomon is true, Simmy."

"So Solomon wasn't real?"

Aiden chuckled. "Oh, Solomon belongs to history, alright. But let's just say people back then were pretty imaginative. You know what my favorite Solomon story is?"

But Flair and Simone weren't interested in a history lesson and soon Aiden fell silent again. Snow began to fall. A clock somewhere in the distance had chimed eight bells as they reached the hotel. Eight. Margaret would be serving Christmas Eve dinner to the out of town families at the House of Gumm at eight P.M. Aiden felt his heart yearning for the Grand Room, a mug of hot chocolate, and a certain pair of sparkling eyes.

The hotel lobby was so packed with people that nobody noticed the Johnsons enter, nor Aiden seating Simone on a couch. "Okay, I'm gonna get our stuff. Should I check out?"

Flair folded her arms, staring at the beautiful red and white Christmas tree adorning the lobby, ignoring Aiden. Simone shrugged.

"Yeah probably not, then the Dominion could know we left. Okay, don't go anywhere kids, be right back." And Aiden ducked into the crowded lobby, heading for the elevators.

"Where exactly do you think we'd go?" Flair muttered under her breath, rolling her eyes in Aiden's direction. "Moron."

Simone was used to Aiden and Flair arguing; that was nothing new to her, but she liked it better when they were throwing their snipes face to face. Not this. This was when things got nasty between them.

"Stop being so mad, Flair," she said. "Aiden never gives anyone credit."

"Don't defend him. Aiden's just a jerk. How is your leg?"

"I still don't feel anything," Simone said, looking at her twisted ankle. "I don't like looking at it either. Can you cover my legs with this?" She handed Flair the gray shawl Margaret gave her.

Flair covered Simone's knees and ankles and sat next to her. Time crept by, and the sisters kept a vigilant eye for any possible Dominion agents, during which time Flair described her battle with the Goons to an enthralled Simone. After a while, Flair noticed many of the hotel guests staring at them.

"Wish they'd knock it off," Flair muttered, glaring at two women passing by.

"Who?"

"These people looking at us!" She stood up, incensed. "If you have something to say, say it!" The women scuttled by, muttering.

"What's *eczema*?" Simone said.

"What?" Flair said, her nostrils flaring like an angry bull.

"That lady told the other one I look contagious, but the other lady said I had eczema, and eczema isn't contagious. What's eczema?"

"A skin disease I think." Flair shook her head, looking ill.

"You okay? You don't look good."

"Either you just learned French or my brain's scrambled from those crystals. Didn't understand a word they said." Flair glared at a couple walking with a stack of Christmas gifts.

"Scrambled?" Simone said, sounding concerned. "Maybe you shouldn't mess with them anymore."

"Maybe. Margaret did say they affect people." Flair stared at the strings on the pouch. "But it felt so right...*okay, that's it!*"

A woman covered her mouth in disgust, and Flair had finally had it. She scooped Simone in her arms and moved to the back of the lobby, sitting on a bench where a large planter hid them from the crowd.

Aiden entered Room 334, not bothering to shut the door behind him. He opened his suitcase and threw his belongings inside, then rushed towards the adjoining room when something stopped him. On the nightstand near his bed was Margaret's book of wisdom.

He picked it up, thinking of the conversation with Jonas and his own theory about the Song of Solomon. If he was right, Margaret would have written this book under the influence of a powerful legendary object. The Wisdom of Solomon residing in this battered old book? The prospect intrigued Aiden and he sank onto the corner of the bed, opening the book. His sisters could wait a few minutes.

An endless parade of holiday travelers continued filing into the hotel, and the story about the chaos at Hotel Quorum was all over the television. Time crept; it had been over thirty minutes since Aiden had gone upstairs.

"How long does it take to pack a couple of bags?" Flair grumbled when she heard gasps of astonishment erupting from the main entrance.

Flair peeked around the planter and saw a man enter the lobby, wearing a dark green suit with patched elbows, his face covered with a green and black mask. Two enormous Goons followed him, cutting right down the middle of the throng of hotel guests. Flair recognized one of them: the long, spindly, yellow-faced man, who had been at Quorum.

"Simmy," she said, glaring. "The big uglies…they're back." Flair eased Simone on the bench and tied the two pouches to her belt.

"I thought you weren't going to use those," Simone said, sounding fearful.

"Yeah, well, maybe one day," Flair said.

Mr. Quick stepped towards the front desk clerk, flanked on both sides by Lanky and an extremely hairy Goon with gorilla-like arms and a thick unibrow over his eyes. Mr. Quick lifted up the mask that covered his face, just enough to show his mouth.

The young woman at the desk cringed. The flesh along Mr. Quick's chin and jaws was raw and stripped, his skin looked dead, his lips were scarred and blistered.

"*B-Bonsoir,*" she stammered, "can I help you, *Monsieur?*"

"Yes you can," Mr. Quick whispered. "Our friend Aiden Johnson is staying in Paris. We're looking for him. Is he here?"

The hairy Goon leaned in towards Mr. Quick. "They're here. I can hear the Purified child breathing."

"So can I," Lanky agreed.

Mr. Quick looked back to the desk clerk, smiling. "Aiden Johnson. Which room?"

The desk clerk gulped, seemingly mustering up as much courage as she could.

"My apologies, Monsieur, but I cannot speak about our guests."

"Really? Well, perhaps you shouldn't speak at all."

Mr. Quick struck, delivering two lightning-quick jabs to the clerk's throat, so fast that it looked like he hadn't done anything. The clerk immediately grabbed her throat, mouthing words, but was unable to make a sound.

Mr. Quick spun the computer monitor around and grabbed the keyboard. His fingers flew across the keyboard at lightning speed, typing in characters, pulling up names, but not finding *Aiden Johnson.*

"Nothing," Lanky said. "These Johnsons, they hide so well."

"Search for recent check-ins," Fuzz said. "We'll search the rooms one by one."

The Goons were oblivious to Flair, who crept behind the large Christmas tree. She took out two red crystals from the black bag and her body illuminated. The mute desk clerk raised her head, watching the glowing teenage girl approach.

Mr. Quick noticed the red glow flashing on the desk clerk's eyeglasses. His fingers continued to fly across the keyboard.

"Here," he said finally. "*332, 334.* One male, two females. Checked in at ten last night. Around the time they would have arrived, correct?"

Without warning, Mr. Quick whirled around and threw a spinning circular blade towards Flair. Flair clicked the red crystals together, forming a red barrier, but she was a second late as the blade sped by her. She dropped her crystals, clutching her left arm, which was bleeding.

"It's her," Lanky said. "Laura's daughter!"

"Flair Johnson," Mr. Quick said to Lanky. "See to it that you capture her this time. I will deal with the boy."

Aiden sat on the bed, book open, nose buried, unaware of how long he had been there. He was reading the poem again; phrases were jumping out at him...

> *Tis he who hears with breath or wind*
> *The melody upon the air.*

"Breath or wind?" Aiden muttered. "Of course..."

There was a sound of commotion that any normal person would have heard, but Aiden was unconscious to it as he went over what he had discussed with Jonas. He was unaware of the soft—*ding!*—of the elevator, the advancing footsteps getting louder, the gasps of horror from guests in the hallway, and the masked man who filled the open doorway behind him.

Fuzz and Lanky circled Flair, each wielding their bo staffs. Lanky twisted his weapon and stiletto blades protruded from each end of the staff, while Fuzz produced a long spiky spearhead. Flair recovered her crystals and Fuzz seemed to give her careful consideration.

"Where'd you get those crystals from?" Fuzz said, sizing up Flair.

"I'm tellin' you, there's a stash of crystals in Paris, at Gumm's old hideout," Lanky said. He stared at Flair. "She knows where it is."

Fuzz looked at Flair, contemplating. "You caught my friends off guard, child, they didn't know you had crystals. Don't suppose you'd be willing to talk this out."

This show of hesitation surprised Flair, and she grinned. "Don't be afraid of me, I'm just a little girl."

Fuzz snorted. "A quick tongue leads to a quick death. We're not afraid, you fool. The Goon Squad always tries to negotiate surrender before we pull our enemies apart, piece by piece."

"We'll see about that," Flair said. She fired the first shot, but Lanky leapt nimbly over it. She fired again and again, but Lanky leapt, dodged or deflected her attacks with childish ease.

"Ahh, she's *slower* now," Lanky laughed. And he was right. Flair felt shaky and uncertain. She aimed the crystal again as Fuzz's spear staff fired out at her. Flair jumped aside as the spear cracked the floor tile.

"You kiddin' me, Lank?" Fuzz laughed. "She's a sloppy, untrained rookie. She's never been in a real fight."

"She was doin' just fine at that hotel," Lanky retorted.

Fuzz's staff had a retractable chain, which Flair only noticed it as the spear flew back. The spearhead narrowly missed Flair, who tried again, aiming, firing, but the blasts were either blocked or dodged by the Goons.

"Pathetic. Come on little girl, "Fuzz chided. "We ain't gotta do this. Give it up."

"Yeah go ahead. Keep talking." Two more crystal blasts deflected off their staffs, knocking holes in the wall. She needed to be faster, she thought. *How had she fired off so many blasts before?*

"Okay, you had your chance," Fuzz said, and leaping forward, spear overhead, he attacked.

Flair darted away from Fuzz and formed a shield that deflected his attack, and then spun into the air, narrowly avoiding Lanky. It was a good thing Flair was quick because any of the crushing blows from Fuzz or Lanky would have finished her. The shield was holding up well, however with each deflection, she felt weaker. Flair realized she couldn't keep this up for long.

Suddenly, an inspired idea struck Flair, and she ran headlong towards the two Goons, red shield intact and somersaulted into the air like a cannonball.

"What the—?"

Stunned at Flair's daring, Lanky was off-guard as Flair slammed him into the concierge's desk. Lanky balanced himself and turned, seeing Flair aiming both red crystals decisively.

Twin blasts struck him in the face, flipping him over the desk and out of sight.

Fuzz didn't move. Now he saw what Lanky was talking about. Flair walked forward, crystals aimed, staring Fuzz down.

Mr. Quick stood silently in the doorway, staring in disbelief. His target was sitting on a bed, reading a book. He detested how easy this would be. He considered creating a distraction just to make his task more sporting. Taking him would be child's play in any case, but Mr. Quick was curious. *Was the boy like his father?*

Then again, Mackleford wanted him alive and in a fight, anything could happen. He readied the drugged darts Ellis added to the Ruijen Staff last month, smirking underneath his mask. *No, he was nothing like Wilbert. Wilbert never would turn his back to an open door.*

"You shouldn't read over shoulders, it's not polite!" Aiden shouted, flinging the diary at him.

The boy had sensed him. He'd lingered in the doorway one second too long. The staff in Quick's hand deflected the book, and a flock of pellet-sized darts whistled through the air, hitting the wall just as Aiden escaped into the next room.

Quick stalked after him, activating his Ruijen, which crackled with power. *Why had he waited?* he wondered, turning into the next room. But his green and black mask hid his smile. Yes, *hunting* was much better. He wouldn't damage him *too much...*

"AAAAAAAAUUUUGGHHH!!!!"

What happened then, Quick wouldn't realize until after several long, painful minutes. Something wet splashed him, and his body seized up in pain, terrible pain, and his staff went flying. He heard the clunk of a bucket hitting him full in the face and saw the shadow of the boy escaping through the same door he had just entered, not before snatching something off the floor. Quick couldn't move, twitching in agonizing pain, lying in a puddle of ice and water.

"So, not weak after all," Fuzz said, looking at Flair cautiously. "You *do* fight like Laura. She was the best Journeyman with those wretched stones. Maybe you're gifted too."

The comments about her mother made Flair pause for a moment. She looked at the crystals, sensing a different surge of energy swelling inside of her.

"Let's find out how gifted I am, ugly," Flair said.

Rapid-fire blasts erupted from Flair's crystals; however Fuzz was ready, deflecting every bolt, although the force of Flair's shots drove Fuzz backwards.

The second Flair paused to re-focus, Fuzz's spear flashed towards her. Sidestepping it, Flair struck back, sending another volley of blasts towards Fuzz, who dove just in time to avoid them. The spear had skewered a small antique couch just behind Flair and the chain recoiled at full speed, slamming the couch into Flair's back and dropping her to the floor.

Lanky had returned to the action, swinging stiletto blades at Flair's heart. Hardly recovered from the couch attack, Flair swung a desperate kick at Lanky, and by chance knocked the Ruijen Staff from Lanky's grip and hitting a button on the side. With a loud, grating screech, the staff activated, and white electricity blazed from both ends.

Flair cursed and dove as the streams of electricity sliced through the lobby, shattering windows and cutting through walls. It sailed across the lobby, landing in the Christmas tree, setting it on fire.

The lobby was doused in mist as the fire set off the sprinklers. Flair was slipping and sliding on her back, looking disbelieving and looking for Simone, but with electricity crackling in every direction and the blazing tree, it was hard to focus. It was perhaps sheer luck that made her flip over and see Fuzz closing in on her.

"Finish her, Fuzz," Lanky said, going for his weapon, "before she kills us all!"

As Lanky deactivated his bo staff, his ears heard whimpering. He glanced past the blaze and spotted Simone covering her face and shuddering from the commotion.

Fuzz grabbed Flair by her arm and flung her in the direction of the fiery tree. Flair clicked the crystals together at the last second, forming a shield and bouncing away from the tree like a rubber ball. She skidded across the lobby, crashing into a potted plant near the entrance.

Flair looked down. The aura was gone; her crystals laid back near the tree. Fuzz was bearing down on her fast, his spear poised for the kill. This was it; she wasn't going to make it. Shuffling backwards, Flair looked towards Simone. She didn't want the last thing she saw to be an ugly Goon.

But instead she saw Lanky, evil and yellow, closing in on her sister, who was covering her face, unaware.

"SIMMY! LOOK OUT!"

Simone peeked, saw Lanky's yellow teeth grinning at her, and screamed.

Except it wasn't a scream. What it was, the sound that came from Simone, was indescribable: a dreadful, grating, rattling cry that dropped Lanky to his knees at once and made him cover his ears. He was in excruciating pain.

Fuzz, likewise in anguish, fell a foot away from Flair. They both trembled and writhed on the floor, gritting their teeth as streams of tears leaked from their bulging eyes.

Simone noticed her scream and stopped, looking both confused and frightened. Flair, wasting no time, scrambled off the floor, grabbing the red crystals as she ran past the burning tree. She scooped up a teary-eyed Simone in front of Lanky, who was still down on the floor.

"What was that?" Flair said.

"I don't know!" Simone sobbed into her hands.

"Come on! Let's find Aiden and get out of here!" Flair skidded to a stop at the elevator, hammering the 'up' button, Simone clinging to her back. Fuzz had gotten to a knee, and Lanky was sitting up. The Goons had gotten their wits back and didn't look happy.

"Simmy, do the *scream* again."

"No," Simone said.

"Simone. Do it, they're getting closer!"

"I don't want to!" Simone's eyes were glazed. "It's scary."

Flair fired a shot at Fuzz, who ducked it, and then another one, which he slapped away with ease. He bounded forward like a raging bear, his face twisted with anger.

"Simmy, they're coming!"

"I don't care!"

"Dammit!" Flair ran for the stairwell just as the spear staff slammed into the wall, narrowly missing them and shattering plaster everywhere. She banged the door to the stairwell open with her shoulder and slammed it shut.

"Lock the door, Flair!"

Flair twisted a tiny deadbolt lock on the door, rolling her eyes as she did.

"That ain't gonna hold them!" Flair said. She took off upstairs, running as fast as she could. The sound of the Goons pounding on the door below echoed up the stairwell.

"Mr. Wilson said if we get into trouble, we should head for the roof and help would be there," Simone said.

"Right," Flair said, heaving deep breaths, "but what *help* is he talking about?"

They rounded the fifth floor when they heard the heavy metal door crash to the cement floor. Lanky craned his skinny head and neck up the stairwell.

"Upstairs!" he shouted.

The Goons covered four steps per stride. Simone, clinging to Flair's neck, looked down, watching the Goons close in with each second.

"Run Flair! Faster!"

The elevator door opened and Aiden tore into the lobby, looking aghast at the carnage that had occurred only minutes before. Flair and Simone were nowhere in sight. *Idiot!* He couldn't believe he actually stopped to read that book. They could have been long gone.

The fire was bright and wild, uncontrolled, and hotel personnel began escorting people towards the exits. Sprinklers doused the lobby in a cool, gray mist. Flair and Simone must be outside, Aiden thought; they wouldn't have stuck around in this mayhem, would they? But what if they'd gone upstairs, looking for him? Simone would have probably insisted on it. What if they were headed to the room right now, with that weirdo in the black and green mask? Aiden froze at that thought and turned back, looking at the door to the stairs.

"NO!" A voice shouted above the din and Aiden jumped. A bellhop was gesturing towards the exit. "Monsieur, zee hotel ees a-fire! The ex-zeet is zere!"

"My sisters are....*No!*" Aiden said, fighting his way to the stairs. "Get out... Move!"

But a minute later, four Parisian firemen had escorted Aiden outside. He paced around the building nervously amongst a crowd of angry hotel guests, watching everyone exiting and hoping to spot his sisters. He would have shouted their names, but if this fire was a Dominion ploy to get everyone out of the building, the Goons would be waiting for that.

The police arrived, creating a perimeter, pushing the hundreds of displaced hotel guests back. Aiden stuffed his hands in his pockets and walked away from the building, craning his neck upwards at the roof, suddenly remembering. Jonas said there would be help for them on the rooftop, however from his view, nothing he could see looked helpful.

As Aiden looked down, something hard cracked him across the face: a huge, misshapen fist attached to a blotchy arm. White stars appeared and he crashed face first to the snowy street, feeling consciousness leave him just as long, skinny fingers grasped him and drug him away.

"They're getting closer!" Simone squealed.

Flair, back aching, rounded another corner, running past the fourteenth floor sign. She felt the entire stairwell trembling as the Goons pounded upstairs. Without bothering to aim, she fired a bolt back down the stairwell, but it was pathetic. It ricocheted off Lanky's staff and fizzled into the wall.

"She's losin' it!" Lanky yelped in delight. "She's gettin' weaker!"

At last, Flair saw the top floor, but the Goons were one floor below, gaining ground. As Flair turned to see their location, she misjudged the final step, tripped, and sent Simone and herself spilling across the top landing. The pouch of crystals opened, and a half dozen of the red and white crystals scattered everywhere. Flair had crashed on her back, and Simone slid towards the roof access door.

"The crystals, Flair! They fell out!"

"Don't touch them, Simmy!" Flair panted.

Fuzz and Lanky reached the final landing, smiling at Flair, who was winded and wheezing.

"Oh yeah, she's done! Can't see her glowin' or nothin'!"

Flair hadn't noticed until then, but Lanky was right. Her red aura, which was so bright earlier, had faded. She aimed at Fuzz, but nothing happened. She let the crystal fall from her hand and grabbed another. No effect.

Fuzz laughed. "Sorry, rookie. It's ain't the crystal, it's you. You're too tired, my dear. It's the end of the road."

Flair, not knowing what else to do, grabbed the nearest thing to throw at them, a large white crystal. As she grabbed it, the faint red glow turned stunning white. The blinding aura slowed Fuzz's progress, and both Goons covered their eyes, backing away from it. Flair felt revitalized, and her eyes blazed bright with energetic fury.

Fuzz charged forward with his spear staff. The red crystal in Flair's left hand ignited, and a magnificent crimson blast brightened Fuzz's hairy chest, knocking him backwards into Lanky. The two crashed into the wall, bounced over the railing and down the stairs.

"Much better," Flair said, smiling. "You alright, sugarplum fairy?"

Simone stared Flair, open mouthed and awestruck. "You are too cool right now."

Flair, half-smiling, snatched the bag and scooped the remaining crystals into it. "Whatever," she said, dropping to her knees. "Climb aboard."

Simone hoisted herself onto her sister, clinging piggyback. Flair kicked open the door leading to the roof. The roof looked icy and slippery; however Flair was nimble and balanced as she skipped out to the middle of the rooftop, looking around.

"Where is he?" Simone said. "I don't see Jonas. I don't see any help."

Flair was in a state of astonishment. "I do," she proclaimed.

What Flair could see that Simone couldn't was a zigzagging, crisscrossing array of red and white beams, which, from Flair's viewpoint, connected the entire city of Paris, building to building, rooftop to rooftop.

"At least I think it's *help*. There's a bunch of light beams everywhere. Connected to the buildings. You can't see it?"

"Aww, no!" Simone said, sounding downcast. "I wish I could see that!"

"It's the crystals," Flair said, staring at the white in her left hand and the red in her right. "The beams are all red and white. But how does this help?"

She didn't have time to consider it. *BANG!* The metal door to the roof was kicked down and went skimming across the snow-slicked rooftop. Silhouetted in the doorway was Fuzz, with Lanky running up behind him. Flair didn't react quick enough and was tripped by the door, crashing face first to the ground. Her crystals went tumbling, the crisscrossing beams disappeared, and once again, she felt fatigued and tired.

"These jokers don't give up," Flair groaned.

Fuzz slipped and skated across the roof, trying to remain upright. Lanky's gangly frame was unable to balance and he fell head over heels. Flair reached for a red crystal and fired a weak blast, and suddenly, she too found it hard to keep her own footing.

"End of the ro—*oomph!*" Fuzz said as his feet went skyward and he landed on his enormous backside. Flair also scampered in place before crashing to the ice.

"Crap! I need that white crystal back," she huffed, realizing why she suddenly couldn't balance herself. White crystals enhanced the five senses, giving Flair a heightened sense of touch, which must have improved her balance. But finding a white crystal on a snowy rooftop? Impossible, yet…

"Flair, look! There it is! But what's it doing?"

Simone pointed to the large white crystal moving on its own, cutting a path through the snow. It stopped, wobbled in place for a moment, then began tumbling again, picking up speed.

"Flair, the crystal! Granny said we can't lose it!"

Flair scrambled, sliding on her hands and knees, chasing the white. With Simone squeezing her so tightly around her neck to avoid falling, Flair's face was turning purple.

"Simm-eee…yer cho…keeng meee! Can't *breeeve!*"

Flair dove for the crystal and nabbed it inches before the edge of the roof. Her aura turned white and she stood, feeling balanced, however, the crystal wriggled fiercely.

"What the…it's trying to get away!"

Flair clutched the crystal with both hands and, incredibly enough, it started pulling her. She was being dragged towards a white beam high above the roof that streamed off somewhere into the dark night…

"What's going…LOOK OUT!" Simone shouted.

Fuzz was right on top of Flair, missing with his Ruijen Staff and losing his balance for the third time. Flair delivered a swift kick to his stomach that sent Fuzz sliding and stumbling towards Lanky. Lanky, who finally achieved balance and had just gotten to his feet, grumbled a few choice words before being steamrolled by the out-of-control Fuzz.

Flair, however, didn't see the collision. Kicking Fuzz caused her to slip, and miraculously, the crystal lifted her into the air.

"Flair?" Simone gasped in awe, squeezing her sister even tighter to avoid falling. "How are you doing this?"

"I'm not doing anything!"

Which was perfectly true. The crystal was carrying the girls towards the beam of white light while Flair's legs kicked wildly in the air. She gripped the crystal with both hands as she was too high off the ground to let go, and at that moment, Flair realized what all of the beams of light were for. She watched mesmerized...the beam of white, the white crystal, inching closer, closer...

They touched and—*WHOOOOOOSHH!*

Flair and Simone were rocketing through the night sky along the thin, luminous beam. Panicked, Simone screamed that same rattling, piercing scream from before.

"Simmy, Simmy, Simmy!" Flair screamed back. "Not in my ear!"

"Oops! Sorry!"

The sisters were soaring over the Parisian cityscape, above buildings and rooftops, gazing at the beauty of the city. Flair grinned, squeezing the crystal even tighter. The air in her face and hair felt exhilarating.

On the rooftop, still on their backs, Fuzz and Lanky watched the girls soar off into the night.

"Look at them," Fuzz said in amazement. They're flying."

"I don't think so." Lanky removed a white crystal embedded in his boot. Within a second, a sizzling sound and smoke arose between his long yellow fingers.

"AARRRRGGH!!!"

His scream split the air and he dropped the crystal, stuffing his hand into the snow.

"Idiot! You know *we* can't touch crystals!"

Ugly blisters covered Lanky's hand and he glared at Fuzz.

"Some of *us* can, just never tried it before! But they used 'em to get away!"

Mr. Quick stepped onto the rooftop, seeing Fuzz and Lanky staring out into the night where the girls just departed.

"Get up!" he commanded, advancing across the slick roof effortlessly. Fuzz managed to keep himself upright, but Lanky continued to slip and fall. "What happened? Where are they?"

"Gone," Fuzz said. "The little one is a screamer, we didn't know. They were cornered, but they flew off the side of the building."

Mr. Quick pulled Lanky to his feet, who collapsed almost at once, still unable to balance himself. "What is he talking about?" Quick growled. "They jumped off the building?"

"No," Lanky groaned, "they *flew* off the building. And *kept* flying. I think they used the crystals to…Hey! Wait, don't touch it!"

But Mr. Quick had already picked up the white crystal. His taped hands smoldered and sizzled, but he didn't react to the pain. He looked around, viewing an array of white streams.

"Star Channels," he whispered and dropped the crystal near Lanky and Fuzz, who jumped back. "Good work you two. Now we wait."

Quick's smoking hand touched his mask and activated something attached to his ear, a small headset underneath his mask.

"The police are surrounding the place," Lanky said. "We gotta bail!"

"NO! We wait! For Mochtier."

CHAPTER FIFTEEN – HEIGHTS AND FIGHTS

A blazing fire at a five-star luxury hotel in Paris on Christmas Eve made the evening news and provided the perfect distraction for Mochtier Mackleford. With the lobby flooded with water, and firemen, hotel personnel, news crews, and angry, displaced guests everywhere, no one paid attention to the quiet man making his way to the stairwell.

Mackleford walked onto the rooftop of the Hotel De L'Escapade, which resembled a convention. Ellis Vicartan paced along the edge, staring at the chaos in the streets below, along with Musclehead and Rico. Man-Child and No-Neck were huddled with Pug discussing the encounter at Hotel Quorum. Lanky and Fuzz sat atop a heating duct, patching up their metal staffs, in quiet dialog with Mr. Quick. There was only one very noticeable Goon missing.

"Where's Fats?" Mackleford asked.

"Out scouting for grub, Mack," Musclehead said. "We told'm ya like Quiche Lorrain'e."

"Thank you. I am starving." Mackleford turned towards Mr. Quick, no longer talking to Lanky and Fuzz, quietly re-taping his hands. "Mr. Quick, you took lead on this operation. Who authorized any attack on the Johnsons? I specifically asked for surveillance only."

Mr. Quick reached into his pocket and withdrew the white crystal, showing it to Mackleford. Although it smoked and sizzled in his hand, he did not react.

Mackleford raised an eyebrow in mild surprise. "Where did that come from?"

"Jonas Wilson, I believe," Mr. Quick replied, pocketing the white crystal and recapping the afternoon for Mackleford: their surveillance of the Johnsons; discovering Wilson at the Expo under the pseudonym, Demetric; Boris O'Reilly and his accomplices interfering; Wilson defeating O'Reilly and his men using a coat of Aurorum, and his escape to Hotel Quorum.

"At that point, we decided to capture and detain the Johnsons, believing Wilson must possess critical information. Upon entering Hotel Quorum, we discovered they were supplied with Crystal Stars, and they subdued us temporarily. Fuzz arrived shortly afterwards, and I elected to take a more active role to ensure capture. But..." he paused, bracing himself for the next part of his report, "they succeeded in escaping. They are now on the loose in Paris."

A cold wind swept across the rooftop and it seemed to match the mood. Mackleford's facial expression hadn't changed, but there was no question he wasn't happy.

"O'Reilly was arrested by the local authorities, but we have detained one of his associates," Mr. Quick continued. "We are uncertain what they know about the present operation."

Mackleford remained silent for so long that the Goons began shifting nervously, when finally: "So, Jonas is alive after all. And the countless times I was assured of his death..."

No one, not even Ellis, looked Mackleford in the eye.

"Nothing changes in this world," Mackleford sighed. "Just as much happens on the way to Paris as when I arrive. What was O'Reilly doing there?"

"Mr. Mackleford," Rico's voice rang out from behind, surprising everyone, especially Ellis. Rico didn't seem remotely abashed; he stepped forward, speaking to Mackleford face to face. "According to my knowledge, Boris O'Reilly is presently out of league with our organization, correct? The Song is a prized possession, there's no question he knows its value. He wants to regain the Song to regain your esteem."

"You seem to know Boris well, Rico." Mackleford gave him a gracious nod and turned to Mr. Quick. "O'Reilly's henchman?

"En route to Germany," Mr. Quick said, "to be processed at the Berlin campus."

"I want a full report. I want to know what Boris knows."

"Should we obtain O'Reilly as well?" Ellis asked.

"No. The French authorities can have his worthless hide," Mackleford said dismissively. "But just so I am clear, the Johnsons made contact with Jonas Wilson and you lost them?"

Mr. Quick nodded. "Correct. Wilson aided them in their escape from our agents."

Mackleford fell silent again. The Goons looked at each other nervously.

"The old guard returns," Mackleford said fondly, although with a touch of remorse. "Margaret, Boris, Jonas. This complicates matters. You boys were correct to take action. I wanted Aiden Johnson to locate the Song and bring it to me. Needless to say, Jonas won't allow that. Find them and bring them to me. Alive. We'll get the information we need out of them."

The Goon Squad exploded, half-excited, half relieved. "Whew!" Pug breathed, walking up and slapping his giant hand on Mackleford's shoulder. "Mack, you had me shiverin' in my sneakers! I thought you was gonna *White Hand* the whole Squad! Which would have been cold-blooded, 'cuz I wasn't even there."

"Pug, you're never there," Mackleford said, and everyone roared with laughter. Except Rico, who stared into the night sky in the direction Flair and Simone had escaped.

"Rico, you have something further to add?" Mackleford asked.

The chatter died when Mackleford spoke. They all turned and faced Rico.

"Things are changing for the worse," he said, "something you said...*the old guard returns*. I'm assuming that means those who have opposed you in the past. Mr. Terravil, Musclehead as he prefers, filled me in on the history of the Journeymen Guild on our walk to Paris. Most of their top agents are in hiding or dead, and the few that remain active are scattered. With their absence, our organization has thrived, but now these events, the Song stolen, the old guard returning....well, there is a tide in Journeymen affairs, and before the flood arrives, as it certainly will, a strong response is necessary."

Mackleford stared at Rico, considering his statement. "Rico is right. East Town and the Gumms are becoming a threat once again. We're going to have to take action."

Rico nodded and turned back to the dark night sky. Mackleford looked at Ellis from the corner of his eye.

"Signs of precognition?" Mackleford whispered. "Did you know?"

Ellis shook his head, looking bothered.

"Well, it's a pleasant surprise. Take him back to Colorado, use the jet. I don't want him in the field until we know what's making him tick. And Ellis..." Mackleford patted him on the back, "well done."

Ellis smiled, but he looked clearly disturbed. He tapped Rico on the shoulder and they stepped towards the edge of the building, talking alone. Mackleford turned to the Goons.

"Okay gentlemen. Two teams. We have a lot of work left to do. Mr. Quick? Which way did they go?"

Flair's feet finally caught the rooftop of a building and she stepped down upon the snow-covered surface with ease. She turned, looking from where they came, seeing the L'Escapade in the distance, seemingly miles away.

"Still in one piece, Simmy?" she said, looking over her shoulder.

"That was the craziest thing ever! How did we do that? Oh man, I can't wait to tell Aiden about that! We were *flying*! How fast do you think we were going?"

Simone was a chatterbox again, bringing a smile to Flair's face.

"Seriously though, I think I'm going to be sick," Simone said. "This would be more fun if I weren't a mutated creature."

Flair's heart sank. "You're not a mutated creature," she said, swinging Simone from her back and cradling her. She examined the white beam, which ended on the side of a wall near an access door. Flair approached the spot.

"How does this work? Is it coming out of the walls?"

Flair dropped the white crystal in her pocket and at once the beams extinguished. She scrutinized the wall, finding a white crystal no bigger than her finger. With the hand that cradled Simone's head, she touched it and the beams ignited.

"I got it. Those beams are created by the crystals, so when I touch a crystal, it lights up. See, Simmy, on the edge of this brick…"

But Simone wasn't looking or listening. Her eyes were half-closed and she looked like she was nodding off.

"You okay, sugarplum?" Flair said, shaking her slightly.

"Uh huh," Simone yawned. "Just a little tired. And cold."

"Okay, let's head inside."

Flair opened the access door and descended a stairwell into a spacious office, which in the dim lighting coming from the overhead windows showed it was dusty and full of cobwebs. No one had been here in years.

"Where are we?" Simone said.

Flair rested Simone on a dusty couch and scouted the room. It was littered with relics and artifacts, glass cabinets crammed with odd items and trinkets. Giant maps of the world, drawings, and photographs were plastered to every wall.

"Looks like Granny's house," Flair said. "Full of old stuff."

Simone propped herself up on her elbows, glanced around, and fell back to the couch in a cloud of dust.

"Can you leave me here and let me sleep?"

"No, we should move. What if we—*shhh*! What was that?"

A crunch of gravel sounded overhead. Simone shot upright.

"You think it's them—"

"I don't know," Flair hissed. "Keep quiet."

The access door creaked, and long, unnerving silence followed. Flair and Simone held their breath, staring at the ceiling. Then laborious, heavy footsteps descended the staircase.

"It *is* them!" Simone whimpered.

Flair gave her sister a hard look. "If it is, scream until their eyeballs explode, okay?"

Simone bit her lip, apparently imagining exploding eyeballs, but nodded.

Flair grabbed two red crystals from the burlap bag. Her red aura brightened the entire room.

"Flair? Is that you?"

Flair immediately recognized the voice. "Jonas! Thank God!"

Flair dropped the crystals in the bag and Jonas entered from the stairwell, gripping his electric baton and wearing what looked like a glimmering green tracksuit that Flair assumed was made of Aurorum.

"I'm glad it's you," Jonas said, as he worked his way through the clutter to stand next to Flair. "I wouldn't have withstood another run in today. When I heard the L'Escapade was on fire, I was praying you'd find the channels."

"The *channels*?"

"Yes, the *star channels*, the beams you saw on the rooftop. Gus and I spent years putting it the network together after Mackleford turned on us. We used it at night so we could get around Paris without being detected." Jonas sat on the couch next to Simone. "So things got a little hairy at the hotel?"

"Yes, very hairy," Flair said. "These Goons play for keeps, don't they?"

She told Jonas about their encounter and escape from the Goons, but Jonas was especially interested in Simone's scream.

"How did you feel when you did that?" he asked. "Were you in any pain? Did you feel sick or hurt or anything like that?"

"No," Simone yawned, "I felt okay, but it scared me. You're not going to ask me to do it, are you?"

"Not at all. You've been scared enough. But this is an unfortunate turn of events."

"What do you mean?" Flair said.

"It's called the *Banshee*, what you can do," Jonas said. "A rare side effect of Purification." He turned to Simone and took a deep breath. "Mack is going to want to capture you."

"Capture? Me?"

"Yes. Purified people are pretty durable. I've seen Goons get shot, burned, hit by trucks, fall from tops of buildings and survive. They're vulnerable to electric shocks, crystals, and most of all, the Banshee. They won't rest until they have you."

Seeing Simone's worried look, Jonas smiled. "Luckily we're here, and we couldn't be in a better place." Jonas sprang to his feet and walked around the dusty room. "This is Jump Point, our old headquarters! We should have come here immediately. It will be like the old days. Every new journey began here."

He grabbed a tattered map of South America covered with drawings, plotted lines, and written instructions, holding it high above his head, smiling.

"I remember this!" he cried. "Our Great Andes adventure! Those are his pinpoints and handwriting! And this," Jonas climbed upon a desk, pulling down a large wooden mask hanging on the wall, "was a tribal mask that Gus won, playing a game of chance in the Congo. It was our first adventure together with Mack and Boris. He saved all of our hides that time!"

Flair and Simone watched Jonas scurry around the room, grabbing various items, each with a story: escapes from exploding ships, fighting savage animals, encounters with deadly treasure hunters. After twenty minutes, he sighed and sat down holding a gigantic spear.

"Forgive me girls, just reminiscing. I haven't been in this room in years."

"Why not?" Simone said. "Don't you like it in here? I know I would if I felt better."

"No, I like it very much, Simone," Jonas sighed. "I just haven't dealt with Gaston's death very…" He looked around, only now realizing someone was missing. "Where is Aiden?"

"We got separated at the hotel," Flair said.

"And you didn't look for him before leaving? This isn't good. You *must* stay together! Let's move! We need to get back to—"

BOOM! BOOM! BOOM!

Several loud crashes sounded above, followed by the thundering of heavy footsteps. Jonas stared up, seeing the ceiling cracking and splintering and turned to Flair.

"You were followed! Dear Lord, we're trapped."

Jonas sprang into action, crystals in hand. Flair whipped out two reds and stood at his side.

"No," Jonas grunted. "Hide, both of you!"

Flair didn't take her eyes off the door. "I'm not hiding from these bozos! I've got these," she indicated the crystals, "and Simmy's got her Banshee. We're good."

"I know Flair, but it's bound to be Mack this time and they might be prepared for the Banshee. We can't let him capture you. I'll keep them busy. We'll think of something, but you two need to get back to Aiden. Hide!"

He glared at Flair as footsteps rumbled down the staircase. With reluctance, Flair obeyed, returning the crystals to the black pouch and pulling Simone underneath a large desk in the darkest corner.

Just as Flair was out of sight, the door was smashed in. Mochtier Mackleford was at the door, eyed Jonas and rushed across the room, immediately snaring him by the throat and slamming him to the floor. Fuzz, Lanky, No-Neck, and Pug stormed in behind him.

Mackleford's silver gloved hand flashed into the air and No-Neck was at his side, dutifully removing the glove and revealing Mackleford's ghastly weapon.

SMACK!!

The sound of Mackleford's slap across Jonas's face echoed across the room. Simone breathed a whimper, however, none but Flair heard it.

"Hello old friend," Mackleford said, his face livid. "What a surprise!"

"M-Mochtier? What are you doing—"

SMACK!! The White Hand had struck again.

"I sent the Johnsons to retrieve my property. Your interference is not appreciated."

"The *Johnsons*? What are you talking about?" Jonas choked. "What *property*?"

"THE SONG OF SOLOMON!" Mackleford roared and the Goons shuddered. "Wilbert Johnson came to you after he stole it from me! *Where is it?*"

"Wilbert?" Jonas stuttered. "Johnson? No, he never—"

SMACK!

Flair's stomach lurched; the third strike was harder, more bone chilling than the other two. Flair clapped her hand around Simone's mouth, feeling her sister's tears dribbling over her fingers. Even from her hiding place, Flair had a clear view of them and could see a white, hand-shaped patch of crusted skin had begun to form on Jonas's face.

"I don't have all day, Jonas," Mackleford snarled. "I don't believe in killing old friends, but you know I will."

"Mack," mumbled Pug. "Look."

Mackleford glared at Pug and then glanced around the room, staring at the maps adorning the walls, the glass cases full of treasures and trophies collected from a lifetime of adventure. Mackleford dropped Jonas on the floor and stood, his smile spreading.

"Well, well, well. Looks like I've finally hit pay dirt..."

"This is it, ain't it?" Lanky yelped. "Gumm's headquarters? We've finally found it!"

"Of course," Mackleford breathed. "The Song must be here. Genius to use those blasted crystals to create a hidden pathway." He dropped Jonas to the floor, wearing an ironic grin. "Smart Gus. He knew Purification would keep me from finding Jump Point, but I've overcome that hurdle. It's a shame he couldn't be here to see his failure."

"You," Jonas breathed, as the crusted skin spread wider, "are the failure Mochtier."

"Really? You've led me to the Song and Jump Point, Jonas. You served the Guild better when you were dead. Make this easy, Jonas. Hand over the Song of Solomon. Save Wilbert's kids while you can."

"You found Jump Point," Jonas groaned, "but not the Song nor the children. They aren't here."

"He's lying," Lanky said, looking around the room.

Mackleford craned his neck sideways, as if listening for something no one else could detect. He stalked around the room, shushing the Goons, and after a tense minute, he frowned.

"He's not lying," Mackleford said, retrieving his silver glove from No-Neck. "Not about the Song in any case, it isn't here. But those kids are. I sense the little girl's heartbeat."

The Goons went to work, tearing Jump Point apart, smashing through cabinets, and toppling anything not nailed down. Mackleford circled Jonas, looking very pleased.

"You went into hiding to hang around dusty old rooms full of ancient trinkets?" Mackleford sneered.

Jonas was silent. He had laid down flat on the floor, his body trembling, struggling to breathe. The crusted skin had spread across his face and down his neck. Mackleford, noticing, knelt next to Jonas, cradling his head in the silver glove.

"Jonas, old friend," he said sympathetically, "it will be only me now."

"What about Boris?" Jonas said, managing a small smile.

Mackleford chuckled. "Ever the jokester, Jonas. A shame everything ended so tragically."

Jonas nodded. "The way we said it would. Remember?"

Mackleford clutched Jonas' hand and pulled, sitting him upright. He looked him in the eye and nodded.

"So much I wanted to tell Gus," Mackleford said. "Never got the chance."

Jonas nodded. "Same here."

Mackleford smiled. "I really thought you were dead."

"That's the point of going underground, right?" Jonas laughed.

"Yes, of course, but really Jonas...*Demetric*? Best you could do?"

Jonas coughed, wheezing and laughing at the same time. "Kept your Goons off my back. Allowed me to build and design."

"Still designing those insane houses?"

"If you have the chance, I built a few designs along the river in Millennium Falls."

"Millennium Falls?" Mackleford said, grinning. "I'll have to take a trip."

The tribal mask had been broken in half and thrown at their feet as the Goons continued plundering. Mackleford picked up the pieces, smiling reminiscently.

"So I guess your plans are nearing their end," Jonas said. "Your point of no return."

Mackleford set the two halves of the mask together. "Gus never understood that there was never any turning back. You know the saying—*none is perfect, but should a man chase perfection—*"

"*—he shall find excellence,*" Jonas finished.

"But I haven't chased perfection to find excellence, but to find perfection itself. That is where I am, on the brink of perfection. I'm going to rebuild this world, Jonas. Everything from businesses to governments to people to products. Refine them, reshape them to be the forerunners of a perfect generation."

"You make it sound good, Mochtier," Jonas replied, shaking his head, "but what you're talking about is worldwide Purification. What happens if you screw up and destroy humanity?"

"Humanity is already destroying itself, Jonas. You know that. However, you're correct, better wisdom than mine is needed here. Once I have the Song, I can proceed."

"Wisdom has nothing to do with it." Jonas's voice sounded more coarse and ragged. "It never did. You're playing God with people's lives. You must stop."

"But you've already said it," Mackleford said, separating the broken mask into two pieces and dropping them next to Jonas. "We've past that point. There is no returning."

"And if the world dies?"

"The world will survive," Mackleford replied. "I'm just giving it what it's been missing."

"I see. I guess it's always best to *shake things up,*" and Jonas's eyes darted towards Flair and Simone, "*when you can.*"

Simone elbowed Flair in the ribs, mouthing something, but Flair stared at her, clueless.

"*Green crystals,*" Simone whispered, nodding at the leather pouch.

Mackleford turned his head. The other Goons shot looks at each other.

Pug nodded. "I heard it too. Look under that desk, Fuzz!" Fuzz knocked over a display case, walking in Flair and Simone's direction.

Flair opened the leather pouch, retrieving two greens. "Hang on to me, Simmy…"

The desk immediately shot up above Flair and Simone's head, exposing them.

"Here they are!"

Flair dropped a green crystal and it rolled towards the middle of the room. The moment it stopped, Jump Point trembled. Mackleford turned, staring at the shining green crystal in the middle of the floor.

"A green!" Mackleford said. "Grab it, Lanky!"

"Heck no, I'm not touching that! Those things burn—"

"DO IT YOU IDIOT!"

But it was too late. The second green had already left Flair's hand, tumbling next to the first. The room was thrown into turbulence. Whatever the Goons hadn't knocked over went crashing to the floor, and the floor had begun to crack, splitting down the middle where the greens rested.

Cabinets toppled and smashed, Goons stumbled and fell. Mackleford, however, seemed to have his legs underneath him, wobbling towards the green crystals. Flair reached for the burlap bag and grabbed a red crystal. Staring at Mackleford, her aura blazed a bright, stunning red. She aimed and blasted several bolts at Mackleford, one finally striking him in the chest, knocking him backwards into a painting of East Town.

"Let's go, Simmy! Climb aboard!"

With Simone clinging to her back, Flair tried to steady herself as she stood, but she was doing no better than the Goon Squad. It was like walking on a waterbed; the sisters swayed to and fro like sailors on the deck of a ship.

A loud—*CRACK!*—sounded and a huge fissure split Jump Point in two, Goons on one half next to Jonas, and Flair and Simone on the other. The green crystals were teetering on the edge, threatening to fall into the void between them. Jonas slid over towards the crystals and pinned them to the floor underneath his body, keeping them from falling.

Flair edged her way along the crumbling floor, but lost her balance and crashed face first, Simone's extra weight adding insult to injury. This was proving to be impossible.

"White crystal!" Jonas yelled. *Of course*, Flair smacked her own head and grabbed a white crystal from the pouch. Immediately, the room felt stable. She prepared to toss it to Jonas, but with another loud crack, the crevice between them spread wider.

"No, Flair, not me," Jonas shouted. "Get out of here."

"Mr. Wilson, we've already been through this—"

"I'm not going to survive this, Flair. Get out of here before the whole building comes down. And retrieve the greens before you go." Jonas rolled off of the greens, now staring at the girls upside down. "You can't lose these crystals."

"How? I can't reach them from here."

"The green crystals are attractors. They will come towards each other. Take one out."

Flair took out another green crystal and stretched her hand towards the greens that were teetering on the edge of a long plank of wood.

To Flair's astonishment, the crystals zipped towards her like two green streaks of light. The quaking and rumbling stopped at once and Flair reached out, snaring the greens out of the air.

All was quiet, except the creaking floor and swearing from the Goons below as they were pelted by falling debris. Jonas was sliding into the crevice, but his Aurorum jacket snagged a jagged piece of the floor. He was literally hanging by a thread over the dark abyss as surrounding artifacts tumbled into it. He looked over to Flair, who was watching with Simone.

"Go, girls!" he said. "Now!"

"Wait!" Flair said. "Margaret wanted me to tell you something."

Jonas looked incredulous. "Earlier would've been better."

"I know," Flair said, frustrated. "She wanted to say she was sorry about everything."

Jonas smiled. "I know. And tell Margie when you see her again—"

But Jonas never finished what he was going to say. The piece of floor snapped, sending Jonas and his half of the room crashing into the dark crevice. Flair ran up the stairs as Simone looked back, watching the interior of Jump Point collapse. Flair banged through the roof door just as the staircase collapsed behind her. Afterwards, a bright green flash, followed by a sonic boom erupted out of the dark. The Aurorum had triggered.

On the rooftop, Flair heard Simone crying. She patted her hands.

"There was nothing we could do, Simmy. We couldn't save him—"

"If we go down, maybe he's okay, maybe he's still—"

"There's nothing but Mackleford and Goons down there!" Flair shouted, fighting her own tears. She walked over to the white stream connected to the L'Escapade. It was flickering.

"Are we going back to the hotel?" Simone sniffed.

"Heck no, that place was on fire."

"So how are we gonna find Aiden?" Simone asked.

A strong shiver ran down Flair's spine that was unconnected to the cold weather. She had been relieved when Jonas found them, but now that he was gone, it dawned on her: they were two little girls lost in Paris, separated from Aiden, not knowing what to do.

She looked at the other star channels. "Let's try another one of these beams. Hold on."

Simone hugged Flair as her sister held up the white crystal, connecting it to another star channel. Flair felt the star channel pull her onto it and they rose into the night sky.

"Not so fast, kid!"

An enormous hand snared Flair's ankle out of nowhere. It was No-Neck, and behind him, Fuzz and Lanky were pulling themselves out of a giant hole in the roof.

Flair pointed her red crystal between No-Neck's eyes.

"Wait! Don't shoot!" he screamed.

"Then get lost, freak show!" she shouted.

No-Neck released Flair, falling to the roof, and the sisters raced off into the night.

Fuzz shoved No-Neck in the back, incensed. "Why'd you let go?"

"That was point blank range, you idiot!"

"So?" Fuzz said. "You let them get away!"

"She might have *killed* me!" No-Neck said. "I've seen it happen."

Lanky, meanwhile, was busy tearing his leather jacket sleeves into long strips. "Here, Quick found these some crystals at the hotel," he said, passing the strips to No-Neck and Fuzz. "Wrap these around your hands, before they get too far!"

No-Neck began wrapping his hands, but Fuzz looked hesitant. "But what if that screamer…y'know, *screams* again?"

"Are ya a Goon or aren't ya?" No-Neck growled, punching Fuzz's furry chest with his fist. "*We* don't *lose*! Wrap 'em up!"

The Goons covered their hands with the leather strips and Lanky reached into his jacket pocket, pulling out red and white crystals and slapping one each in their hands.

They looked at each other, seeing themselves bathed in faint auras. No-Neck stared around, finally seeing star channels coming into focus.

"They took this white one." No-Neck raised his crystal, connected to the white beam, and sped off after Flair, followed by his cohorts.

Flair and Simone were thousands of feet above Paris, soaring into the night on the arcing white star channel. Flair stared downwards at the maze of white and red channels below heading off in various directions, and trying to focus on any one of them made her dizzy.

"I'm lost," Flair said. "I can't tell what goes to what."

"Well, figure it out quick! The Goons are back!"

Simone pointed backwards to their left and Flair turned in that direction, seeing No-Neck, Lanky and Fuzz coming up fast, riding star channels.

"Man, these guys grate my nerves," Flair grumbled. She saw a red channel approach from above. "Okay hold on, I'm gonna try something. Please let this work."

Reaching out with a red crystal, Flair touched the red channel, and it pulled her. She yanked her left hand off the white channel as the red carried her in another direction, away from the Goons.

She heard Goons yelling instructions to one another and saw Lanky reach out with one of his gangly arms, grab a passing flagpole, and swing onto a white channel running alongside Flair's red. His metallic staff was out, and razor-sharp stilettos extended from its tips.

"Flair, he's coming!"

Flair turned and saw the silver gleam of Lanky's staff flash past her face, narrowly missing. Fuzz soared in behind him, his spear flying like a javelin. Flair swung her legs wildly to avoid it.

"Go faster Flair, they're trying to harpoon us!" Simone yelled.

"Yo, stop screaming in my ear! If you wanna scream, scream at them!"

The silver chain retracted the spear back and the chain wrapped around Flair's leg. Suddenly, Flair went flying as she and Simone had been yanked off the star channel.

"I have them!" Fuzz bellowed to the others in triumph.

"Forget what I said, Simmy!" Flair shouted, as Simone drew a breath. "Don't scream!"

It took an extreme amount of restraint for Simone not to scream. They were dangling upside down in a sickening spin, with their bodies turning in every direction. Flair felt Simone's grip tighten around her neck and chest. Buildings were rocketing by at a speed Flair couldn't believe. She began swinging her body from left to right, trying to catch whatever star channels were passing, but they were zipping by far too fast. She looked ahead and saw rooftops closing in fast.

"Crap! Simmy, hang on!"

Maybe it was the possibility of slamming headfirst into a brick roof that helped her, but Flair's swinging momentum finally catapulted her to the same white channel Fuzz was riding, directly in front of him. They were staring face to face, and Fuzz was astounded.

Several red crystal blasts snapped the chain and then Flair aimed at Fuzz. With a flash of red, he plummeted off the channel into the rooftop of a building, tumbling head over heels before smashing face first into a brick wall.

Flair laughed and Simone cheered. Flair scissor-kicked, rotated on the star channel so that they now faced forward, and zoomed off. No-Neck was closing in beneath them and to the right. A red channel was just above Flair, and she took it, soaring upwards, away from the Goon as he sailed to the left and out of sight.

"We lost them!" Simone squealed with joy. "They're gone, Flair!"

The red channel zipped between two buildings, and Flair took another white channel, searching for a place to land. "Those guys can really move. Why are they so fast?"

"Their crystals are bigger than yours," Simone said. "Man, Granny is gonna be so mad we lost those—LOOK!"

Simone's pointed finger flashed next to Flair's face and Flair turned to the left, seeing No-Neck racing beside them. With a swing of his staff, several small pellets launched in front of Flair, which scattered and exploded.

"Watch out, Flair!"

"Stop backseat driving!" Flair shouted. "I've got eyes too!"

Flair passed a red channel and held up the red crystal, which took her and Simone in another direction, away from the explosions.

"Simmy, it'd really be stellar if you did your thing, you know…"

But Simone shook her head as another spray of pellets exploded underneath them. The smell of burnt leather came up to Flair's nostrils. She looked down and saw that her pink leather boots were smoking.

"Ouch! Damn, this jerk is going to get it! These were new boots!"

"Shoot them back!" Simone cried.

"I can't!" Flair said. She was unable to fire any sort of attack at the Goons, riding on the red channel, with the white crystal clutched in her left hand, useless for attack. She looked around, scanning for another white channel, and saw one crossing below her.

"Okay, I'm going try dropped to a channel down there."

Simone looked down, uncertain of how far the fall was. "Um, are you sure?"

"If you're not gonna Banshee these bozos, I gotta do what I gotta do!" And without any further warning, Flair yanked the red crystal off the red channel, freefalling.

The plummet was frightening. They were hurtling towards the ground and Flair realized she'd misjudged how far away the channel was. She threw her left hand and the white crystal into the path of the channel as it passed, but it didn't catch.

Simone heard her sister scream every curse word in the book; they were freefalling towards an alleyway and certain doom.

Flair released the white crystal and grabbed another red from the pouch. She was going to create a shield; their only hope. Simone was choking her, blood was swelling inside Flair's face; the street was less than a hundred feet away; her hands struggled with the reds…holding them steady…they touched thirty feet above the asphalt.

A bright red halo flashed and Flair and Simone smashed into the alleyway, ricocheting off garbage bins and parked cars like a giant red pinball. The halo broke after the final hit, and the girls flew into a pile of cardboard boxes covered with snow. Flair took the brunt on her left shoulder, sparing Simone altogether, but the shield did its job.

"Owww," Flair groaned, grabbing her shoulder.

They heard voices. "They fell over there! Check that end." The Goons were close.

"Simmy," Flair said, taking out another white crystal and scooping Simone off the ground, cradling her. "Don't make a sound. I think we can hide out this way."

Flair took off down the alley, her footfalls barely making a sound. After twenty minutes of dashing between houses and buildings, Flair finally collapsed on a bus bench. The voices of the Goon Squad had died out a while ago and snowfall had returned. Simone was shivering as she asked: "So what now?"

Flair rolled her eyes. She didn't know *what now*.

"I don't know," Flair grumbled. Jonas was gone. Aiden was missing. What Flair wanted was someone to tell her what to do. She sat Simone next to her.

"Maybe…maybe…wait!" Flair said, looking inspired. "Mr. Nefflin is still here, right?"

"How are we going to find him?" Simone said.

Flair's mind searched for the answer, but none came. "I don't know," she moaned "I don't even know where we are."

"Are we still in Paris?"

"I think so. Paris is a big city like New York. Hey, I have a map!" Flair reached into her pocket for a map of Paris she purchased at the Expo, but instead pulled out the business card Jonas had given them.

"Jonas's house! That's it Simmy! That's where we were going. I'm pretty sure Aiden will find his way over there and ..."

"How? How does Aiden know where it is? *You* have the address."

Flair smiled. "C'mon Simmy, Aiden's smart. He'll find a way there. Just relax."

"How can I relax? And forget Aiden for a second, what about *us*?" Simone snatched the card from Flair. "We don't have a way to get there. We don't know where *Chart Trees* is!"

"You don't even know how to pronounce it," Flair said, smirking.

Simone didn't offer a comeback. Her eyes were watery, mouth trembling, looking as if she was ready to explode. Flair pulled her into a comforting hug.

"Alright, I'm sorry, that wasn't funny. I was trying to get your mind off the crappy day we're having. Aiden always does that and I guess I'm not very good at it. Rainier. I forgot about Rainier. He'll know how to get there. We just need to get to a phone. I lost mine back in Jonas's room."

Somewhere, a bell tower they could not see began to chime. *What time was it anyway?* Flair thought. She listened, counting the chimes all the way to twelve.

"It's midnight, Simmy" Flair sighed. "Merry Christmas." And she cradled her sister into the glow of the white crystal's aura, indistinguishable in the snowfall.

CHAPTER SIXTEEN – RENDEVOUS IN CHARTRES

Aiden awoke in the passenger seat of a very dusty car. His vision was blurry, his head was pounding, and the maniac behind the wheel wasn't making matters any better. He rose up, looking around when the car swung around a corner, slamming his head into the cold metal door.

"Owwwww!" No sooner than Aiden groaned, a soft voice spoke.

"Thank God you're awake! Aiden, I'm sorry. I didn't know that would happen."

Aiden recognized the voice instantly. He had just spent the whole week with that voice.

"Gloria? What are you doing here?"

"Helping," Gloria said. Her sparkling eyes darted from mirror to mirror like a criminal in a high-speed chase. "Where's Flair and Simone?"

"I don't know." Aiden touched his cheek and flinched. "I lost them."

"We'll find them." She didn't take her eyes off the road, but reached over to Aiden, grabbing his hand. "I'll fix everything, don't worry."

"Well, what's going on?" Aiden groaned. "Why are you here?"

"Margaret told me what happened. I know about Mackleford, about the Journeymen, about the Dominion, about everything."

Gloria's pronouncement didn't seem to surprise Aiden. "Okay, but that doesn't explain why you're here."

"I'll explain, but we need to get safe. You're being followed."

Gloria was speeding around corners, maneuvering the snowy streets with ease; clearly she knew her way around Paris. Aiden was in too much pain to protest. He leaned back in the chair, opening and closing his mouth to stretch his jaw.

"Are you okay? Does your head hurt? I have aspirin."

Aiden's head was indeed ringing with pain, and his jaw felt loose. He reached up to squeeze it; it felt wiggly and tender.

"Ugh…think my jaw is broken."

"You hear that?" Gloria barked. "You broke his jaw! Happy now?"

Aiden stared at Gloria, perplexed. *Who in the world was she talking to?*

His answer came when he turned around and glanced into the backseat. Three pairs of goggling eyes peered at him. The Purified children from Margaret's house were lying in the backseat, and one of them looked happy indeed, sneering at Aiden.

"What? You brought these things?"

"They aren't *things*, Aiden!" Gloria snapped. She drew a breath, as if preparing to give alarming news. "They're my brothers."

"*Your brothers?* Ouch!" Aiden's hand shot towards his cheek. He had forgotten his swollen jaw, and opened it so wide, it was like being punched again.

"Yes. Raul, Ramon, and Alfredo. My *older* brothers, Mackleford's first victims, attacked before you or I were born."

"Older brothers?" Aiden murmured, trying to make sense of it.

The tall brother wearing the bucket hat was mocking Aiden, hitting himself in the jaw and pretending to be unconscious, his long gray tongue flapping in his mouth. His brothers squeaked and laughed.

Aiden scowled. "Well one of your brothers sucker-punched me!"

"It was Alfredo," Gloria sighed, sounding like an embarrassed parent. "All I told him was to bring you to me."

The brothers continued laughing. Aiden quietly unbuckled his seatbelt, sitting upright; Gloria noticed nothing.

"Alfredo?" Aiden said. The tall brother grinned, tapping his own jaw with his fist.

"Yes, he's a sweetheart, but sometimes he's a little over-protective and—"

But before she finished, Aiden flew towards the backseat, reaching for Alfredo's neck. Alfredo squealed and shoved one of his brothers in Aiden's path before reaching over the top of Aiden's seat and taking a swipe at him.

"Aiden!" Gloria shouted. "AIDEN!"

A wild backseat scrum ensued: Aiden and the three Gannares brothers, grabbing, punching, and clawing every inch of each other they could. Aiden was bent over backwards, one hand wrapped around Alfredo's neck, with the other two brothers twisted around him, pounding in him the chest with their heavy fists.

"Stop!" Gloria screamed, struggling to control the car through all the commotion. "You idiots, we're gonna crash!" But no one was listening. Aiden was still throttling Alfredo's skinny neck as Alfredo was gagging, urging his brothers to drag Aiden into the backseat.

Gloria slammed on the brakes and everyone lurched forward. Aiden flew forward, ramming his shoulder into the dashboard.

"SIT BACK!" she snapped at Alfredo, who had sprung forward after Aiden. Alfredo jumped at her scream, ramming his head into the roof of the car. Gloria had Aiden pinned to his seat and her eyes were so intense, Aiden had no choice but to relax.

"Look, I'm sorry, Aiden" Gloria breathed. "I can fix your jaw! What I can't fix is us flying off the road! So everybody cool it!"

Aiden and Alfredo glared at one another for several tense seconds, and finally, Aiden righted himself in his seat and buckled his seatbelt. Gloria released him and drove on.

They rode in silence for several blocks, Aiden staring at Christmas decorations as they passed, his brain feeling like churned butter. Everything was happening too fast: Goons attacking, sisters missing, Gloria and her *brothers*, the Song of Solomon and its secrets, his splitting headache and swollen face. And his father. His father caused all of this mess. If he had never given them that invitation, they wouldn't be here. The question Aiden couldn't answer is why did he do it.

Gloria reached under her seat, retrieving something black, green and shiny. "Where'd you get this from?" she asked. It was Mr. Quick's Ruijen Staff.

"What? Oh, off one of those Goons," Aiden replied. "He attacked me with it, but I got the drop on him. Figured it's better in my hands than his."

"Nice job," she said, twirling it in her hands. "You should hold on to this. You may need it." She tossed it to him and Aiden fixed the baton to his belt.

"So, your brothers were attacked by Mackleford?" Aiden said, rubbing his left shoulder.

Gloria nodded, driving through an intersection, her eyes still darting everywhere.

"I guess that explains your parents."

Gloria blinked. "What explains my parents?"

"Why they don't want me and you hanging out together. They saw what happened to my mother and they've already lost three kids to Mackleford. They don't want to lose you too."

Gloria nodded her head. "That's mostly right, but mainly, they think you're dangerous."

Aiden stared at her with utter astonishment, looking almost offended.

"It's stupid, I know," Gloria continued. "I was twelve when I found out I had brothers, when I found out about Purity, the Dominion, Mackleford. Anyway, that Christmas, I went into our basement where my parents kept them. I just wanted to play with them, get to know them. But our dads were down there, planning something. Soon as they spotted me, they threw me out, but not before your father said something…"

Suddenly, Gloria tensed all over, looking fearful.

"What did he say?"

She answered him slowly. "He said *Aiden's going to do it*. And that's when my dad exploded."

"*Aiden's going to do it?*" Aiden repeated, twisting in his seat and facing her. "Aiden's gonna do *what?*"

Gloria said nothing, but a strange expression crossed her face as she looked into Aiden's eyes: a plea, desperate, but hopeful. Aiden looked away, staring back through the windshield, feeling his heart racing…

"It took me a while to ask my dad what your dad meant," Gloria murmured. "He said I was mistaken, but I know what I heard."

"So what am I supposed to do? What makes me so dangerous?" Aiden said. He thought he already knew, but he wanted to hear Gloria say it.

"You gotta understand, Aiden. Our parents were working together for Gaston Gumm and so was half of East Town. Kids included, all except for the Johnson kids. So naturally, my dad thinks your dad was up to something with you and Flair and Simmy, and he thinks you know more than you do, even though I told him you don't. So he sure as hell doesn't want us getting cozy, just in case."

"Like I said, he's trying to keep you safe."

Gloria shook her head. "I can take care of myself and he knows it. It's something else, but honestly I couldn't care less. If he wanted me safe, he shouldn't have quit the Guild. My father knew Gumm was close to finding the Purity cure, just like he knows Mackleford is close to completing his plans of Purifying the whole world."

"*Purifying the whole world?*" Aiden bellowed, opening his mouth wide, causing his jaw to hurt again. Behind him, the Gannares brothers howled, kicking the back of his seat.

"Yes, the whole world," Gloria said. "Mackleford's been at it for years. The original Guild members think he's creating a Purified Army, but it's worse than that. Mackleford wants to jumpstart evolution. He thinks he is some kind of pioneer, saving the human race from itself. I read his whole plan. He trying to genetically engineer a perfect man so he can use him as a prototype, and the closer he gets to that, the closer we get to Purified Armageddon."

Aiden took a breath and steadied himself so he didn't shout out again. "*Purified Armageddon?*" he whispered. "And you sit around having pie-eating contests…"

"That's because all the old timers think we've won!" Gloria said. "That the Dominion's been falling apart for months…"

"Jonas said my parents changed everything…"

"Changed *everything?*" Gloria laughed, shaking her head. "Then he has no idea what the Dominion became after Gaston Gumm died. They're beyond powerful. They've got everything they need. Money, connections, resources, everything they need to do whatever they want. Two years ago, your mom and dad organized a sting with us youngbloods, infiltrating their colleges. When we got to their Colorado campus, that's where we learned what they were really up to. *Project Revolution*, their worldwide Purification plan."

Aiden couldn't believe what he was hearing; it was too incredible.

"But we discovered one piece of good news. They have a cure. In case they screw up and they need to hit the restart button, they developed an antigen. A Purity cure that would cure any Purified person. That's Simone, my brothers, your dad—"

"Mackleford said he would cure Simmy," Aiden said.

"Margaret told me," Gloria said. "She said Mackleford needs what your father took from him. Not sure why, but he does.

Mackleford isn't a public person, but he's come out twice this year looking for it. Whatever it is, he wants it bad."

Aiden shifted in his seat and winced from his injured shoulder. He was starting to understand Gloria and didn't like the feeling. Gloria reached out, caressing Aiden's shoulder. Her touch was soft, soothing. He leaned back, shutting his eyes.

"What's Mackleford looking for?" she asked. "Margaret said something about a *song*."

"It's called the Song of Solomon," Aiden said. "A wind chime."

"A wind chime? What good is that?"

Aiden felt relaxed, calmer from Gloria's touch, and sensed brightness coming through his closed eyelids. He opened his eyes and saw a bright aura surrounding Gloria, giving her an angelic appearance. He jumped.

"Don't worry," Gloria said, removing her hand from Aiden's shoulder and showing him a white crystal. "I'm taking most of the energy from this one."

Aiden looked at the crystal warily. "I don't understand. Most of the energy…"

"If you know what you're doing, you can control crystal energy."

"What are you doing with it?"

"Whites speed up the healing process." She smiled, stroking his chin with the glowing white crystal, and his jaw felt immense relief. "Anyway, you were saying something about a wind chime…"

Aiden leaned back, recounting everything he knew about the Song of Solomon. As he finished, words that Jonas had said echoed in his mind.

You have heard its results…a small tribe becoming a powerful nation, almost overnight… Since that first campus opened, Restoration's growth was incredible. New campuses were springing up yearly…

It made Aiden wonder. Despite what Gloria believed, his parents had hurt the Dominion by stealing the Song, slowing their progress, maybe preventing worldwide Purification. *So if Mackleford wanted it back…*

"My hotel room is just outside Paris," Gloria said, breaking his concentration. "We'll patch you over there."

"No. I need to find my sisters. I'll get patched up later. Jonas said he lived out in Chartres. They're probably waiting on me."

"Chartres it is," Gloria said.

Aiden glanced out of the window as they drove outside the city, leaving Paris behind. His mind drifted to what Gloria had said. Apparently their fathers had concocted some job for him—*Aiden's going to do it*—but never told him about it. *Journeymen schemes.* This was what Jonas had warned him about. Yet, a gnawing feeling of responsibility was erupting inside of Aiden, as if he needed to finish an unknown job.

"My brothers don't like being close to crystals. They have a bad effect on Purified people."

"So I've heard. Put it away, I'm better." Gloria shoved the white crystal in her jacket pocket and the Gannares brothers relaxed.

"They've suffered so much," Gloria said. "Over twenty years in a cellar. No friends, no school, no normal life—"

"They're not the only ones without a normal life," Aiden said, meeting her eyes briefly. Gloria's expression showed she understood his meaning and her face tightened.

"I'll be different when this is over," she said. "Once my brothers are cured. Once Mackleford pays for what he's done."

Their eyes met again and Aiden saw that same hopeful look return, blazing across her face. He wasn't going to let it pass this time.

"And I'm the guy?" Aiden said, smirking. "Aiden's going to do it. I'm supposed to take down Mackleford. You think that's what my father meant?"

"Yes," Gloria replied. "I do."

It took Aiden a moment to respond, as his frustration for this whole ridiculous mess was rising. He couldn't believe how inconsiderate all of them were. So he was supposed to take down some crazy, psychotic freak of nature and his organization? And his father had actually *planned* for him to do it. He shook his head, chuckling to himself.

"Well, sorry to disappoint everyone, but I'm not in the revenge business."

"Revenge?" Gloria snapped. "What are you talking about? What revenge?"

"You said this ain't over until Mackleford *pays for* what he's done," Aiden said coolly. "Sounds like revenge to me."

"Well actually it's called *justice*, Aiden!" Gloria shot back. "If a man does the crime, he does the time, not because it's revenge, but because it's right!"

"Revenge, justice, whatever," Aiden said, still wearing a smirk that seemed to infuriate Gloria all the more. "You act like it's as easy as that."

"When you look at what he's done," Gloria said, her voice rising, "it *is* as easy as that!"

"Maybe for you, but I'm no killer."

"Oh, and *I am*?" Gloria shouted, unconcerned with her brothers' increasing squeals. "Look at what he's done! Your mother, your father, Simone! What's he gotta do to get your attention? Shoot the dog?"

"I don't have a dog," Aiden replied.

"Oh, nice! Soooo predictable! Smart aleck sarcasm. Is that all you're good for?"

Aiden rounded in his chair, facing her. "Look, I didn't ask for this! You've been dealing with this a lot longer than I have. A week ago, I was grading essays."

"And a week later, you can take down the most dangerous organization in the world! Doesn't it mean anything to you that your father trusted you to—"

"Are you kidding?" Aiden laughed. "This crap is his fault! It'd be different if he ever told me about his great master plan, but he told me nothing! Nothing! He sent us in blind!"

Gloria stared at him, speechless for a moment.

"The blame game?" she said in disgust. "Really? Please tell me that's not all you've got."

"You tell me, Gloria!" Aiden shouted. "You tell me, what am I supposed to do?"

Gloria didn't answer immediately. They had shouted so much, Alfredo, Ramon, and Raul were covering their ears and kicking their chairs. She stopped the car, turned in her seat and gave them a silent apology. She looked at Aiden, hers eyes again brimming with hope.

"You're supposed to save us."

Aiden and Gloria held their gaze momentarily before both looked back to the road. Those words, and that look in Gloria's eyes, had finally done their job. By *us*, Gloria meant everyone Mackleford had hurt and would hurt: the citizens of East Town, his parents' friends, his entire family, Gloria's family. His father, confined to a bed, barely alive. Gloria's brothers, plagued for decades. People in hiding, like Jonas Wilson. He saw his mother's scabbed, withered face in that coffin, staring at him.

What had been troubling Aiden, but what he now understood, was his father's dedication to fighting the Dominion rather than living a simple life. Aiden knew there would be no simple life for anyone if Mackleford were allowed to continue. Margaret was right. Mackleford was one of those men T.E. Lawrence spoke about: a madman who would dare to act out his dangerous dreams, to make them reality. A madman with ideas that had yet to happen. Dangerous ideas.

The whole world, Aiden's own voice echoed in his head.

A madman who had to be stopped.

As luck happened, a couple out on a midnight stroll came upon Flair and Simone and gave them use of their cell phone to call Rainier. The old cabbie picked the girls up at a quarter past one, shocking Flair as he opened the cab door, revealing a shiny new wheelchair.

"Do not ask where I got eet," he said, smiling. "Eetz best you don't know about zee business we conduct here."

"But, I don't..." Flair stuttered. "How did you know we even *needed* another wheelchair? I didn't say anything."

"We all have eyes and ears," Rainier said, winking. "Some see and hear further than others. Let's get going. Where to?"

Flair handed the address to Rainier and they were off. They rode in silence, Simone fast asleep and Flair thinking. With Rainier knowing Simone's wheelchair situation and the Goon Squad finding them at every turn, she had the uneasy feeling of being watched.

The trip to Chartres was short with Rainier driving. Within a half-hour they were cruising through a beautiful city that reminded Flair of East Town. They passed buildings, churches, houses, peering through the darkness and snow, searching for the street Jonas lived on. Then, as they rounded another corner, Flair gasped.

There was no question they had found the place. Rainier's cab stopped outside the strangest home Flair had ever seen. It didn't look like it belonged in France: a three-story house, brightly colored in red, gold and green, with long, slanted roofs topped with small statuettes of strange people smoking long, odd looking pipes. The porch was trimmed in white and gold, with small glass lanterns hanging above. Simone woke as the cab stopped, and in her excitement of seeing Jonas's house, forgot she couldn't walk, swung open the door and tumbled out of the cab.

Rainier helped Simone up, settled her into the new wheelchair, and located the front door key inside a statue of a bald monk. Then, with a hearty "*Adieu*", he gave them a long bow, leapt into his cab, and was gone.

Flair and Simone entered a cluttered living room: wire, bags of clay, planks, wooden blocks, and twisted moldings were scattered haphazardly throughout and there were dozens of unfinished models of peculiar houses. There was little space to walk as cardboard boxes, Styrofoam, bubble wrap, and plastic were strewn across the floor. And somewhere in the middle of this mess, a grandfather clock chimed out. It was two o'clock.

Simone was examining one of Jonas's model houses when Flair grabbed her arm, pressing her finger against her mouth.

"Someone's here," she whispered, holding the white crystal up in her hand, pointing to her ear with the other.

"I know," Simone breathed. "I feel something, it's like, like..." Simone couldn't find a word to explain it, but she felt humming all around her, as if the air itself was vibrating.

Simone gasped, pointing towards the grandfather clock against the far wall, and a moving reflection of a man on its thin pane of glass. Someone was on the other side of the wall.

Flair held her breath; she was exhausted and another round with the Goons was the last thing she wanted. *Where else could they go?* She steeled herself, gripping the crystals.

"Who's there?" the reflection said.

Flair's heart leapt. "Aiden!"

Flair dropped the crystals and flew through the room. Aiden ran around the corner and they crashed into each other. Flair embraced Aiden with all her might, slamming her head into his jaw, causing him to groan.

"Aiden! I don't believe it!" Simone exclaimed, bouncing happily in her wheelchair. "Flair said you would be here, but I didn't believe it!"

Gloria walked around the corner, hands in her pockets, grinning at the reunion. "Told you it wasn't the Goons, Aiden. My brothers would have sensed them."

"Gloria? What are you doing here?" Flair swung her head around towards Gloria, ramming her brother's jaw again. Aiden howled and grabbed his swollen face.

"Whoa!" Flair said, seeing Aiden's blackened eye and swollen cheek. "What happened to you?"

"In pain," Aiden moaned. "Explain later." He worked his way over to Simone, looking her over. "See you got another wheelchair. You okay?"

"Stellar," Simone sighed. Aiden knelt and hugged her and Simone squeezed him back as tight as she could.

Gloria stepped through the clutter on the floor, looking around. "Where's Jonas?"

Flair and Simone shook their heads sadly. Aiden rolled his eyes in frustration. "What happened?"

For the next half hour, they traded stories: Aiden's encounter with Mr. Quick, Gloria in Paris with her brothers, the fight at the L'Escapade, and Jonas falling at Jump Point. Flair and Simone had Gloria captivated with their escape from the Goons not once, but twice.

"Incredible," Gloria remarked. "The Goons are the Dominion's best soldiers. Escaping them once is hard enough. Bravo, Flair."

Flair's pale cheeks reddened. "Margaret never told us crystals did all of that stuff."

"Not to kill the buzz," Simone said firmly, "but let's not stand around celebrating. We're lucky to be alive. So what's next? Because I'd like to get back to *walking* if that's okay!"

Aiden laughed. Simone's trademark spunk was on display. He stood up, pacing. "Simmy's right. We need a plan."

"The crazy thing is how they keep finding us," Flair said. "No matter where we go, they just keep popping up."

"They're tracking you," Gloria said. "Goons can sense Purification."

"I don't understand why the Goons are interfering before we even find the stupid thing," Aiden remarked.

"Because Jonas got involved," Gloria responded. "Either him or Nefflin. That's why I work alone."

"Mr. Nefflin?" Flair said. "He doesn't seem like much to worry about."

"Nefflin's loose lipped, especially when he's drunk," Gloria said, clearing clutter from the couch and sitting. "We need what Mackleford wants, that's the first order of business. Find anything at Jump Point?"

"Nothing," Flair sighed. "I wish we would have had more time to look around."

"I don't think your dad would've taken it there anyway," Gloria said. "Too dangerous. He would've taken it somewhere Mackleford couldn't get to."

Flair sank on the couch next to Gloria, who pulled her into a one-armed hug. "Any ideas, bro? Where do you think it is?"

"I was just going to say the same thing Gloria said. Somewhere hard to get to that only Pops knows. But wherever it is, I don't think we should give it to him."

"What do you mean?" Simone said.

"Yeah," Gloria said, taken aback. "What *do* you mean?"

"You serious?" Flair said with a baffled expression. "The only reason we came out here was to find that thing and give it to him. For Simmy. We're not leaving her like this!"

"Flair, Mom and Pops sacrificed their lives for the Song. Clearly, it's too powerful. We can't just hand it over."

"Actually, Aiden's right," Gloria said. "We need a plan B, but without this Song thing, we've got nothing. With it, we have something we can use against Mackleford."

"But what if he's lying?" Simone yawned. "Jonas said we can't trust him, and if there isn't a cure, and we give it to him for nothing—"

"Simmy, you're not staying like this," Flair interrupted. "Aiden, is that thing more important than our sister?"

"Nothing's more important than family," Aiden said. "But we can't give it to Mackleford."

"I'm glad you and your father think alike, Aiden," came a voice from upstairs. Aiden remembered the voice the instant he heard it.

"Dillinger?" he said.

Everyone turned, watching a sandy-haired man in a shabby military jacket descend the stairs, a red aura surrounding him. Carson Dillinger walked the outer rim of Jonas's junky living room, flexing his blue and yellow gloves, with circular red crystals imbedded in the palms. His eyes were locked on Gloria, and it wasn't a pleasant look.

"And just who in the hell are you?" Simone said.

Gloria shifted on the couch as if to stand. Carson raised his gloved hands, aiming directly at Gloria. "Don't move Gloria. Or I'll blast you."

The Johnsons stared at one another, mystified at this threat. Gloria scoffed, rolling her eyes.

"Okay, Carson."

"What are you doing here, Dillinger?" Aiden said.

"Relax, Aiden," Carson said, winding his way through the living room. "I'm one of the good guys. But Gloria, I thought I told you to stay out of this."

"And I thought I told you my father's name is Nick, not Carson," Gloria said.

"Your father told you to stay out of it too, sweetie pie!"

Someone else entered through a back door, also glowing dark red. Everyone turned, this time facing a young girl with waist-length, jet-black hair, wearing a thick sweater, a skullcap and glasses so thick they might have been goggles. Her red, white, and blue gloves were also aimed at Gloria.

"Sonya Martinez," Gloria breathed and looking unhappy. "Haven't seen you in while."

"Probably why I'm alive. I see you're still backstabbing the Guild."

"Backstabbing the Guild?" Aiden and Flair mouthed to one another.

"Really, Sonya? When will you accept that you were wrong about me?" Gloria faced Sonya, slowly crossing her arms. Sonya's fingers flexed and she looked wary.

"When Goons fly. But until then, keep your hands where I can see them."

Gloria stared curiously at Sonya, as if determining whether or not to take her warning seriously. She looked at Carson, who also kept a steady aim on her. Finally, with a snort of laughter, Gloria unfolded her arms, throwing them in the air in mock fashion, as if surrendering to the police.

"Carson, Sonya, do you really want these problems?" Gloria said in a scathing tone. She didn't seem remotely concerned about Carson or Sonya.

"Don't threaten me," Sonya said, her voice dangerous.

"Then put your gloves *down*," Gloria commanded. "*Now!* Before I do it for you."

Carson's jaw was clinched, Sonya's nostrils flared, but neither of them moved.

"Look, nobody wants a fight, okay?" Carson said in a calm voice. "I won't use crystals if you don't. Just trying to figure out why you're here is all."

"You know why," Gloria snarled. "This is a chance for us to get the cure. You think I'm missing out on that?"

"We told you she doesn't care, Carson, but you don't want to listen." A high-pitched voice came from behind: another young girl, blonde, short and slender, bathed in a hazy red aura.

"Cool it, Lyric," Carson admonished. "I'm handling it."

"Oh great, Sonya *and* Lyric!" Gloria laughed. "Nothing ever changes! Still drooling over Carson, still blaming me and my family for everything that goes wrong!"

Sonya smiled. "But this time we have proof, sweetie pie. You told Mackleford where to find Wilbert."

"What are you talking about?" Gloria replied. "See what I mean, Carson? Pay attention, idiots, I want Mackleford worse than any of you!"

"Yeah, but you want the Purity cure even more, don't you?" Sonya countered.

"So what's your point?" Gloria snapped.

"That means you ain't above making a deal. You got thirty seconds to spill it before I do."

Gloria looked affronted. "Shut up, Martinez, you're out of your mind!"

"You got away with your act in Montecito because we didn't have any evidence, but you showed your true colors."

"I told you to shut up, Sonya!" Gloria said. "I'm not taking any more crap from you! Your hands aren't exactly clean either."

At that moment, Sonya took a slender black device the size of a credit card from her belt. Carson and Lyric frowned, but Gloria looked worried. Aiden noticed the change in her expression.

"Remember these?" Sonya said, flipping the device between her fingers. "Wilbert gave them to us two years ago when we infiltrated the Dominion."

"What's that?" Flair asked.

"It's a tracer," Sonya said. "Dominion tech, useful for keeping tabs on their agents and recording data. Wilbert, your dad, stole a few, figured we would need them since we were undercover. Each one is unique, made for one person and one person only. I don't understand all that techno mumbo-jumbo about global digital whatever, but I know they work. Guess who this one belonged to?"

Gloria's nervousness was evident to everyone. She didn't answer.

"No guesses? Well, allow me to enlighten the room. It's yours, Gloria. Thought our tracer system was trashed after Montecito? Well, I got Edison to fix it. I knew it'd be useful again and I traced this back to its owner. You. Want to know where *you've* been?"

"You know I lost that in Montecito," Gloria whispered.

"Right, except the problem with your lie, *shnuck-ems,* is that these devices are voice activated. You remember? Only *you* can activate it, and boy," she laughed heartily, "has it been *active*, and strangely, always at the scene of a crime."

"Sonya," Carson said, "get to the point. Where has it been?"

"Canterbury Springs last May, and in Woodwind last week," Sonya said.

The room fell silent. Gloria looked ill and stunned.

"Canterbury Springs?" Aiden muttered. "Mom and Dad...?"

"What happened at Woodwind?" Lyric asked with a frown.

"Forgot to tell you," Carson said. "Someone caused a snow slide."

"That avalanche that almost killed us?" Flair shouted.

"It must be—" Gloria was shaking. Her nerves had fallen. She looked scared and worried, but Sonya pressed on, feeling confident.

"The Dominion? Is that what you were about to say? But we found red scorch marks on the trees. Dominion agents don't use crystals, Gloria. Sloppy, so sloppy."

"Look," Gloria said, "if I wanted to take the Johnsons out, they wouldn't be standing in this room."

"Oh, is that a fact?" Flair said, suddenly turning her full attention to Gloria.

"I didn't mean—Flair, come on, I'd *never* hurt you or your parents!"

"We knew the Gannares' were dirty," Sonya continued, "but we never thought for a second you'd betray Wilbert and Laura."

"I didn't tell Mackleford a damn thing!" Gloria shouted.

"So who did?" Sonya said, pressing forward. "No one else wants the cure as bad as you, you just said so yourself. Did Mackleford promise you the cure? Is that why it's easy for you to stab us in the back?"

"How dare you?" Gloria spat. "My brothers have suffered more than any of you could possibly understand!"

"Your brothers were attacked before you were born!" Sonya shouted, louder than ever. "The worse of it was over when you were in diapers! You didn't watch it happen! Only one person in this room hasn't had to bury a parent, *precious*, so don't lecture us on suffering!"

The room fell into a jarring silence. Gloria and Sonya glared at one another with hatred. Simone stared at the carpet, afraid to look at anyone. Flair was heaving; her golden brown eyes were like smoldering fires, glaring at Gloria. Lyric looked paler than ever, sick to her stomach.

"Gloria." Aiden took a deep breath, calmly walking towards her. He was going to make sense out this nonsense, put everyone's mind at ease. Gloria hadn't betrayed his parents. She couldn't have. This girl Sonya, whoever she was, was mistaken. "Gloria?" he said again.

Gloria blinked at the sound of Aiden's voice, as if he had awakened her from a trance. She didn't meet his eyes. She looked completely lost as to what to do next.

"Yeah. That's right, don't look him in the eye, Gannares," Sonya said. "He'll see right through you, just like Wilbert did."

Gloria was silent. Flair's breathing was becoming choppy, erratic.

"Any more lies you want us to swallow, honey?" Sonya said, a vengeful smirk playing on her lips.

"No," Gloria said, finally looking at Aiden, her eyes remorseful. "I'm sorry about this."

And what followed those words happened in seconds.

Gloria moved with unfathomable speed. In one motion, she slid to the floor, legs apart, and whipped around in a pirouette like a gymnast. Her feet kicked two model houses on either side of her, which launched in opposite directions towards Sonya and Lyric.

In the second it took for Sonya and Lyric to blast the model houses into splinters, Gloria's hands flew in and out of her jacket pockets and now donned sleek golden gloves, dotted with red and white crystals, with large blood reds in the center. Before Carson, Sonya or Lyric could react, Gloria had twirled to her feet, spinning like a top, and rattling off red blasts like an automatic rifle.

The room, which had been quiet and dark, became a fireworks show. Lyric dove to the floor as Sonya formed two red shields. Carson still hadn't moved until a bolt flashed near his face. He created a glowing red shield that deflected the second and third bolts into the wall. However, Gloria's attack was quick and precise; three successive bolts broke his shield and a blast in the chest knocked Carson backwards, demolishing a large model house.

Gloria's attack ended, and before anyone could breathe another breath, she had reached into her pocket, retrieving something sparkling, as bright and blue as the ocean. Aiden watched amazed as Gloria tossed it in the air in the midst of everyone.

Sonya reacted first, screaming incoherently, and turning to run. Lyric was on her feet and squaring up against Gloria, not seeing the blue crystal above her. Carson, dumbfounded, blurted out, "Lyric! Watch it! She's got a blue!"

The blue crystal hit the ceiling with a thud and seemed to stick there. It flashed once, brilliant and stunning, and Aiden could see Lyric's face bathed in blue light, staring up, frozen in terror. The room started to spin, and as it did, all sights and sounds went hazy…

    …black

       …dark

          …quiet…

…
"…wake…"

"…you hear me…?"

A voice was fading in and out, like a radio out of tune.

"Simmy…come on…"

Simone heard a voice lightly echoing in her ears, as if it were coming across a cavern. Her head throbbed with the worst pain she'd ever felt. With difficulty, she opened her eyes, finding herself stretched out on a long chair. She was regaining her senses as what felt like a thick, prickly mist was leaving her body.

Though she had only flown twice before in her lifetime and was disoriented, Simone knew she was aboard an airplane. It was blinding inside the plane's cabin, so bright that she shut her eyes almost the instant she opened them.

"You're okay, Simmy. I've got you."

"G-Gloria? Is …wha'…happened?"

"How do you feel? Are you feeling nauseous?"

"Nauseous?" Simone muttered. "Whas'sat mean?"

"Feels like you gotta throw up."

"Oh…um…yeah," Simone croaked. "My head hurts super bad." She attempted to open her eyes again, seeing a blurry woman with auburn hair standing in front of her. "Ugh!" she moaned.

"I know, sweetheart," Gloria said, stroking Simone's forehead. "Keep your eyes closed for a few minutes and you'll feel better."

Simone shook her head. "Nothing's gonna make me feel better. This is the worst."

"I don't have anything to help you," Gloria murmured. "You might feel like this for a bit, but it'll go away."

"Why? What's happening to me now? More Purification stuff?"

"No, not Purification," Gloria said. "Well, not directly anyway. Side effects of a blue crystal. Blue crystals produce unconsciousness."

"They knock you out?" Simone asked.

"Yes, pretty much. However for someone who is Purified like you, it has a more drastic effect."

"Granny Gumm—" Simone began, but she lurched forward and vomited all over the floor. Gloria grabbed her shoulder to stop her from pitching her whole body out of the chair.

"Take it slow, Simmy."

"No," she sputtered. "Granny Gumm said no one knew what blue crystals did, only that if we ever saw one, we should run."

"She's right about running," Gloria said. "If you're close to a blue when it's used, it'll put you down for hours. Like everything else with Crystal Stars, it depends on how much physical energy you have. Your energy is pretty low right now, so you've only been out for six hours. Your brother and sister, they'll probably be out a little while longer."

"What about you?"

"It's different for me. I know how to protect myself."

"Granny said only Dominion agents had blue crystals," Simone mumbled.

"Granny doesn't know everything," Gloria said. "And don't worry about the Dominion. We're on our way to get the cure!" She spoke in an upbeat tone, trying to sound cheerful.

"Where's my brother? Where's Flair?"

Gloria didn't immediately answer, which caused Simone to open her eyes and look at Gloria. Her hair was disheveled, her eyes were bagged, heavy with sleeplessness and a certain amount of guilt.

"We had to go," Gloria said. "They didn't come with us."

"But, but *you* had the blue crystal!" Simone shouted. "You *are* Dominion!"

"No, Simmy. They didn't understand, I couldn't make them understand, so…"

"So you killed them?" Simone said with a slight whimper. "You killed Aiden and Flair?"

"No, of course not," Gloria said with a nervous laugh. "Blue crystals just knock you out, remember? They're fine."

"So why didn't you bring them too?" Simone said, looking leery.

"I just don't need any more interruptions. Besides, Aiden has a job to do. We're going to need that Song of Solomon for this to work."

"Why?"

"Because we need it to get the cure from Mackleford, sweetheart—"

"But we can't give it to him! Jonas said—"

"Never mind what Jonas said, I've got everything under control."

"No, you don't!" Simone snapped. "I'm not stupid, you knocked everyone out! They said you were working for Mackleford and they were right!"

"That's enough!" Gloria shot back, and the youngest Johnson flinched. "You're coming with us. Unlike some people, I keep my promises. I'm going to get you cured!"

"I don't care about the STUPID cure!" Simone shouted, and with that shout, she had heard it. The Banshee Cry, the same unnatural sound she made at the hotel. It was just as scary as it was before; it even seemed to have rattled the cabin. But Simone didn't care much about scary voices at the moment. She was beyond angry.

Gloria looked nervously at the cockpit door. "Simone, calm down, don't lose your—"

"I WANT MY FAMILY! NOOOWWW!"

The Banshee was deeper and much clearer, and suddenly the plane jerked to the left. Simone and Gloria went flying out of their seats, crashing into the cabin walls.

Everything was loud, chaotic; the plane was spinning, tossing end over end as the cabin shuddered. "Don't *scream*, Simone!" Gloria yelled through gritted teeth.

The wheelchair went crashing to the rear of the cabin, and the only thing keeping Simone from joining it was the armrest she had grabbed. Her legs were flailing behind her and as she looked up, she could saw Gloria pinned face first against the roof of the plane.

Simone couldn't help feeling this was the end and somehow *she'd* done it; her Banshee scream had done something to the plane. She looked to Gloria, wanting to say something, apologize, anything. But Gloria wasn't panicked; she had rolled over onto her back, lying flat on the roof of the plane, her arms pinned down.

Gloria retrieved a white crystal from her pocket and Simone felt a powerful surge of energy rush through the plane. Shining bright and under control, Gloria maneuvered towards the cockpit and opened the door. Someone was slumped in the pilot's seat and Gloria shook him, rousing him from what looked like a seizure.

The door slammed closed and Simone held on in silence as the cabin continued to shake. After what was perhaps only a few seconds but seemed like an eternity, the rumbling subsided. Simone felt the plane leveling off, and she fell into a chair. A couple of minutes later, Gloria stumbled out of the cockpit, her hair even more disheveled, her face devoid of color. She slumped into the chair directly in front of Simone like a rag doll, breathing hard and trembling.

"M-my brother Raul…flying the plane, Simmy." Gloria said, her chest rising and falling, as beads of sweat glistened on her forehead. "If you scream like that, well, you know what happens when you scream like that, so, if you don't mind, try not to do it again."

CHAPTER SEVENTEEN – THE KNIGHT'S END

Bright sunshine flooded Jonas's cottage, beaming through the curtains, casting light on five bodies strewn across the floor. Slowly, the victims of Gloria's attack stirred. A sunbeam hit Aiden's face and he awoke, propped his flat cap on sideways, and stood.

He had no idea what had happened and was having trouble piecing the events together. One minute, they had all been talking; next, there was a blinding blue light. Now it was daytime and he was picking himself off the floor. He looked around the room, seeing the others waking up, Carson first, then Sonya. Sonya crawled over to Lyric, shaking her. Carson nudged Flair with his foot.

"Come on sister, wake up." Carson croaked. "Where's your other one, Aiden?"

"My other what?"

"Your other sister."

Aiden's blood ran cold. His blurred eyes scanned Jonas's workshop.

"Flair, where is Simone?"

Flair was on her hands and knees, looking sick. "I don't know. I can barely think."

"She's not here." Carson said, looking around the room. "Her wheelchair's gone."

"So is the tracer," Sonya grumbled, scattering items on the ground and finding a piece of paper that caught her interest.

"Simmy! Where are you?" Flair called, jumping up.

"Easy does it, sister," Carson said, grabbing Flair by the arm. "You're gonna fall. Go slow, let your balance come back—"

"Oh great," Sonya muttered from her knees.

"What is it?" Aiden and Flair said in unison.

"Gloria." Sonya threw out her arm, handing the paper to Aiden.

On the back of one of Jonas's designs was a hastily scribbled note. Aiden read it aloud.

I'm sorry you guys don't believe me, but right now we don't have time to argue. Aiden I know you understand what I am trying to do. I am going after the cure and I've taken Simone with me so I can cure her too. I'll tell you where we are once you have the Song of Solomon. It is the only thing I will be able to use in a bargain.

Aiden's voice trailed away as he finished. He felt dead, empty, like his entire world had just ended. *I've taken Simone with me* he read again. Simone was gone, Gloria had taken her. *Kidnapped her.*

A roar of fury broke the silence. Flair had gone into a rage, stampeding through the room, throwing over everything in her path. True to Carson's warning, she lost her balance within seconds and crashed through a pyramid shaped model home. Aiden, still stunned, only watched as Sonya and Lyric attempted to calm Flair down.

"Flair, stop, settle down—"

"GET AWAY FROM ME!" Flair bellowed, and her face was so livid, they obeyed without another word. Carson stepped in between them.

"It's okay, let her flip out now so we can deal with her later."

"What's *that* supposed to mean?" Flair whipped around at Carson, her amber hair dancing like golden flames. Carson looked at Flair for a moment, then turned his back on her, patting his jacket pockets.

"Your anger is no good to us," Carson said in a lazy voice. "At least not this kind of anger. You're just ranting and raving."

"Ranting and...?" Flair snarled. "Look, pal, my sister—"

"I'm not judging," Carson said, and he started sifting through the clutter on the table. "I'd be pissed too. So go ahead, break some more stuff, fall down a few more times, but let me know when you're done so we can find Simone."

Flair, incensed, reached for the burlap bag on her hip.

"Don't bother, sister," Carson said, now on his knees, lifting the sofa and looking underneath it. "You can't use crystals when you're all riled up. Your mother taught me that."

The words *your mother* seemed to calm Flair. Her anger faded as she stared at Carson, breathing heavily. "M-my mother? My mother taught *you*?"

"Yep," Carson replied. "I was taken under her wing when I was a kid. We all were. Sonya was trained by Summer."

"Still hasn't finished, the old bat." Sonya said, grinning.

"Lyric's dad schooled her," Carson continued. "But I was lucky. No one understood crystals better than Laura, except Gus Gumm."

Carson got to his feet, approaching Aiden. He nodded with compassion and clapped him on the shoulder before moving past him. His sympathy seemed to shake Aiden from his trance.

"What kind of training did my mom do?" Flair said, momentarily spellbound.

"Everything," Carson said. "How crystals work, different attacks, how to get the most power out of the whites. She was the best. Every single Goon was scared of Laura Johnson."

"What about Gloria?" Aiden asked. "She seemed pretty advanced. Who trained her?"

No one answered right away. Carson, Sonya and Lyric stared at one another.

"Gloria's different," Lyric said.

"Gloria trained Gloria," Sonya said.

"We don't know where she learned the stuff she knows," Carson said. "It was like, one day she knew nothing, and then she knew everything and she ain't sharing. But Gloria won't hurt Simone, that much I'm sure about."

"Maybe she won't," Sonya said, "but she's up to no good. You heard her. She's still obsessed with the stupid cure! And that *Song* thing? Is that what your dad took from Mackleford?"

Aiden nodded, his gaze became distant. His mind had switched back to Simone, wondering where she was.

"Well he ain't getting it, whatever it is!" Sonya said, approaching Aiden. "Understand? If Mackleford wants it, he can't get it, and that's that!"

"What is it, though?" Lyric asked Aiden. "What does the Song of Solomon do?"

Aiden sighed and, once again, went through the entire conversation he had with Jonas and his theory about the Song of Solomon. Sonya and Lyric looked skeptical, but Carson nodded.

"I was out there with Wilbert and Gus Gumm. I've seen way crazier stuff than the Wisdom of Solomon floating around this planet." He turned to Aiden. "Hey look, I'm sorry about this, bro.

Believe me, I tried to prevent it. We haven't exactly been getting a lot of help."

"What do you mean by that?" Flair asked.

"The old timers," Carson said. "They just don't listen. Margaret for one, she should have told you everything before Simone's attack, she never should have told Gloria *anything*, and sending you to France without our protection was insane. And then there's Wilbert."

"What about my father?" Aiden said.

"Well, I mean he wanted you involved, right? You have his Key, don't you?"

Carson went into his jacket, pulling out an identical metal key to Aiden's.

"There's five keys and Gumm didn't just give them to anybody. Only Journeymen who can protect them should have them. No offense Aiden, I'm sure you're an awesome son and all but, c'mon, you weren't ready for this. Your father kept your whole family out of this business for your entire lives, and then suddenly, he drags you in. What gives?"

Aiden frowned. *Aiden's going to do it* echoed again like a song stuck in his head.

"Knowing Dad, he must've felt like he didn't have a choice," Flair said.

"Carson, you said yourself Mackleford would eventually track them down," Lyric said. "Maybe Wilbert thought it was time they knew."

Carson finally located what he had been looking for in the wreckage of the model house he had crashed through: his cell phone. The battery was lying beside it, detached. He replaced it and powered it on.

"Maybe," Carson said. "Wilbert definitely wanted you to know everything sooner or later, so Margaret filling you in makes sense. Giving you his Cornerstone Key doesn't."

The cell phone buzzed in Carson's hands, the display flashed, "AM".

"Oh great," Carson sighed. "Lyric, it's your dad. Here comes a lecture." And with an eye roll, Carson answered the call with the 'speaker' function. "Hey Art—"

An anxious voice spoke the second Carson answered. "Carson? What the hell is going on? We've been calling you for hours! Margaret just told us about the Johnsons' daughter, Mackleford—"

"Gloria used a blue on us, Art."

"A blue?" the man choked. "Gloria? Good Lord! Is everyone okay? Where's Lyric?"

"I'm here Dad. I'm fine."

"Everyone's fine," Carson said. "Aiden and Flair are here, but Gloria's taken off with Simone."

"Simone?" the man on the phone breathed. "But why?"

"Why does Gloria do anything, Art?" Carson replied.

"But what's Simone got to do with the cure?"

"She wants to trade my sister for the Song of Solomon," Flair said, "and then trade the Song for the cure."

There was a deep sigh from the phone. "I'm so sorry, Flair," Art said, sounding sympathetic. "I hate first time meetings under these circumstances, but in our line of living, you get used to it. I'm Art Middleman, Lyric's father, an old friend of your parents. I'm sorry for what you're going through, however this sort of thing is expected, *Carson*, since we don't have the type of unity we once had. The Journeymen have always been a cooperative group."

"Riiiight." Carson stuck his finger in his mouth, pretending to gag.

"Carson, have Marcus to bring Aiden and Flair to me," Art continued. "We've just arrived in Town. We'll hide them, we'll find Simone. We cannot risk anymore missteps."

Aiden looked at Carson, shaking his head. "Thanks, but no thanks Middleman. I'm not going back to East Town without Simone. I can handle myself."

"Aiden, we've already had enough rash and hasty decisions to last us an entire year. Things are spiraling out of control. I'll handle Gloria and get Simone back. We want her safety as much as you. Wilbert and Laura were great members of the Journeymen and—"

"My father *is* still alive, you know," Aiden said, cutting off Art.

"Of course Aiden, of course," Art said with a frustrated sigh. "Listen, as you can plainly see, you're not equipped to handle the Dominion. Your sister's been Purified and kidnapped. I need to restore order before things get worse. Right now, I hate to sound callous, but you're just in the way and a danger to everyone else. Just get back to East Town if you know what's good for you."

"Know what's *good for me*?" Aiden replied. "Listen, I'm not going anywhere but to find Simone, you understand? And you can keep your opinions about me to yourself."

"Get a grip, Aiden!" Art shouted, sounded insulted. "You're in over your head, you have no idea what you're dealing with. I'm trying to keep you safe!"

"Dad, you said don't make rash and hasty decisions, maybe we should think—"

"Quiet, Lyric!" Art snapped. "And you make sure you are on that plane too! Running off, leaving the country without telling us anything? Your mother's been like a cat on hot bricks since yesterday."

Lyric sat down, her pale cheeks turning bright red.

"You Youngbloods are becoming more of a hassle every day!" Art shouted. "You're reckless, you're making things worse and you're going to end up dead! Think about your parents and your families for once! Now, tell me about this Song of Solomon. What is it and where is it?"

"Y'know what," Aiden laughed, "I should've had you figured in five seconds flat! Getting on the phone, sounding all concerned, but you wanted information all along. Pops didn't trust you guys, and now I see why. I'm done with you, fella. You can hang up now."

"W-well…" Art stammered, "very cheeky! I see you've taken on the tone of the Youngbloods! Fine, it's your life. You think you can handle the Dominion? Done a great job so far, haven't you? Just one thing, whether you trust me or not, your parents sacrificed *everything* for that Song of Solomon, so handing it over to Mackleford after all of that would be the stupidest thing you could do, son!"

"Hey, you ain't my dad, so don't call me son!" Aiden said. But Carson's phone flashed and the call was gone.

"See what I mean?" Carson laughed. "Margaret sends you three out here, all alone with no help, but *we're* the reckless ones."

"That guy had a lot of nerve," Aiden said, incensed. "Who does he think he's talking to?"

"That's the old timers for you," Sonya said, shaking her head. "They're always lecturing us, but they fly by the seat of their pants all the time."

"Exactly," Lyric chimed in from the couch. "Did you hear him, Carson? *Make sure you're on that plane, young lady!* And my *mother*? Please."

"And what's wrong with that?" Flair said in admonishment. "You should be happy you have a mother that cares about you."

"Diana is *not* my mother!" Lyric snapped. "She's some woman my father married. A Goon killed my mom when I was five."

"Alright, alright, we're wasting time. Are you good?" Carson had walked over to Flair, who stopped glaring at Lyric and nodded her head.

"Good. Lyric, Sonya, find Mike and Libby. Meet me at De Gaulle and keep an eye out for Nefflin. Aiden, Flair, let's go."

"Go where?" Aiden asked.

"A nightclub. Information broker. Someone who will know where Gloria went."

An hour later, Carson parked a red pick-up truck in front of a large three-story building. If this was supposed to be a club, it was the strangest Aiden had ever seen. No glowing neon, no rhythmic music. It was a square, ugly structure that looked like it had survived a few wars and the people loitering out front didn't look like partygoers: wild-looking men with eye patches, broken, scarred faces, some missing limbs, dressed in tatters, openly brandishing weapons. And to top off the scene, a gruesome statue of a spear-wielding skeleton slaying a medieval knight stood front and center.

"This is a nightclub?" Aiden asked.

"Not what New Yorkers are used to?" Carson said. "The Knight's End has a unique clientele, as you can see. It's a club for people that don't wanna be found. Most of these dudes are disowned and wanted dead, not alive. So here, they get protection in exchange for information, but they aren't opposed to running an occasional job."

"Outcasts gotta eat too," Aiden said.

Carson grinned. "Right. The adventure crowd comes here looking for news, intelligence, hired hands. There's assassins in there, criminals, mercenaries, spies, even legit businessmen. Matter of fact, this is where Jonas came before he settled in Chartres. Anyway, these dudes know everything about everything."

"Everything?"

"There's a dude inside that knows who will win the next five Super Bowls."

"I'm here to find my sister," Aiden said, "not get Super Bowl picks."

Carson fixed his jacket collar. "Listen, I don't know how it will go down inside. I doubt you'll receive a warm welcome, so stay on your toes."

"Why not? What did we do?"

"It ain't what you did, it's who you are. You're a nightmare, Aiden. An unfamiliar face. You could be anybody: a buyer, a seller, a snitch, a spy, a cop, a killer, or some dude from Brooklyn looking for his kid sister."

"Can't you just tell them who I am, save us another headache?"

Carson turned in his seat. "You don't get it yet." He took a breath, his eyes searching for the words. "They don't trust anyone, not me, not you, not even themselves. They won't care what I say. I could've been tricked or set-up, I could be selling them out. Point is, we're not just gonna stroll in there and get easy answers."

"So is there any point in this?"

"Yes. Because somebody inside knows where Gloria went. We'll work the room, just be patient. Crap, I should have brought Lyric now that I think about it. Margaret said you got *starsick*, with the crystals." He turned to the back seat, looking at Flair. "You any good with crystals, sister?"

"My name is Flair," Flair replied. "And, yes, I'm good enough."

Carson opened the glove compartment and retrieved an old pair of black and white leather gloves covered in what looked like dried blood.

"Excellent, Flair, we might need you." He tossed the gloves to Flair. "Put these on. Find a couple of crystals that fit inside the palms."

Flair scrunched her nose, looking nettled. "Ugh! Is this *blood*? I'm not putting these on!"

"You know how to make shields?" Carson said. He slid a red crystal into the palm of his glove and a bright red aura ignited.

"You touch two crystals together," Flair said.

"Okay, that takes two hands, one for each crystal. Now, look at those gloves. There's small reds stitched into the fingers. On their own, those little ones don't do jack, but when you have a red in the middle, all you need to do is make a fist," Carson balled his hand into a fist, and a bright red disk shone in front of Carson, "and we've got ourselves a pretty strong shield."

"But this is someone's disgusting blood!" Flair said. "Whoever wore these probably died wearing them. No thanks."

"And you saw how Gloria blasted us?" Carson continued. "Okay, she couldn't have done it without her gloves. Your speed, accuracy, focus, everything is better with gloves. The leather conducts crystal energy better, your attacks are more potent, shields, everything…"

Flair's expression showed she was unmoved.

"When your mother was found," Carson said, "she didn't have her gloves. Left them at your grandparents. If Laura had them, we wouldn't be here and she would be…" He broke off, shaking his head, and giving Flair a very serious look. "Look, you'll need those if we have to blast our way out, and the way things have been going lately, I'm almost counting on it."

Flair grimaced and slid the gloves on with disgusted look. Carson nodded and swung his door open.

The moment they stepped out of the car, Aiden half-wished he had a pair of gloves too. The crowd of hoodlums turned their attention towards them, glaring at them in silence. Aiden noticed his sister pocketing two crystals from the burlap bag.

"Okay, keep cool. They won't make a move unless we do." Carson was talking under his breath, all the while smiling and nodding at the degenerates. "Wait here, I'll see if one of the regulars can get us in."

Carson walked ahead of Aiden and Flair towards a skinny man wearing a tan overcoat with dozens of pockets, a pair of goggles propped on his blonde head, and with the exception of the goggle-shaped outline around his eyes, a face filthy with black soot. He was talking to a group of bare-armed, tattooed men, but the moment he saw Carson walking his way, he quickly excused himself.

"Carson Dillinger, as I live and breathe!" the skinny man yelled, giving Carson a firm handshake. The two exchanged pleasantries, but Aiden could tell the man was tense. He shot glances back to the surly tattooed men, who hadn't taken their glares off of Aiden and Flair. Carson placed a hand on the man's back, steering him towards the Johnsons.

"Someone you gotta meet, Ed," Carson said, walking over to Aiden. "Edison Ingram, Aiden Johnson, Wilbert's son. Ed here is our own personal *Mr. Wizard,* master of gadgets and gizmos."

"M'pleasure," Edison said in a squirrely voice. "Your dad was a cool cat, I liked him." Aiden flinched; he didn't bother reminding Edison his father was alive. Edison shook his hand, wearing an odd, insincere smile on his face. "And this young lady is?"

"I'm his sister, Flair," Flair said. "Wilbert's daughter."

He gave Flair a small nod of the head. *"Enchanté, mademoiselle!"* He turned to Carson, still displaying his overdone smile. "So Carson, what are we doing today?"

Carson looked leery at Edison. "We need info, we've uh—got some questions about a missing girl, but are you okay, Ed? Something wrong?"

"A missing girl?" Edison gasped. "Why that's just fascinating!" He clasped his hands together playfully.

Aiden was getting annoyed at the behavior. And was he mistaken, or did he see Edison *wink* at Carson?

Carson hadn't missed it either. "What're you winking at me for?" Carson said.

"Oh. Did I wink?" Edison chuckled, beaming at them.

Aiden had had enough. "Look, my sister was just taken and we don't know where—"

"What a shame, what a shame," Edison said. "But who's in the truck, Carson?"

"Huh? No one." Carson looked at Aiden and Flair, puzzled.

"Wouldn't lie to me, would you Carson?" Edison slapped a hand on Carson's shoulder and squeezed it a little too hard.

"Ow! 'Course not, Ed," Carson said. "What's wrong, someone after you?"

Edison twisted his mouth into a sarcastic smirk. "You don't have a Purified kid in the back of that truck?"

"No!" Carson said, completely unnerved. "That's why we're here. Their sister is the Purified girl. Gloria Gannares ran off with her and we're trying to find out where."

"Really?" Edison whipped off his goggles and began scratching his head. "Well, that was a bad edit, wasn't it?" He threw his head back, cackling to the heavens. His whole persona seemed to change immediately, becoming much less irritating and much more insane. "Sister's Purified, eh? Shoulda said so off the bat."

"C'mon Ed, Nefflin must've told you."

"Nefflin?" Edison gasped. "Neff's in town?"

"Yeah," Carson said. "He's the one who brought them to Paris."

"Ya don't say!" Edison barked, looking utterly amazed. "Nice of him to let me know, the dirty sneak! How long have you been in Paris?"

"They've been here since yesterday." Carson shook his head. "So wait Ed, you haven't heard from Nefflin? He hasn't been here?"

"Heckers! 'Course not, wouldn't have put on this ding-dang show if I'd known!" He finally shook his head exasperated and looked at Carson. "Welp, y'know Neff around the holidays! Probably found himself a friendly lady to play *'What's in the box?'*" He cackled again.

"But we need Nefflin once we know where Gloria went."

"Pay no mind to that puzzle, Carson m'boy! If Neff's in Paris, we'll find him. But why is Gloria kidnapping little children? She ain't still monkeying around about that cure, is she?"

"You're close, but it'll take way too long to explain. She's got an eight-hour head start, and without knowing where she's going we can't figure out what she's doing, so we need some info. Can you get us inside or at least find out for us?"

Edison glanced at Aiden, Flair and Carson with a look of utter cynicism. "Heck no kid! I'm not putting my neck in a noose!" He snapped his goggles back over his eyes. "No one's talking to these two even if I got them in, and *you*, you're definitely a scratch. Journeymen've been in and outta here all week and no one's dealing with them. Something's up with the Guild lately."

"Like what?" Carson asked. "Wait, who else has been here?"

"No offense," Edison said, jabbing his thumb into his own chest, "but I'm closed to the nose 'til I know the score. Understand I still gotta work with a coupla you guys. And besides, you never know who's...*HOLY MACK-A-ROLLIE!*"

Edison's eyes appeared to be popping out of his head as they had fallen upon the metallic rod slightly hidden beneath Aiden's jacket. He threw open Aiden's lapel, his mouth wide and slack-jawed.

"Unreal! Is—is that from a Goon?" Edison asked.

Carson, seeing the Ruijen Staff attached to Aiden's belt, was equally astonished. "Geez, Aiden! Where on earth did you get that from?"

Aiden had forgotten all about the staff. He unhooked it from his belt. "*This*? Oh yeah, I got it off one of those—" But Edison snatched the staff before Aiden could finish, eyeing it with wonder and lust.

"I've seen that one," Carson said. "Those markings. It belongs to Mr. Quick."

"Mr. Quick?" Edison breathed. "How did you manage to obtain it, Aiden?"

It was fitting that this was Christmas morning, because Edison looked like a ten-year-old child unwrapping the top toy on his wish list. Aiden's eyes narrowed and he held out his hand, taking the Ruijen back. Edison returned it, looking disappointed.

"Well, no big deal," Aiden smiled. "Last night at the hotel. They ambushed us, and he was shooting stuff all over the place with this thing so I just doused him with the ice bucket. Electrocuted him. He dropped on the spot, I grabbed this and bailed."

"What about the other Goons that were with him?" Carson asked, incredulous.

"What other Goons? It was just him."

Carson and Edison looked stunned and glanced at each other knowingly.

"Wacky," Edison grunted. "Goons are excellent tacticians, never attack alone. Ever. Something must have made Mr. Quick forget himself."

Carson nodded. "Yeah, he underestimated you, Aiden, a mistake he won't make again."

Aiden considered the two men, who still hadn't taken their eyes off the Ruijen. "So, never gotten one of these off of a Goon before?"

Edison began bouncing on his toes. He was breathless, his face giddy. "Are you kidding? Aiden, it's like you've taken Mr. Quick's right arm! These things are custom made for each Goon. Gosh darn it, I mean, how do you even do something like that? Fingerprint recognition? Body heat index? Who knows? And have you seen them in action? *Geez Louise!* The science in these things is incredible! Groundbreaking! The Holy Grail of next level technology! Whoever created these gizmos has cracked codes we've never ever thought of! Aiden, please…I beg of you! May I…? Just for a couple of days. For research, I pinky promise I'll give it back!"

Aiden and Carson looked at each other, exchanging smiles. Aiden turned to the transfixed Edison. "It's been short circuited, I'm sure. From the water. Probably broken now."

Edison's face slackened. "Oh, oh no, I certainly hope not," he said with a fearful voice.

"Well, how's this?" Aiden said. "You want this thing, I want inside. Make it happen."

Edison bit his lip, looking at Aiden for a moment, and then without a word, took off, cutting a path through the men towards the entrance.

Carson patted Aiden on the back. "Wilbert would've been proud. Good job."

The moment the trio entered the Knight's End, the music abruptly stopped and all conversations ceased. Aiden, Flair, and Carson found themselves staring at a gallery of rogues. A hundred cutthroats gathered around filthy tables in an enormous, dimly lit barroom. Every eye was fixed on them. No one was smiling.

The Knight's End looked vast and endless from where they stood. Two more massive floors loomed overhead; its inhabitants had also stopped what they were doing and leaned over the wide balconies, staring. A quartet of men with musical instruments silhouetted against a roaring fireplace had been playing a jaunty Christmas song, but now they, along with their audience, were craning their necks to get a look at the trio.

The only sound came from the creaky, wooden ceiling fans spinning above. Several seconds had passed and the discomforting sight of bullet casings littering the floor increased Aiden's heartbeat. His muscles were tense, his mind was frenetic. He looked at Carson from the corner of his eye.

"Now what?"

Carson wore a casual smile, appearing in control, waving to someone. "We'll get called over," he whispered. "That's the way it works. Just be patient and see how—"

But Aiden was feeling very *Simone-like* at the moment and couldn't help himself. He didn't want to wait to be addressed.

"Look, I need some help here!" he blurted out. "My sister was kidnapped—"

"What's your name?" the barkeeper asked. His voice was clear, strong, and stern. Aiden deduced a Midwest American accent, the man somewhere in his thirties.

"Aiden Johnson. My father was Wilbert Johnson. You might know him."

A number of men glanced at one another at the mention of Wilbert's name, but no one spoke. A commanding voice rang out from a dark corner far behind the bar in a language Aiden didn't recognize. The barkeeper listened intently and nodded.

"No one here knows anyone named Wilbert Johnson."

"Well, no offense, but there's a couple hundred people in here. Maybe you're wrong."

A smattering of laughter was extinguished by the voice in the dark corner. The bartender gave his translation.

"He says to get out and don't come back unless you're ready to die."

Aiden was resolute. "I'm not leaving until I get what I came for."

The sound of chairs shifting and men readying weapons was all Flair needed. Before Aiden could even look at her, Flair's hands flew into in her pockets for the red crystals, which fell somewhat naturally into the center of her gloves. Carson repeated Flair's move just as the men in the bar had gotten to their feet, pointing guns at the trio.

Their auras glowed bright in the darkened bar, casting light upon the barkeeper's face. He wasn't what Aiden expected: handsome, with soft, curly hair. He yelled something in French and everyone lowered their weapons.

"I told them to hold off. Put your crystals away."

Aiden shot Flair a *don't you dare* look, which Flair acknowledged with a nod. Carson pressed his back against their shoulders, raising his gloved hands.

"We're just trying to find his kid sister," Carson said. "We're not a threat."

The voice from the corner sounded again and the handsome barkeeper grinned in amusement. "Well, if you're Wilbert Johnson's son, you should *sing for us*," he said.

Aiden was taken aback. *Sing*?

"You know the song, don't you? Wilbert's son should know it. So sing."

Aiden stared at Flair and Carson, who looked bewildered. He glanced around the bar, as if one of the hoodlums could give him a clue, but they just stared, hands on their weapons.

"What song is he talking about?" Flair asked. "The Song of Solomon?"

"I think he's talking about an actual *song*," Aiden whispered.

The barkeeper held up a finger. "You've got one minute, then be ready to use those crystals."

Black-hearted laughter echoed around the barroom as Aiden racked his brain...A song? And *something his dad knew*. But his father never taught him any songs he could remember except *The Itsy Bitsy Spider*...

"What song, Aiden?" Flair nagged.

Stall him, Aiden thought. *His father knew it, but he didn't...*

"Can I at least get a hint?" Aiden asked.

"No," the barkeeper barked.

...maybe something his father had always sang...but he was always humming or whistling, probably thousands of songs. Aiden strained harder.

"Thirty seconds, Mr. Johnson."

What? It hadn't even been fifteen. But it didn't matter if he had been thinking for an hour, Aiden was clueless...

"Come on pal, I just had a long night..."

"*Fifteen seconds...*"

"...and it's too early in the morning..."

"*Ten seconds!*"

Suddenly, two words clunked into place in his brain. *Night? Morning?*

A memory...two little old men in suits, a tall woman in a black dress and veil, his father, all gathered around a table. They beckoned to Aiden and he stepped slowly towards them as they began singing a slow, mournful tune…

"*Five seconds…*" The ratcheting of weapons, clips being loaded sounded around them…

"*A lonely night!*" Aiden yowled in a horrible tone that made Flair jump. The bar room froze. Aiden stammered along, choking words out: "…*becomes a vacant morn…*"

Flair, Carson and the handsome barman stared at one another with raised eyebrows.

"*The men of darkness, once more reborn…*"

"What?" Flair said, staring at her brother.

"*Our weapons black and grey, steel and flesh*
"*The journey never ends, our souls will never rest!*"

"You know the song?" Carson said, stunned.

"*Ten thousands like us have gone before…*"

A wild haired old man wearing a thin blue blazer cluttered with medals spun on his barstool. He tapped his cane in rhythm and his froggy voice crooned along with Aiden's.

"*Faceless soldiers in a nameless war!*"

Others from around the bar had risen to their feet, joining in.

"*The shadowed life we live, deceiving truth and kin…*"

A group of men upstairs were singing, banging mugs and glasses on the tables.

"*No mercies we give, and death, our only friend!*"

The chorus of the song rang throughout the bar; everyone was singing. The four-man band in front of the fire had struck up, keeping in tune with the hundreds of singers. Aiden had already stopped.

"The war was cold! Those days of old were fought on bloodied knees!"
"We sold our souls, the brave and bold, to know that home was free!"

"The gentleman in the back wishes to talk to you!" the barkeeper yelled over the raucous singing. Aiden stared into the dark corner as the bartender led them past drunken men who seconds ago had murder in their eyes but now raised glasses, bottles and mugs to Aiden, slapping him on the back and belching the song in harmony.

At the booth was a small old man with a grubby beard, wearing a brown derby hat and a black button-up shirt, short sleeved, revealing that most of his right arm had been amputated just above the elbow. He was drumming his fingers, humming the song as Aiden approached.

"Well done, Aiden." He was American, Aiden deduced. The man held out his only hand, motioning to the booth seat. "Please, sit."

The three slid into the booth as the old man leaned on his stump, peering at Aiden.

"Everybody's right," the man said. "You definitely favor Wilbert."

Something struck Aiden, another one of those recollections that had been coming back to him. This wasn't the first time he'd laid eyes on this man.

"We've met before, haven't we?" Aiden said.

The old man snorted. "We most absolutely have."

"But I don't remember when."

The old man laughed again. "I'll wager you're tired of that feeling too. Your mind is full of these instances, Aiden, and I'll explain, but first, enjoy this. Look at this happiness you've brought. You've filled these men with warm memories. Many of them haven't heard that song in years."

"Happiness?" Aiden said. "That song sounds extremely depressing."

"Perhaps, but for them it harkens better times. Do you know what the words mean?"

Aiden nodded. "It's a tribute to espionage."

"Indeed it is," the old man said, turning and facing Aiden more directly. "Most of these men are former spies, relics of the cloak and dagger days of the Cold War. Old, tired, unwanted by family and country. Ever sung that song before?"

"Never," Aiden answered, "but you knew that, didn't you?"

"I knew you weren't as familiar with it as with *Here we go round the mulberry bush*," the old man laughed. "But how, Aiden? Millions of songs in the world, how did you know the right one?"

The memory had come to him so suddenly, Aiden hadn't stopped to consider it. But the sly look in the old man's eyes told Aiden that this man knew things about him.

"I remembered my father singing it to me, with some other people, but I'm not sure when or where." He had never learned it but he knew the song as clearly as he knew the old man's name.

"It's because you, like your father, have a unique condition. I've forgotten the technical term. Similar to a photographic memory."

"I keep having memories and I can't figure them out," Aiden replied. "But every word of that song is clear. As clear as your name. John Brown. From Los Angeles."

"John Brown?" Carson said, amazed. "Wait. You're *thee John Brown?*"

John Brown smiled, ignoring Carson, who was now staring reverentially at the old man. "Your brain is a puzzle box. Things you've seen, read, heard, or experienced have been purposely locked in your mind and will come forth when needed. I don't know the condition better than your father; he, of course, having the same ability was able to use it perfectly.

"So in this case, your father gave you that song and told you when needed, it would be there. Your mind simply recalled the information. Like a computer pulling up an old file. You've seen it in Wilbert before Carson, yes?"

Carson nodded. "Yeah. So he has some sort of super memory?"

"In a childish manner of speaking," John said. "But to classify it that way makes it sound like he has super powers. It's merely a neurological condition."

"Condition?" Aiden said, concerned.

"Nothing life threatening, Aiden, I assure you. Just makes you unique."

"Okay, how do I use this *condition* to find my sister?"

"You don't. You'll need me for that. Your unconscious mind gathered nothing after Gloria used the blue crystal on you. Oh yes," John said off Aiden's stunned look, "I'm aware of what happened at Jonas Wilson's residence. But your sister isn't all you're looking for, is she?"

"Wait a second," Flair said. "You know where the Song of Solomon is?"

"Not me," John said, pointing at Aiden. "Him. Somewhere in your brother's brilliant brain is the location of what you and also Mochtier Mackleford seek. In the right place and time, much like today, you'll remember."

Aiden's eyes sprang open, as he just realized something.

"My father never came to Paris to find Jonas, did he? He came here to talk to you."

"Incredible," John said. "Your mind is as sharp as Wilbert's! Indeed, your father often traveled under false purposes, as well as false names, to conceal his intentions. As you are aware, Survival International was his usual cover."

"And what about Jonas?" Aiden said, thoughtfully. "After he went into hiding, did he also travel under false names and false purposes?"

John Brown cocked his head to one side with narrowed eyes, surveying Aiden. Aiden knew he was deciding whether or not to divulge what he knew about Jonas. He sat silently for at least a minute before answering.

"Jonas couldn't have spent the rest of his life hiding in France. He was an adventurer, accustomed to world travel. We created his 'Demetric' alter ego, otherwise he would have been stuck in France, which would have been intolerable for him."

Aiden's mouth hung open for a second, and he breathed a soft "of course." He straightened up, smiling. "So, why did my father want to visit you?"

John stared at Aiden for a moment, mystified, before he broke into a laugh. Aiden smiled and nodded and it seemed they were sharing a private joke, tapping their noses and winking.

"You figured Jonas' secret, didn't you?" John said with a loud slap on the table. "I stand corrected, you're sharper than Wilbert! Okay, this one's for free. Wilbert wanted to verify the authenticity of a relic he had in his possession. I assumed it was something he was selling or had just purchased it and believed himself duped. Only after the sinister event in Canterbury Springs did I realize what it was."

Aiden's eyes boggled. "So you saw it? It was authentic? The Seal of Solomon, the Ring of Aandaleeb—"

John chuckled. "No idea. I'm no historian, Aiden. I have people for that. The man I commissioned to review the item confirmed it was certainly ancient, over three thousand years at the very least. Seemed good enough for Wilbert."

"Three thousand years?" Flair gasped, sounding impressed.

"That must have been it then!" Aiden said. "But where did Pops—"

"In its own time, Aiden," John said, patting his shoulder." Today, you have a more immediate issue. Gloria Gannares and your sister's whereabouts. This will most certainly require an exchange."

John looked across the table at each of his three visitors expectantly, clearly waiting for someone to do something.

"What does that mean, an exchange?" Flair said, looking to a squirming Carson.

"Ahh—Mr. Brown, these two, they had no idea they would be coming here and…"

"Carson, this was not your caper, it was Wilbert's. I'm sure he made the proper arrangements in case Aiden found his way here."

"What're you talking about?" Aiden asked.

"At the risk of sounding crude, I'm talking about *payment*," John answered.

"But they don't have that kind of cash," Carson replied.

"Wilbert understood, he sent them on this errand. Now be quiet, Carson." John looked slightly irritated, but smiled at Aiden. "I am a broker by occupation. I am paid for my services."

"Normally in the hundreds of thousands." Carson muttered. "Look, sir—" But the old man shot Carson a look that cut off whatever he was about to say.

Aiden looked at John, helpless. "I'll gladly pay you Tuesday?"

"Not quite the answer I'm looking for," John said, not amused.

"My family doesn't have that kind of money, Mr. Brown."

"And your father gave you nothing at all?"

"Nothing. Except—" and then he remembered. "Wait a sec, Pops did give me money. Aiden reached into his inside pocket, searching, and finally retrieved the black envelope.

"You see, Carson," John said. "Wilbert's always prepared. Let's have a look."

Aiden dumped his father's lucky coins out of the envelope and spread them across the table. A tinge of guilt prickled in his stomach watching John pick through the coins. He didn't know if John was taking advantage of him. The coins might be worthless, but they were important to his father, and he wasn't sure if he wanted them given away. However at this point, Aiden felt as if he had no choice. The longer they delayed, the worst things were likely to get for Simone.

John selected one of the coins Aiden never identified: the half-dollar sized coin displaying the head of a pig. The old man flipped it in his fingers, looking almost rapturous.

"Ah yes, this will do nicely," he breathed, gazing at the coin. "Objections?"

Aiden hated not knowing what the coin was, but didn't delay. "Where's Simone?"

John plopped the coin into his breast pocket and beckoned the bartender over.

"Gloria has departed for Argentina to visit an old acquaintance. I've never met the man personally, but I've heard of him. He is known as 'the peaceful one' in his circles." The bartender handed John an envelope.

"Argentina?" Aiden said. "That's where the Gannares' are from. Gloria said there was some sort of family situation going on."

"That's no family situation," Carson muttered. "She went to see El Sereno."

"Indeed, indeed," John said, nodding. He reviewed the envelope's contents and passed them around the table. There were security images of a plane on a runway and a sheet of phone records. "Gloria is an exceptional and resourceful schemer," John continued. "She arranged a private plane and proceeded to steal it, no doubt being flown by her eldest brother. The Guild's previous encounter with El Sereno was quite disastrous. Strange place to take your sister."

"Who is El Sereno?" Aiden asked, looking at Carson, who appeared comatose, staring straight ahead. John glanced from Carson to Aiden then back to Carson, slightly amused.

"As you can tell from Mr. Dillinger's sudden change in demeanor, El Sereno's a sticky little wicket. On paper, he's Hector Cessano, president and CEO of a thriving pharmaceutical company in Argentina. Completely clean as far as the US Government and Interpol are concerned, but— "

"But he's not clean, is he?" Aiden said.

"Of course not. The business is a front for something. But what?" John shrugged. "Now, understand something Aiden, I gather and sell information and frankly, I am the best at what I do. Pick anyone within three thousand miles of this building and I'll tell you his bad habits, his bank account number, and what he fears the most. I know exactly what time the Prime Minister of Great Britain went to bed, or what the King of Pakistan had for lunch last Wednesday. But I have no clue what Hector Cessano—El Sereno—and his cohorts actually do on that *campus-slash-compound* in Argentina. He is very good."

Aiden turned to Carson, who looked like the rug had been pulled out from under him. "Pharmaceutical company? Gloria said she knows where the cure is. Maybe it's there. Carson?"

"Um...maybe," Carson mumbled. Aiden was getting frustrated. He didn't need Carson spacing out on him now. Flair reached out to Carson, grabbed his wrist and shook it.

"What's up?" she said. "What happened out there?"

"We just wanted to check it out," Carson said with a faraway look. "Find out who El Sereno was and his connection to Mackleford. It was after Morocco, we interrogated Dominion agents. One guy dropped El Sereno's name. We put together an undercover team and..." His voice trailed away.

"And?" Flair shook his arm, prodding him to continue.

"We were compromised. We ended up losing a lot of our younger Journeymen. El Sereno is cruel. He doesn't know compassion. He has this pit out in the jungle…" Carson swallowed and broke off the story, and then he took a deep breath to steady himself. "Anyway, if that's where Gloria's gone, I can get us in."

John showed mild surprise. "Still remember the where the back door is?"

"I'll never forget that place," Carson said.

John stood up. "Well then, fun times await! Is that all for today, Aiden?"

"One last question," Aiden said. "Would these guys really have shot us if I didn't remember that song?"

"Naturally," John said simply.

Aiden looked unsettled. "Oh. Well, then, yes, I think that's it for today. Thanks."

John tipped his brown derby. "Until next time."

CHAPTER EIGHTEEN – OF FLIGHTS AND DREAMS

"Montecito? Think I've heard of that place—"

"Yeah, I bet you have," Carson said with a grin.

It had been over an hour since John Brown had departed the small booth, and now Aiden, Flair and Carson stared across the table at a frightening looking group of rogues and brutes. Seated was a man who appeared to be the group's leader, wearing a thick leather jacket and a red baseball cap.

"Now listen," Carson said, "we already have transportation. A simple three-day operation. One day to get in, one day to get the targets, and—"

"Ain't Montecito in South America somewhere?" the man in the cap said, frowning as if a sudden realization hit him.

Carson sighed. "It's in Argentina."

"Yer talkin' 'bout El Sereno, ain't cha?" The man in the baseball hat pushed back from the table and stood as his associates grumbled, shaking their heads and throwing their hands in the air, muttering "stupid Journeymen".

"Ain't enough money in the world to tangle with El Sereno," the man in the cap said. Carson groaned, watching the men leave, but suddenly spotted another group of mercenaries, rose from the table, and chased them across the room.

Flair felt Carson had done the asking all wrong. If El Sereno was this dangerous, they might have to try something other than a straightforward request. Five minutes later, another group of burly mercenaries were seated at the booth, and in another five minutes, they left in a hurry after hearing the name El Sereno.

"Sit tight," Carson said. "I see a bounty hunter from Australia I know."

But within an hour, every mercenary, thug, and adventurer in Knight's End had heard what Carson was up to, and a procession had been queuing at the booth, telling Carson not to bother. When they were finished, Carson had buried his face deep into his folded arms on the tabletop.

"It's fine, it's fine," Carson said, looking up, sounding courageous. "I was hoping for some hired hands, but with the three of us, plus Lyric, Sonya, Mike, Liberty, we'll convince Ed and Nefflin to tag along. Plus I got guys in Argentina that owe me favors—"

"Like those Russians you said owed you a favor?" Flair said. "They said they'd sooner go back to Siberia."

Carson ignored Flair. "It won't be easy, not the best situation, but hey, it can't possibly get any worse."

The next man who approached made a liar out of Carson. He was a tall and dark-skinned, wearing a dashiki, and spoke with a deep, heavy African accent.

"Carson Dillinger. So nice to see you again."

Behind the man was a short woman with braided hair, wearing a winter coat along with a vicious scowl, glaring at Carson as if she wanted to strangle him with her bare hands.

Carson's face went blank. "Oh. Hi Maylock. Hello Ms. Bando."

"*Hello Ms. Bando?*" barked the woman. "That's all you have to say?" And she proceeded to rattle off a torrent of swear words that made Flair cover her mouth in amazement.

"Okay, I know I missed the deadline," Carson moaned.

"Be careful, Carson," Maylock said with a wide smile. "I don't want to be taken as an unreasonable man. Missing a deadline is a day, a week, maybe a month. It's been two years."

Carson sat forward. "You know Maylock, your deal isn't exactly a walk in the park. I need a crew, supplies, and transportation at a moment's notice. That's a lot of prep work."

Maylock sat down, pulling out another chair for Ms. Bando, but not taking his eyes off Carson. "You know how much I love your excuses, Carson. Luckily your friends are not as clever as you are."

"My friends?"

"Yes, your Journeymen friends. Lyric, Sonya, Liberty, Michael. They've joined us."

"What do you mean, *joined you?*" Carson muttered, his face growing paler by the moment.

"Can you believe our fortune?" Maylock said, smiling. "We spotted them at the airport as we were leaving town. I would have said Christmas came early, but it *is* Christmas! Lo and behold, Santa delivered! They're outside in the van, itching to get started."

"You found him!" came a squirrely voice from behind. Edison Ingram sauntered up to the table and jumping into the booth next to Carson, grinning ear to ear. "Told ya he was still here!" he laughed, slapping both Carson and Maylock on their shoulders. "Maylock didn't think you'd hang around for too long, but I said Carson and I go *waaay* back! He'd never leave without saying g'bye!"

Edison leaned into Carson and whispered. "Promised me half-a-hundred if you were here. Sorry buddy," he giggled. "You know how it goes!"

"Thanks Ed," Carson muttered.

"Yessir, Carson is a hard chipmunk to catch, but we caught 'em, Ms. Bando," Edison said, winking at the short woman.

"Edison Ingram, another friend of Carson, Elena," Maylock said to Ms. Bando. "He's kind enough to accompany us to complete Carson's half of our bargain. Shall we?"

"Who, me?" Edison said, taken aback. "Nah, I never go on their little misadventures. But I'll take my finders fee, thanks!"

"But Edison, you and Carson, how did you say—*go waaay back*," Maylock said with a leering smile. He snapped his fingers and three large men with big rifles slung over their shoulders stepped forward. "He needs supplies and transportation. Some of your specialties, right, Edison? Welcome aboard!"

"Er…it's really Chuck and Neff that handle…" But Edison was hoisted to his feet by one of the gunmen and shoved along as Maylock nodded to Aiden and Flair.

"More friends of yours?" Maylock said. "Put them in the van too."

"They're clients," Carson said, warning Aiden with a look. "At least they were."

"Well then," Maylock said, "consider yourselves properly warned from making deals with Carson Dillinger. His customer service is deplorable."

With a grouchy Edison leading the way and Carson murmuring "that's what you get!" in his ear, Aiden, Flair, along with Maylock, Ms. Bando and their henchmen exited the Knights End. They headed towards a black van surrounded by a dozen large men wearing dashikis.

If Aiden didn't know things had gone from bad to worse before, the looks on the faces in the van said it all. Lyric hung her head, looking defeated, and Sonya was angrier than Aiden had ever seen anyone. Sonya beckoned Carson over and whispered something to him, after which Carson asked Maylock for a moment alone with his *clients*, to which he was told, "Make it fast".

"What's the deal Carson?" Aiden said. "Who are these guys?"

"I owe 'em," Carson said, "for Morocco. A *'scratch my back, I'll scratch yours'* deal two years old. They're picking a bad time to cash in."

"So what now?"

"Ms. Bando's problem is going to take weeks to fix. It's why we haven't done it yet, too much has been happening." He sighed. "I'm sorry. I'll get you on a plane. I'll let Art know what's going on. He'll try and—"

"We're not going home without Simone," Aiden said. "Right Flair?"

"No way, Jose." Flair replied.

Carson almost laughed. "Do I need to remind you," he said, jabbing a thumb at the old building, "that bar room full of gun-toting he-men wouldn't step one toe inside of Montecito? Don't be ridiculous."

"You knew my father, Carson. What would he do?"

Carson shook his head. "That's different. Wilbert was trained and Simone is his daughter."

"Well I'm not trained," Aiden replied, "but she's my sister. And at this point, I am her father as far as that goes. So, two things—"

"Aiden, c'mon, I admire bravery, but this is—"

Aiden spoke right past Carson's protest. "One, did Sonya find Nefflin?"

There was a bit of commotion behind them and they turned to see Edison being shoved rudely into the black van. Carson looked grim.

"Yes," Carson said. "She said Nefflin's at the airport in the hangar where he parked his plane, hiding out from Maylock's bunch."

"Thirty seconds, Dillinger!" yelled Maylock.

"Good. And two, tell me where that back door is."

Carson turned from Aiden towards Maylock, who glared back. "I swear you two are as crazy as your parents!" Carson snarled at them. "El Sereno has a two-hundred man private army in a fortified compound! Towers with guns, snipers, twenty-five foot walls—"

"Can't just knock on the door and ask for Simone, can we?"

Carson wasn't amused. He reached around and grabbed for something behind his back. "Flair? You've seen the Star Channels, right?"

"Yeah," Flair said. "Those crystal beams we travel on. They took us to Jump Point."

"Exactly." Carson pulled a slender silver pistol from his waist and slapped it into Flair's hand. "This is a Channel Gun, in case you need to make one. Here, let me show you."

He guided Flair's hand on a small sliding door and opened a small chamber at the top. "One crystal at a time, make sure it ain't too big. Fingernail size should do the trick." He clicked the chamber closed. "Then you just aim and fire. Can shoot about a hundred yards—"

Maylock threw the van door open. "Time's up, Dillinger!"

"Thirty seconds!" Carson yelled. He slapped a dirty rabbit's foot keychain into Aiden's hand. "Go to Nefflin. If he can't talk sense into you, he'll fly you to the Montecito airstrip. Under the tower is a storage shed. Open that and there's a tunnel that leads into the compound."

Aiden nodded. "Got it. Thanks."

"And don't let the name fool you," Carson said. "El Sereno ain't peaceful at all. In fact, it would actually be a great idea to get to Gloria first."

"Gloria?" Flair shot back. "I'm not going over there for her! I'm going for Simone, and God help Gloria if she gets in my way!"

Carson laughed. "Do me a favor, sister. Don't take any chances with Gloria."

"Why?" Flair said tetchily. "Don't want me bruising up your little girlfriend?"

Carson was taken aback by Flair's attitude, but smiled and reached his hand to Flair's chin.

"Just can't lose anymore Johnsons this year," he said softly, tugging her chin.

Flair's pale cheeks reddened and she smiled, watching Carson march off to the black van. Aiden glared in Carson's direction, then looked at Flair.

"He basically said Gloria would kick your ass, so what are you smiling for?"

Five minutes later, the black van departed, but not before an apparent escape attempt by Edison. However, as it turned out, Carson had told Edison what Aiden and Flair were doing, and Edison wanted to return the Ruijen Staff to Aiden.

"These guys'll just take it from me anyway," Edison said before being dragged back to the van by the large men in dashikis. "Besides, I've been to Montecito. You'll need this!"

As Aiden and Flair were clueless on how to get back to Paris, much less find Charles De Gaulle airport, they abandoned Carson's truck and phoned Rainier. The trip back to Paris was tense and quiet. Neither Aiden nor Flair had spoken since leaving the Knight's End. By the look on Flair's face, Aiden knew she was focused on Simone, but for him, his mind was swimming in many different directions, not the least of which was what John Brown had told him.

It all made sense now, Aiden thought. His memories were things lost inside of his puzzle box of a mind, and had been triggered by these recent events. He understood that, but how was he supposed to find the Song of Solomon in his memories? He hadn't heard of it until Jonas told him about it, and determining where his father might have hidden it was impossible. He settled into his seat as Rainier took the road leading to Paris.

"Truly sorry about Simone," Rainier said. "Gloria is obsessed. Zat girl is bad news."

"Why did she go to El Sereno, Rainier?" Aiden asked. "What's over there?"

Rainier took a moment before answering. "Well, Mackleford and Cessano *are* partners, Cessano makes drugs and Gloria is looking for zee cure, no?" He waved a hand and shrugged. "As simple as zat, maybe. But, we also know *some-zing* else. Cessano is smitten with Gloria. He'll protect her."

"He'll fail," Flair murmured.

"Flair, if I may make a suggestion," Rainier said, looking at Flair in the rear view mirror, "focus on Simone, do not tangle with Gloria. That girl can get nasty."

Simone gazed at fluffy white clouds as they passed her window. The sun was settling on the horizon and shone on Gloria's face, who was snoring three seats ahead of her. Simone was desperate to find a way to help Aiden and Flair locate her, but *how*? She didn't know where she was going, and it wasn't like she could leave breadcrumbs. As she looked around the plush interior of the plane's cabin for some clue that might help her, she spotted a pair of goggling eyes peering from behind the long couch in front of her. It was one of Gloria's brothers.

"Hi!" she gasped, sitting up. The brother ducked and slid behind the couch. Simone smiled at him; in the sunlight, he didn't look as scary as he did that night in East Town. In fact, there was something wholesome about him. He peeked again at Simone, who sat as still as she could. Then, she heard him speak.

"Please don't scream. That was very painful earlier."

Simone nodded. "Okay," she whispered. "I'm sorry."

"Your name is Ramona?" asked the brother. His voice had a rattling, squishy sound, but Simone made out what he was saying very clearly.

"No, it's Simone, Simone Johnson," she said. "You don't have to hide. I won't scream anymore, promise. What's your name?"

The brother considered Simone for a moment. Then with one quick, fluid movement, he set his long fingered hand on the back of the couch, sprang up and catapulted himself over it. He plopped on the seat, Indian style, his elbows on his knees, gazing at Simone.

"Yes, I thought your name sounded similar to mine. I'm Ramon Gannares. How old are you, Simone?"

"Um…eleven. I'll turn twelve this March."

"Twelve. That's how old I was when Mackleford did this to us."

"That means," she whispered, drawing with her fingers in the air, "you're thirty-three years old. Aiden had said you were attacked twenty-one years ago, that's how I know. But you still look like a kid. You know, except for the—" She broke off, feeling guilty and embarrassed.

Ramon smiled. *"It's okay, I know I look terrible. You don't look too bad though."*

Simone giggled loudly, causing Gloria to stir in the seat in front of her. Apparently, neither Simone nor Ramon wanted Gloria awake as they both fell silent until she had settled in her chair and started snoring again.

"I don't want to wake my sister. I've wanted to talk to you alone, ever since we were at Margaret's. What has happened to you is fascinating. You can hear us and still speak in your own voice. That's rare for a Purified person."

"It is? But why? I don't understand."

"Purification has disabled me and my brothers' ability to speak properly, but we can still communicate with some who are Purified. Many Purified are like us. You heard us that night at Margaret's home, remember?"

"Yes," Simone said, "but how?"

"Purification opened the extra sensory part of your brain, the part most people cannot use. You have the ability to hear words that form in the mind. You can think of it like reading minds in a way."

"But...but I can't read minds. I don't know what you're thinking about."

Ramon shook his head. *"Were you able to understand people in Paris? Think hard."*

Simone sat back and thought, staring at Ramon, remembering the women from the hotel. She assumed they had been speaking English and Flair wasn't paying attention.

"I was. I could understand these two ladies, but Flair said she thought I'd learned French or something. But I don't know French. I didn't understand the people on television."

"Because you're hearing what their mind is expressing, even if you cannot understand the language. The same way you can hear me and my brothers, although we cannot speak."

"How do you know all of this?"

"Trial and error, learning from others. There are Purified people all over the world. Not members of the Dominion, just sad cases like us, failed experiments. Our sister has dragged us from one side of the planet to the other looking for the cure. We have met so many and learned much about Purification, but much of it is unnecessary. There's nothing she can do."

"You said I could be cured," Simone said. "But one of your brothers said I couldn't."

"You can, yes," Ramon said. *"It's a theory of mine. It's your skin, it flakes away. It isn't solid like ours. Notice our skin doesn't flake. That shows Purity isn't part of you yet, Simone. It's trying to escape your body. But you're running out of time. Have you noticed your ankle? Your brother told Gloria it had been broken."*

Simone looked at her leg and gasped. Her ankle, which had been horribly twisted and swollen, looked perfect.

"It's better!" Simone whispered. "But I don't get it."

"There are six stages of Purification. In the third stage, the entire skeletal system is transformed and strengthened. It's healed the broken bones in your ankle, but in a few days you'll complete the sixth stage. Purity will take hold permanently."

Simone looked worriedly at the pale, flaking skin on her arms.

"Don't worry about it," Ramon said, leaning back on the couch. *"This may be one time that my sister is right. For your cure, that is."*

Simone and Ramon talked for another half hour about their misadventures in Paris before Gloria stirred awake after a rough bout of turbulence. Ramon hid behind the couch as Gloria stumbled into the bathroom. He waved goodbye to Simone and slipped back into the cockpit.

Minutes later, Gloria exited the bathroom and entered the cockpit, speaking on the radio, arranging transportation to a city called Montecito. Ramon was right. Simone could tell Gloria was speaking in Spanish and understood her perfectly, but not the man over the radio.

"Raul, we're landing in Cordoba," Gloria said, pointing to a map in front of him. "There is a closed runway here, a little beat up, but that shouldn't be any problem, right?"

Raul grunted at her, waving her away like an annoying fly and focused back on the reddening sky as the sun was setting.

"We'll be landing in a few, Simmy," Gloria said, returning to the cabin and sitting on the couch Ramon had previously occupied. "I know you are anxious to get on the ground. We've been flying almost a whole day."

Simone said nothing, staring out of the window. Gloria looked annoyed.

"Well, you don't have to talk to me, that's fine," Gloria snarled. "But when it's over and you're cured, you'll thank me."

"What if you're wrong about the cure?"

"I'm not wrong! Do you think I would take you from your family if I wasn't positive? This is the closest I've ever been to getting it. I just need you to cooperate. Okay?"

"Like I have a choice," Simone muttered. She went silent again, leaned back in her seat and closed her eyes. Gloria's face soured as she rose and returned to the cockpit, slamming the door behind her.

Flair stood on a short runway at Charles de Gaulle airport, watching large jumbo jets scream off into the gloomy gray of an overcast Parisian afternoon. Marcus Nefflin and Rainier exited a hangar, pointing to something on a map with an official-looking man in a green and gray uniform. The man saluted them as he left, which made Nefflin and Rainier break out in laughter as they walked over to Flair.

"Gloria stopped in Sierra Leone," Nefflin said. "Refueled. They're flyin' a Falconer 8800, twin-engine jet, business class. Ain't pinned down where she's stoppin' next, but she'll be on the ground in Argentina inside o' five hours."

Aiden, meanwhile, was settled in aboard Nefflin's plane. Exhausted and wanting nothing more than to lie back and sleep, he was bothered, and it wasn't about Simone, or his memories.

In his own head, he was admonishing himself—*Aiden, think about your sister and not that stupid relic!* But he couldn't help the historian in him. Just knowing that seven months ago, his father had been carrying a three thousand year old artifact had his heart racing. He wanted to see it, hold it, feeling intrigued and ashamed at the same time.

Aiden slept almost the entire flight to Argentina, not even waking when the plane landed for refueling, but the journey wasn't as restful as he had hoped. When he closed his eyes, he saw visions of Simone as an infant, on her first day at school, at cheerleading competitions, at his mother's funeral. When he tried to ignore them, his dreaming became worse. In Aiden's last dream, he awoke on the floor in front of the fireplace, attempting to push the Cornerstone Key back into its brick, hoping by doing so, this would all go away.

But behind him, Aiden had the feeling of being watched. He turned slowly, and with a jolt, saw a frightening old man with leathery skin, covered in dark tattoos across his arms and chest watching him. Trembling and trying to remember how the man got there, he realized the old man was speaking to someone else in shadows. A familiar voice spoke out.

"He won't remember until it is time to remember."

It was his father's voice.

He turned, staring past the old man, looking for his father, who was nowhere to be found.

"How is this possible?" the old man's withered voice asked.

"He and I share a unique gift," his father said. "But don't help him until he is ready. Make sure he is worthy."

Aiden stared into the old man's eyes, frightened. The old man moved in closer.

"KNOCK IT OFF!" Flair screamed, and suddenly the old man and the voices were gone, replaced by blinding white light. Aiden felt something was pinching him extremely hard.

"OW!" Aiden shouted, grabbing for his leg. "What are you doing?"

Flair was seated in front of Aiden, throwing a blanket over her head.

"You keep kicking my chair," Flair said, incensed. "You're dreaming, dumbbell."

Aiden shot a look over his shoulder. White sunlight blinded him.

"It's still day time?" Aiden slurred. "Thought we would've been further along by now."

"We *are* further along," Flair yawned. "You've been sleeping since we took off, something I'd like to do myself. It's already the next day."

"Already the next day?" Aiden pressed his face against the window, faintly making out a ragged landscape underneath the wispy clouds. Everything was green.

"We're already over South America?"

"Yes," Flair sighed, sitting up, exhausted and irritated. "We've landed and refueled twice. I haven't slept at all. Mr. Nefflin says in another hour we'll be landing in Argentina. He had a rough time when we stopped in Brazil. I'm surprised that didn't wake you. They wouldn't take our papers at first, but he called Margaret and she wired some money to him."

Aiden rubbed his eyes, still looking groggy. "I can't believe I was asleep that long."

"Yeah, you were babbling about some old man. I figured your super brain was telling you something about the Song of Solomon, so I left you alone."

"What was I saying?"

"I dunno," Flair grumbled. "Jibber-jabber. Don't you remember?"

"Kinda," Aiden muttered. "It was…weird. Same old man I told you about, the one I've seen in my memories before, except this time—" Aiden froze, his face brightened, and he sat upright, his eyes fixed onto his sister.

"What's wrong?" Flair asked.

"How long until we land?"

"I don't know. About an hour. Why?"

"Because I think…no, I *know* where Pops hid *the Song of Solomon*."

CHAPTER NINETEEN – EL SERENO

Just before dawn in Montecito, Argentina, an exhausted man was out of his bed, searching his sprawling villa for his cell phone, which had been ringing nonstop for ten minutes. Muttering curse words under his breath, he finally found the phone in his study, quickly answering.

"Whoever this is, this better be important," he croaked.

Mochtier Mackleford's distinguished voice replied. "Excellent! I'm glad you answered, Hector."

"Mackleford? Do you have any idea what time it is?" the groggy man said. "What the devil is this about?"

"I'm modifying our arrangement, Hector. My men are coming tomorrow for the shipment."

Either from sleepiness or confusion, the man didn't immediately answer. "The shipment? What happened? Why the change, Mackleford?"

"There are developing circumstances I can no longer ignore," Mackleford answered. "East Town is active once again."

"East Town?" the sleepy man yawned. "Well, I'm sorry about *your* problems, but *our* agreement doesn't change. The last time you sent your men…"

"That was due to your lack of security," Mackleford finished, "but your cooperation was rewarded. This matter involves the timeline of our venture."

"I don't care," the man grumbled. "Nothing changes."

"That's unfortunate. I was hoping you'd help me with the Johnsons."

"The *Johnsons*?" the man said, suddenly awake and alert. "*What* Johnsons?"

"*Those* Johnsons," Mackleford said, sounding amused. "They've been proving troublesome."

"But you put down Wilbert and Laura."

"Their children, Hector. Their three children, the youngest of which happens to be a *screamer,* who is coming to you now, being escorted by that other *unresolved pain* of yours."

The tired man was silent, but only for a moment. "*She* is coming here? Why?"

"Why does Gloria do anything?" Mackleford said. "But more importantly for you, the older brother and sister won't be far behind."

The tired man fell so quiet he might have hung up. After a minute of silence:

"What do you want?"

"Just fill up my two trucks," Mackleford said, "and make sure the screamer is muzzled and drugged with the strongest sedative you have and send her along. My men will handle it from there. Oh, and the Song of Solomon, should it find its way there, although I don't expect it to. The remaining Johnsons are yours."

"Okay." The tired man was no longer tired, although his voice became a whisper. "Let's make certain we understand each other, Mackleford. And I think we do or you would not have mentioned the Johnson children. We each get what we want, correct?"

"I wouldn't dream of robbing you of your moment, Hector."

Flair stared at Aiden, open-mouthed and astonished. Aiden could tell she had a lot of questions running through her mind and didn't know which one to ask first. Without warning, she erupted into a fountain of babble that would have put Simone to shame.

"Wait, so you *really* know where it is? *Seriously*? So what John Brown said is true, you can remember stuff from a long time ago that Dad told you? That's insane. I thought he was crazy, but if he's serious, why would Dad put you through that? I mean, did he know that you would need to find it one day and—"

Aiden finally reached up to Flair and covered her mouth as he had done to Simone many times. "Relax, *Simmy*. You're gonna talk all the oxygen out of the plane."

Flair moved Aiden's hand away and composed herself. "So, it was this dream? That's how you know?"

"Yes and no. I started figuring it out when we realized Pops lied to Margaret."

"What?" Flair exclaimed in shock. "When did Dad lie to Margaret?"

"We just found out, remember? John said Pops never came to Paris to find Jonas, but that's what Pops told Margaret."

Flair's mouth hung open. "Oh wow, that's right, I forgot about that. But why would Dad lie?"

"Well, it's obvious," Aiden said, "he didn't want Margaret to know about his meeting with John."

"But Margaret wasn't telling Mackleford our every move. Gloria was."

Aiden paused a moment at Flair's last statement, making Flair eye him suspiciously.

"Well, he was worried about Margaret talking to Gloria. No one in the Guild trusts her, right?"

"Right! And that's what I don't get!" Flair stopped speaking, her eyes staring into space. Aiden knew she was imagining doing something violent to Gloria. "She's played us for idiots this whole time, Margaret as the biggest one. Why does Margaret trust her if no one else does?"

"It's not about *trust* for Margaret. She said the *Youngbloods* only came around when they wanted money; they didn't involve the *Old Timers* anymore, right? Margaret used to be important, now everybody's kicked her to the curb."

"Everybody," Flair said with a nod, "except Gloria."

"Bingo. I'll bet you Gloria was at her house every day, cleaning, cooking and picking her brain for information. You heard Rainier, Gloria's the most active Journeyman out there, taking on every assignment, every mission, searching for the Purity cure. Hell, Sonya said the same thing. With Gloria around, Margaret feels important, helping the Guild's most active agent, even though no one trusts her."

"Right, right," Flair whispered. "She didn't know. She just wanted to be useful and Gloria took advantage of it."

"Of course. Helping Gloria kept Margaret in the thick of things, and Gloria got exclusive information. It was a *win–win*."

Flair sighed, shaking her head sadly. "And Margaret told Gloria where Mom and Dad were, and Gloria ran straight to Mackleford—"

Aiden steadied himself, looking Flair directly in the eye. "Look, you ain't gonna like hearing this, sunshine, but I believe Gloria when she says…"

"*HER?*" Flair's voice reverberated around the cabin, cutting Aiden off. "Oh, but of course you believe *her*!" And Flair took on a sycophantic, groveling posture and voice. "Oh, perfect Gloria, my queen! Can I serve tea with you? Can I clean your dishes? Can I kiss your—"

"Look," Aiden said, cutting Flair off, but smirking at her cruel imitation of him, "just because I don't think she sold our parents down the river—"

"In case," Flair shouted, raising her voice above Aiden's, "you haven't been paying attention, Sonya had the evidence and Gloria stole it back from her, dummy!"

"You keep forgetting I can read people," Aiden said, smiling. "Listen it's not…"

"Enough with the *I can read people* crap!" Flair yelled. "I'm not ten anymore, Aiden! She's the reason we're travelling to who knows where to deal with whatever this maniac El Sereno can throw at us! Why don't you *read* that?"

"I know what she's doing with Simmy is rotten, but Gloria didn't lowball Mom and Pops. Not a chance. Either she's being setup, or Mom and Pops messed up."

"Okay," Flair said shakily, "let me get this straight. Mom and Dad, from everything we've learned about them, were the top Journeymen. They hid us from the Dominion without having to go underground. They were the ones Gaston Gumm trusted. They found the Song of Solomon when everybody, including Gumm, failed. But you think they screwed up, and this was just one big, happy accident?"

"Or Gloria's being set up," Aiden said in a steady voice. "It's obvious there's something wrong inside the Guild, Flair. First, Boris O'Reilly had way too much information on Pops and Jonas. John Brown confirmed Jonas wasn't really in hiding and O'Reilly already knew that. If they're supposed to be good, how does O'Reilly know their every move? There's this stupid *Old Timers, Youngbloods* rivalry going on. Too many loose ends to blame anything on one person."

"But what about the tracer thing Sonya had?" Flair argued. "It was in Canterbury Springs and Woodwind, and it could only be used by her."

"Come on Flair, even you have to admit that was too easy. That's what makes it look like a set up. A big piece of evidence like that? How did Sonya even find it? Was it just lying on the ground? There's more to her story than that."

Aiden could tell he was getting through to Flair, but she still looked mutinous. "We're just gonna disagree about your precious little princess. So whatever. Where's the Song?"

Aiden wanted to continue defending Gloria, but backed off. "Fine. Remember the book Pops borrowed from me, the one I found in East Town, *Lionel Vann and the Headhunters*?"

"What about it?"

Aiden took a breath, searching for the right words. "It wasn't the first time Pops had borrowed it." Aiden already knew the answer, the puzzle pieces had clicked a while ago, but explaining it was different.

"So? What does the book have to do with it?"

"The old man in my dream was a headhunter," he said, standing up, pacing the cabin. "And I must have met him once. In the middle of my book, there's a map leading to a village in the heart of the island of Borneo. I thought it was a made-up place, but the map was so detailed, almost like it existed. In the story, it was one of the world's last vestiges of headhunting."

"And you think this place exists?"

"If the old man is real, then maybe so is the village. Pops took the book last summer, just before he went after the Song, which means he had it in mind for something. Anyway, there's one quick way to find out."

Aiden stood and approached the cockpit, with Flair on his heels. Peering in, he saw Nefflin in the pilot's chair, staring blankly ahead with a hazy sort of shimmer surrounding him. Aiden noticed a shiny white crystal hanging around his neck.

"Nefflin? You okay?"

Nefflin looked to Aiden, glassy-eyed. "Me? Yeah, jus' tired is all." He was breathing evenly, his voice was haggard. "Flyin' fer twenty hours really burns ya. The crystal keeps m' wits on." He spun the crystal in his hands, and then brushed his hair out of his eyes robotically. Aiden and Flair exchanged nervous glances.

"But good news, you two," he stammered in a monotone drawl. "Looks like the Falconer landed in Cordoba. Gloria must know someone there. Means the Montecito airport's ours. It's been abandoned for years, 'cept when we've used it."

"You look wiped out, pal," Aiden said. "We're okay, right?"

"'Course," Nefflin cracked. "Do this all the time. White crystal, keeps th' brain on high alert, ya know? Hard t' fall asleep while yer wearin' one."

"Okay, well we have a question for you. Did the Journeymen and the Dominion ever mix it up or anything down in Borneo?"

"Borneo trouble?" Nefflin muttered, his eyes searching. "Journeymen've kicked up dust from one end of the planet to the other."

"But with the Dominion? Any confrontations with them in Borneo?"

Nefflin frowned, seemingly upset at not knowing where the question was going. But then, recollection glinted across his red eyes. "Oh yeah," he said slowly, the words leaking out. "Them bloody headhunters. How could I forget? That was a nasty time for them Goons, I'll tell ya. They got their clocks cleaned on that one."

Aiden and Flair looked at each other. "What do you mean, Mr. Nefflin?" Flair asked.

"The Dominion tried to take over th' whole stinkin' island," Nefflin croaked. "Malaysia, Indonesia, everything, can ya bel'ee that? 'Course, ain't the first time they tried to hi-jack a country, just like Morocco, remember? Lessee, lessee. Borneo was twelve years ago. Your dad got a tip about Dominion scientists requestin' a lab in the South Pacific. Thought they found Purity bubblin' to the surface of a river, so they moved in and tried to push the locals out..."

Nefflin's slow, droopy speech was making Aiden antsy. "Okay, so what happened?"

"Folks wernt too happy with the Dominion's plans for their ancestor's homes," he droned on. "Called up a group o' headhunters still dabbling in that old life. Yer dad got along real good with one o' 'em, can't remember his name though. Anyway...man did they ever do a number on the Goon Squad."

"They took out the big uglies?" Flair said.

"Hell yeah," Nefflin snorted. "Never seen 'em take it in the shorts like that. Gus said they were just off their game. Come t' think of it, that's the last time I saw Gus." Nefflin stopped talking, looking slightly disconsolate, and for a moment he seemed normal, but his glazed stupor returned a second later. "Yep, Mack himself couldn't stop 'em from runnin' out of there, tails between their legs, when they started takin' heads."

"Taking heads?" Flair gasped, covering her mouth.

"Well, what did you expect?" Aiden said, slightly annoyed. "They're headhunters!"

"Couldn't've been one taller than five-foot-five. Took out six, seven Goons a day." A grin broke over Nefflin's face. "Stackin' their heads all on top of their houses like a warnin'. You can imagine, Mackleford was pissed." Nefflin turned, looking at Aiden and Flair. "What's this about anyway?"

But Flair and Aiden were nodding at one another, satisfied.

"Sounds like a place the Goons don't want to visit again," Flair said.

"And a perfect place to stash the Song." Aiden replied. "Especially if Pops was good friends with them."

"What?" Nefflin looked normal again. "You think that Song thang is there?"

"I do. We're going to take a detour there, but after we get Simmy."

Simone and Gloria were being jostled unmercifully in the covered bed of a pickup truck bounding along a bumpy road. Absent from the truck were Gloria's brothers, whom Gloria had left behind on the airplane. Gloria told Simone that Purification wouldn't go over well in El Sereno's compound, as many of the men, including El Sereno, were scared of any contact with Purity.

Simone discovered just how afraid El Sereno's men were. After sitting on the airport tarmac for almost four hours, several men with rifles arrived in a sedan, took one look at Simone, and refused to ride with her. It took another four hours for the truck to arrive, after which, Simone and Gloria settled into the bed of the truck.

"Sounds like your friend is scared of me," Simone said.

"Maybe, but he won't turn you away."

"Why not?"

"Don't worry about it, he won't. It's the one ace I have up my sleeve." Gloria checked the time on her phone. "Inside of two hours, we'll have the cure."

They sat in silence as the truck rolled and bumped along for another half hour before coming to an abrupt stop. The doors slammed and in a moment two men stood at the back of the truck, dressed in military camouflage, cleanly shaven, with pistols aimed.

The smaller of the two was young, no older than twenty, smiling sheepishly at Gloria. The larger man had a number of silver badges glittering across his left shoulder. He also stared at Gloria, but with more of a leer.

"I don't know what this game is, Gloria," the larger man said, removing Simone's wheelchair out of the truck, "but coming here was a mistake. The boss isn't happy."

"You're hired help, Gustavo," Gloria sighed. "Don't worry about it, it's above your pay grade."

"Hired help?" Gustavo tapped one of his shiny badges and said in a boastful tone: "Try new chief of security."

"Congratulations," Gloria scoffed. "But since you admitted you don't know what my game is and you're clearly an idiot, why don't you just shut up, *chief?*"

Gustavo scowled, hearing Simone chuckling from inside the truck. The younger guard struggled to hide the smirk on his face, infuriating Gustavo even more.

"Get them out!" Gustavo ordered, shoving him in the back. "Gag that little one!"

"Gag the little one?" the younger guard repeated. "Why?"

"She's supposed to be gagged! She's a *screamer!*" He pointed to Gloria. "Let's go!"

Gloria glared at Gustavo and began to stand when the other guard raised his pistol a little higher, looking concerned.

"What do you mean she's a *screamer?* What does a screamer do?" He sounded scared.

"They dance the tango!" Gustavo growled, holding out a black bandana. "What do you think? They *scream*, idiot! Just strap her into the wheelchair and tie this around her mouth."

"I'm...I'm not touching her."

"Would you prefer *the Pit?*" Gustavo said. This question appeared to do the trick as the younger guard moved with haste, taking the bandana from Gustavo. "That's better!" Gustavo banged his hand on the truck. "Let's go, Gloria! Let's not keep the boss waiting!"

The younger guard reached nervously into the truck, snatching Simone under her arms and throwing her into the wheelchair. He took up the bandana and yanked it around her mouth.

"She's not a sack of flour, don't treat her that way!" Gloria barked at the guard, who ignored her, quickly and roughly zip-tying Simone's arms to the wheelchair. He was having a difficult time, as Simone kept throwing his hands away until Gustavo aimed his gun at her.

Gloria was incensed. "Can't handle a little girl without pulling a gun on her?" The younger guard paid no attention, wiping his brow with his sleeve and finishing tying Simone down.

"Weapons!" Gustavo barked, shaking a small basket at Gloria. "Let's go, I know you have them. In here!"

Gloria retrieved her golden gloves, four red crystals, and two white crystals from her inside jacket pocket and dropped them in the basket. Her eyes and hair and temporarily shined as she touched them, and Simone once again sensed an enormous surge of energy.

Gustavo secured Gloria's wrists behind her back with a plastic zip-tie, and they set off walking. Simone was wheeled ahead, bumping along the rocky soil for a hundred yards through thick foliage, until they finally arrived at a chain-link fence topped with barbed wire. A large metal gate to their right swung open.

They stepped onto a massive campus, which at first glance, reminded Simone of Aiden's college, Rittmoor University. A string of old brick buildings created the outer boundary of the campus, with taller, more modern buildings in the center. Activity was high throughout: people dressed in suits, medical scrubs and smocks milled around an enormous stone courtyard, walking to and from various buildings. But what stood out to Simone were the dozen or so large, curved towers overlooking over the complex. They were tall, thin, and daunting. Silhouetted against the sky, they looked like the fingers of a giant monster.

Simone turned to Gloria, who had just laughed, wearing a look of mild surprise and amusement. "Made a few changes, haven't you?" Gloria said, staring into one of the watchtowers, where the shadow of a guard paced. "Nice towers."

"Shut up and walk," Gustavo barked.

Gloria grinned. "Cess doesn't need all this extra security. Why the redecorating job?"

"Probably above my pay grade," Gustavo sneered. He steered them into what appeared to be a small storage shed and slammed the door behind them.

Gloria fumbled around for a light switch, found it, and instantly the room was saturated in intense, neon blue. She surveyed the room, which was empty except for a half-dozen crates scattered around the room. She used the sharp edge of one of the crates to break her zip-tie around her hands, then quickly approached Simone, removing the gag from her mouth.

"So sorry Simone, I had no idea, I mean I did tell them you were Purified, but I never told them about the Banshee. They should have sent someone used to handling..." She cut her apology off. "Are you okay?"

"Absolutely, Gloria!" Simone sniped. "I'm doing fantastic!"

Gloria sat down on a crate, her eyebrows wrinkled in deep confusion. "Someone told them we were coming here," she muttered. "Someone who knew about the Banshee. But who? Mackleford doesn't know I'm here. Does he?"

Simone gazed around the room, shielding her eyes from the intense blue lighting. "What is this room? And why are the lights blue?" Simone asked.

"I, I don't know, not sure," Gloria said, staring into space. Simone slumped in the wheelchair. She was angry with Gloria, but a coherent and focused Gloria was better than this.

After hours of waiting, the door banged open and three men with rifles beckoned them. Gloria wheeled Simone outside, and it took Simone a moment to adjust her eyes. It was nighttime; darkness and silence had fallen over the campus. It was no longer bustling; the people in suits and medical clothing were gone, replaced by an entirely different sort.

Loitering throughout the compound were dozens of clean-cut, but rugged men in black and gold uniforms, and every eye was on Simone, staring at her as Gloria pushed her along. Simone had been gawked at when she was in Paris, but for her, this felt worse. In Paris, people looked at her with a mix of confusion and sympathy. But these men, these military men in the compound, were clearly terrified.

They reached a three-story brick building standing against the thick jungle, with a long porch in the front. The guards led Simone and Gloria up a set of steps towards the porch as there arose buzz of chatter and excitement. From the left of the building, walking up a dirt path that led into the jungle came a dozen guards supporting a fifty-foot long wooden platform. Four more men followed, each controlling a pair of vicious dogs, restrained by chains and muzzles. Behind them were two more men dragging two guards dressed in tattered, bloody uniforms. Simone recognized them.

"Hey Gloria look, they're dragging that security guy and his little buddy." Then, realizing it, she gasped. "Oh, wow..."

The two men had been mutilated, and it was clear what had happened. Simone was at a loss for words. She gulped, watching the dogs as their handlers took them into the rows of buildings and out of sight.

The bodies of the men were left at the foot of the building, and a final group of men approached, led by a tall, slender man dressed in black. He was middle aged and quite handsome with a perfectly trimmed mustache peppered with gray, and unusually bright blue eyes. But as Gloria looked at him, he gave a brief appearance of a wounded animal. The look quickly faded as he drew a deep, bracing breath.

"They're not dead, my dear," the tall man said in a quiet, constrained voice. He climbed the steps of the porch, never taking his eyes from Gloria. "I called them off so Gustavo and Miguel could fully enjoy their punishment."

"Punishment?" Gloria shouted. "Why?"

"I told my men to never admit you again," he said, nodding to Gustavo. "He claims to have forgotten as it was so long ago. But I never forget. And to top it off, he brought this Purified *thing* into my camp."

"But, I...You *knew* we were coming! And she's not a *thing,* Cess, she's—"

"Do *not* call me by that name, Miss Gannares!" he said coldly. "You no longer have that privilege."

"Fine then, *El Sereno!*" she replied angrily, and he looked wounded once again. "She's not a *thing,* so I'll appreciate it if you don't call her that!"

El Sereno bristled, but recovered, looking at Simone, who was still staring at the bloodied men with disgust. He sat in a nearby wicker lounge chair and reclined into its cushions.

"Not as bad as your brothers, is she?" El Sereno remarked, although indifferently. "I suppose you want the *cure.* You have to know by now that no cure has ever existed and quite possibly never will."

"Don't play me, Cess," Gloria said. "We both know what's going on here. You can't hide anything from me, so let's cut to it. I want the cure. I'll do whatever it takes to get it."

El Sereno chuckled, gazing at Gloria, stroking his shaven chin, lost in a moment. He was certainly enamored. He looked back to Simone to break the spell.

"Offering yourself, Gloria?"

"I don't think you'd take me back even if I was."

"No," El Sereno muttered, with a wistful longing in his eyes. "No, I would not. Even if I was so gullible to trust you again, I have remarried. Jessica, you remember?"

"Oh yeah, Jessica. She's quite a little teakettle. Bet your hands are full with her." Gloria moved over behind Simone, stroking her hair. "Well I have something better than Jessica or me for that matter."

El Sereno fixed his eyes on Simone again. Simone wasn't sure what was going on, but she knew it wasn't good.

"Who is she?"

"Simone. *Johnson.*"

"Really?" El Sereno said with a long, icy drawl, looking at Simone with frightening delight.

"Her brother and sister are on their way after they get the Song of Solomon. They'll be looking to trade the Song for their sister. A *cured* sister."

El Sereno spoke, not taking his eyes off of Simone. "The Song of Solomon has been missing for months, Mackleford himself can't find it. They know where it is?"

"Of course they do. Aiden won't tell me, but for his sister, he'll bring it."

"Aiden, is it?" El Sereno whispered, and as Simone looked at El Sereno repeat her brother's name, she saw his eyes gleaming eagerly. "And what if he doesn't bring it?"

"Well, I'm sure he's coming for his sister back just the same."

"And you think he'll come *here*? Does he know who I am?"

"I'm sure he has been told everything he needs to know," Gloria said. "Carson is helping them. You remember Carson, don't you?"

The wicker lounge chair creaked as El Sereno got to his feet, walking the length of the long porch, slow and measured and alone. He returned to the group, exhaling with a deep sigh. "You've done well, Gloria. But you've done it for a cure that doesn't exist. Why don't you tell me what you are really after?"

"Spare me your lies, Cess," Gloria said. "I know what goes on here. I've been to Colorado. I've seen the shipments myself, what goes in and out. And I have it on good authority that you just shipped crates of it to Mackleford."

"Crates of what?" El Sereno laughed. "Those orchids Mackleford wants to develop?"

"Orchids?"

"Yemen orchids. Remember? We picked them, during that—" El Sereno paused, grimacing, as if recalling something painful. " — that unfortunate business in Morocco."

"My contact has seen their journals!" Gloria shouted. "Their logs! Your shipments were called *the cure*, Cess!"

"I believe Mackleford uses the flower as a part of his experiments to improve deformities for his Goons. A *cure* in a manner of speaking, sure, but for Purity?" He shook his head.

Gloria stared at El Sereno, her mouth slackening.

"Please be sensible, Gloria," he said. "Mackleford guards the secrets of Purity, it is the backbone of the Dominion, even his very life. Cure it? My God, it would destroy him if a cure were ever discovered! If I were producing the cure here, wouldn't I use it against him? You know me better than that."

Gloria turned away. "But, it has to be here, and my brothers need it, they don't deserve—" Emotions overcame Gloria. Simone watched her as she fell apart, trembling, unable to speak.

"They are lost, my sweet," El Sereno said, soothingly, stroking the hair out of her face. "But, come Gloria, no more tears. It disgusts me as well, but Mackleford has won. Purification is upon us and the world is at the mercy of its own destiny. We must accept and prepare for the inevitable. Rodolfo, Ernesto, take them and feed them, show them kindness. I have one final piece of unfinished business to conduct, and then, it will be time for El Sereno to retire."

The Cessna touched down on an uneven runway as darkness began to creep upon the jungle. Aiden was first off the plane, glancing around at his surroundings. The airport was nothing but a narrow strip of concrete with a small tower teetering to one side, looking as if it could collapse at any moment. The storage shed and access tunnel would be just below it.

Flair, full of passionate energy, bounded off the plane after Aiden. "Let's move, bro. I wanna talk to Gloria. Mr. Nefflin, you coming?"

"I'm comin', I'm comin'!" Nefflin yelled, standing at the door of the sounding annoyed. "You try flyin' for twenty-two hours straight and see if yer just ready and rarin' to go!" Nefflin tucked his white crystal inside a pouch, shoved the pouch inside his boot, and straightened up. The exhaustion on his face couldn't be more evident.

"Maybe we should wait until morning," Aiden said, "when we've all rested."

"Nah," Nefflin grunted. "Night's the best time to attack. Cover o' darkness, everyone's sleepin'. The element o' surprise."

"What do you mean *attack*?" Aiden said. "We ain't getting into a gunfight with a compound full of desperadoes. Simmy's in there!"

"Well what didya think we were gonna do? Tiptoe in, get your sister and stroll out the front gate? This is El Sereno we're talkin' about."

"That's exactly what we're doing," Aiden said. "I'm done throwing caution to the wind. We need a plan that doesn't involve waking up half of Argentina. We're not soldiers, Nefflin."

"So what's your master plan then, Johnson?" Nefflin sneered. "No, wait, Flair, let's hear 'im out." Nefflin held up his hand to Flair who had opened her mouth to protest.

Aiden looked uncertain. He didn't actually have a plan. "Well, we could go in quiet, scout it out, look around, then—"

"Pokin' around is the fastest way to get caught!" Nefflin protested. "They got cameras, patrols, and big ol' watchtowers surroundin' the joint—"

"And that's why we take it slow. We go in there with some kind of hare-brained attack plan, they might take this thing to another level. I'm going to assume everything you said about El Sereno is true. Ruthless, cold-blooded, bad to the bone, right? We go in there crystals blazing, Simmy's as good as dead."

Aiden looked at Flair and Flair nodded in agreement. Nefflin wasn't as agreeable.

"Well, ain't how we used ta do things, but what the 'ell do I know? I just fly planes." Nefflin pulled a long thin metal baton from his waist.

"What's that?" Flair said.

"'Lectric baton. We'll need it in that tunnel. For them pesky black widders. They love that tunnel."

"The pesky black *what*?" Flair asked.

CHAPTER TWENTY – *"SUBTERRANEO"*

It was a sauna: dark, dirty, and claustrophobic and Aiden's sweaty clothes were glued to his skin. Legs heavy with fatigue, he marched on, Nefflin ahead zapping bugs and Flair behind complaining every step of the way.

"Quit whining, Flair," Aiden said. "This isn't as bad as the tunnel under the Grand Garden, and the one at Quorum was way worse than that, although there weren't any bugs in there, compared to this one, which is full of 'em."

"I've been avoiding these tunnels so far. Of course the one I can't is full of bugs."

The walk took over an hour, and along the way, Nefflin zapped anything that moved. It was exhausting work inching along, and their backs pained from hunching under the low ceiling. The air was hot and suffocating as Nefflin had been eliminating hordes of insects with the electric baton, leaving an acrid stench in the air.

"Took us a year to dig this damn tunnel," Nefflin said as he killed another large horde of insects. "Forgot how long it was, but we're almost there. Just a few more feet."

A few more feet seemed too much for Aiden as his lungs were begging for fresh air, but at last, the tunnel began to climb. Nefflin grabbed the white crystal from his boot, placing it on the chain around his neck. His body glowed white, which was especially intense in the dark tunnel.

They reached an overhead beam running left to right, and like a man twenty years younger, Nefflin grabbed it and hoisted himself to a landing just above, and turned to help Aiden and Flair.

No longer hunched, the three stood on a wooden floor that expanded ahead into darkness. Nefflin pressed a finger to his mouth.

"We're here," he whispered. "Right underneath the compound. Glad they never found the tunnel."

"What's above us?" Aiden asked.

"Used ta be barracks." Nefflin said. "No telling what's up there now."

"What?" Aiden whispered. "You snuck in through the *barracks*? Why weren't you ever caught?"

"Had folks on the inside, o' course," Nefflin said. "Wilbert's plan."

"Well, we don't have folks on the inside now, so what if there's guys sleeping up there?"

"Well this ain't no easy shin-dig, son!" Nefflin grabbed his white crystal, shaking it in Aiden's face. "That's why I got this, so I can hear what's goin' on. Relax. I'll go ahead, take a peek. If it looks dangerous," Nefflin broke off, looking unsure. "Well, we'll try an' find another way. Or maybe it is a smasher an' grabber like I said. Wouldn't be so bad either, Martinez said yer sister's pretty handy. If she's half as good as yer mom, we're golden."

Flair grinned. "You want a red crystal, Mr. Nefflin? I've got a whole bag of them."

"Nah, Flair, this zapper'll be enough. 'Sides, those reds give me headaches."

Nefflin was nimble and light on his feet as he dashed ahead, and his bright aura illuminated his surroundings: a smooth wood floor in what looked like a hallway, with gray cement walls and ceiling. At the end of the hall, a thin rope dangled from the ceiling.

Nefflin grabbed a metal case, placed it under the rope and climbed on top. His head disappeared into the ceiling and Aiden deduced from a creak that Nefflin was climbing up through a trap door.

Suddenly there was a loud crash, and Nefflin's legs flew up into the ceiling and out of sight. Aiden pulled Flair down and slipped back into the dirt tunnel. He held her there as they heard bangs and zaps of electricity.

"They have him!" Flair shouted.

"Shhh! Quiet!" Aiden whispered, pulling her further down the tunnel.

"We have to help him!" Flair said.

"Wait!" At once, flashlight beams danced along the cement walls, and Aiden and Flair pressed their backs flat against the tunnel wall, listening. There were sounds of scuffling above them, shouting, a door slam, and rapid footsteps.

"Can't you hear what's going on?" Aiden said. "Get your white…"

Flair plunged into the pouch, retrieving a white crystal, sliding it into the back of her glove as Carson had done.

The noise above continued. Flair's aura was blinding bright as she stared at the ceiling, following the action above with her eyes.

"I hear them talking, but it's all Spanish, I can't under...oh, they're chasing him!" She pointed back down the tunnel, opposite from the trap door. "Yeah, they are chasing him over there...Ooooh! They're shooting!"

Aiden heard muffled gunfire above and moved quickly. He grabbed the beam and hoisted himself to the wooden floor above them. He turned to help Flair up, but much like Nefflin, Flair sprang up easily onto the wooden floor. They both ran to the end of the hallway and stared up at the trap door, which was open.

"Hear anyone up there?" Aiden asked

"It sounds like..." She frowned, looking utterly confused. "Like scratching".

"People? Breathing? Voices?"

Flair listened again, and after a moment, she shook her head. "Okay, let's go." Aiden leapt and grabbed the edges of the opening with both hands and pulled himself upwards.

He was standing in a long, narrow room, no longer a barracks, but an office. Tall cabinets and stacks of boxes hid the walls and a row of cubicles was stationed in the center. At the far end of the room stood a large desk. Aiden ran over to it as Flair entered into the room from below.

The desk was littered with papers, files, and strangely enough, record album covers. Aiden grabbed the closest one, a copy of Frank Sinatra's *Strangers in the Night,* and saw what was making the scratching sound: an old phonograph sitting on a small table in the corner. The needle was skipping at the end of the record. Aiden turned back to the desk.

"Look for anything about Simmy or Gloria," he said. "And keep your ears open, in case they come back."

"What about Mr. Nefflin?"

"He's a big boy. Let's do what we came to do, but *listen* for him."

"That would be a lot easier if that stupid scratching would stop."

Aiden turned around and switched off the phonograph, then froze, gazing at the revolving record as it finished spinning.

"What is it?" Flair said.

"*Strangers in the Night?*" Aiden muttered to himself. "Strangers in the Night, Flair. He knew we were coming."

"What makes you say that?" Flair said, only half paying attention to Aiden. She was examining a set of blueprints over the clutter on the desk. "Hey bro, take a look at this."

Flair slid the blueprints over to Aiden. It was a layout of the entire compound, and the scale of the buildings showed how large the compound was. Flair drew her finger over dotted lines on the diagram that connected to various parts of the facility, pointing to one word written over and over: *subterraneo.*

"I'd bet this is the whole campus," Flair said confidently. "And I know this word means *underground,* and I'm betting these are underground tunnels."

Aiden stared at the blueprint for a long time until, finally, looking around the room, he pointed to a small rectangle in the corner of the compound.

"Here's where we are," Aiden said. "See, here's the tunnel we used, and look." He pointed to a word indicated by arrows that directed off the page—*alarma.* "There's an alarm in that tunnel. I bet we tripped it. They were ready for us."

"Mr. Nefflin didn't know," Flair moaned. "I hope he's okay."

Aiden looked grim. "From what Carson said, El Sereno's the type of guy that's going to find out what you came for first. Let's hope so, because I don't know how to fly a plane."

"Right," Flair said, punching Aiden in his shoulder, "*and* we don't want Mr. Nefflin dead, jerk! What's this?"

One of the connected passageways had an squiggly line drawn through it in red ink, heading to a room on the opposite side of the facility. Aiden looked around on the desk and found an uncapped red ink pen.

"Someone just drew this. It's probably where they took Simmy. Carson said they'd be scared of Purification. They probably stuck her down in here to keep her away from—"

"Wait," Flair grabbed Aiden's arm, cutting him off. "Footsteps." She straightened up, pointing at the door. "Straight ahead, their voices are getting closer."

Aiden glanced around the room, looking for an escape, and nodded to a nearby window above a metal cabinet. They quickly moved towards it, climbing onto the cabinet, and Aiden tried easing the window open quietly, but an ear wrenching — *CREEEEAK!*— sounded instead.

"Not good," Flair hissed.

The door burst open and a dozen men in camouflage flooded the office. They stared at Aiden and Flair, looking stunned and uncertain. Finally one man pointed and shouted, aiming a pistol.

Flair clenched her hands into fists, creating two bright red translucent shields, repelling gunfire away from them. With each deflected bullet however, the red shields flickered.

"Hurry bro! These shields ain't gonna hold!"

Aiden hopped out of the window, landing on a stack of green crates piled high against the outer wall. He reached back inside for Flair, watching her shield herself with one glove and rip off powerful blasts with the other. The guards at the doorway took cover, allowing her to escape through the window. Aiden pulled Flair onto the crates and they climbed to the roof of the building.

"We gotta move before they surround us," Aiden said. "That building leads to those underground access tunnels you saw." He pointed at a white building with a slanted roof about fifty yards away.

Flair nodded to Aiden. "Ok. I'll handle them, you go."

"What do you mean—" Aiden began, but Flair had already taken off across the top of the roof and disappeared over the side. Aiden shook his head with a smile as he heard men shouting and Flair's blasts hitting their targets. Steeling himself for the twelve-foot drop to the ground below, he leapt, crashed, and rolled to his feet. He was running flat out, seeing bright flashes of red illuminating the buildings in front of him.

Aiden reached the slanted roof building, twisted the doorknob but found it locked. He lowered his shoulder, rammed it into the door again and again until the door flew open.

He stumbled into the room, which looked to be a storage shed, filled with large planting pots, bags of soil, and gardening tools. Aiden turned back to yell for Flair, but what he saw had words failing him.

He was watching his sister whirling through the air like a crimson blur, firing crystal blasts, deflecting gunfire, and sending many of the guards on the run. She finished the last of the armed men with a powerful headshot, causing the man to somersault into the air and crash face first into the ground. She backpedalled into the room and Aiden slammed the door behind her.

Aiden was stunned. "Did you just kill that guy?"

"No," Flair said. "I don't think so."

"But I just saw—"

"I'll tell you in a second. How do we get into the tunnels?"

Aiden had forgotten all about the tunnels while watching Flair. They searched behind the tools and bags of soil, tossing pots aside until Aiden found a tiny seam in the wall behind a metal rack. Throwing the rack to the floor, Aiden pulled a metal handle protruding from the wall and opened a door. The space behind it was four feet in height, and Aiden and Flair ducked into it, closing the door behind them.

Flair followed Aiden down a narrow staircase and into a sweltering passageway, with floors and walls of metal.

"So those guys—"

"They were still moving after they fell," Flair panted. "Couple of 'em tried to get up, had to put them back down. Jonas said up close and personal, crystal shots can kill, but from a distance, it's like they just took a punch from Mike Tyson."

Aiden patted her on the back. "Well, that was impressive, sunshine. How'd you get so good so fast?" Flair returned an embarrassed smile to her brother, and Aiden knew why. He rarely complimented Flair on anything.

"Well, Carson was right. These gloves really help. What's it called when you shoot a gun and your arm flies backwards?"

"Recoil?"

"Yeah. Without the gloves, my arm kept doing that. It was starting to hurt. But these gloves," she gazed at them admiringly, as if they were a long-lost friend, "I don't know, seems like it doesn't happen as much. I think it's the leather. Although I wish they were hot pink so they'd match my boots."

They jogged on, and within a minute, arrived at a fork in the passage. There were three doors lined up in front of them, with hallways continuing to the left and right into total darkness.

"Which way?" she said.

"It's right at the third fork," Aiden said. "But here, we go left."

"You sure?"

"Yeah, I'm sure," Aiden replied. He wiped sweat from his forehead as he gazed down the dark tunnel. "The same way you can use those gloves, I can see that map. Photographic memory like John Brown said. Come on, let's go."

They crossed the fork to their left, jogging down the dark passageway.

"*ALIVE!* I said after they tripped the alarm! *I want them ALIVE!*"

"It wasn't me, boss! I didn't shoot! I heard you!"

Simone and Gloria were seated at a small folding table in an empty room in front of two untouched plates of grilled steak fajitas. Gloria had appeared to be lost in a distant gaze, every so often murmuring apologies to her brothers' names. But the shouting and noise seemed to have snapped her out of stupor. El Sereno was screaming at the top of his lungs, and from the sound of it, furniture and other items were being thrown and smashed in the next room.

At once, there was the unmistakable crack of a gunshot, a howl of agony, and a door slamming. Simone's pale fingers covered her mouth as, second later, the door burst open with El Sereno storming in, wiping blood off of his hands.

"Good help is hard to come by," he growled. "As is the truth."

Gloria didn't say a word. She stared between El Sereno and two men posted at the doorway, who were shaking and pale with fear.

"I must hand it to them," El Sereno said with trembling lips. "Whether it's Mackleford or the Guild, they all know my weakness. *You.* I almost believed *YOU!*" El Sereno bellowed, and with one swing of his arm, the table between Simone and Gloria flew across the room, smashing into a wall.

"I have no idea what you're talking about, Cess!" Gloria said with defiance, her voice growing as loud as El Sereno's. "I'm playing this straight! I only want the cure!"

"I should have realized you were lying," El Sereno said softly. "It was so obvious. You gave yourself and the child far too easy. But it doesn't matter. None of it matters now."

"What do you mean?" Gloria said.

"Mackleford's Goons have arrived with their abominations. I just hope they don't find Aiden. I want to deal with him in my own way."

"Aiden?" Gloria choked. Her face was chalk white.

"Aiden is here?" Simone whimpered.

"Yes," he said, looking at Simone curiously. "What do you think, child? Give him a taste of my hospitality? Let's see the kind of man your brother is, yes, and I'll show him the kind of man I am." And he turned his back on them, yelling his two guards. "Gunnar! Take these two from my sight. Give them *suitable* accommodations until I can decide what to do with them. Octavio! Please introduce Mr. Johnson and his darling sister to the dogs!"

Aiden and Flair pushed ahead, sweat saturating their clothes. Aiden directed them at each turn, with Flair's aura lighting the way. They had walked for nearly ten minutes when they stopped, hearing sounds above them: people running, barking instructions in Spanish, and vehicles starting.

"What's going on up there?" Flair said, an ominous shiver running through her.

Behind of them, they heard slams, bangs, doors opening and shutting, more voices. This time, however, the voices echoed inside the tunnel.

"Let's keep moving," he said, turning back around and grabbing Flair's arm. They broke into a trot, but after a few feet, there was a loud thud and the metal walls shuddered. Something extremely heavy had hit the tunnel floor in the blackness ahead. There were two more thuds, and Flair gloved hand gripped Aiden's arm, digging crystals into his skin.

"You hear that?" she gasped in his ear.

"Ow!" he said, shaking off Flair's vice like hold. "That loud crash that could have woke the dead? Of course—"

"No, it's something else," she whispered. "Breathing. Scary breathing."

"Nothing you can't handle, right sis?" Aiden said, clapping her on the shoulder.

Flair stared at him, half-incensed, half scared. "I don't know what it is! It stinks though, smells like seaweed."

"We've gotta be close to that second fork," Aiden said. "The tunnel starts curving before you hit it, and we're in that curve right now."

Flair wasn't listening; she was trembling "Seaweed? Just like it was at—" And then realization came over her, and her eyes widened. "Oh crap!"

Now Aiden smelled it too. Whatever the smell was coming from, it was very close. Aiden and Flair peered ahead, trying to detect movement in the darkness as they heard an unnerving scratching, scraping noise echoing everywhere.

"They're just around the corner," Flair whispered, pointing ahead.

"Let's go back," Aiden said, turning promptly and marching up the tunnel. "We'll hide out in those rooms we passed."

They had only walked twenty feet up the passage when Aiden froze. Two enormous white dogs were standing in the glow of Flair's aura, and two more walked next to them, teeth bared, white spittle glistening around their jaws. A half-dozen more pairs of eyes gleamed behind them, and a chorus of growls rumbled through the tunnel like thunder.

"Cordobas," Aiden gulped. "Wow, I thought they were extinct."

"I don't like the way you said *Cordobas*," Flair said. "What are Cordobas?"

"A breed of fighting dogs. Extremely vicious." Aiden stood between Flair and the dogs, shielding her. "In *Lionel Vann and the Third Legion*, Vann and Manfred Boley had to get around a pack of them."

"Who gives a damn about Lionel Vann?" Flair hissed. "Which way?"

"Whatever's in front of us can't be worse than this," Aiden said. "Go ahead, I'll keep them busy."

Aiden grabbed Flair's arm and pushed her up the tunnel, and Flair walked ahead. She glanced backwards as the darkness slowly engulfed her brother. No less than fifty feet later, she finally saw what was making the scratching, scraping sound.

Flair recognized the three creatures that met her in the narrow corridor. Grunners. But these weren't the same monsters that she fought at Hotel Quorum. These were larger and uglier, with scaly blue-green bodies, six crablike legs, and large, silver pincers on their sides. Their skin was scabbed and scarred like battle armor, and each had identical raised markings on their backs, as if the creatures had been branded.

Flair, on pure reflex, blasted them with her crystals, but the red bolts merely ricocheted off of their armored skin and only seemed to infuriate the creatures. The grunners leapt off the floor with incredible speed, aiming their pincers at Flair.

Flair shielded herself just in time, and the beasts slammed into two red barriers, knocking Flair to the floor as they bounced into the walls.

Hurried footsteps were behind Flair, and she flipped over to see Aiden and the pack of dogs bearing down on him. Bypassing Flair without giving her notice, Aiden and the Cordobas slipped on the ocean-smelling slime covering the floor and went skidding around the corner, colliding with the Grunners.

Trapped in a narrow tunnel with a menagerie of beasts might have spelled doom, but as it happened, the animals turned their attention onto one another. A grunner snared one of the Cordobas by its leg with its sharp pincers and with a bone chilling—*SNAP!*—broke it cleanly. Breaking the dog's leg only seemed to anger the Cordobas, and the pack leapt upon the three grunners in a snarling, bloody frenzy.

Seizing the opportunity, Flair, shields still intact, slipped around the melee and up the tunnel. She saw Aiden backing away from the creatures, looking disgusted.

"What the hell are those things?" Aiden shouted.

"Some Purified fish, crab combo," Flair sputtered. "Whatever they are, those dogs are tearing them up."

Suddenly, the snarling, snapping white mass slammed into Flair's barrier, shoving her back about five feet. She held her ground long enough to allow Aiden to scramble to his feet. The Cordobas were flat against the red shields, pressing forward as Flair was sliding backwards, unable to stop their momentum.

"Aiden! Help!"

Aiden grabbed Flair's back, pushing, but the Cordobas continued driving them down the tunnel. A lone grunner flopped in between the dogs, but they ignored it. They seemed furious that they weren't able to break through the red shield that stood between them and their prey.

"I can't hold them…" Flair grunted.

Aiden looked down the tunnel, squinting, and spotting a door twenty feet away.

"Hold on, there's a door here!"

"Open it!"

Aiden sprinted to the door and grabbed the knob. Sure enough, locked, and ramming his shoulder into it had no effect. He squatted down, examining the lock.

"Dead bolt, pin and tumbler," he breathed. "If only I had—"

He searched absently around him for a substitute for a nail file and paper clip. He ran back to Flair, grabbing her wrists and pushing with her.

"Got anything metal on you?"

"Like what?" she said through clinched teeth. "You think I just keep bits and pieces of metal laying around?"

Aiden looked down, noticing the metal buckles on Flair's boots. "These'll work!" He reached down, ripping two buckles from the boots. Flair's red aura brightened.

"*What in the world!* Aiden, are you serious?"

"Lock picks. I'll buy you new boots!"

"Oh, I'd better get *more* than that!"

The boot buckles ripped free, leaving straggling threads. Aiden ran up the tunnel, biting the buckles, twisting and bending them in his teeth.

"All things considering," Aiden said, "this is payback. You said you saved my butt once, I'm just returning the favor."

"We're saving each other right now!" Flair grunted. "Unless you want to trade!"

Picking the lock was proving impossible. Flair's aura was the only light, making it difficult for Aiden to see, and the heat was stifling. Beads of sweat stung Aiden's eyes and Flair's buckles kept slipping from his fingers.

Flair appeared around the curve in the tunnel, inching closer. "Come on bro! You didn't destroy my boots for nothing!"

Aiden hadn't picked a lock since he was thirteen, and back then he didn't have vicious dogs bearing down on him. He turned just enough to see the backs of Flair's heels.

"It's not easy! Your stupid buckle isn't working!"

"Shut up talking about it!" Flair commanded. "Make it happen!"

Aiden wedged the first part of his makeshift tool into the lock. He took the smaller piece of the buckle from between his teeth and went to work on the pins. This lock would have five pins, the first would be the easiest. *There!* It clicked and slid into place.

"Hurry!" Flair cried, sounding panicked. She was ten feet away, digging her foot into a small groove in the floor; but instead of giving her extra stability, it caused her to stumble. The dogs and the lone grunner gained more ground before Flair recovered her footing.

The second pin gave way. The barking and raging of the dogs was unsettling. Aiden left the piece in the lock, wiped the beads of sweat from his face, and continued. The third pin would be the hardest. It was sitting up the highest and was the most difficult to push into position.

Aiden's hand shifted. The bright aura was nearly there. He pushed up. The third pin slipped and caught hold. And the fourth pin fell quickly after.

Flair was four feet away, and Aiden felt the heat coming from her aura. Eyes closed, teeth gritted, grunting incomprehensibly, giving every last ounce of her strength. Seeing his sister fighting so hard against the Cordobas gave Aiden a calm sense of purpose.

Picking locks was easy. Flair was the one fighting.

He jiggled and twisted the boot buckle until finally the last pin fell into place. The lock clicked and the door swung outward into the tunnel. The room was dark and, with the exception of two large lamps emitting a purplish hue, empty.

Aiden stepped behind Flair, grabbing her around her waist. "Come on, sunshine, turn them this way."

"What are you talking about?" Flair spat. "Just get in there..."

"No. There's no exit, we'll be trapped. Besides," he said, looking at the large lamps, "I don't know if it's safe. Just turn them the left."

Although she had no idea what Aiden had in mind, Flair obeyed, guiding the Cordobas towards the wall, and Aiden twisted her waist further around until they both were pinned flat against the open door. The dogs still pressed against the shield until the lone grunner flopped into the room, thrashing around as if searching for more prey.

Three of the dogs turned and pursued the grunner, leaping away from the Flair's shields, which lightened her load. She pushed against the remaining Cordobas, directing them into the room as Aiden slammed the door.

Flair collapsed flat on her back, arms splayed. Her hair resembled a frizzy, stringy mop, and she was heaving as if she had just finished running a marathon.

"Are you okay?" Aiden asked, hovering over his sister anxiously. "Can you stand?"

"Of…course…not…you…idiot!" Flair panted, her eyes shut tight.

"Great," Aiden groaned. He stared at Flair's pouch, bracing himself for something. Then reaching down and opening it, he removed a white crystal.

"What's up?"

"Take a breather," Aiden said, looking curiously at the white aura surrounding him. "I need to check something and I need some light."

He took one step and was hit with that same woozy sensation he felt in the Cranberry. He stumbled up the tunnel until he slammed into the blood-strewn wall where the melee began. The heat and dizziness was bad enough, but the stench of the dog and grunners was overwhelming. His aura flickered, his footsteps echoed inside his head like the clanging of a bell. But he needed to focus, he needed to make sure he wasn't seeing things…

Pinching his nose, Aiden kicked one of the dead grunners onto its side, examining its raised markings in the quivering light. It wasn't made with a branding iron as it had appeared. It was grown into its scaly skin, a part of the creature itself. The markings were in the shape of a fat letter P, a marking Aiden immediately recognized. He fished inside of his pocket, retrieving his father's lucky coins. He pulled out the heavy copper piece with the symbol that perfectly matched the markings on the creature's back.

He turned away from it, overcome by the smell of death, fighting the urge to let go of the white crystal, but he finally dropped it, deciding to hold onto his lunch instead.

"You good, bro?" Flair's voice and her bright aura approached. "What are you looking at?" She leaned over him with her hands on her knees, staring at the grunner Aiden was inspecting.

"This." Aiden touched the raised marking on the creature. "I thought I recognized it when those things attacked." He showed Flair the coin, rolling it between his fingers.

"Where did you get that from?"

"One of Pops' lucky coins," Aiden replied. "I looked it up at the library, but—"

Flair interrupted, looking completely confused. "But that's *Prestigeon*."

"I could never find—" Aiden continued, but then stopped. "Wait, what?"

"Prestigeon. I told you about them, remember? They're buying up all my labels."

Aiden looked disbelieving, staring back and forth between the coin and his sister.

"Prestigeon," he whispered. "Pops was trying to tell me...."

"Oh God, not again," Flair said, throwing her hands on her hips. "Another riddle?

"No," he said quietly, staring at the dead grunner. "I thought he didn't want me to, but he *wanted* you to know. Pops knew you knew, he knew I needed you just like he needed her!"

"He needed who? What are you talking about?"

"Mom."

"What about Mom?" Flair was worried, but Aiden was enlightened. He understood now, everything fit together. He looked at his sister, seeing her in a whole new light. He reached out, gripping Flair's shoulder.

"Mom would be proud of you."

And without her saying anything, Aiden could tell those words had affected Flair in a deep way that perhaps even she didn't realize. He always knew his sister better than anyone, even better than their own parents. Flair was gazing at him now, taken aback.

"What do you mean?" she said.

"Everything you've done. The way you handled those things back there, taking care of Simone, saving us in Paris. This is *you*, Flair. You're a fighter. And if there's one thing we knew about Mom, she was a fighter. She was tougher than everyone, even Pops.

I'm just saying she'd be really proud of her daughter right now. Just like her brother is."

Flair stared at Aiden, silent and stunned. Her expression was odd, somewhere between hopeful and anguished. Her lips trembled and her amber eyes glittered with welling tears. Her chest heaved and then with a shudder, Flair wept, softly at first, but increasing in intensity and volume. Hard, painful sobs that Aiden felt. That shook him in his gut.

He hadn't expected this. *Why was she crying?* He thought he had paid Flair a compliment, giving her strength and encouragement. But he didn't react right away because something had just occurred to him. This was the first time Flair had cried since their mother died.

"I th-thought I had more time with Mom," Flair sobbed, her breath catching in her throat. "I hate myself, Aiden! *Why was I so stupid?*" She broke down again, louder, deeper.

"You're not stupid, Flair." He looked at her teary face, searching. "You're, you're just…"

"I am stupid! I m-miss Mom so much, and it hurts all over, *everywhere!* And I can't stop it from hurting!"

Aiden reached up, stroking the strings of hair from the front of Flair's face.

"Except when you're fighting, right?"

Flair's face was blank, but she nodded.

"Then Mom's there with you, sunshine. Right in the action. Keep fighting with her."

"She always wanted me to be like her, Aiden," Flair said timidly. "I should've been."

"Parents are crazy sometimes. Expectations—"

"You lived up to yours," Flair sniffed.

"Please! My sister's Purified and kidnapped, we're halfway around the world trapped in a criminal's compound, and just got attacked by extinct fighting dogs. That's hardly living up to expectations. Okay, tell me about Prestigeon."

Flair looked disoriented, still wiping tears from her eyes. "They own lots of companies," she sighed. "That fancy drink water company, *Flagen?* They own that. They own a couple of art galleries too. Fancy restaurants, places like that."

"Okay, why are they minting their own money? Why would Pops have it? And who is this guy on the back?"

He held the coin up, wiping dirt off of the man's face with his thumb and showing it to Flair. Just then, Flair's head jerked to one side.

"What was *that*?"

"What was *what*?"

Flair stepped down the tunnel, turning her head as if searching for something. She stared at Aiden's coin.

"Do that again, with the coin," she said, frowning. Aiden's thumb wiped the face of the man again.

"That," she said, holding up a finger. She saw the white crystal on the floor. "You need the crystal to hear it. It sounds like something unlocking and locking."

Aiden swiped his thumb again, listening for it, but it was no good.

"Where is it coming from?"

Flair stepped over a grunner corpse and ran down the corridor to the left, back the way the came, Aiden following behind her. A hundred yards later, they were staring at an enormous black door made of smooth steel, large enough to drive a truck through it, displaying an overlarge Prestigeon logo.

Aiden flicked his thumb across the coin, watching. Now he heard it, the sound of a bolt sliding in and out of place, but nothing moved. He flicked the coin again, pushed on the door, trying to slide it and lift it from different angles, but it wouldn't budge.

"Impossible," Aiden heaved, pacing and steadily swiping the coin. "There's no handle, no unlatching mechanism. This door is solid steel." He shoved the door again to no avail.

"Enough with the muscles," Flair admonished. "We need your brain."

Aiden pressed his face against the door, examining it. He slid his fingers all across the door's cool, smooth surface. Finally, across the left of the Prestigeon logo, he discovered three tiny grooves in the metal. He beckoned to his sister.

"Over here, Flair." She stepped forward and her aura brought the tiny grooves in the door to light. Peering into the grooves, Aiden could see silver mesh.

"This company is *fancy-shmancy*, right?"

"That's a dorky way of putting it, but yeah."

"The door is unlocked, but its needs something to open it, and I think this is a microphone." Aiden placed his mouth right next to the door and said "Prestigeon!" in a clear voice.

Nothing happened.

"It needs a password," Aiden said. "*Mackleford!*" No response. "*Dominion!*"

Flair glared at the door like it was another enemy. She was concentrating on a word as Aiden continued to throw passwords at it. "Come on, sunshine," he said after a minute, "what would they use for a password?"

"Purity," Flair said.

At once, the giant "P" flashed bright blue. The hallway shook as the large black door slowly rose, revealing a room bathed in a brilliantly powerful fluorescent red.

Inside were thousands of flowers, and their odor was overpowering. Aiden's eyes began to water and he coughed terribly, but Flair had taken off running down the hallway.

"Flair?" Aiden shouted. She was already around the corner and out of sight.

"*Jeez!*" she coughed, walking back, recovered from the effect. "What in the world is that?"

"Orchids," Aiden said simply. "But I've never heard of them smelling like an onion factory."

Flair wiped her stinging eyes. "Why are they in a room full of red light?"

"Exactly. And they had that empty room back there that we saw. It had black light and UV lamps. Horticulturists use UV rays to cultivate flowers."

"Cultivating them for what?" Flair said.

"I have no idea."

Aiden squinted, walking further into the room and examining the orchids. They were seated in long rows of planters, which had all been welded to the floor. The lights above him were also in fixtures that had been welded to the ceiling.

Aiden was inspecting the flowers when the room jolted violently, followed by a deafening grinding noise. Aiden fell to his knees; the noise in his ears was deafening.

"What's going on? Flair?" But Flair couldn't hear him. She was standing outside the room, in a state of shock, staring at the entire room, along with her brother, rising into the air.

Aiden looked back towards the door as he tried to regain his feet, watching Flair's astonished face as it dropped out of sight. He was floored once more, this time slamming his head cruelly against the edge of one of the metal planters.

A giant black box swung precariously in midair as a large crane maneuvered it towards the back of a large flatbed truck, watched by a dozen of El Sereno's men.

"Wait!" the man operating the crane shouted. He stepped outside of the cab, staring up at the box. "Look there, we've got a door open."

The box tilted to one side and Aiden fell ten feet to the ground, crashing in the center of a cement courtyard.

Within seconds, he was surrounded by uniformed men, some wearing black and blue uniforms with the Prestigeon logo on the front, others in black and gold military uniforms. They all aimed automatic rifles at Aiden as he rolled over on his back.

"Oh crap," he muttered. Dazed, head pounding, Aiden heard his name echoing across the complex. He was disoriented, being hoisted to his feet, and shoved along. Aiden vaguely made out a jeep stopping ahead of him, and a tall, slender man dressed in all black getting out of the passenger seat. He walked up directly to Aiden, raising a fist. There was a swish and a loud crack, another jarring pain on his jaw, and the world went black.

CHAPTER TWENTY-ONE – INTO THE PIT

Gloria awoke, vision blurred, head pounding. She didn't remember it happening, but knew she'd been drugged. She was in a dark room that had one other occupant, a sleeping Simone, below in her wheelchair, head hanging, so that all Gloria could see was her drooping curls falling around her pale skin.

Gloria was in a worse condition: suspended in the air by a rigging of chains covering the ceiling. With thick cuffs around her wrists and ankles, looking like a marionette caught in its own stringing. She tried grabbing the chains and hoisting herself upwards so she could sit on a loop of chain hanging behind her. But drenched in sweat and drained of strength, she lost her grip and fell. Slowly, she began losing consciousness.

"What's this place?" Simone asked. The jangle of Gloria's chains had awakened her, and looking around, her face turned. She was staring at a gruesome collection of machetes, saws, hatchets and knives hanging from the walls, some covered in dried blood.

"Simmy, you're awake!" Gloria heaved. "This place? You don't want to know."

But Simone had a feeling she knew, and shivered at the thought. She wheeled backwards so she could see Gloria's face.

"What kind of guy is El Sereno?" she asked.

"Sometimes he's okay, but mostly, he isn't. He knows everything about being cruel."

"What's going to happen to us?"

"You'll be fine Simone, don't worry. As for me, my fate's up in the air," she said, staring at the chains suspending her from the ceiling, "no pun intended."

Simone chuckled, closing her eyes. "Nice one, *Aiden*," she sighed.

"What about Aiden?" Gloria said.

"Nothing, he always makes me laugh when I'm scared. Like the whole day after my mom's funeral. You guys are a lot alike."

"I know," Gloria said, breathing deeply. "I...like Aiden. I really do. He feels *me*, the person that I used to be. He's the…missing part of…" She was drifting into unconsciousness; her breathing was becoming erratic.

"Don't go to sleep. Keep fighting until Aiden saves us."

Gloria mustered a small chuckle. "Now you're making me laugh. Aiden is going to leave me to rot. Come on, I kidnapped his sister."

"Well, okay, that was pretty lame, but you wanted to cure me and your brothers."

"I was your age when I found out about my brothers," Gloria said, her voice sounding more ragged. "When Gaston Gumm died, my parents lost it. They had done a good job of hiding things from me, but after he died, they stropped trying." Her voice cracked, and Simone thought she heard the faintest whimper behind it.

"They told me everything, who they were, about the Gumms, the Guild, the Dominion. About Mackleford. About my brothers. When I met them, it destroyed me. I thought I was an only child forever, I begged for brothers and sisters, used to say, 'Mom, can't I have just one little brother or one little sister?' Come to find out, I'm the little sister."

Tears rolled down Gloria's nose, making a small puddle underneath her. Simone thought about herself, *the little sister*. What if she never knew Aiden or Flair existed? Then discovered them, and found out what happened, what Mackleford had done? What would *she* have done?

The silence had crept back in, and Simone saw Gloria hanging motionless. She had to wake her, keep her talking. "I talked to Ramon," she said, and Gloria perked up.

"You did?"

"Yeah. On the plane, you were asleep." And Simone recanted their conversation to Gloria, who was alert for most of it, but drifted as Simone finished.

"He said I could be cured. He said he can't be cured, but he thinks I can."

"There's no cure," Gloria muttered. "It doesn't exist."

"Yes it does! Aiden will find it for us."

"No, Simmy. This place was my last hope and I was wrong. Cess can't lie to me. Besides, like he said, why would Mackleford create a cure that would destroy the Dominion?"

"But he did," Simone said. "The Goons talked about it at Jump Point."

"What do you mean?" Gloria said.

"Well, now that I think about it, we're they talking it or thinking it? How am I supposed to tell the difference? It's weird. If I see their lips move, I'll know, but I was under a desk—"

"Simone," Gloria interrupted.

"Oh, sorry. Well, one of the Goons said that this new guy was perfect, that he had got the cure that they always wanted."

"Perfect?" And Gloria suddenly sprang to life, popping up, jangling the chains. "He said the new guy was *perfect*?"

"Yes," Simone said, smiling at the sparkle returning to Gloria's eyes. "And he said he got the cure everybody—"

"Forget the cure," Gloria whispered. "He's done it, Simmy. Mackleford's done it. We've gotta get out of here..."

Using what was her last ounce of strength, Gloria grabbed the chains, pulling herself into a handstand, stretching her legs over the loop of chain she tried to grab earlier.

Simone gazed on in amazement as Gloria twisted her torso, pulling the chain loop tight. With a loud—*clink!*—the chain snapped free from the ceiling, bringing a smile to Simone's face.

The chain swung back and forth, dangling over Simone's head. "This is really going to hurt," Gloria sighed, and nodded to the chain. "Okay, Simmy, grab the end of that and pull."

Something released as Simone complied. All at once, Gloria and the snakelike network of chains crashed to the floor with a loud clang.

Gloria got to her knees, groaning in pain, but smiled at Simone. "Nice work, Simmy. Now, if only I had some crystals..."

Simone began hopping in her wheelchair. "Oh, oh, oh! Look behind me, in the wheelchair pocket! That's where Flair was keeping them!"

Gloria grimaced, crawling over to Simone. She peered into the back pocket of the wheelchair at several sparkling red and white crystals, which must have spilled from Flair's bag.

"Jackpot!" Gloria said. She leaned over and kissed Simone on the head as she grabbed two white crystals. "Let me heal up for a minute, and then we're getting out of here."

Footsteps echoed throughout the metal hallway. Flair was running as fast as she could, disoriented, her mind affected and bogged from the overwhelming stench from that room—the room that had somehow risen into the air, taking Aiden with it. She didn't understand what had just happened, but now wasn't the time to think.

Shouts echoed along with those footsteps: voices in pursuit. She sidestepped the grunner-dog carnage at the fork in the tunnel, running past the door where she and Aiden had trapped the dogs. She reached the end of the corridor, finding the door that Aiden said Simone might be behind. She shook the handle, but it was locked.

"Simmy! Simmy!"

A half-dozen men rounded the bend and threw something at Flair, which clanked against the metal walls, before coming to near Flair's feet: a small metal canister spraying mist into the air.

Suddenly, Flair's throat closed, her muscles felt like stone, and before she could think, she had collapsed on the floor. It was intensity beyond imagination, far worse than the smell of those flowers. Struggling to breathe, she raised her hand, aiming at the shadowed figures slipping through the hazy corridor. The first shadow pointed, yelling something in Spanish.

But before they arrived, someone behind her had grabbed her right hand, attempting to remove the white crystal. She reached up to grab the crystal, but a gnarled hand slapped hers away. Flair was too weak, unable to resist.

Or was she? At once, her throat un-seized and she felt much lighter. The shadowy men crept closer, only yards away. Flair lifted her left hand as high as she could, firing a barrage of crystal blasts that ricocheted off the metal walls. One found its mark as someone squealed in pain, and the rest of the men, apparently wanting no part of it, dispersed. The gnarled hand grabbed Flair's jacket collar and dragged her back down the tunnel.

Two minutes later, after being hauled up a ladder and carried through two rooms, Flair was dumped on a soft pile of white clothing.

"Gotta take yer white off when the gas gets tossed, young lady."

"Mr. Nefflin?" Flair croaked.

"Come on, Flair, breathe!" Marcus Nefflin stood over Flair, waving something large in her face, fanning cool air all around her. The effect was instantaneous. With each passing rush of air, Flair felt better.

She sat up blinking, propping herself on her elbows. "What happened?"

"You got hit with a Calico Cocktail, nerve toxin, one of Ed's old concoctions. Hell of a way to stop a Goon back in the day, but they're immune now. It only affects folks holdin' whites, which you learnt the hard way. Take it off next time."

"Where have you been?" Flair asked, standing and looking around the dark room, only lit by a small lamp. "And where are we?"

"I've been *here*, but hell if I know where *here* is," Nefflin replied, tossing a trashcan lid can on the pile of clothes. "If you ask me, it's where they do laundry, with these clothes all o'er the place. Been waitin' on things to die down, keepin' quiet in case they started searchin' the place."

"How did you get away? We just knew you were caught."

"I *was* caught. When I came up outta that hole, there was nothing but El Sereno's guys up there. Zapped a couple, got away, but they know this place better'n I do. I cut 'round one corner and knocked my head into a darn pole! I woke up handcuffed, watchin' El Sereno beat some joker half to death, shot 'im in the knee, then ran into the next room, hollerin' in Spanish. But then he said some'n in English. Think he was talkin' ta Simmy."

"You heard her?"

"No, but I heard 'im say 'let's see what kind of man your brother is' or something like that. Right? So who else could it be? Well, at that point he went back yakkin' in Spanish, and about five minutes later I heard dogs growling."

"Dogs," Flair grumbled, briefly remembering their encounter with the Cordobas.

"They forgot all about me once they realized you two were here. That guy he shot in the knee passed out, so I grabbed his keys, uncuffed m'self, and slipped into the next room to see who he was talking to, but they were gone. So I walked across the yard and hid over here."

"Nobody saw you?"

"Heck no. Like I said, they were lookin' for you two, didn't give a damn about nothin' else. By the way, where is Aiden?"

"I don't know. We found something down there, a room with a lot of flowers and it was all in this weird red light. Aiden was checking it out, and then, and I don't know how, but the room went flying up into the air."

"It didn't do it on its own if that's what yer thinking. I don't know if you saw that giant crane out there sitting against the edge of them trees. I heard 'em rev that big sucker up 'bout a half hour ago. When I crept outside to look, it was carryin' somethin' in the air, a big black box."

"Aiden was inside," Flair gasped. "They captured him!"

"Must've. Someone fell outta that thing and hit the ground hard. They jumped 'im. I ducked back in here, that's when I heard you screamin' for Simone down below." Nefflin was scratching his balding head. "That room sounds like a portable lab. Seen 'em before. You said they had flowers in 'em?"

Flair nodded. "Yes, they did. Aiden said he thinks they're doing something to the flowers, like experiments."

"What's that gotta do with it?"

"I don't know. Let's just find Simone. Where'd you hear El Sereno talking to her?"

"We'll go, but first, let's get some of these on," Nefflin said, pointing to the pile of clothes. "We're too noticeable in these clothes. We need to be insuspick, er, introspecial, or in…"

"Inconspicuous?" Flair asked, frowning.

"Yeah. That."

Within five minutes, both Flair and Nefflin were dressed head to toe in gold and black military camouflage, Flair even finding a cap that contained her huge mane of sweaty hair. She wrapped it tightly, tucked it under a hat, and they set out, sneaking across the sprawling courtyard, making their way towards a large one-story building off to the side.

Flair finally had the feeling that she was on a corporate campus of a large pharmaceutical company. The interior landscaping was gorgeous. Large fountains stood in the center of a stone courtyard and there were small planters with exotic plants growing around the small coterie of older buildings along the perimeter.

But the rest of the complex looked like a prison compound. The enormous outer wall loomed over the campus, and every fifty yards stood the watchtowers that Nefflin said had been constructed since the Journeymen last infiltrated.

They entered a dining hall, and Flair's stomach grumbled as they passed tables with unfinished dinners that El Sereno's men left behind. Nefflin marched around the tables and entered a hallway ahead.

"I was here and there's where I heard yer sister," Nefflin said, pointing to two adjacent rooms. Flair entered the second room, feeling anxious. There was nothing remarkable in the room at first glance, but then as she was about to leave...

"She was here," Flair gasped, hovering over a feathery pile of dead skin underneath one of the chairs.

"Must've been really scared. Purity comes out more when yer scared."

"What do you mean?" Flair said, turning on Nefflin. "What does that mean, Mr. Nefflin?"

"Ain't good. The more scared you are, the faster Purity pumps through your system. Yer sister wernt bad like most Purified, suspect you and Aiden had 'er relaxed. But ever since she's been with Gloria, I'm guessin' she's not doing too good."

Flair's face darkened when she heard Gloria's name. "I swear when I get my hands on that lousy—"

"Easy, Flair, easy. They obviously took them out of here." Nefflin looked grim. "And I think I know where. Come on."

Water was splashing somewhere, reminding Aiden when he was twelve: that one scorching Brooklyn summer when he had cracked open a fire hydrant and gave the neighborhood kids a cool treat. He stood in front of a hydrant, dousing himself with water. It felt good, but it was getting to be a bit too much. The water was pounding him, invading his mouth and nostrils. He was struggling to breathe, trying to turn away from the water...

He snapped awake. He wasn't twelve, this wasn't Brooklyn. He was tied down to something hard and flat, upside down, with blood rushing to his head. He was gasping for air, but couldn't breathe. His face was covered in a soaking wet cloth. *What was going on?*

Someone screamed at him, there was laughter. His heart banged against his rib cage, feeling like it would explode at any moment. Aiden tried to make sense of where he was and what was happening, a deluge of water flooded down his nostrils and into his mouth.

He twisted and turned, trying to grab whatever was doing this, but then realized his arms were tied behind his back, trapped between his body and the flat surface. His lungs were burning, screaming for fresh air to breath, but he could only suck in the sopping wet cloth stuck to his face. Suddenly his body swung like a pendulum, and he was upright.

More shouting. His head was pounding. He was punched in the stomach, and flipped upside down again.

A jarring voice rang in his mind. It was his father, speaking to him as if he was across a valley, distant, but clear.

"You can only endure pain when you understand."

"But why am I doing this?" Aiden heard his own voice asking.

"Even in the worst situations, there is a purpose, the solution, and the reason why you must endure." And he saw his Flair and Simone's faces, as vivid and alive as if they were in the room, and he felt emboldened.

He was wrenched up again, his head again banging off the wooden slab.

"Where is the Song of Solomon, Aiden?" a quiet voice said. "Do you have it? It won't spare your life, but it might spare your sisters."

"Why not mine?" Aiden mumbled. "What'd I ever do to you?"

A hand yanked the wet cloth from Aiden's head. The tall man, the last person Aiden saw, was standing before him, an intense hatred emanating from his cold blue eyes like heat from a radiator.

"You," El Sereno said, turning away from Aiden, "have done nothing, Aiden Johnson. But you are an educated man, so you're aware of the phrase, *the sins of the fathers are now visited upon the sons.*"

Aiden nodded. "Alright then, what did my dad do?"

"A little history first, Aiden, so that you may comprehend. Fighting has always been in my family. My father and grandfather trained me. They were both cage fighters back when it was illegal in most civilized countries. They built a marvelous empire: gambling, fighting, along with other unseen, nefarious activities.

"To inherit my birthright, I had to defeat my father in the cage, man to man. And I did. I stopped just short of killing him and he gave me my inheritance proudly. I believe great wars should be fought with weapons, but men, worthy men, they settle their personal business man to man, fist to fist.

"Of course, the world doesn't think this way. Men will insist upon kidnapping and threatening family. My father was such a man, but not me. I have always despised that. Some mocked me, said I was too kind. Too peaceful, called me *El Sereno*. Although it served a purpose, for as I began to overtake Argentina and South America, my name gave my opponents the mistaken idea that I was seeking some peaceful cooperation. They could not have been more wrong. They underestimated me to their demise.

"But my son, my only son, Reynaldo. Also a fighter. Too good for this world, my world. My father's world. My grandfather's world. He was the greatest of the Cessanos. He was our pride. As a praying mantis, quick and deadly; as a cobra, fluid and precise; as a tiger, strong and relentless. I kept Rey far from my world; I wouldn't allow him to know it. However your father, trying to discover how Mackleford and I are associated, captured my son while he was in your country training for his first match."

And now El Sereno looked like a different man. His bright blue eyes darkened and his voice trembled as he continued.

"He tortured Rey for information. Instead of coming after me, Wilbert Johnson went after my son. Needless to say, his efforts were pointless. Rey knew nothing about my world. I raised him away from it, and your father knew that. After he was through with him, he discarded him, left him to die, and went into hiding. That is the type of scum your father was. A coward."

Aiden's mind was flummoxed. *His father, torturing a man, leaving him to die?* His eyes were locked onto El Sereno's vengeful gaze.

"I asked myself the same question your father must have asked himself," El Sereno whispered. "What would I do to the son of my son's murderer?" And it was then that Aiden noticed El Sereno was holding a long, thick blade, over a foot long, razor sharp.

"I would give him the honor of avenging his father's cowardice. I would give him the chance my boy didn't have."

And immediately, El Sereno flipped Aiden over, slamming him on his stomach, cutting the plastic zip ties binding his arms together. Aiden turned over and sat upright.

"So, Aiden Johnson, let us see if you are a man and a fighter, or if you run and hide as well as your father."

Aiden began sizing El Sereno up for the first time. Though he was easily twice Aiden's age, his body was lean and muscular. He wouldn't be a pushover.

"I'm from Brooklyn," Aiden said bravely, "I ain't afraid of a fight."

"Me? No, Aiden, not me. Though I would love the pleasure, I'm an old man, and my hands have already shed blood today. But my beauties have been waiting for a good fight."

The dawn sky above was mired with storm clouds, though the horizon was a soft orange, light and clear. A cool and comfortable mist was falling, but the air felt heavy with anticipation. Aiden and El Sereno walked side by side through the center of the complex amidst an entourage of a hundred men, murmuring, passing money and scraps of paper to one another.

A wide, dirt pathway led them into the jungle. Aiden stared up at tall, slender trees stretching into the sky and spotted a loudspeaker above, one of several that were propped up around the compound. Another Frank Sinatra song, *I've Got You Under My Skin*, blared with a tinny warble.

"What's with the Sinatra? You his biggest fan or something?"

El Sereno turned his head, looking at Aiden with his large blue eyes. Aiden laughed.

"Everyone called you *Ol' Blue Eyes* growing up?"

El Sereno smiled, staring into the steadily brightening sky. "My mother. It was her nickname for me, as well her father. The only blue eyes in the family. Sinatra pays tribute to her memory. Do you have children, Aiden?"

"No."

"A shame, but fitting. We are the last males in our line. With your death, your family name dies as well."

"My father is still alive," Aiden remarked.

"Is he? What life does he have? Is he truly alive as he rots in his hideout?"

Aiden smirked. "You wouldn't understand."

"Well Aiden, you are a teacher, aren't you? Maybe you can teach me something before you die."

Two hundred yards away, lurking in shadows, Flair and Nefflin watched Aiden, El Sereno and the entourage disappear into the dense jungle.

"Where are they taking him?"

"The Pit," Nefflin said, blinking his bleary eyes.

"Carson said something about a pit. What is it?"

"Not a happy place, sister."

"Why? What happens there?"

Nefflin didn't answer, regaining that faraway look, but this time there was a trace of dread behind it. Flair shook his arm and Nefflin snapped out of it.

"Fight for yer life. Fight to the death."

Flair's mouth went dry. "Aiden has to fight to the death?"

Nefflin nodded.

"We gotta help him," Flair said. "Let's go!"

"This is our chance to get Simmy. Everyone's outta the way."

"Right…right." Flair stood up. "You get Simone, I'm going after Aiden."

Nefflin grabbed the loose sleeve of Flair's jacket and pulled her back to the ground. "I swear you Johnsons are psychos! A hun'red dudes with machine guns, Flair? We oughta get your sister and Gloria first."

"No," Flair said, pulling away from Nefflin. "Aiden might be dead by then."

"You'll be lucky if you're not dead with 'im!"

Flair leapt up before Nefflin could react. She scanned the jungle trees and retrieved Carson's channel gun from the pouch.

"Then let's hope today's my lucky day!" And she pounded off into the jungle.

After a half-hour, the procession came to an abrupt stop, and the men created a wide gap for Aiden and El Sereno. They reached a clearing of trees, and in the center of the clearing was a massive hole, nearly the size of a football field with jagged edges and a fifty-foot drop to the bottom.

El Sereno stared into the Pit as his men fanned out around the perimeter and the murmur of voices died down. Everyone was quiet; hats removed and heads bowed. The only noise came from birds tweeting and cawing and the occasional shuffle of someone's feet.

"This is our proving ground," El Sereno whispered to Aiden. "Where we fight. Where my father taught me. Where my son learned the rules of combat. Where these men were trained. Whoever enters here does not come out unless he is worthy. Those who cannot make it out, we do not bury them. They remain there, unworthy but not forgotten. I salute you with this honor, Aiden Johnson. Brave men, much braver than your father, breathed their last here."

And with that, El Sereno took a spool of rope from one of his guards, turned towards the Pit, and cast it high into the air. Aiden watched as the rope spiraled and uncoiled, landing somewhere in the dark center. El Sereno reached down, picked up the slack of the rope, and handed it to Aiden.

Aiden looked back, seeing four guards grasping the other end of the rope. Understanding, he snatched the rope from El Sereno, looping it around his waist.

"I'll be right back," Aiden sneered, and he lowered himself, descending into darkness.

It took him a half-minute to reach the bottom, and as his feet touched muddy floor, he turned and looked to the top. The sunlight edging through the trees didn't reach down here: it was as black as nighttime. It was all Aiden could do to see his hand in front of his face.

"Don't know what kinda guys you're used to dealing with," Aiden yelled, "but dogs don't faze me."

Aiden could have just been spewing brave words, but he did feel confident. Dogs might've been a shock if he hadn't dealt with them earlier. And that was in a tight, confined space, but here in this arena of sorts, he would have the freedom of movement. He remembered being chased by neighborhood dogs as a kid, always more fun than frightening.

"But Aiden," El Sereno said, smiling, "who said anything about *dogs*?"

And suddenly, another Sinatra song cut through the air. *Call Me Irresponsible* was blaring through a pair of loudspeakers Aiden noticed far above the Pit, fixed to a tree.

"Oh, that was *irresponsible* of me to not mention it!" El Sereno laughed along with his men. "No, Aiden, I've moved on from dogs. My beauties will deal with you."

On the far side of the Pit, opposite from El Sereno, a large gap opened in the circle of men. Something was coming through the opening, right where the sun peeked over the rim.

There was a heavy sliding sound, and Aiden saw a long wooden plank being lowered into the Pit. The men stepped back, making more than enough space for whatever was coming. They cackled, they serenaded, but Aiden wasn't paying them any attention. His heart was pounding. *What was it? One of those big grunners? Another purified monstrosity?*

He ran up to the ramp, having a mind to break it. If the thing had to be dropped into the Pit, it might be injured and that could give Aiden a fighting chance. But the sounds of machine-guns being readied forced Aiden to retreat.

Through the streams of dawn light, he could make out three fat silhouettes restraining something in chains. An animal, large and long, four stumpy legs attached to a muscular frame. It had a long, fat tail as big as its body, which swished back and forth, giving the three men all they could handle.

A Komodo dragon.

Aiden remembered seeing a Komodo dragon for the first time during a field trip to the Bronx Zoo when he was ten. The tour guide said they were stealthy hunters and had powerful bites. Aiden recalled not being impressed at the time, but that was when the Komodo was behind a glass cage.

Once the three chubby animal handlers managed to steer the Komodo on the ramp, it seemed to know what to do from there. Its forked tongue flicked happily as it stomped down the wooden plank. Aiden wiped his face, looking at the large lizard hastening its approach into the Pit, working out a strategy for tackling the monster, when something occurred to him.

El Sereno had said *beauties.*

As in more than one.

His eyes turned to the top of the ramp. Two more Komodos were being wrestled into place.

"Beautiful, no?" El Sereno screamed over *Come Fly With Me.* "They are brothers, I raised them since hatchlings. Their bites will not kill you immediately, but they will cripple you long enough for them to savor a nice meal."

The guards crooned along with Sinatra, pointing into the large pit at Aiden, and the three large lizards bounding down the ramp.

"I can't say my beauties are undefeated, they have suffered loss. Their sister, at the hands of a Journeyman. But it seems to have inspired them, as every opponent since then has been ripped into pieces."

It was still dark, so dark that Aiden barely made out the last Komodo reaching the bottom. No sooner did its clawed foot step off the wooden ramp was the ramp removed, leaving Aiden with no way out, staring at three humongous beasts.

The lizards fanned out with their snouts up, sniffing the air for their prey. Aiden backed away, his brain firing on all cylinders.

It was noisy in the Pit, men singing and laughing; Sinatra's voice now echoing *My Way* off the walls. Aiden figured the beasts wouldn't hear him if he didn't make any noise. He was trying to remember the zoo guide on his field trip—*was a Komodo's vision based on movement?* Ok, Aiden thought to himself: *Against the wall. Stay quiet. Think fast.*

But then there was an ear splitting—*crack!*—loud enough to be heard over everything. Looking down, Aiden saw he had stepped onto a human bone, by the looks of it, a forearm. Aiden turned and saw he was standing at a mound of human remains, ten-feet high.

The very sight of it caused Aiden to stumble and crash on his back at the foot of the pile of bones. The bones teetered slightly as the men above gasped and cheered.

Aiden turned around; the Komodos were alerted to his presence, moving in, angling themselves in front of Aiden, cutting off any escape. Aiden wanted to think, but the Komodos weren't giving him a second. They charged in, their fat, meaty legs pounding across the muddy ground.

Aiden scrambled off the ground, ran and leapt over one of the Komodos. The tip of his sneaker caught its long tail, and Aiden lost his balance, crashing headfirst into the mud.

All three lizards turned at once and went charging back towards Aiden. His hands and feet slipped in the mud, unable to gain traction. The first Komodo reached him, openmouthed and snapped. Aiden avoided the slimy fangs by inches but was close enough to smell its hot breath, which stank like rotted meat left in the sun.

"Hear that, Mr. Johnson," El Sereno laughed. "We're playing your song!"

"Start spreading the news....I'm leaving today..."

Aiden heard *New York, New York* creeping into his ears and made the mistake of paying it any attention. A *swoosh* sounded through the air like a bullwhip, and he caught the full brunt of a Komodo's tail in the stomach, knocking him on his back. The horde above cheered.

Another Komodo closed in, looking for which piece of Aiden it wanted to sink its teeth into first. Aiden got to his knees, crawling away as the dragon mounted another run at him. Aiden spun his body around, away from the snapping fangs.

WHAM! He had crawled face first into another massive tail, which clubbed him in the nose like a baseball bat. His face stung, warm blood trickled from both nostrils, but he couldn't react. At that moment, a heavy paw clawed his legs, and he felt a burning pain. One of the Komodos had bitten him. He yanked his leg away and kicked the beast in its face.

"I want to wake up in a city that doesn't sleep..."

No! Stop listening to the stupid song! A patch of sunlight had brightened the bottom of the Pit, and he got to his feet, limping towards it. Through his watery eyes, he got his first good look at the Komodos.

They were even worse in the light than in the dark. Three huge, ugly, flat nosed monsters, one brown, one green, and the biggest, a nasty yellow. He limped sideways, his wounded leg oozing blood with every step. The lizards were matching his moves, pinning him in.

Even if he could run, there was nowhere to go. Three of them, one of him, and the catcalling men above were letting him know. *This was it.* This was how his life was going to end...

"I'll make a brand new start of it...in ol' New York!"

The stupid song was back in his ears...the last song he'd ever hear...

"If I can make it there..."

But then, those lyrics, those words hit Aiden's heart like one of Flair's crystal blasts.

"I'll make it...anywhere!"

Anywhere, Aiden thought. *Anywhere.*

It wasn't a stupid song. Frank was right. El Sereno was nothing he hadn't dealt with before. The scene may be different, and yes, there were vicious Komodos dragons attacking him, but El Sereno was just like the tough guys where he'd grown up.

He looked around. The Pit? Just Brooklyn without buildings. The screaming men above? Old hags screaming from their balconies. These three animals in the mud with him? Dogs, bullies, gangs, whatever stood between him and what he had to do, whether it was going to the corner store, catching a train, or walking Flair to school.

He'd never been afraid, he'd always handled Brooklyn's witless thugs, and this Argentine thug would be no different. Flair and Simone needed him; he needed to make it.

"It's up to you! New York, New York!"

It was up to him.

He felt empowered. Defiant. He was ready to strike back at these beasts, at El Sereno. He wanted to laugh into those cold blue eyes.

Aiden dodged the jaws of the green Komodo, turning as the beast almost nipped his waist. He sprang backwards off his injured leg, swinging a kick, and smacking the beast in the mouth.

Something snapped. The Komodo's jaw. Aiden saw the beast writhing on the ground and heard El Sereno's audience groan above him.

"I want to be a part of it...New York! Newww Yoooorrk!"

The falling mist had become a solid patter of rain and the other Komodos charged. Aiden slipped in the mud as they collided with him, crashing at the foot of the pile of human bones.

Aiden lost the squeamishness that had plagued him earlier. He needed a weapon, and any of these bones would do. He grabbed the closest bone as the large yellow Komodo was poised to strike. A skull, wobbly attached to a spinal cord—*WHAM!*—cracked the lizard across the head. It was undeterred, however, lashing back for another bite. Aiden reacted, swinging the skull back and feeling it disappear from his hand. He blinked at his empty hand, perplexed until he realized the skull had somehow wedged into the dragon's mouth.

"King of the hill....AAAY- NUMBER ONNNNE!!"

Without thinking, Aiden climbed the pile of the bones as the yellow lizard thrashed, unable to free the skull from its mouth. Halfway up, he steadied his feet and leapt into the air like a pro wrestler, landing with his full body weight on the Komodo's head.
CRUUNCHH!!
The skull went skidding across the Pit, but Aiden couldn't assess the animal's condition. His jump had triggered the tower of human remains to crash over him like a tidal wave. Large skulls and heavy bones crashed into his head, and the world was spinning once again. He felt blackness upon him.

"I'm gonna make a brand new start of it....IN OL' NEW YOORRRK!!"

Frank had brought him back. He could hear the shocked, calamitous yelling of the men above him, but he didn't pay it any attention. He picked and kicked himself through the cold bones, and there was the yellow komodo. The animal lay quiet, unconscious.

"AAANNND....if I can make it there...I'm gonna make it....anywhere!!"

Aiden didn't take a moment to celebrate. The brown Komodo was rushing forward, its ugly black eyes gleaming at him. He reached down and grabbed a large femur and swung.

The femur hammered the side of the dragon's head and snapped in half. The beast staggered and fell. Without hesitation, Aiden leapt into the air again, and with all his might, plunged the broken femur bone straight through the Komodo's neck.

He wrenched his arm away savagely, separating bone from beast. He stood, dirty, bloody, and spun and glared at El Sereno, who stared at him with a mix of shock and fury. Aiden slammed the broken bone, splattering mud.

"ANYWHERE!" he roared at him.

But following Aiden's euphoria were the sounds of a hundred rifles being readied. El Sereno was staring psychotically into the Pit as his men trained their rifles at Aiden.

His victory meant nothing. He was going to die no matter what.

But something small and red flashed overhead, whistling through the air like a firework. Everyone looked as it struck a tree opposite from El Sereno's end of the Pit.

Next, there was a rustling sound, like a bird dashing through the trees from branch to branch. El Sereno and his closest cohorts looked above; whatever was moving was just overhead, and they watched the leaves jostle and flutter until a gleaming green crystal fell at El Sereno's feet.

"Green?" El Sereno said, but the tremors had already begun before he could react. The crystal rolled away, tumbling into the Pit. El Sereno's men stared, confused, trying to hold their balance, when shouts erupted from the men on the other side.

Everyone turned and, with a thrill of amazement, saw a girl donned in military fatigues, bathed in a red glow, hurtling through the air towards them like a specter. Flair tossed another sparkling green crystal, aiming towards the center of the Pit.

El Sereno's face turned the color of chalk. "No!" he screamed. "Shoot her down!"

Machine gunfire exploded from everywhere, and Flair, ready for it, clenched her left hand, creating a bright red shield that deflected the bullets away. She yanked her hand off of the Star Channel and splashed down in the center of the Pit just as the second green crystal sank into the muddy floor.

It was bedlam. The ground underfoot buckled and the Pit was collapsing on every side. Several of El Sereno's men lost their balance, nose-diving fifty feet to the bottom. Those that remained atop were haphazardly firing their weapons. Flair rushed to her brother's side, raised her gloved hands towards them and red bolts exploded like fire, causing chunks of earth to crumble beneath the feet of El Sereno's men, hastening their plummet.

El Sereno was clinging to a tree trunk, pointing to men, screaming instructions.

"Come on bro, let's go!" Flair shouted, as guards stumbled her way.

"Can't," Aiden heaved. "V-venom…can't move…"

The Komodo's venom had finally overcome Aiden. His limbs were stiff and rigid. Only able to turn his head slightly, Aiden couldn't see what was happening, but felt himself sinking waist deep into one of the several fissures the eruption had spawned. He saw a blurry image of his sister flash past him, fighting El Sereno's men. A Komodo slid by, engulfed in an enormous pool of mud collecting in the center, barely feet from him.

The last guard standing was hammered by a haymaker from Flair and skidded across the ground into the same swirling mud pool that threatened to consume Aiden. Flair danced over to her brother, who was sinking deeper.

"Aiden! Your hand!"

Aiden heard Flair's voice faintly calling him, but couldn't do anything. He couldn't move; his body was as stiff as a corpse, and he felt the Komodo's hot venom filling his chest and arms. Everything was tightening; his breathing was shallow. He knew he needed to hold on, he knew Flair and Simone needed him, but he was fading fast.

Flair chanced a brief glance skyward, staring at the red star channel sixty feet above. But it might as well have been a mile away for all the difference it would have made. She had no way of getting Aiden close to it.

But her thoughts were cut short as an enormous gunman with a powerful assault rifle riddled the floor with a cavalcade of bullets. Flair activated her shields, repelling the gunfire, but by the shield's brightness, they were weakening. The longer this scene continued, the longer they remained in the Pit, the greater the chances of neither of them getting out of there alive.

It had to be done. Flair could think of nothing else. She had been warned and didn't know what to expect, but she couldn't see any other way.

As the gunman took cover behind a tree to reload, Flair reached into the leather satchel and removed another green. The third one. She stared at it, back at the gunman, and then dove for Aiden's hand as she threw the green crystal into the air.

Whatever Flair imagined would happen, she wasn't prepared for what did. For a brief second, just before the third green crystal hit the ground, Flair thought she might've been able to pick the gunman off with a clean shot once he stopped to reload again. But all thoughts disappeared from her mind the moment the crystal landed.

The ground beneath their feet seemed to have vanished; the eruption that preceded it felt like a giant bomb had exploded around them. In one split second, the earth had torn wide open like the jaws of a giant monster and Aiden, Flair, guards, dirt, grass, Komodos and all were swallowed into a large, churning abyss.

How far they had fallen until Aiden grabbed Flair, neither of them knew. But when Flair felt something grab her ankles, she looked down and saw Aiden clinging to her boots for dear life. She looked up into a whirlpool of dirt, making out a thin red beam that was somehow closing in on them. The same tree that Flair had attached the crystal was also being swallowed into a raging sea of earth.

Flair held out her right glove, and the large red crystal linked with the beam, and they zipped skyward. The beam was taking them out of the danger! Or was it?

Beneath them, the jungle was being swallowed up by an ever-widening hole that matched the speed of Flair's Star Channel. If they didn't reach safety, she and Aiden would be devoured just the same.

"Faster, Flair, faster!" Aiden screamed.

Flair heard Aiden's urging, reminding her of Simone exact same words, and how the Goons travelled faster on the Star

Channels back in Paris. Simone thought it had something to do with the size of the crystals. It gave Flair an idea.

"Hold on tight, bro!" Flair shouted, and felt Aiden squeezing her boots.

She held up her second glove, and intertwined her fingers so the red crystals in her palms touched, and—*WHOOOOSHH*!

Aiden and Flair took off like a rocket, barreling along the channel at breakneck speed. Trees below them became green blurs until they leveled off with the rest of the jungle. They were far ahead of the crumbling chasm, but the end of the channel was approaching fast. Unable to stop, Flair yanked her hands from the channel, sending them freefalling to the jungle floor.

Flair held her fists out, creating two giant red shields, but they gave way on impact, and Aiden and Flair tumbled and bounced, crashing into a cluster of trees.

The ground was trembling ferociously, but Flair wasted no time, leaping up and running towards the giant earthen mouth, watching trees being swallowed before her eyes. She opened the leather satchel and grabbed the largest green she could find, and held it out, focusing.

Aiden tried standing, but the ground was tossing him like a wild bronco. "Flair," he yelled, "what are you doing?"

"We gotta stop this before it destroys everything!" Flair yelled desperately. She shut her eyes, focusing as more jungle collapsed into the void. "Simmy's still in there!"

Aiden didn't understand what she was doing and was about to pull her away from the brink when suddenly the rumbling subsided and stopped. Aiden stared into the dark hole, watching three green sparks streaking towards them.

Flair caught the greens deftly and stared at them, amazed at the damage they caused. She stuffed them back into the leather satchel.

Aiden sighed with relief, spun his sister around, and hugged her for all he was worth.

"Thank you…"

"Riddle me this butthole," Flair panted, grinning, "how does it feel to have your sister save your butt twice?"

"Great," Aiden breathed. "Really great."

He released Flair and they both stared in awe at the great chasm. The void was canyon sized, hundreds of feet deep.

Then, without warning, Flair turned and ran back towards the campus, retching and vomiting. Aiden laughed at first, but then felt his own stomach reeling, and ran in the opposite direction.

He finished coughing and spitting and staggered over to Flair. "Here," and held out a white crystal in his hand. "I think the good vibrations from this thing are gone."

"What? Oh!" Flair took the crystal in her hands. "How did you...?"

"When that joker with the big gun was hammering down on you, this fell out of your pouch. When I grabbed it, everything felt a hundred times better."

Ten minutes later, they entered El Sereno's campus, which had sustained incredible damage. The older buildings were destroyed, sitting in clouds of dust and smoke and one of the new watchtowers had collapsed in a heap. A guard, clutching his head, wobbled from one building to another, otherwise the place was devoid of movement.

At last a lone figure limped across the campus to meet them. Marcus Nefflin, covered head to toe in white dust and ash.

"So, havin' fun with green crystals, ay?" Nefflin grumbled. "Ya almost killed everybody! These buildings ain't indestructible, y'know!"

"Hey we didn't know, okay?" Aiden shouted at Nefflin before Flair could.

"Keep yer voice down!" Nefflin whispered, pulling them behind a large pile of rubble. "Simmy's on the other side of the campus. But we won't make it if those overgrown meatheads hear us!"

"Overgrown meatheads?" Flair said, frowning.

"Yeah. The Goon Squad jus' arrived."

CHAPTER TWENTY-TWO – THE GIRL WITH THE GOLDEN GLOVES

Flair looked like she could've thrown up again.

"The last time we ran into them, we were lucky to escape," she groaned. "What are they here for?"

"Sight-seein', and I hear the jungle is lovely this time of year!" Nefflin snapped. "How the hell should I know why they're here? I'm jus' along for the yuks and giggles, r'member? If ya listened to me we woulda been outta here by now!"

"Oh please!" Flair said, fuming. "You got hijacked the second you stepped out of that trap door! If we listened to you, we'd be dead!"

"Knock it off, both of you," Aiden rebuffed calmly. "We're doing great."

"You call this doing great?" Flair and Nefflin said in unison.

"I do." Aiden turned to Nefflin. "Simmy and Gloria still alive, right?"

Nefflin nodded.

"Okay. And thanks to Flair, most of El Sereno's guys are out of commission. Simmy is able to put the Goons down with this Banshee thing—"

"If you can get her to do it," Flair said, "but she wouldn't for me."

Aiden waved his hand impatiently. "She'll do it. We just need to get to them and we're home free. Where are they?"

"Past the center courtyard," Nefflin said, "hangin' out in one of El Sereno's torture chambers."

"Torture chamber?" Aiden asked. "She's okay, right?"

"Yeah, s' far as I can tell."

"What about Gloria?"

"Don't worry about her, loverboy," Flair said, "She isn't coming."

"What're you talkin' about?" Nefflin said, puzzled. "We ain't leavin' without Gloria."

"Great, another Gloria fan!" Flair snapped. "I don't give a damn what you drooling suck-ups say! She kidnapped my sister, that little chickadee can walk home."

"Oh, no, *you* don't get it," Nefflin said. "Didn't you hear me? The Goons are here. When you need firepower, you don't leave the bazooka behind!"

"Watch it happen!" Flair sounded dangerous and Nefflin backed up a little. "If you didn't notice, I just wasted half of the great El Sereno army—"

"And almost got killed too, I'd bet," Nefflin shot back. "Ya think a coupla greens—"

"If you two don't mind," Aiden interrupted, "we'll save this discussion for when life and death aren't on the line." When neither Flair nor Nefflin protested any further, Aiden slapped Nefflin on the back and said: "Lead the way."

Although he was glad the argument ended, thoughts of Gloria were making Aiden feel sick. Gloria had kidnapped his sister and deliberately brought her to this compound; out of all the places in the world to pick, Gloria had chosen a murderous criminal's backyard. And now Aiden thought he knew why.

El Sereno held some vendetta against his father and the Johnson family because of the death of his own son. Even more unsettling than his father possibly committing murder was that Gloria knew this. Was Gloria's plan to dangle them like a gift in front of El Sereno's cold blue eyes, hoping he'd trade the cure for their lives?

The sun was fully up, shining over the campus, and Aiden got his first good look at El Sereno's compound. The damage was significant, although most of the newer buildings remained intact. The trio crept through the chain of older buildings along their way towards the center courtyard; the thick black dust and smoke that hung in the air provided excellent cover.

Minutes later they stood near the smoldering remains of a collapsed building which had a clear view of the large stone courtyard. Standing in the center were the Goon Squad members.

"Geez, they're big!" Aiden exclaimed, staring at the four enormous men directing a platoon of Prestigeon personnel. They were moving large green crates from the four tall buildings that surrounded the courtyard, loading them into two big delivery trucks.

Nefflin moved forward, squinting through thick black smoke. "The big guy with the tattoos on his arms is Musclehead, their leader."

"Those two," Flair pointed at two Goons inspecting crates, "chased us from Jump Point."

"The guy in the leather jacket is No-Neck, tough sucker, big mouth. The skinny guy next to him is Danny Lankershim, Lanky. Used to be one of us."

"He was a Journeyman?" Flair said, astonished.

"Yep, but he turned on us," Nefflin said. Aiden felt a jolt to his heart at the words *turned on us*, thinking of Gloria. "And the kid with the big hands is Man-Child. Wow, thought they had 'im in Morocco."

Aiden stared silently, scanning every corner of the courtyard. They couldn't go through the buildings or behind them. Any way they might try would spell doom.

"We can't get past here without being spotted," he muttered.

"Obviously," Nefflin growled. "Now ya wanna smash and grab?"

"I don't think we have a choice," Aiden said. "We'll do the smashing, you do the grabbing, and we'll meet back—"

"Shhh!" Flair whispered. "Look!"

A dozen men appeared from a haze of black smoke opposite them, limping into the courtyard, looking the worse for wear. And to Aiden and Flair's complete astonishment, the first man in the group was...

"El Sereno?" Flair gasped, watching the tall man hobble over to an amused Musclehead. "Are you freaking kidding me?"

"Oh yeah," Nefflin said grimly. "El Sereno's a survivor."

"And he's gonna head straight for Simone," Aiden said. "Let's move."

Aiden, Flair and Nefflin quickly crept through the haze of black smoke until they could go no further. They had reached the edge of the courtyard and Nefflin pointed to the building catty-corner from their position where Gloria and Simone were, and right in-between were Goons, El Sereno and a few dozen guards.

"This is impossible," Flair said. "Even if we could fight the Goons off, which I doubt, we're not gonna get to Simone before El Sereno does."

But Aiden was no longer looking at the Goons or the courtyard. He was staring straight up into the sky, smiling.

"We're not gonna fight them, we're going over them," he said simply, pointing to the rooftops of the tall buildings surrounding the courtyard.

"We're gonna do what?" Flair said.

Aiden pointed from the rooftop of the nearest building to the one opposite. "If we go up and over the courtyard, these sightlines are so tight, they won't see us unless they're staring straight into the sky. And why would they? All the action's on the ground, they're talking to each other, they got their green crates to load. So if we go above…"

Aiden looked down, seeing Flair and Nefflin were staring at him, utterly confounded.

"Well, it worked for Lionel Vann," he remarked. "Remember? In *The Defender of the Gods*?" They continued to stare at him. "Oh come on, it was only his best book!"

"I ended up in the emergency room playing your *Vann Fan* crap, and that's when we were in a kitchen."

"Flair, after what you just did, this is cake! Where's that thing Carson gave you?"

Flair reached into her waistband, pulling out Carson's out the channel gun. Aiden nodded. "Good. Make us an elevator going up."

Flair, shaking her head, fitted a white crystal inside the gun, aimed, and shot it into the edge of the rooftop of the closest building. She pressed another white crystal into the ground with her boot, creating a white star channel, nearly invisible in the bright sunlight.

She handed a white crystal in Aiden, who reluctantly accepted it.

"Okay," Aiden said queasily, "ladies first."

Reaching out with her right glove, Flair zipped into the air, looking like a red ghost gliding along an invisible wire. She sprang onto the roof easily and trotted across the rooftop to get a view of the courtyard.

Flair knew immediately that Aiden was right. From this angle, no one would see them unless they were staring straight up into the sky, and why would they, as the Goons argued heatedly with El Sereno. Their voices echoed upward so that Flair could hear them clearly.

"I'm not stopping just 'cause you got your butt kicked by a couple of kids," Musclehead said. "I got deadlines and things to do, Cessano! Sort it out when we split!"

"Mackleford and I had an agreement!" El Sereno screamed. "We each get what we want, and I want my men to search the campus! Mackleford won't be happy if they escape!"

Musclehead seemed to find his last comment amusing.

"Mack's not taking your call, Cessano!" he said. "Just tank their plane, that should keep 'em from escapin', right?"

"Don't you think I've done that already? It doesn't solve *my* problem. But maybe if I stop these trucks at the airport, maybe he'll take my call then! What do you think?"

Musclehead rounded on El Sereno, his eyes flashing.

"Then you'll be messin' with me. You sure you wanna do that?"

Their argument continued as Flair jammed one white crystal into a crack on the rooftop, aimed with the channel gun, and fired another white across the courtyard to the building directly opposite them. Nefflin came running up, having ascended to the roof, with Aiden wobbling behind him, looking green around the gills.

"You really need to get used to these," Flair said.

"I'll be...fine," Aiden burped. He was standing perfectly still but felt like he was on a rollercoaster.

"Let's not dilly-dally," Nefflin barked, and he leapt off the edge of the roof, the white crystal in his hand caught the star channel, and he glided smoothly to the other side.

Aiden was next. Pale and queasy as he was, he still made it across the expanse, Nefflin grabbed him as his feet caught the rooftop. Aiden staggered. His stomach couldn't take much more of this.

But as Flair prepared to glide over, Aiden fell to his knees retched so loudly that it reverberated across the entire camp. Everyone in the courtyard turned and looked up.

"Dammit, kid!" Nefflin said.

El Sereno's eyes darted into the bright blue sky. "There!" he shouted, pointing to Flair first and then to Aiden and Nefflin.

Musclehead spotted Flair gliding over the courtyard. Grinning, he raised his Ruijen Staff high into the air.

CRAACKK!

A bright yellow bolt sizzled through the air, aiming where Aiden and Nefflin stood. They dove as the bolt ripped the rooftop apart, sending chunks of concrete flying in every direction.

There was a blinding white flash, followed by a sound wave that made the hairs on Aiden's neck ripple. The white crystal had shattered and the Star Channel was gone before Flair made it across. Her legs kicked and flayed as she plummeted to the courtyard.

Flair barely reacted, closing her hands into fists at the last possible second. The shields activated inches above the ground, but disappeared when Flair's body struck the courtyard floor with a sickening thud.

Pain surged through Aiden as if he'd hit the ground himself. He ran to the roof's edge and looked. Flair was lying on the ground, motionless.

"FLAIR!"

Aiden lurched forward as if he were going to leap off the roof, but Nefflin pulled him back, just in time to avoid another thunderbolt from Musclehead.

"Get back boy! Wanna get disintegrated?"

Aiden yanked away from Nefflin, searching for a way down, and spotted an access ladder on the other side of the roof. Another crackling bolt of energy forced him to the floor.

No-Neck and Lanky looked at the prone body lying face down in the dirt.

"Who is that?" Musclehead said, pointing towards Flair with his staff.

"The Johnson girl, Laura's daughter!" yelled No-Neck, and he pulled his Ruijen Staff, proceeding with caution.

"*That's* who you had trouble with?" Musclehead chuckled.

"Shut up, you weren't there!" No-Neck growled. He was halfway to Flair when a red bolt blasted his weapon out of his hand. Shocked and enraged, No-Neck spun and two more red bolts to the chest knocked him flat.

The source of the blasts came sprinting onto the center courtyard: Gloria, enveloped in a red aura, pushing Simone's wheelchair with one hand and firing on Musclehead and Lanky with the red crystal gripped in her other hand. The Prestigeon men wanted no part of this, dropping the crates and scattering in every direction.

"*Gannares!*" El Sereno and Musclehead shouted together. Musclehead aimed his Ruijen towards Gloria.

"Gloria, look out!" Aiden shouted.

But Gloria was on top of it. Without breaking stride, she grabbed a second red crystal from the wheelchair pocket, flipped it into the air, and caught it in her right hand. A bright shield formed just as Musclehead's energy beam struck.

But rather than deflecting the beam, Gloria's shield seemed to absorb its energy. Musclehead stared uncertainly as Gloria skidded next to Flair. The crystals flickered like a broken neon light, and, raising her arm, Gloria hurled them at Musclehead, hit the ground and shaped Flair's left glove into a fist.

Musclehead cursed and ran for it.

The crystals tumbled where Musclehead just vacated as the shield activated around Gloria, Simone and Flair. There was a bright flash, followed by two enormous explosions that rocked the courtyard. The Prestigeon trucks were blown backwards across the stone pavement and crashed into the building opposite them.

Seconds later, the haze of smoke left behind from the blasts was clearing. El Sereno had been thrown over twenty feet into the air by the dual blasts, but the old man was on his feet before any one else. His face was possessed, manic, crazed. No-Neck's staff had slid next to him, and he grabbed it and charged towards Gloria. Aiden, watching from above, yelled a warning to Gloria, whose back was turned.

"Gloria! Watch—"

But a third explosion shook the area before Aiden finished, as one of the trucks erupted into a ball of flame. Its front grill flew through the air, smashing into El Sereno, and sailing him out of the courtyard.

Gloria looked up towards the roof where she had heard Aiden's voice and smiled.

"Aiden! Get down here, I need you!"

Aiden and Nefflin hadn't yet moved, but at Gloria's word, they leapt into action, both streaking towards the roof ladder.

Gloria grabbed a white crystal from the wheelchair pocket and hoisted Flair to her feet.

"Flair? Can you walk?"

She pressed the white crystal against the back of Flair's neck, and a white aura brightened around both of them. Flair snapped alert and winced, clutching her left knee as she tried to walk.

Gloria knelt, bringing the white crystal to Flair's knee. From the look on Flair's face, her pain was subsiding, but she began to glare at Gloria as she administered to her knee. Flair jerked away from Gloria, turned and saw her sister, and limped towards her.

"Simmy!" She fell into a hug, nearly tipping the wheelchair over.

"Thank God you're alive!" Simone squealed. "Gloria said you dropped three greens. You didn't really, did you? Granny said that it was dangerous!" Flair patted Simone on her head, looking at her skin, which was more pale and withered. She whipped around at Gloria.

"Get away from us," Flair snarled. "As far as you can."

But before Gloria could reply, Aiden and Nefflin ran up, both out of breath. Aiden gawked; the once beautiful courtyard looked like a battle zone. Every window on the surrounding four buildings was shattered. Large cracks split the pavement. Bodies strewn in every direction. The two large trucks were over turned, the green crates and their spilled contents of orchids littered the area. A deep crater stood in the center where Gloria had thrown the red crystals. Members of the Goon Squad were sprawled everywhere, from the looks of it, one of them had been blasted into the upper floors of one of the buildings, as Aiden saw a pair of enormous legs and boots hanging out its windows.

Gloria looked at Aiden; her eyes looked like they were on fire, and Aiden had mixed feelings at the moment. He was angry with her for kidnapping Simone and was unsure of what else she might be capable of…Mainly, however, he was glad she was all right.

"Aiden, look, I'm…"

Aiden shook his head. "I don't want explanations, I want to leave. Let's get out of here before these guys come around."

Too late. The Goons had come around. Lanky, Man-Child, and No-Neck got to their feet shakily, and Musclehead dropped from the upper window, landing in the center of the cracked courtyard.

But Gloria wasn't paying attention to Musclehead or to any of the Goons. She was staring at the orchids that had spilled from their crates, and suddenly her face looked illuminated.

"Perfect…" she whispered. "Perfecting them—" She grabbed Aiden by the collar, shaking him. "These flowers, I think they have something to do with the cure!"

"We can't worry about that now!" Aiden yelled. "Which way is out?"

"You don't understand, Aiden, if we stop Purification, we stop Mackleford—"

Musclehead fired another crackling energy attack at the group, missing. Flair, limping ahead, struck back, firing three red bolts at him, but her attacks didn't seem potent. Musclehead's bo staff slapped the shots away with ease. With one giant sweep of his weapon, he formed an enormous white belt of blazing energy.

"We're sittin' ducks!" Nefflin shouted. "Get movin'!"

Nefflin grabbed Gloria by her arm and Aiden sprinted across the courtyard with Simone's wheelchair as Musclehead's energy whip snapped against the pavement. Musclehead swung his weapon again, forcing them inside one of the courtyard buildings, before extinguishing the giant whip.

"This ain't our fight, boys," Musclehead screamed to his fellow Goons. "Let's get our work done and go!"

He walked over to the truck that hadn't exploded, and incredibly with just one hand, pulled it upright. The truck bounced and wobbled on all four tires, and No-Neck rushed around to the back of the truck, side by side with Musclehead.

"Man-Child! Lanky!" No-Neck yelled to the other two Goons. "Quit messing around and let's split!" He was tossing broken and unbroken crates into the truck as fast as possible.

But Man-Child and Lanky weren't listening. Man-Child was holding a bleeding gash across his ribs and Lanky's mouth was dripping blood. The look in their eyes suggested they had no intention of leaving.

"Not 'til I get some!" Lanky declared. He snatched his Ruijen Staff off the ground, and Man-Child scooped up No-Neck's staff lying next to the unconscious El Sereno. Together, the two giant men charged towards Aiden and company.

Aiden stared at the Goons through the shattered glass doors. "Move!" Aiden shouted. "Through here." He pushed Simone's wheelchair through the lobby, glass crunching underfoot.

"Bring it down!" Lanky roared to his companion. And with a nod, Man-Child swung his staff horizontally through the air, releasing a barrage of small black pellets, which exploded and ripped into the building's outer wall. Without hesitation, Man-Child whipped the staff around again, showering the building with more exploding pellets. The entire building teetered.

Aiden and the others dove into a nearby hallway as more earsplitting explosions rattled the building. From their view could see the courtyard clearly through a large window frame that held remnants of broken glass.

"He's gonna drop the building on us!" Nefflin screamed.

"Keep them inside, Lankershim!" they heard Man-Child shout. Aiden looked outside, watching Man-Child climb on top of the smoking remains of the damaged truck and continue his bombardment. "Don't let them walk out of that door!"

Lanky ran over to a flanking position, opposite of Man-Child, blocking the only other possible exit. Leaving the building would mean facing Lanky or entering Man-Child's line of fire.

Dust was raining down on them and everyone coughed. The building creaked and groaned, reeling from another blast from outside. At that moment, Aiden looked around, counting... *Gloria, Simone, Nefflin...*

"Flair?" His heart stopped. Flair was nowhere in sight. He looked back towards the lobby, but there was no sign of her. "FLAIR! Where's Flair?"

"She must be outside!" Simone cried. Another explosion. "Aiden! Go get her!"

"Get her?" Nefflin said. "Hell, inside ain't no better than outside!"

Gloria grabbed Aiden's arm. "She's badly injured, her energy is drastically low. Her attacks won't have the same punch."

"We cain't stay in here," Nefflin growled in Aiden's ear. He was stating the obvious, as the building didn't seem like it would take much more pounding, and if Flair was still out there, she needed help...and fast.

Aiden looked at Lanky, twirling his bo staff and cackling. They'd have to go through him; it was their only way out. He looked at Nefflin, who had that same reckless look in his eye, nodded, and sprang ahead, right through the back door, charging towards Lanky.

But at that moment, shooting rattled from above. Guards in the watchtowers were raining gunfire down on the courtyard, forcing Aiden to backpedal and retreat back inside, while a tall man in black shouted, pointing in their direction. El Sereno's men were back on their feet as their leader bellowed commands to his men, limping across the center of the courtyard.

"Hey, idiot!" Lanky barked at El Sereno, rising from the ground, dusting himself off. "They almost shot *me!*"

"Forget it, fool!" Musclehead yelled, now flinging stray flowers into the back of the truck. "Mack'll do worse if we lose this shipment! Let's go!"

Aiden quietly hoped Lanky and Man-Child would follow Musclehead's warning, but they acted as if they couldn't hear him. And from their position, with both exits covered and the watchtowers pinning them down, there was no escape.

"Simone," Aiden said, turning to her. "I know you don't like it, but you're gonna have to scream…"

Simone shuddered at the thought, but it was only a matter of time before the building collapsed on them all. She nodded, drew a deep breath and…

CRASH!

Something flew through the broken windowpane, sailing back inside the building and sliding across the floor, stopping next to Nefflin. It was Flair.

"Where in the world were you?" Aiden shouted.

"I was trying to get a crate of those flowers," Flair breathed, pushing up from the floor.

"You were…" Aiden stammered. "Are you insane?"

"Well, *she* said it was the cure, I had to try…"

"What's in your hands, Flair?" Simone asked. "Those don't look like flowers."

Everyone stared at Flair's hands as the building trembled. In one hand she held the Ruijen Staff that Aiden had taken from Mr. Quick; in the other, a pair of golden gloves, bedecked with red and white crystals.

"No Simmy, but I found these," she said, "next to that El Sereno guy."

"Hallelujah!" Nefflin breathed. "We're saved!"

Gloria stepped forward, holding her hand out. "Thank God. My gloves."

Flair stared at the gloves, saying nothing.

"Flair. Please."

Everyone silently watched Flair, who hadn't as much as looked at Gloria.

"So," Gloria said, pacing around Flair, "what are you going to do? Let this building crush us, let everyone get shot to death, or hand me my gloves?"

Flair glared at Aiden, waiting to see whom he would side with. Aiden didn't look as if he wanted to make that decision, but...

"Just do it, Flair," he said quietly.

"She's our ticket home, sweetheart!" Nefflin growled. "I told ya we need her!"

Gloria eyed the gloves like a hungry tigress. But Flair didn't take her eyes off Aiden. "I can't beat her, bro. If I give these to her, and she decides to double cross us..."

"I'm not your enemy, Flair," Gloria shouted, "but we're running out of time!"

Another chunk of the building crumbled behind them, this time close to Simone. Flair stared up; the ceiling could give at any minute. Gloria looked at Aiden with a "now or never" expression.

Flair flung the gloves into Gloria's chest. "This isn't settled between me and you, precious," Flair said.

Without hesitation, Gloria put them on, igniting her blazing red aura. She walked next to Flair, but didn't look at her, keeping her eyes fixed ahead.

"You're wrong about me," she said, "but it'll wait." And with that, she burst off into the courtyard.

It didn't take long for Gloria to make her presence felt. Her first order of business was those watchtowers. Two echoing blasts boomed from her golden gloves, hammering the towers and sending their occupants plunging through the open window to the ground.

El Sereno turned towards the towers and watched Gloria dashing across the courtyard, launching powerful blasts that knocked over several guards at once. She flipped and spun, dropping men from every angle, and even fired at El Sereno, brushing him back from a fallen rifle. El Sereno kept his distance from the weapon, instead sending men in her direction.

"Shoot her!" El Sereno screamed, his face manic, possessed. "The man who kills her will be as a son to me!"

But they couldn't. Gloria was a human blur, moving at top speed, blasting off crippling attacks and creating enormous shields that deflected everything they fired at her.

"Ya see?" Nefflin snickered, elbowing Flair in the ribs. "Now that's talent!"

Flair stared, totally mesmerized at Gloria's speed and power, but shook herself out of her trance, narrowing her eyes.

"What are we, cheerleaders?" Aiden said before turning Simone's wheelchair towards the door and pointing over her shoulder at Lanky, who was screaming obscenities at Gloria. "Simmy, you're up!"

Simone opened her mouth, but didn't scream. Horror had fallen over her as she stared up at the ceiling. Several giant cracks had suddenly split along the entire ceiling and with a resounding roar, the building collapsed around them. Nefflin leapt over Simone and Aiden pulled Flair to the ground, shielding her with his body, bracing for the impact.

But there was no impact. No pain. Did the building fall? There didn't seem to be any bricks or beams crushing them, not even dust cutting off the air. Through Aiden's shut eyelids, everything was bright red. He slowly opened his eyes, looking above him.

A large crystal shield surrounded them, and stacked on top of the glowing barrier laid jagged chunks of debris.

"Good job, sunshine," Aiden said, grinning at Flair. "Guess that makes it three—"

"Don't thank me…" Flair said, showing Aiden her hands, which were empty of crystals.

"But—then how?"

Nefflin was already bent over, pulling Simone's wheelchair through a gap ahead. Small chunks of concrete tumbled along the top of the barrier as Aiden and Flair crawled after them.

Aiden contorted through the gap, followed by Flair. About twenty feet away was Gloria, her right hand aimed in their direction, straining, as if holding a tremendous weight. They were momentarily stunned, realizing what happened. Somehow, Gloria had thrown a barrier over them inside of the building before it collapsed, and held it up while they escaped.

"How did she do that?" Flair said, breathless and amazed.

"You guys okay?" Gloria grunted. But she didn't wait for an answer before opening her right hand. The red barrier disappeared, dropping the remainder of the building in a heap. The maneuver seemed to have taken something out of Gloria, because she staggered, disoriented and weak.

Man-Child roared in frustration, furious that no one was crushed under the rubble of the building, and fired the explosive pellets at Gloria. Gloria's glove closed in time to activate a shield, but it wavered in brightness. Behind her, Lanky was charging, and with a twist of his wrist, exposed the stiletto blades on his staff. Gloria fired, but the blast had nothing behind it as Lanky slapped it away easily, shouldered his staff, and aimed to spear Gloria like a knight in a joust.

Gloria's right hand activated another red shield, but Lanky's spear pierced her defense, slowly and steadily. Gloria stared at Lanky in shock, watching the razor sharp stiletto inching ever closer to her throat, with Lanky grinning from the staff's other end.

"Not this time, Gannares!" he said. The tip of the blade pricked Gloria's neck, drawing blood. She twisted away from it, dropping to one knee as another bombardment from Man-Child hammered her shield to the left.

"AIDEN! WHAT ARE YOU DOING?"

What Aiden was doing was rushing towards Lanky, barely hearing Flair's cry. No weapons and no ideas, but he had to do something.

But Aiden never reached Lanky, for at that moment a deafening roar filled the air. Everyone, including the Goons, stopped what they were doing, turning eastward towards the sound.

Out of the bright blue sky, a helicopter came screaming into the compound, its silver rails scraping the outer wall, barreling towards Man-Child, who stood on top of the overturned truck with a stunned expression on his face. Just as he made to run for it, three silhouettes sprang from the copter and barreled into the courtyard as the explosion from the crashing copter ripped the air and sent everyone ducking from flying shrapnel. The smoke dissipated slowly, and all heads turned to see who had just joined the battle.

Raul, Ramon, and Alfredo, the Gannares Brothers, walked through the haze of black smoke, grunting and pounding their fists into their hands.

"It's about time!" Gloria shouted at them.

Two days ago, if anyone had told Aiden he'd be excited to see the Gannares Brothers after Paris, he would have laughed in their faces, but their sudden arrival seemed to turn the tide. The Brothers were a force; dashing between El Sereno's guards like a pack of cheetahs, performing handsprings and back flips, surprising men from behind with crushing haymakers. Ramon, the shortest brother, leapt right next to Simone and smashed his fist into an astonished guard's face. Simone struggled to contain her excitement. She had never wanted to scream so badly.

"Come on, Aiden," Flair shouted. "This way!"

There was so much going on, Aiden had become a spectator, but at Flair's word, he grabbed Simone's wheelchair and sprinted towards her. He looked around for Gloria, who, in the commotion of an exploding helicopter and the Brothers arrival, seemed to have disappeared.

"Where's Gloria?"

"Sorry," Flair said, "not really concerned about her! Mr. Nefflin!"

Nefflin was holding his electric baton, standing over Lanky's twitching, electrocuted body. He spun, not towards Flair, but to another bellowing voice somehow rising over the medley of noise.

"GET UP!" El Sereno shouted. "AFTER THEM!"

Nefflin backpedaled, scanning the area. Musclehead and No-Neck continued heaving crates into the truck as if there wasn't a blazing wreck of a helicopter thirty feet away. Lanky turned over, pushing himself up from the ground. El Sereno's men were crawling out from their places of cover.

"Where's Gannares?" Nefflin said.

"She's on her own!" Flair shouted.

Lanky crawled to a knee, his yellow teeth fixed in an ugly snarl, and picked up his Ruijen Staff. Alfredo grabbed Flair's arm, and Raul grabbed Aiden's, pulling him away from the courtyard.

"Mr. Nefflin, we're leaving! Bye!" Flair shouted. Nefflin took one final backwards glance, turned and followed.

It was ten minutes of non-stop running; the compound was certainly bigger than Aiden had imagined. They pelted through the campus, tripping and stumbling but never falling, ducking between buildings and around large planters. The Gannares Brothers led the way, crashing through fences and clearing the way for Aiden and Simone's wheelchair, while Flair and Nefflin pulled up the rear. They reached a steep embankment and began climbing.

"After we get out of here, then what?" Flair asked.

"Any ideas, Neff?" Aiden gasped, rolling Simone up the embankment.

Nefflin didn't answer. He looked every bit of a man in his fifties that had just nearly run a mile in a stifling jungle. Out of breath and wheezing, Nefflin collapsed at the top of the embankment where they discovered a gravel road running between the jungle and the campus. Flair had just reached the top, limping badly, when a loud roar came over the trees behind them. The big Prestigeon truck was barreling down the road, with Musclehead behind the wheel.

The Gannares Brothers were jumping and cheering, pointing at the vehicle as it passed them in a cloud of dust. Aiden didn't understand until he the dust cleared away. Gloria was clinging to the top of the truck, her flaming auburn hair whipping wildly in every direction.

A crystal blast at the passenger door shattered the window, and Gloria prepared to swing into the truck, but the truck bounded over a bump in the road. Gloria bounced from the roof to the hood, hitting the gravel road with a crunch.

The truck smashed through a large metal gate, the Prestigeon logo glinting as Musclehead picked up speed on the highway. Gloria was on her feet, enraged, sprinting for the gate. Everyone followed, exiting the compound, running past a sign: *NUEVO MUNDO FARMACEUTICO.*

Gloria looked ready to pursue the truck on foot, but turned back, racing up to Flair, who was stooped over, clutching her leg.

"Channel Gun?" Gloria snapped.

"What?" Flair snapped back.

"*A Channel Gun!* Do you have one?"

"Oh, wait…" Flair fumbled around her back, feeling for the channel gun, which was tangled in her clothing.

"Come on!" Gloria said, shaking her hand at Flair. "Hurry!"

Flair finally freed the gun and Gloria snatched it, tore two red crystals from her golden gloves, slapping one into the gun. She aimed, pulled the trigger, and the crystal whistled through the air. She pounded the other red into the trunk of a nearby tree.

"Come on, come on!" she pleaded, gazing at the crystal as if her life depended on. But after a few seconds, she screamed in frustration, slamming the channel gun into the mud.

Aiden, not holding any red crystals couldn't see what made Gloria upset, but Flair could: a thin luminous beam, stretching into the distance, but not attached to the truck, which disappeared in the distance.

Gloria turned on Flair. "Faster next time! We could have caught them!" she shouted, before walking away.

"Cool it, Gloria!" Aiden said, restraining Flair around the waist.

A sound arose from somewhere inside the campus, the loud rumble of engines revving, which didn't go unnoticed by anyone in the group.

"Here they come!" Nefflin wheezed. "Let's hustle!"

Gloria's mind seemed to be elsewhere. She was still gazing in the direction where the truck had dipped beneath the horizon. "They're taking them back to Colorado," she muttered. "To their main lab. I can beat them there, I just need—"

Gloria turned her head, distracted by another sound in the distance, a low, rhythmic humming, followed by the screech of metal-on-metal.

"That's it!" she said, and sprinted off down the highway, not waiting, not explaining. The others stared at each other, bewildered.

"Where are we going?" Aiden yelled ahead, as everyone scrambled to follow.

"The train!" Gloria shouted.

"What train?" Flair said.

"The train that runs from here to Córdoba! Come on!"

Gloria ran up the highway, darted into a gap in the trees, and followed a dirt road, heading in the direction of a locomotive's whistle. The others were behind her, whippy ferns and tall brambles of dried grass scratching them as they tried to keep up with Gloria.

In a clearing ahead sat a small train station, and departing it was a sleek, shiny passenger train tugging a dozen coach cars full of people. The engine was slowly chugging out of the clearing and into the surrounding jungle as several of its passengers stared out of their windows, puzzled at the group of people running frantically for the train.

The rumbling engines were just on the other side of the trees. Aiden felt his heart pounding; they were falling further behind the caboose. Just when it looked like they wouldn't catch it, the train lurched and the brakes squealed.

Aiden saw a chubby man waving from the engine; evidently, the conductor spotted them and stopped the train. Although it allowed everyone to get onto the train, including Simone and her wheelchair, Aiden wanted to put as much distance between themselves and El Sereno's men as possible.

"We need to talk to the conductor," Gloria said to Aiden after the two of them helped an exhausted Nefflin onto the caboose. "If Cess finds out where we are, he'll stop this train."

A loud roar of engines erupted and everyone turned, staring out the window. Five jeeps filled with El Sereno's men burst through the clearing. Aiden grabbed Simone's wheelchair.

"Keep moving!" he yelled ahead.

They sprinted through a dozen coach cars, knocking into passengers the Gannares Brothers leading the way, with Aiden and Simone pulling up the rear. It They reached the final coach, finding its passengers cowering in their seats, looking wary.

Aiden pushed past one of the passengers towards an open window and poked his head outside. The jeeps were gone but several of El Sereno's men were clinging to the side of the train and entering through the caboose.

"We're gonna have company!" Aiden yelled.

They stared at one another for several seconds, grim-faced. Aiden continued up the aisle, taking Simone to the front of the car where there was a small docking station for wheelchairs.

"We're gonna have to fight it out here, Simmy," he said. "Stay put."

The Gannares Brothers were muttering and squeaking to each other, and together with a nod, they leapt over the tops of the seats, stepping on the heads of the frightened passengers, heading towards the previous compartment of the train from where they came.

"Where are you going?" Gloria asked. Ramon looked at Simone and grunted, then slid the door open and disappeared into the next coach car.

"He said they're going to head them off," Simone said. "Give us time."

"Excellent!" Aiden's respect for the Gannares Brothers was growing. He pulled Nefflin next to him by his elbow. "See if you can work your magic so this conductor keeps us on schedule," he said. Nefflin gave Aiden a short nod and climbed through the door leading to the engine.

Gloria stood behind, staring avidly at Aiden as he secured Simone's wheelchair. "Neff, wait up," Gloria said, following him into the engine compartment.

Aiden kissed Simone on the forehead after Gloria disappeared into the engine car. "You'll be fine here, Simmy. I'm going to help the brothers. I won't let anyone get back here."

"Just don't be mad at Gloria, Aiden," Simone yawned, looking very sleepy. "She did it for her brothers. She's the little sister. She had to."

Frosty air escaped from Simone's nose and Aiden watched her drift to sleep. He walked past Flair who was glaring at her knee, holding a white crystal and trying to nurse it as Gloria had, but it seemed ineffective.

Passing through the car door, Aiden stood on the ramp connecting the coach cars, watching an incredible brawl going on in the next car. El Sereno's men were unsuccessfully trying to get through the Gannares Brothers. He grinned, felt something brush his arm and turned. Gloria was there.

"What's up?" Aiden said.

"My brothers need my help," Gloria said as Raul sent a guard tumbling over the heads of frightened passengers and into a window. There was a curious look in her eye.

"I was thinking the same thing, but looks like they've got it covered," Aiden said.

"Maybe." Gloria said, pushing past Aiden and stepping to the other coach. Aiden grabbed her arm.

"What's going on?"

Gloria didn't meet his eye. "I'm not coming with you guys."

Aiden stared at her, momentarily speechless before uttering: "Why?"

"It's Cess," she said, shaking her head. "He can do a lot more than just stop this train. He can shut down Argentina. He has that kind of power in this country. You need to get out and I'm the perfect distraction."

"I don't care what he can do," Aiden said, almost shouting. "We need to stay together, we can't keep separating like this. We need you!"

Gloria turned as another guard slammed into the window of the railcar behind them, followed by a joyous chorus of grunts. She looked back; Aiden hadn't taken his eyes off of her. She leaned close to him, patting his hand.

"You don't need me. This is your show, city boy. You'll be fine."

She knelt, grabbing a rusty coupler that attached the two cars, preparing to disconnect it. Aiden dropped to a knee as well, snatching her hand away.

"You wanted the Song of Solomon to get the cure. We're one plane ride away from it and you're leaving?"

"Because I need to play my part to make sure that it happens."

Aiden stared in disbelief. "Play your part? Don't be stupid. Get your brothers and come on."

"No! Cess will slow you down. I'm going back."

"What happens when we get to Mackleford? I can't fight like you."

Gloria smirked. "Well, yeah, you got that right!" She laughed, leaning in, seemingly studying his face.

"Right, so you need to—" Aiden began, but Gloria cut him off.

"Don't," Gloria said. "Stop. You have a job to do, Aiden. You know it now, don't you? And stop worrying about fighting; your dad wasn't great with crystals either." She moved closer. "Your talents are better than fighting. And those are the talents we need right now."

Although her face was filthy and her auburn hair was sweaty and plastered to her face, she looked as stunning as the day they first met, and her eyes had never shone brighter. Aiden's heart slowed as he stared into them. He felt relaxed. And somehow, without either of them realizing it, they were as near to each other as two people could be without touching.

"I still gotta get the Song, get Simmy cured, and face Mackleford. This is far from over." Aiden took a deep breath. "But I have the craziest feeling that—"

"—you're gonna be just fine." Gloria finished with a smile.

"Yeah, but I'm just—"

"—worried about me," she finished again. "I've been fighting the Dominion since I was fourteen. Relax."

Their faces were less than inches from each other, their eyes saying what words couldn't. Gloria broke the gaze first, looking down, and re-clutching the coupler.

"Just save some of the cure for my brothers," she said, tears welling in her sparkling eyes, "and a piece of Mackleford for me if you can!"

Aiden touched Gloria's face, wiping tears from it, and gently pinching her cheek as she had done so often to him. He couldn't resist, and she didn't even try. They kissed. It was soft, warm, like a beam of golden sunlight.

All their senses seemed to disconnect from the world; smells, sights, sounds all vanished, except for the touch of their lips, which was all too brief. The coupler had turned in her hand, and she was departing. They stretched towards each other, longing to keep hold, to connect, to stay with the other as long as possible. Aiden felt it was more than railcars pulling them apart. Life and circumstances, cruel and hateful, were tearing her from him.

Finally, it was gone, and the world returned with a loud rush, although the golden warmth still clung in the air, and he felt her tears lingering on his face. She didn't look at him anymore; she jumped, turned, and disappeared into the departing railcar.

Aiden stared at the top of the railcar. The Gannares Brothers had taken to the roof, whooping, cheering, and smacking high fives. Then Ramon pointed and elbowed the others, who turned and looked down at Aiden, still kneeling. Aiden didn't know why, but one-by-one, the three brothers gave him a thumbs-up salute. Aiden stood and returned the gesture, watching as the car faded further, further and further away, until it was nothing more than a black dot on the horizon.

CHAPTER TWENTY-THREE – THE SONG OF SOLOMON

Two hours later, one hour outside of Córdoba, Simone was in rare form. Asleep.

But two hours earlier, she had been awake and alert, yammering non-stop about everything that just happened in Montecito, reliving every single story to her audience of terrified passengers, who couldn't understand a word she was saying.

However, Nefflin, who was seated next to Simone, had been tinkering with Mr. Quick's Ruijen Staff, activated some mechanism and sprayed a cloud of yellow mist into the air. He was out cold before the staff rolled off his lap and hit the floor, and Simone, slurred "that hellllicopterrr wasss soooooooo cooooooool…" before dropping off. The gas had spread throughout the coach car, knocking everyone else out cold, except for Aiden and Flair, who were seated in the back, far away from the mist.

Aiden was glad for the peace and quiet so he and Flair could discuss their next move. Nefflin had already gained the conductor's cooperation to keep the train on schedule, promising a hefty pay off if they arrived safely in Córdoba, where Gloria had left behind the stolen airplane. When Aiden told everyone Gloria stayed behind to keep El Sereno's forces occupied while they escaped, Flair was the only one who didn't praise Gloria's effort. Her anger hadn't cooled and with her frizzled amber hair and furrowed brow, she gave the impression of a lioness ready to pounce. Aiden decided it would be a good idea to keep Gloria's name out of the discussion.

"Let's say you're right," Flair said, "and the Song is where you think it is, and we get it. How do we know where to go from there? Mackleford never told us."

"He never told us because he thinks Pops told us where he stole the Song from. That's why Mackleford came to us in the first place, which means he believe we'll know where to go once we've got it."

"So that doesn't answer the question. Where do we go once we have it?"

"Restoration College, Colorado. Gloria said it was the only campus that had a Dominion presence. That's where Mackleford will be."

Flair's eye appeared to twitch involuntarily at the mention of Gloria's name. Aiden cursed himself inwardly for forgetting and switched subjects.

"It's gonna be incredible, isn't it? The Song of Solomon, over three thousand years old. Wonder how it held up so long?"

"I just wanna know how it gives people wisdom," Flair said.

"It doesn't," Aiden said with a roll of his eyes. "It's like a rabbit's foot, a lucky charm. If you believe it brings you wisdom, then you feel wise." He shook his head. "Stupid superstitions. Still, you don't run into a three thousand-year-old artifact every day. Its age makes it priceless no matter what it is, and if it was really owned by Solomon...?"

Aiden recapped the life of Solomon for the next half-hour, and as Flair was already tired, a history lesson was just what she needed to put her to sleep. As they arrived in Córdoba, the passengers awoke, feeling drugged, but none the worse for wear. Nefflin had evidently taken very good care of the train conductor, as he shook his hand over and over again, giving him a big hug, and even arranging their cab ride to the Cordoba airport. Once arriving at the airport, in what was by now customary for the Johnsons, Nefflin disappeared for twenty minutes and returned with the proper credentials for the next leg of their journey.

They stepped into the cabin of the Falconer 8800, a sleek private jet, wall-to-wall with plush leather chairs and couches. Although the seats were inviting, Aiden sat in the cockpit with Nefflin instead, while Flair parked Simone next to one of the plush leather chairs and sank into it, exhausted. Simone didn't dare tell Flair, but she just so happened to be sitting in the same chair Gloria had sat in on their flight to Argentina.

In contrast to the events of the week, the flight to Borneo was uneventful. Aiden woke Flair and Simone as the plane prepared to land in a city called Seria. They exited the comfortable, air-conditioned plane into scorching, sweltering heat and stared at the surrounding landscape.

The Borneo jungle was far different than its Argentinean counterpart. Dense and thick, it reminded Aiden of the lush Grand Garden back in East Town. Thinking of the Grand Garden reminded Aiden of all he had learned and discovered in the past week: the truth about his parents, the Guild and the Dominion, Gloria and her brothers. But one thing still remained unresolved: Simone's Purification looked worse than ever. Her skin felt more rigid and scaly, and she was sleeping more and more.

"Purity's takin' hold," Nefflin said ominously. "R'member she wernt so bad at first, but now, the way she looks, all that sleepin' she's doin'? She's full-blown Purified." Simone was snoozing in her wheelchair, and even as Flair wheeled her off the plane, moving from the cool-air conditioned plane to the blistering outdoor heat didn't seem to register with her.

Nefflin hailed a taxi and they were off, travelling over uneven highways, passing through bustling cities and small rural towns, before finally taking a detour down a narrow, dirt road. Leaves and branches encroached on the cab, forcing all windows up. It was a stuffy, sweaty, bumpy ride for what seemed like an hour before the cab driver began speaking animatedly to someone over a CB radio.

"What's he saying, Mr. Nefflin?" Flair asked.

"Dunno. Don't speak the language."

"He's talking about me," Simone mumbled.

Everyone jumped, not realizing Simone was awake. Aiden looked into the back seat. Simone was pale and shivering.

"How do you know?" Aiden said.

Simone explained, as Ramon Gannares did, about her ability to understand the essence of all speech. Aiden, Flair and Nefflin looked amazed.

"And what's he saying about you?" Flair asked, glancing at the cabbie.

"He's saying he's got an infected *thing* with him," she uttered miserably. "He's afraid I'm going to infect him."

"She's not an infected thing, *jerk*!" Flair growled, punching the driver in the arm. The driver turned to strike Flair back, but she had already slotted a red crystal into her gloves. The glow from the crystal and the manic look in Flair's eyes seemed to make the driver think twice.

The road finally came to a dead end and there didn't seem to
be anywhere further to go. Trees surrounded them on all sides and
overhead; they were so tightly clumped together, only traces of
sunlight crept through. The cabbie yammered something at them,
swung his door open, jumping out of the cab with the engine still
running and pointed straight ahead into darkness.

"He says we're supposed to go with them," Simone said.

"Go with *who*?" Flair asked. "There's nobody—OH!"

Flair jumped in her seat. Out of the corners of the jungle grotto,
a dozen men emerged from the darkness. They were thin and dark-
skinned, dressed in loose clothing, their large eyes peering into the
car with trepidation.

The driver gestured to them, got back into the cab, slammed
the door and shifted the car into reverse. "He's telling us to get out,"
Simone said weakly. "He's not staying around. He doesn't like it
here."

Aiden grabbed the door handle, but then paused as Flair and
Nefflin each reached for their doors. Something was nagging him
other than the frightened cab driver. He was following his father's
same footsteps: the room under the Grand Garden, to the Knights
End and John Brown, and now to Borneo, where his father had been
months ago. He had an empty feeling in his stomach, realizing
wherever he was going, there was no point bringing along a tired
Nefflin and his little sisters, one sick, one injured.

This was something he had to do alone.

"Don't come with me," Aiden said to Flair.

"What? Why?" Flair said, looking suspicious.

"There's nothing more you guys can do. Go back to the plane,
get Simmy out of the heat. Neff, send another cabbie, someone a lot
less jumpy."

"You don't have to do this alone," Flair said.

"Yes, I do."

Flair studied Aiden's face for several seconds before nodding
to him. "Okay. Let's go back to the air conditioning, Mr. Nefflin."
She reached over and around the passenger seat, giving her brother a
hug and kiss on the cheek. "You be careful, clown boy."

So the cab reversed, zooming out of the dark corner of the
jungle, carrying Nefflin, Simone and Flair, leaving Aiden alone with

the small troupe of men, who beckoned Aiden ahead, guiding him into darkness.

They led Aiden through a dark passageway covered in foliage, which twisted and turned several times until they walked out onto a sloping, grassy hill, heading downwards towards a river.

Just like in Montecito, Aiden now found himself walking through a jungle amongst a throng of men, but these weren't scowling or armed; they just stared at him as if he were a curiosity. They led him through a winding pathway that Aiden would have never noticed on his own, shooting curious glances, mumbling things under their breath that Aiden wished he could understand. After walking for a while, the troupe stopped in front of a rocky riverbank.

A wooden canoe with a long red roof ambled towards the riverside, led by a young man, small, skinny and dark-skinned, wearing long khaki pants with muddy cuffs, and a paper-thin white tank top. His eyes were large and haunting, and stared into Aiden's as if trying to see his soul.

"Mr. Aiden Johnson?" the young man said as the boat bumped against the muddy shore.

"Yes. I am, I mean, that's me. Aiden." He gulped, removing his flat cap, trying to be extra respectful, though he was unsure why.

"My name is Kenji," the man said. "My grandfather's sampan boat. His nephew, Omar." He nodded to a bald man sitting in the front with a long pole, and then to a shirtless man chewing a long root. "My cousin, Jinak."

"Nice to meet..."

"They don't speak English. We are here to take to you my grandfather's home."

Omar said something in his language, interrupting Kenji. He nodded.

"Have you any weapons? Weapons are not permitted."

"Um, oh yeah." Aiden held out Mr. Quick's gleaming Ruijen Staff. The locals on the muddy shore gasped and muttered as the driver rattled out more instructions to Kenji.

"Omar says drop the staff and leave it there," Kenji said, pointing to the riverbank. "They will not trouble it. It shall be there when you return." Aiden looked back at the men who had led him to the river and with a firm thrust, planted the Ruijen Staff into the muddy soil in the midst of them.

Aiden climbed aboard the boat, which sagged at the additional weight, and sat on a small stool. The bare-chested Jinak sat under the red roof, lifted a wooden string instrument from the chair opposite him and began to play a somber melody. Omar murmured something to Kenji, and, with a push of his pole, the sampan reversed into river.

The surrounding scenery was breathtaking, although Jinak's slow strumming gave the trip an ominous feeling. The river fell under the shadows of thin columns of trees, and their green, leafy branches only revealed patches of blue sky. There were waterfalls at every bend in the river, large and small, splashing over the tops of high cliffs, trickling down along the leaves and into the river.

Fifteen minutes along, the men had done little more than look at each other in what was, with the exception of Jinak's music, unnerving silence. Kenji and Omar spoke briefly to themselves, and Aiden, though unable to understand the language, did understand something.

"I heard my father's name," Aiden said to Kenji. "What's he saying?"

"He said your father came through here seven months ago with a lot of hope in his eyes. He gave something to Noteki."

"Who's Noteki?"

"My grandfather. The famous headhunter."

Aiden looked at Jinak, Kenji and Omar, and felt their eyes on his throat.

"You must be proud," he gulped.

They floated along the river for another half-hour; Kenji lit lanterns and hung them at the front and rear of the boat. The sounds of the jungle drowned out Jinak's song, unsettling Aiden as darkness crept in. Finally, Omar turned the boat through an inlet, and another minute he stopped in front of a large house.

Aiden's eyebrows raised; it wasn't anything like he expected. The house was white, trimmed with a rustic red, and had a picket fence, a porch and a garden in the front. It wouldn't look out of place in a small American town.

Kenji jumped ashore and helped Aiden to the riverbank.

"What you are here for," Kenji said, shaking his head, "Noteki will not give you."

"Do you know what I'm here for?"

"No," Kenji said.

"So how do you know he won't give it to me?"

"Because my grandfather owes your father his life, and your father asked him to never give it to you."

"You're joking?" Aiden groaned. "He told him *not* to give it to me? Why?"

"That you'll have to ask my grandfather."

Kenji led Aiden inside, and if the outside of the house made Aiden closer to home, entering it gave him the exact opposite feeling. The inside was dark and eerie and there was a crisp smell of age, like a mixture of mildew and mothballs. The house seemed alive, creaking and moaning, as if voicing its disapproval at Aiden's intrusion. It had a lived-in look, yet was a house no man would want to live in. After Kenji departed, Aiden kept staring into the dark, shadowed corners, having the feeling of being watched.

He entered a small living room, whose carpet was worn almost to the concrete floor underneath. There were wooden carvings, statues and ceramic vessels stationed on low shelves and tables around the floor, with only a small couch and a rocking chair for sitting. As Aiden's eyes began adjusting to the darkness, he looked along the walls, and his heart skipped a turn.

All along the walls were severed heads of all shapes and sizes. Blackened, ugly, with hideous mask-like expressions. And skulls littered the floor in many corners. Aiden felt compelled to run, but as he looked for an exit, a door opened behind him and he jumped.

"Good evening, Aiden Johnson," a withered voice croaked.

The owner of the voice was tiny, possibly smaller than Simone, and reminded Aiden of a monk. He almost didn't look real: an ancient man, skinny, with leathery brown skin covered in dark tattoos. His bulbous eyes had large gray irises, looking as if they could see everything at once. He was quite toned and wore nothing except a loincloth tied around his waist. His balding head seemed to glow in the candlelight.

"I am Noteki, a friend of Wilbert Johnson, your father." He gave Aiden a quick once-over before flashing a curious smile. "You have your mother's look. A surprise."

"Funny," Aiden said. "Everyone who knows my father says I look like him."

"My eyes see things differently." The old man tottered over to the rocking chair and sat. "In you, I see Laura's spirit, her zest for living, her love for people. Your physical likeness to Wilbert is irrelevant to me."

He spoke with the nerve of an old respected warrior and had an air of authority and self-assuredness. It made Aiden take a moment before speaking.

"So, according to your grandson, you're not going to let me have it."

Noteki shook his head. "What your father gave to me was his to give. He sought it, obtained it, and earned the right to decide its destiny. Not you. You have never experienced what he has experienced, his sorrow and his devastation. So no, you can not have it."

Aiden stared quietly for several seconds at Noteki, calculating in his mind. This was another riddle his father had set up, a test. He had to prove himself.

"Well, maybe I haven't experienced the same sorrows as my father," Aiden said, "but my family has been dealing with his mistakes, so that should count for something."

"*Mistakes*?" Noteki snapped, raising an eyebrow. "Your father made mistakes?"

Aiden felt uneasy at the old man's tone, but continued on anyway. "By taking the Song? By hiding his family? Most definitely."

"You dishonor your father," Noteki replied. "You have no idea what you speak of. Wilbert made a noble sacrifice."

"It was brave," Aiden said, "but it was the wrong move. His wife is dead, he sacrificed his own life, and it gained him nothing."

"The Song is safe," Noteki said, "far away from Mackleford and his atrocities."

"But Mackleford pushes on anyway. And my father's actions left his family in danger and unprepared and at the end of the day, solved nothing. He was wrong."

The old warrior's brow crinkled as he considered Aiden. After a moment, he walked into one of the shadowy corners, retrieving large bucket of liquid with fat gnats zooming around it. He returned to Aiden and put the bucket under his face. Aiden winced. It had an overpowering sweet odor.

"Taste this," Noteki said.

"What?" Aiden said, gagging.

"Dip your finger into this and taste."

"Why? What is it?"

"Taste and you shall know."

"I'm not tasting that! Are you nuts?"

Noteki dropped the bucket and Aiden jumped back to prevent whatever was sloshing in the bucket from splashing on him.

"Do you understand the senses, Aiden Johnson?"

"The senses?" Aiden replied. "What are you…"

"The five senses!" Noteki said, his voice cracking. "Sight, taste, touch, smell, hearing!"

Aiden looked puzzled, but nodded for Noteki to continue.

"They are our doorways to understanding the world. The greatest of these is taste, for the other senses are disconnected from mind, body, and spirit, but what a man tastes becomes a part of him. A man can see this bucket, hold it in his hands, hear the gnats, smell its stench, but until he tastes it, he knows not its foulness!"

"You're crazy!" Aiden shouted. "No one's drinking that crap!"

"And that is why, Aiden Johnson, you have no place to judge your father," Noteki said, pointing a reproving finger. "You have yet to taste his sorrows, so how could you? Wilbert tasted the sorrows, and it angered him! You have not tasted enough sorrows or felt enough pain to be angry, and until you have, you will not understand Wilbert Johnson! Should I be moved by the convictions of a boy who could not protect his sisters? You were trusted and you failed!"

Aiden was quiet, watching Noteki as he snatched up the bucket and turned, giving a reproachful glare and walking back into the dark corner.

"We never needed protecting," Aiden said. "Protecting us from the Dominion was his biggest mistake."

"You do not understand!" Noteki jeered. "Do you know how many children of Journeymen were kidnapped and Purified and killed? Your father kept you alive—"

"Sure, he kept me alive, but he let Mackleford to stay in business, and look where that's gotten the Guild. Look how close Mackleford is to Purifying the world. Talk about not understanding!"

"So you believe that you would stop him?" Noteki replied. "Mackleford and his Dominion?"

Noteki's reply was not with the sneering amusement as before. There was a definite yearning in his voice, a composed, hopeful look in his eyes. For a moment, Aiden's gaze fell. He had read the old warrior's body language in that very moment and had already translated its meaning.

Aiden's going to do it.

This old man was just waiting to hear how.

"Have you ever heard of anyone ever stopping a group like the Dominion by hiding from them?" Aiden asked. The old man remained silent. "We can't only protect our family, Noteki. We have to develop and nurture them. I know that my father started out doing that, training me. I don't know what stopped him, but one of his trainings stuck. He taught me to read people. He said to start with a person's shoes, then their hair and their clothes. Watch their hands, look into their eyes. And you can read anything on anybody. Read 'em like a book, and know what makes 'em tick."

"What does your father's trick mean to me now?"

"Take your grandson, Kenji," Aiden said nodding towards the front door. "He's suffered, just like you, but he's proud of it, just like you. I guess you've both been drinking from that same bucket of crap or whatever, but the point is, you two draw your strength from the same place: your family. You see, that's how you stop guys like Mackleford. You don't hide from him; you bring your people around you, get your strength behind you and go at him. Together.

"A couple of weeks ago, I thought I knew my family, but I didn't. We're like people I've never met before. Flair is a heart and soul warrior, Simone is whip-cracking sharp, and I guess I care more about people than I thought. My father's failure was not trusting in us. He put his faith in secrecy and safety, not in his family. But that's not what I'm gonna do."

As Aiden finished, Noteki stared him, contemplating. Aiden could tell he was making his mind up about the matter. Then the old man stood up.

"Follow me," he said.

The tiny man entered another room, turned a switch and dim light filled the area, illuminating a sight that made Aiden cringe. In the center of the room on a round wooden table sat a large mound of skulls. But these skulls were enormous, the size of beach balls, too big to be human. Aiden realized to whom these skulls belonged.

"Goons."

"Yes," Noteki said. "Mackleford's atrocities. Your father defeated them, but he refused to take their heads."

"Thank you, Pops," Aiden breathed in a sigh of relief.

"So *we* did," Noteki continued. "His conquests are here. Mackleford's atrocities fear us. They will not come back."

"Perfect place to hide the Song."

"Yes," Noteki said, and the same finger that reproved Aiden earlier now pointed into the center of the stacked skulls. "It is *there*."

"Of course it is," Aiden groaned, not bothering to hide his tone.

"And you must take one," Noteki said, again nodding at the skulls.

Aiden stopped cold. "A *skull*? I have to take a skull?"

"Yes," Noteki continued. "To defeat Mackleford, you must embrace the strength of family, very true. So embrace your father's strength. Honor his sacrifice."

"You're really testing my patience today," Aiden sighed. "Okay, let's have it."

The old man scooped up a large, grey-white skull with large teeth and a round top like a basketball. He walked over to Aiden and dropped the skull in his hands. It was heavy.

"Gee," Aiden said in mock gratitude, "I don't know what to say."

"You may have it," Noteki said. "It is there."

Where the skull had once been sat a crumpled burlap sack. Aiden set the skull on the floor, reached into the space, and removed it. It was much like the burlap bag that held Flair's crystals. *Was there anything in it?* It felt so light.

He opened the bag, pulling a brown thread tied to an artfully crafted wooden stem, upon which were sculpted, red and gold ornaments cut into five shapes: a circle, a triangle, a crescent, a diamond, and an eye. Hollowed tubes of wood and smooth stones hung alongside of the glass.

Aiden examined the item for several quiet moments. When imagining this moment of discovery, he thought he would be nervous, but he wasn't. A three thousand-year-old mythical relic in his hands, yet he felt a strange sense of fulfillment, as if he had finally found what he'd been searching his whole life for.

In the center of the relic was a small, round gemstone. Aiden walked underneath the overhanging lamp, examining it. Etched along its surface were elaborate symbols and characters of which Aiden had never seen. But in the center, though worn and faded, the largest symbol was unmistakable.

The Star of David.

Aiden stared at it, transfixed for several moments. Holding the Song of Solomon in front of his face, he took a breath and blew a puff of air into it.

The sound of the chimes filled his entire head. Whatever apprehension he had felt had evaporated, being overcome by the clarity of the soft tinkling. It was music such as he had never heard before.

He turned to Noteki, who had settled down on a chair in the corner of the room, staring at him. "It's beautiful, isn't it? You've heard it, haven't you?"

"Yes. The Song works the same for everyone, yet all men hear different things. Some will hear the path of their desires. Others hear truth, wisdom, and peace. You possess a power that will clear great barriers from your path, but—"

"But when I confront Mackleford, he'll have it too."

Noteki nodded. "But you obtained this by proving your wisdom is greater than his, and what strengthens you far exceeds what strengthens him. Your family was meant for this."

"You mean Flair and Simone?"

Noteki patted him on the shoulder. "Indeed, Wilbert failed there, but you haven't."

Aiden took a long look at the Song of Solomon, the gleaming red and gold glass, the adorned wooden tubes, and the smooth river stones and placed it carefully into the burlap bag.

"To save your sister, you must give up the Song. But to give up the Song is to give up the world. Do you know what you are going to do?"

"I do," Aiden said confidently. "The element of surprise."

In no time at all, Aiden was sitting in a taxi, on his way to the airport where unbeknownst to him, Flair had been pacing nervously on her bad leg.

Aiden's mind was on his mission. A sense of purpose was rising inside of him. He knew exactly what he had to do, where to focus his energy, how to explain his plan. Flair hobbled up to the cab as Aiden arrived at the airport, almost tackling him with a hug when the cab door opened.

"You found it?" she whispered. "The Song?"

Aiden held up the burlap bag, clenched in his fist, looking over to the plane.

"Is everyone ready? I want to make sure we make it back in time."

"Back in time?"

"Yeah, in time for the Reading," Aiden said, throwing his arm around his sister and helping her to the plane. "We still have Granny's book, remember?"

Flair smiled, almost laughed. Aiden frowned, looking puzzled.

"You just called Margaret *Granny*."

"Did I?" he said, grinning. "How about that?"

CHAPTER TWENTY-FOUR – IN THE GARDEN OF ANCIENT WISDOM

"When the world was new, men lived in a paradise. And that paradise was a garden."

Mochtier Mackleford walked down a long hallway at Restoration College, with Ellis Vicartan besides him, scribbling in a spiral notebook. It was nighttime; their heeled footsteps echoed as a janitor operated a whirring floor polisher across the hardwood floors, buffing them to a high shine.

"And the ancient wonders of the world, Ellis—those seven legendary creations of mankind? The greatest wonder of all was the Gardens of Babylon, indescribable in their beauty and splendor." They stopped at an elevator, Mackleford pressing the down button, Ellis's attention still on his notebook.

"Scholars doubted whether these gardens actually existed," Mackleford said as the elevators doors opened and they entered. "Paradise they relegated to the status of myth. They asked how could men with limited technology construct such a marvel? They don't understand that both gardens were created through great and ancient wisdom. The wisdom of Paradise, the wisdom that nurtured Babylon, the world's greatest kingdom. Mankind has desired to return to Paradise. To re-build perfection. But even with today's ingenuity, their failure is obvious."

The elevator doors opened. Mackleford's office was dark except for the soft, blue glow of the giant aquarium. Ellis was still jotting something down as Mackleford slid behind his desk.

"Their new kingdoms have failed because they did not embrace that wisdom as we have. For wherever that wisdom is embraced, it blossoms as the garden."

Something clicked behind the desk, and a great rumble shook the room. A seam in the glass aquarium divided, opening wider and wider, revealing a long, expansive hallway, enveloped wall-to-wall and ceiling to floor by more of the aquarium. The two men entered the hallway, heading towards a blinding bright light shining at the end.

They exited the hallway into what could be called a garden, but "garden" wouldn't do it justice. It was theatrical: a dazzling display of breathless beauty, an arena immense in proportions, magnificent in splendor. There was no visible source of light, but the entire place was as bright as a July afternoon. A domed roof twenty stories high covered vast, twisting waterfalls splashing into lakes in each corner. Palatial structures of stone connected with bridges of fine metals. There were enough flowers and trees to fill a city park.

Mackleford ascended a large circular-stepped pyramid made of pristine white marble that stood in the garden's center, regarding his creation while Ellis sat on a metal bench at its bottom. An artfully hewn four-way stone arch awaited Mackleford at the top, and he reached up into its center. Drifting between the fingers of his silver glove was a strand of thick brown thread hanging from the archway, the bottom of which was frayed, as if something had been ripped from it.

"This is greatness! Perfection! This will be our headquarters, our Jump Point! When Babylon embarked on her road to greatness, she too birthed a magnificent garden. Here is our legacy to the world, where all shall come to share knowledge, seek wisdom, and find perfection. Here they will shed their stunted, crude humanity and have their true mankind restored!"

Mackleford's voice was rising, echoing throughout the cavernous garden. "It will be found here, in our garden of ancient wisdom, in our new birthplace of men, in our new paradise! How shall Journeymen, or enemies, or anyone stand against us?"

The next twenty-four hours zoomed by in a flash. Perhaps it was the tension of the imminent meeting with Mackleford, or the anticipation of curing Simone, but before they knew it, Nefflin announced they were flying over California and would be landing within three hours. They were back inside of the United States for the first time in a week, and Aiden, who until a week ago hadn't flown on a plane in his life, was finishing his fourth plane ride, hoping it was his final one for a while.

Denver International Airport was bustling, jam-packed with holiday travelers returning home from Christmas, so Nefflin's arrangements took longer than usual. He had entered and exited the airport twice, spoken to at least a dozen different people before finally emerging from a rental car stand, jogging over to Aiden with a package wrapped in brown paper.

"Margie's care package, sum'n for m' troubles," Nefflin told a curious Flair. "And speaking of troubles, time t' make some payments. It's been one expensive world tour. " He slapped a set of car keys into Aiden's hand. "You're all set, Aiden, everything's there."

"Wait," Flair said, looking mortified. "You're leaving?"

"Gotta pay the piper, Flair," Nefflin said. "B'sides, you don't need me to hand that thang to Mackleford."

Flair opened her mouth to speak, but Simone, who was looking worse than ever, stirred in her wheelchair, distracting her.

Aiden looked at the car keys with apprehension. "Thanks, Nefflin," he said, shaking his head. "We'll call you when we're done."

"Yer doin' fine, son. Startin' ta see your dad in ya." And Nefflin hugged Flair and Simone, turned, and disappeared into the crowd.

It was an unsettling car ride. Flair, seated in the back, clutched an ice cold Simone who lay sleeping in her lap. Aiden didn't seem to have a handle of the car, his knuckles straining against the steering wheel as he gripped it with both hands, his eyes locked in on the road. The car skidded into the rumble strips on the side of the highway, creating a loud, grinding sound in the car, which woke Simone.

"What happened?" Simone whispered. "Is it the Goons?"

"No, it's 'Hot Wheels' Johnson!" Flair said. "Can't you take it easy, bro? You're gonna kill us before we even get there."

"It's only my second time driving," Aiden said. "Not as easy as it looks on TV."

Flair and Simone both stared at each other and then into the rear view mirror, meeting their brother's eyes.

"Remember when Pops was driving a cab?" Aiden explained. "He let me behind the wheel once. But who needs to drive in New York? Parking is a pain in the neck. So much easier just to take a cab. Man, I hate this."

"I thought you had your license years ago," Flair said, sounding scared.

Aiden responded with a fearful laugh as he swerved the car back onto the road.

Restoration College was a one hour drive from the airport, but it took them two hours to arrive with Aiden behind the wheel. The campus was large and isolated, surrounded by rows of pine trees, manicured hedges, and a giant man-made river. Aiden crossed over a stylish wooden bridge that led into the main campus, gazing at three tall, shimmering buildings of glass standing in the center. The car jerked to a violent halt in a parking lot just over the bridge, and Flair unclicked her seatbelt and bolted through the door at once.

"Remind me to walk when you're driving!" Flair said, pacing around the lot for several seconds, trying to get a hold of herself. Aiden frowned at Flair as he left the driver's seat, heading towards the trunk of the car.

"Can't be worst than zooming around on Star Channels."

"Trust me, it is."

"Are we here?" Simone asked. She had stirred at the sound of her brother and sister sniping at one another. "Can we hurry? I am so over this."

Aiden rummaged in the trunk for a few moments before slamming it shut and tightening the cord around the black burlap bag that held the Song of Solomon. He unfolded the wheelchair, Simone crawled into it with Flair's help, and the Johnsons entered the campus.

The dead wintery morning and hazy sunlight couldn't disguise the fact that Restoration's campus was gorgeous, abounding with smooth, granite fountains featuring mythological creatures and statues of perfectly chiseled men and women. There were giant archways throughout the campus, and the trio of buildings Aiden saw as he drove onto the campus came into clearer view.

"Check it out," he said to Flair, pointing at the buildings

The three buildings were entirely of glass and shaped like chess pieces: a knight, a bishop and a rook. Their frosted panes gave them a mystical look, reflecting the pale blue sky above. Flair limped along, glancing bleary-eyed into the distance, as Aiden pointed out a stadium, athletic fields and a large building that appeared to be a gymnasium.

"This place is huge, bro," Flair said. "How are we going to find Mackleford?"

As if on cue, a voice called *"Aiden Johnson!"* from a loudspeaker mounted to a light pole above.

Aiden and Flair turned their attention to the speaker. "That's me," Aiden replied. "Where to?"

"The Bishop Building. Straight ahead."

The bishop-shaped building towered over the others, glimmering ten stories into the sky, with an enormous Restoration College logo displayed over its entrance.

"Once you enter, take the second hallway to your right."

As they walked along, Flair tugged at Aiden's sleeve. "Listen, I've been thinking—"

"That's the scariest thing I've heard all week," Aiden said.

Flair continued, without letting the remark bother her. "You're gonna give it to him, aren't you?" she asked.

Aiden didn't respond. He looked sick and stumbled over a seam in the concrete.

"The wheelchair ramp is to your right!" the voice called out as they entered the shadow of the building, and Aiden made for it.

"You okay, Aiden?" Simone asked.

"Splitting headache," Aiden replied, adjusting his flat cap. "Turns out flying all over the planet isn't all that."

"Listen Aiden," Flair said, stepping in front of him and taking the wheelchair, "we can't let Mackleford have it."

"You mean this," Aiden replied, extracting the burlap bag from his jacket.

"We're only doing this because of Simmy, but after what we've seen—"

"But you just said it," Aiden replied. "We're doing this for Simmy. How much time do you think she has? Besides, Pops expects me to do this."

"You really think so?" Flair said. "But why? Carson said Dad sending us after the Song doesn't make sense."

"Just because it doesn't make sense," Aiden said with a slight hiccup, "doesn't mean there isn't a reason."

"Okay. What reason then?"

Aiden stared at the Restoration logo on the building's tinted glass door, reaching for the handle. "The Song of Solomon isn't the problem. Pops wants me involved. That's why I have these crazy memories, why I knew that song in the Knight's End. Pops believes I can stop Mackleford."

They entered a gorgeous lobby, immaculate as the campus outside. The smell of floor polish hung in the air and the surrounding walls were decorated with portraits of faculty members and student announcements. A large map of the campus hung on the center wall, underscored with three words in large, brass letters:

RESTORE   RE-EDUCATE   REFORM

Aiden slumped towards the map, noticing the six wide hallways, three to his left and three to his right. He entered the second hallway to his right, Flair just behind him.

"But why you?" Flair said. "John Brown said Dad has that memory thing too. Why didn't he just do it himself?"

"Proceed down the hallway! There will be an elevator on your left about three-quarters of the way! Take it to the basement!"

"It's not just the memories. It's something else. That's why Pops gave them to me, because he tried but couldn't do it. Only I could…"

Aiden had slowed his pace, but his mind was soaring. Something about this line of thinking was bringing him closer to the truth…why it *had* to be him. It was hazy, vague, and yet he was close…

They reached the elevator and Flair jabbed the down button. A dull hum from below signaled the elevator car's approach.

"You sound like Jonas—"

"What?"

"He said Dad meant for us to save them when the time came."

Aiden nodded in agreement. "Maybe that's the reason. I mean, look where we are. Look what you can do, what I can do—"

"What about what Mackleford can do? This worldwide plague? There's more at stake here than just us."

"Relax, sunshine. Just follow my lead and don't get nervous."

A soft—*DING!*—sounded and the elevator doors opened.

Seconds later, the Johnsons stood on plush carpet in an expansive office, bathed in the shimmering glow of an enormous aquarium that stretched across the back wall. Someone was waiting there; Aiden and Flair remembered the man, both having met him in the L'Escapade hotel.

"Disarm yourselves," Mr. Quick said in his coarse voice. "Your gloves, girl," he said to Flair, shaking a small basket. "In here." While waiting for Flair to comply, he turned to Aiden. "And you have something that is mine."

Aiden took the Ruijen Staff from his waist and passed it back to Mr. Quick, who gave it a once over, then hooked it to his belt. His masked face stayed with Aiden until Flair dropped the pair of crystal gloves and the channel gun into the basket. Mr. Quick walked around the back of the wheelchair, removing the crystal pouch from the back pocket and dropping them into the basket.

"Very good Mr. Quick...Bring them in."

Mr. Quick pointed them towards the aquarium wall and they entered into the long, bright corridor, whose exit was a football field away. Simone's head lolled to one side; the light from the aquarium walls brightening her cracked, graying skin. Her eyes, tired and red, gazed at the swimming sea creatures, which brought a smile to her face.

"Last year, Mom took me to an aquarium park," Simone whispered. "It looked like this."

"Mom hated the ocean," Flair remarked.

"I know, but we were there for three hours...she even petted a shark with me. Their skin is so rough."

Simone's shaky hands reached towards her face, caressing her own scaly, dry cheeks. "Do you think I'm gonna end up like Mom? Am I gonna die too?"

Flair took one of her hands off of the handles, sweeping a tear off of her cheek. "You're not gonna die, Simmy. It's almost over."

They crossed a threshold into blazing brightness, and it took a while for Aiden's eyes to adjust. It reminded him of the Grand Garden, except this place was a hundred times bigger. He knew they were underground, but they might have been in a city park. He looked up and saw standing in various locations around the domed garden: Musclehead, No-Neck, Man-Child, Lanky, Fuzz, along with several other Goons he had never seen, all watching them.

In the center of the massive garden was Mackleford, standing under a giant archway at the top of a circular, stone-stepped pyramid. A short, stocky man in a sweater vest and tie and a young man in a white smock flanked him, and twenty more figures, the same black-clad masked men that had met Aiden that night in the

House of Gumm stood two-by-two at attention, trailing down the pyramid steps in front of Mackleford, creating an aisle.

Mackleford stepped towards the edge of the pyramid's capstone, smiling and throwing his arms wide, reminding Aiden of Jonas showing off his model homes at the Expo.

"You are on the first campus of Restoration College!" he shouted. "We started with three professors, twelve students in a four room building on this very spot. Today, this campus alone houses two thousand students in sixteen dormitories, and schools of fine arts, mathematics, technology, and architecture. Our advanced science programs are world class. Twenty-seven state-of-the-art laboratories, courses in metallurgy, biotechnology, chemical physics, organic chemistry, and this living arboretum. Aiden, you, as an educator, would love to work here!"

"Well, considering you murdered my mother," Aiden said frankly, "I kinda doubt that."

Mackleford's smile faded immediately, being replaced by a grim, stony expression. "Very well. Where is my property?"

Aiden thrust the black burlap sack into the air.

"Good," Mackleford said. "Bring it up."

"Simone first!" Aiden croaked, although with force and authority.

The Goons looked at Mackleford, who was indifferent to Aiden's command. His silver glove gripped Dr. Standis on the shoulder.

"Certainly, Aiden. A promise is a promise. Dr. Standis will see to your sister. Please," he said, beckoning him forward.

There were at least thirty steps to the top, and Aiden groaned as he began to climb, glaring at the doctor as they passed each other midway. Flair limped behind Aiden, wincing. Standis reached the bottom first and tended to Simone, while Aiden, giant beads of sweat glistening over his forehead, trudged up each of the giant circular steps.

"You had me worried, Aiden," Mackleford said, "but I'm glad you made it. Everything will be easier for everyone going forward."

Aiden and Flair reached the top of the pyramid and turned, looking down on Simone, a hundred feet below. He passed the black burlap bag to Mackleford, who opened it and extracted the ancient wind chime by its thread, holding it above his head. He stepped under the archway and tied the stripped threads together before turning to Aiden.

"You don't look so good, Aiden."

"Try going to four countries in five days, from freezing snow to hot jungles and see how you look."

"I've done so," Mackleford laughed, "many times throughout my life."

Aiden stared at Dr. Standis tending to Simone. "So, there is a Purity cure?" he said. "Not a myth after all. Your partner El Sereno thought it didn't exist."

"Partner?" Mackleford laughed again. "Cessano's an underworld criminal, a far cry from a partner of mine. I have need of Argentina's unique climate and his facilities. He's a tool, just like the Gannares girl I used to buy his cooperation."

"All pawns in the game," Aiden said, shaking his head.

Mackleford smiled and nodded. "You're no Journeymen, Aiden. You're a man of understanding as am I. That stupid girl is so desperate for the cure she'd swim to the bottom of the ocean for it. And Hector Cessano perfected my antigen under his very nose, not that it will be necessary any longer. As far as your sister, she isn't weakening. She's getting stronger. Dr. Standis?"

The doctor was examining Simone, checking her eyes and having her stick out her tongue. After a moment...

"Early stage four," Standis announced. "Beginning on the muscular system."

"You see?" Mackleford said. "Nervous, respiratory, skeletal...each system stronger than a week ago. And the unique enhancement Purification created in her. The Banshee. Another of my students exhibited this same remarkable trait. Simone has been improved."

"She'll improve herself in her own way, Mackleford," Aiden said.

"I don't blame you, Aiden," Mackleford said pleasantly. "I don't blame any of you, not even your father. We're programmed products of a repressed humanity. The natural evolution of mankind has been interrupted for thousands of years, beginning when Herodotus hid the secrets of true wisdom. You have no idea what we've been robbed of, Aiden. We should be gods by now, instead of the failing creatures that we are."

"Gods?" Aiden said, almost with a laugh. "Getting ahead of yourself, aren't you?"

"You wouldn't say that if you've lived my life."

"Gaston Gumm lived your life, didn't he?" Aiden said. "I'm sure he'd disagree."

"He did," Mackleford said, nodding. "But as incredible as Gus was, he didn't understand mankind is craving for a new era. Instead, he continued the suffocation of the human race, as did his predecessors. Aiden, imagine for a moment if Hippocrates hadn't pioneered modern medical thought, or if Tesla didn't revolutionize the world through electricity. That is how mankind has been robbed."

"It's different," Aiden replied. "Purity is dangerous."

"Dangerous?" Mackleford laughed again. "No, Purity is volatile, but that is its most beautiful and essential characteristic! Purity is power and life and it shall be the blood of the new humanity. Sustaining us, strengthening us, cleansing our minds and bodies, keeping us from sickness, injury, and death."

"And turning people into ugly Goons," Aiden said dryly. "You forgot that part."

The Goons looked insulted but kept their silence. Mackleford balked as well, but his cool smile returned.

"Don't worry, I'll show you something regarding that," he said. "But before I do, answer this question for me. Why is this world dying?"

"Who says it's dying?" Aiden countered.

"Aiden, please," Mackleford said, somewhat irritated. "We are men of understanding, don't insult our conversation. Your hometown of New York is rife with immorality. You've just rubbed shoulders with the scum of civilization. Turn on your television and watch: economic crisis, unsafe schools, corruption everywhere. Why?"

Aiden didn't respond.

"Because something is broken," Mackleford said, tapping his chest, "in here. Deep inside every man, woman, and child. We should have progressed beyond this weak shell long ago. We haven't, the collective conscience of the world senses it, and we're rebelling."

Aiden looked thoughtful for a moment. "I got it. You've given up on people, Mackleford. You gave up on the world. But I haven't, nor did my father."

"Ah, a father's conviction," Mackleford said with a smile. "Son, the world gave up on itself long ago. You just haven't accepted it. This is why I must act while humanity still has a chance. I will heal what ails us, revolutionize our race, and give life meaning once again."

"It's incredible," Aiden said, sounding contemptuous. "You can talk about healing, humanity, and life…" And Aiden's voice trembled, thinking of his parents and Simone. "And at the end of it all, you're just a murderer. You're really that blind."

"No, *you've* been blinded by your father, and by Gus," Mackleford said in a cool, steady voice, although his silver glove was clenched into a tight fist. "I will be the savior of this world, Aiden Johnson, and you will be witness to that."

"The only thing I'm witnessing is your failure, Mackleford. You just haven't accepted it."

"I've failed?" Mackleford shouted. "Look around you! Your predecessors are either in hiding or dead in their graves and where am I? I have long ago proven their failure and now I shall prove it once again! Let me introduce the forerunner of the next millennium. Rico! We have visitors!"

Far in the distance, from behind one of the twisting waterfalls, a hulking figure emerged: the tall, muscular Rico. Everyone turned in his direction.

"Here is the power that has been hidden from us for centuries," Mackleford said. "Rico is perfect. No deformities. Nothing but raw, unadulterated power."

Rico walked past the Goons, who all stared on admiringly, and the dozens of Black Masks turned their heads at once, also watching Rico stride impressively towards the pyramid.

With everyone's attention on Rico, Aiden eased next to Flair. "Hey sunshine," he whispered into her ear. "I need you to do something."

Flair didn't respond. She was also fixated on Rico, her mouth slack like a salivating hound.

"Flair?" Aiden repeated. "Flair, hello, can pick your tongue up off the floor for a second?"

"Huh—uh, what?"

"Focus please…"

"I'm trying bro, but look at him!"

Aiden was flummoxed. "What are you talking about? He's a Purified Goon!"

"Oops, oh yeah…"

"Just listen—"

Rico arrived at the foot of the pyramid. Dr. Standis, open mouthed, had temporarily stopped examining Simone to gaze at Rico along with everyone else. Rico nodded him away from the wheelchair and approached Simone, staring at her with a curious expression. Finally he stood back and motioned to Dr. Standis to continue his treatment.

"What do you think?" Mackleford said, turning back to Aiden and Flair. "Quite an upgrade over the old models. You see, Aiden Johnson, Rico will master this world, destroy mortality and lead the march of the new humanity for the next two centuries as the old human race fades into obscurity. Failure? This is my crowning achievement!"

"That's what this is all about, isn't it?" Aiden said. He turned his back on Mackleford, staring down the pyramid at Simone and Dr. Standis. "Destroying mortality. You're afraid of death. I heard you flipped out when your father died."

Dr. Standis was hovering over Simone, holding a long syringe, whispering to her. Simone, head drooping to one side, was unresponsive.

Aiden stared at the needle. *That must be it*, he thought. *The cure.*

"You really think you know me, don't you, Aiden Johnson?" Mackleford said quietly.

Aiden turned back to Mackleford. "Well, I mean, you're an obvious guy, Mackleford. Trying to create the perfect man. Running from your father's death and your own. You ain't so complex—"

"You don't understand death as I do," Mackleford interrupted, with no hint of a smile on his face. "You have no idea what it's like to be on a deathbed. I do. Death has threatened me many times over. My father died a lonely, penniless farmer, no wife, while his only son paraded around the world, seeking fame and fortune. I often wonder what his thoughts were as he waited for death. Probably wishing his son cared about more than riches. You see, you don't think about how much money you've made when you're dying in a bed, oh no, you think about your life and what it meant. I don't fear death, Aiden. On the contrary, I fear life and not making enough out of it."

"Listen to him," Rico said as he ascended the pyramid. "The wisdom in his words is timeless."

"Yeah, especially when you've got Solomon on your side," Aiden said, staring at the chimes twisting in the center of the archway. "Maybe it's time we changed that. Simmy! NOW!"

And Simone, to everyone's surprise, shot upright, opened her mouth wide, and let loose with a loud, deafening scream. The Banshee.

It was the first time Aiden had heard it and even for someone who wasn't Purified, it was an unnerving, bone-chilling sound. The scream echoed around them so loudly that even Flair dropped to a knee, covering her ears. Dr. Standis, in complete shock, stumbled sideways, dropping the needle in Simone's lap before falling to the floor.

Aiden looked around the arena-sized garden as the Banshee Cry faded. The Goons weren't cringing as Flair and Carson had described. Instead, there was the sound of deep laughter rising up into the domed ceiling.

"Well done, Mackleford," Man-Child's slimy voice chanted from his perch above. "Always two steps ahead."

"On the nose again, Mack!" No-Neck bellowed.

Flair looked around. The Goons were all on their feet, arms folded, smiling.

Ellis Vicartan held a steady smile on his face, glancing around at all of the Goons, seemingly making sure none of them had succumbed.

"It worked Mochtier," Ellis said after a few nervous moments. He extracted a pair of earplugs from his ears. "We anticipated you, Mr. Johnson. You couldn't have been more obvious. Just like your father, too simple-minded to—"

Ellis looked at Mackleford, who was staring at Aiden, who was no longer wearing his father's old flat cap. That was in his left hand. In his right: a bright red crystal, aimed directly at the Song of Solomon.

Mackleford's jaw was rigid.

"You know, I've been around those wretched stones for over sixty years. You think I don't know *star-sickness* when I see it? The moment I saw you sickly and weak-kneed I figured some pitiful plot was underway. Was this the best your father could come up with? Smuggle a stone under your hat and attack me with it? Or am I to believe that you, a historian, are willing to destroy a three-thousand year old artifact?"

Aiden's face shone with sweat, his eyes darting between the Song of Solomon and Mackleford.

"You can't destroy the world if I destroy the Song," Aiden said. And he didn't waver though his stomach was boiling. His mind was focused, and the red crystal brightened.

"What is this?" Mackleford said. "Your *own* conviction? Is this supposed to frighten me? I could kill you where you stand!"

"And the Song goes with me."

Aiden felt the stare of every eye in the place, but he dared not turn. This was between him and Mackleford, and he needed to remain focused.

"They say a wise father knows his own child, Aiden," Mackleford said, "but it seems Wilbert misjudged you. You've seen beyond the fog of lies he perpetrated against you, haven't you? He didn't hide you for your own sake, but for the sake of his own plans. He'd have you destroy this powerful relic to serve his own misguided ideals instead of serving humankind. Certainly you have seen this…So, was he right? Are you the one who will finish the Dominion? If so, then destroy it!"

Aiden face tautened, but he didn't budge. He looked at Flair, who gave him a look as if to say, *if you're going to do it, do it…*

After a tense moment, Mackleford shook his head. "For a moment there, I thought you were going to do it. I expected more from Wilbert. Mr. Quick, take that stone from this fool. If he tries anything, have the Black Masks tear his sisters apart!"

But before Mr. Quick could move a muscle, a red blast ignited from between Aiden's fingers. It was instantaneous but seemed to happen in slow motion. Bright red energy illuminated Mackleford's sneering face…a beam rushed forcefully towards the wind chime twisting innocently under the archway…contacted the relic, striking a skinny wooden tube in the center, splintering it…and the resounding blast of particles and energy exploding into a blinding ball of light.

The Song of Solomon shattered into a thousand pieces.

Everyone was still as all eyes fell on Aiden, glowing dimly in a hazy red aura. Mackleford was pale, staring at the surrounding debris in horror.

"You idiot!" he breathed. "You damn fool!" he screamed. "You, your entire family...you're dead to me now!"

Mackleford, his face livid with rage, snatched off his silver glove, revealing the White Hand. The ghastly weapon flashed to Aiden's throat, and Aiden raised his right hand, the red crystal still firmly between his fingers, and caught Mackleford's hand.

"AAAAAAAAAAAAAAA!!"

Mackleford's scream was blood curdling. The red crystal was between their hands, and Aiden, seeing his advantage, gripped harder, interlocking fingers with Mackleford's. The red crystal had no chance of escaping.

Aiden felt heat, but wasn't sure if it were coming from the effects of the White Hand—as he saw his own skin on his hand blistering—or from the crystal's effect on Mackleford. Mackleford looked astonished; his rage had vanished, replaced by fear. The White Hand was smoldering and Aiden's only thought was to squeeze tighter and not let go.

"Ellis! Rico! Someone..." Mackleford called pitifully.

Mr. Quick grunted something incomprehensible, and the Black Masks reacted, rushing up the smooth marble steps alongside Rico. Aiden, using every ounce of strength he could muster, twisted his and Mackleford's arms downward, aiming towards the center of the Black Masks and Rico, focusing.

A powerful red blast ripped through the center of the charging mass of humanity, bowling Mr. Quick and the Black Masks over and finding its mark smack dab in the middle of Rico's alabaster chest. The Black Masks flew everywhere, but Rico was unaffected. He kept storming up the marble pyramid, stomping over Black Masks as he went.

The blast had thrown Aiden and Mackleford on opposite ends of the capstone. Aiden's arm was in so much pain that he dropped the crystal.

"FLAIR! DON'T JUST STAND THERE! DO IT!"

At Aiden's words, Mr. Quick, who was trapped underneath a pile of his Black Mask cronies, turned and looked. Flair was standing near the bottom, an empty basket at her feet.

The gloves were back on.

No-Neck and Lanky also looked towards Flair, who was immersed in a striking, blazing red aura. Bolts scattered through the air from her gloves like sparks from an exploding firework, and the Goons ducked for cover.

Rico reached the top, looking at Aiden on his left and Mackleford on his right. Mackleford slumped over to his side, inched towards the archway, towards the remains of the Song of Solomon. He sifted his fingers through shards of the destroyed relic, looking crestfallen and collapsed onto his back.

Aiden could see the White Hand was no longer shiny. It was charred and bony; the skin was withered and hung from Mackleford's hand like a loose glove, as if the flesh beneath his skin had disappeared.

"Something is wrong," Rico said, his eyes falling on first on Aiden, then Aiden's right hand. "You're not what you seem, Mr. Johnson." Rico picked Mackleford up, cradling him in his arms, and headed down the pyramid.

Aiden stared at his own hand, whole and perfect. He had touched the White Hand, and yet he didn't feel any different. But he didn't waste any time thinking about it. The Black Masks were getting to their feet.

Aiden crawled towards his father's flat cap, which he had dropped after the blast, retrieving a green crystal from inside. He looked down the side of the stone pyramid, searching and spotting Mr. Quick with his cohorts at the bottom of the stone pyramid. Their eyes met, and the masked man stood, whipping out his Ruijen Staff and preparing to charge.

However, Aiden's next move made Mr. Quick pause. Aiden pointed the green stone straight ahead, almost like he was preparing to fire a charged attack with it. Mr. Quick cocked his head to one side, almost in a mocking fashion, as if Aiden didn't know what he was doing.

But something was wrong. Mr. Quick froze, tightening his grip on his Ruijen, which twisted and torqued in his hand. He was struggling, trying to keep hold, but it finally slipped free, flying at top speed towards the crest of the pyramid and Aiden.

Aiden caught the staff in mid air, looking down on the masked man. He couldn't see Mr. Quick's facial expression, but imagined it was one of utter astonishment. Aiden twisted the staff and swung it indiscriminately towards the Garden's palatial structures.

Dozens of black pellets whistled through the air, striking two artistic marble columns that held up one of the terraces. The pellets exploded, leveling the structures in an instant, collapsing the terrace on top of No-Neck and Lanky.

Aiden didn't stop there. He swung again at another stone structure, where several more stunned Goons stared on. They too were slow on the uptake and plummeted to the ground as the monuments were demolished. Ellis dove for safety next to the pyramid's plinth as debris rained over them.

Standis wheeled Simone out of harm's way to the opposite side of the pyramid as Flair continued her ferocious attack, firing jets of red at falling Goons and Black Masks. Musclehead jumped to their defense, leaping over one hundred feet through the air, landing next to Flair. His staff ricocheted off Flair's left hand shield as Fats, who was incredibly fast for his size, advanced from the other side, deflecting her rapid-fire blasts with his staff.

Fats' action saved his comrades from Flair's bombardment and several Goons jumped at this opportunity to retreat to the exit.

"*Brothers!*" Ellis screamed out. "What are you doing? Your lives and your future are here! Take care of each other! *We are all we have!*"

A few Goons froze in their tracks while others continued to scramble towards the aquarium corridor. Fuzz, Pug, and another tall Goon stared at each other. Ellis' words seemed to inspire them.

"*We're all we have!*" they said to one another. "GOON SQUAD!" roared throughout the chamber, as a half-dozen of the retreating Goons came charging back.

"The boy is the true threat!" Man-Child shouted to his fellow Goons. "Get the boy!"

The host of Goons, joined by Fats, ran straight towards the marble pyramid and leapt upon it at full speed. To Aiden's surprise, their collective force was enough to shake the entire structure. Aiden crashed to his chest and watched the Ruijen roll across the marble surface until with a—*click!*—twin streams of white energy screamed forth from both ends of the staff, slicing uninhibited across the underground garden and into two waterfalls in opposite corners.

It was the loudest sound Aiden, Flair, and Simone had ever heard. An ear-splitting crackle filled the arena as two metallic structures hidden behind the waterfalls glowed orange and exploded, spitting white-hot metal into the air. The garden hadn't yet stopped shaking from the explosion when the wreckage rained from above.

"Move out, Flair!" Aiden yelled, watching a searing chunk of metallic debris heading towards her. She leapt out of the way, as did Musclehead, just as it collided at the base of the pyramid.

Everything was happening so fast, Aiden had almost forgot the Goons were still coming for him. A frightening sound roared throughout the cavern as torrents of water gushed from overhead, pouring from the two giant holes in the ceiling where the waterfalls had once been pleasantly splashing.

Pug, Fuzz, Fats, and the other Goons were undeterred, still climbing for Aiden, who had recovered the Ruijen Staff and swung the energy beam towards his attackers. Pug took the full brunt of the beam in his chest and launched off the platform, soaring over the heads of Goons and Black Masks, landing hundred feet away in the branches of a tall tree.

Aiden swung again. Man-Child flattened himself against the steps, leaving Fats a sitting duck. The beam flashed where it struck, and Fats went bouncing down the stone steps like a giant beach ball.

A splashing sound filled Aiden's ears and he looked down where Fats had fallen, realizing. Water was everywhere, rapidly rising. Mackleford's Garden was flooding.

Aiden pressed a button to deactivate the energy beams and dashed to the other side of the pyramid where Simone had been. Dr. Standis was pulling Simone's wheelchair up the side of the pyramid and Aiden descended the steps, aiming the Ruijen.

"Did you give it to her?" Aiden shouted, barely able to hear himself over the roar of the water.

Standis mumbled to himself, staring in horror at the amazing destruction surrounding them like a man who was in over his head.

"The cure, Doctor!" Aiden barked again, tapping Standis with the Ruijen Staff.

But Standis was at a loss for words. He walked backwards, slipped awkwardly off the step, and splashed into the rising water. He didn't look back as he swam for his life.

"I did it," Simone said. She held up the hypodermic needle before tossing it and rubbing her arm. "He dropped the needle and…I think I found a vein, like a blood test, right? But I don't feel any different. It didn't work."

Man-Child and Fuzz were closing in as the water continued to rise, covering five steps of the pyramid. Aiden glanced; Musclehead and Flair were still squaring off, now on a crumbling terrace beneath a destroyed statue. Aiden rolled Simone in that direction, towards the backside of the second step and froze. Ellis Vicartan stood above him on the capstone.

"Brothers, he is mine!" Ellis shouted to the Goons, squaring his shoulders towards Aiden. In his hand was a blue Ruijen Staff and with a flick of his wrist, activated it with a loud hum.

Aiden looked at the Goons standing on the marble step just below him, blocking any avenue to escape.

Aiden held Mr. Quick's staff in front of him, trying to reactivate the white beams at Ellis, but there was no reaction. Ellis leapt down to Aiden's step and landed with a shudder and separated his staff into two short batons.

With one swing of Ellis's arm, Aiden went sailing. Before he knew it, a heavy boot pinned him to the ground, and Ellis began hammering on him. It was all Aiden could do to hold onto the staff for protection, when a resounding—*SNAP!*—split Mr. Quick's staff open.

From within the staff, amongst a multitude of black pellets, a bright green crystal rolled out onto the marble step of the pyramid, and the structure began to tremble.

So, you placed a green inside?" Ellis said. "So that's how you drew it away from Quick."

The black pellets were spilling onto the marble step below, each exploding with a loud *BOOM!* Ellis seemed to be ignoring this, his eyes locked onto Aiden's.

"You think you can manipulate my weapons against me?" Ellis snarled. "I created them, you imbecile!"

Ellis raised his staff for a deathblow and Aiden caught one of the black pellets before it rolled over the side of the step and threw it into Ellis's face. The resulting explosion was enough to distract Ellis from his attack.

Aiden sat up and rushed, shouldering Ellis in the ribs and trying to knock him off the step, but Ellis was so strong he hardly budged. He continued rubbing black soot out of his eyes, cursing and staggering. Unaware of where he was going, he crashed into Aiden and they both toppled over the side, along with something else that had slipped out of Aiden's pocket.

The green crystal—the one Aiden used to take the Mr. Quick's Ruijen—fell into the rising water, sinking through the surface, creating bubbling ripples that began to slosh back and forth, larger and larger.

"Aiden! Help!"

Aiden turned to see Flair in trouble, kneeling on the top terrace beneath two red shields that were weakening under Musclehead's pounding assault. He swung a vicious blow with his Ruijen Staff and Flair's shield broke. She went skidding across the terrace floor, which was beginning to flood.

Aiden was in a quandary: Simone, nearly overtaken by the rising water at the step below, Musclehead was advancing on Flair, as giant waves rose and crashed all around. Aiden turned his attention to Simone, who, while craning her neck to keep her face above water, had fallen out of the wheelchair and into the water.

"Use your arms Simmy, swim over to me!"

Aiden tried to make his way to his sister. Having never swam in his life, the best he could do was wade along the step until his foot finally lost contact with the surface, and he slipped into the water. Simone, however, had taken swimming lessons and was kicking her legs wildly, working her way over to…

Wait? Aiden thought. *Simone is kicking her legs?*

"Simmy! You can move your legs!"

"I can?" Simone looked curiously at her legs underneath the water, and suddenly realizing: "I CAN! MY LEGS WORK! AIDEN! I'M CURED!"

Simone's scream exploded like dynamite, but it wasn't harsh or frightening. In fact, it sounded jubilant, exultant, heroic! A euphoric *WOOOOOHOOOOOO* echoed throughout the domed garden.

At the moment she screamed, something happened to the remaining Goons. Each of them swooned on the spot, toppling wherever they stood and crashing into the water. Ellis's face wore a shocked expression before he fell, splashing face first, out cold.

Aiden grabbed Simone's fingertips and pulled her into a hug. Her face was already clearing, the gray skin diminishing. She was still kicking her legs, hitting Aiden in the shins and knees.

"Mission accomplished!" Aiden said. "Now, let's get Flair and get the hell outta here!"

He turned, searching for Flair but instead spotted a pale face bobbing in the water. Rico, with Mackleford's limp body hefted across his broad shoulders, looked calm despite the water nearing the ceiling of the domed roof. The two met eyes briefly.

"This isn't finished yet, Mr. Johnson," Rico called to Aiden. And then the alabaster face disappeared underneath the surface of the water.

And as if on cue, Flair was swimming over to them, a smile on her face. "What was that?" she said to Simone. "It knocked out all the uglies!"

"It was me," Simone squealed in delight, "because I can swim! I mean I can kick my…I mean my legs! They work! I can move my legs, Flair!"

Flair let out a whoop of her own, laughed and jump-splashed into a hug with Simone. Flair kissed her sister on the cheek, which showed patches of smooth, unblemished skin.

"Your face!" Flair sighed, kissing Simone again. "I missed this face!"

Another minute of celebrating, they realized they were the only ones still conscious and the water was still rising. Suddenly there was movement, and soft splashing sounds echoed around them; Goons were emerging from underneath. It was an eerie feeling, sitting amongst those floating bodies, with the domed roof rising closer and closer.

"How are we going to get out of here?" Simone asked.

There didn't seem to be a ready answer. They stared at each other and at their unfavorable circumstances. Their own ragged breathing was all they could hear, and how much longer would they hear that?

"There!" Aiden shouted. "I see—" and he sprang away through the water, doing his best impersonation of a swimmer. He was gone just for a moment and returned holding something shiny.

"I believe this is yours," Aiden said, handing the channel gun to Flair. Flair smiled, ripping two red crystals from her glove. She slotted them into the channel gun, shooting one into the archway atop of the pyramid, almost engulfed by the rising water, and firing the other through a large hole in the splintered dome.

Aiden couldn't see what the crystal had made contact with, but Flair's smile indicated that she had a star channel.

"Simmy, grab a hold," Flair said.

The three of them clutched one another in a giant hug. Bloodied, soaking wet, freezing, they rose from the water, ascending the star channel. They whisked through the cracked dome and into what looked like a giant concrete riverbed. Aiden looked down at the domed ceiling, realizing where they were.

"The river we saw on our way in," he proclaimed. They landed on the slanted cement riverbed. "That's where all of that water came from."

"Who cares? How do I look?" Simone said. Through the remnants of dead skin, Aiden could see Simone's cheeks were pink and flushed. The scales around her neck were subsiding, shrinking back into her skin.

"Excellent, Simmy," Aiden said, climbing out of the riverbed and reaching his hand out to help Flair and Simone. "You did great in there. Never been prouder of you. You too, Flair. You had them on the run."

"Wait, where's the thing?" Simone said. "The Song? Is it lost?"

"Aiden destroyed it, Simmy," Flair said. "You must've missed it. That's what set Mackleford off."

"No, I didn't," Aiden said. "It's right here." He retrieved a burlap sack from his jacket, reached inside, and pulled out the Song of Solomon. "How about that? Not even wet."

Flair was stunned.

"B-but I *saw* you destroy it. How…"

"That wasn't the *real* Song of Solomon," Aiden said. "That was the fake, the one hanging up in Granny's Garden."

"The fake one? But how did you—"

"Nefflin did it. I had him radio Margaret after we left Borneo. She overnight mailed to Denver. By the time we landed, it was already there. Nefflin left it in the trunk of the rental car."

"Mailed?" Flair said, a confounded look on her face. "Overnight?"

"Yes. The crazy thing about it, the Song…I could kinda feel when it wasn't nearby. I wanted to keep it in the car, but I figured if I could tell it wasn't there, so could Mackleford. Knew I needed to keep it close," he said, patting his jacket pocket.

"You didn't *really* think he was gonna destroy it, did you?" Simone scoffed, performing a cartwheel in front of them. "Ain't that thing like a thousand years old or something?"

"Wait? *You* knew?"

"It's *three-thousand years,* Simmy, and of course she knew. Simmy was part of the plan. I didn't know if the Goons would be there, what with the Banshee and all, but in case they had some ear plugs or something…anyway all I needed was a distraction."

"But the Banshee didn't work! They were ready for that!"

"I just said that, sunshine," Aiden sighed. "Try and keep up. I just needed Simone to distract everyone so I could get the red crystal under my hat."

"That's why you looked sick the whole time we were in there?" Flair said, incensed. "Why weren't you glowing red?"

"I kept it wrapped in the burlap. Still made me sick though."

"And why didn't you tell *me*?"

Aiden gave a dramatic roll of his eyes and looked at Simone, who giggled. "We've been through this already," he sighed.

"Need to know info," Simone said, patting Flair on the back.

"Plus you're a bad actress," Aiden said. "You would have given us away."

"I'm not a bad actress!" Flair shouted.

"We remember your Scarlett O'Hara from your eighth grade play," Simone said, mimicking a horrible Southern accent. *"Frankly my dear, I don't give a damn!"*

"Language, young lady!" Aiden said with mock-reproof, and the two of them laughed.

"Whatever to both of you! You guys stink!"

Simone was still dancing circles around Aiden and Flair like a maniac when there was a sudden tremor. Underfoot, cracks formed along the cement, with mud seeping through them. The three of them froze and without thinking, grabbed each other's hands and sprinted across the campus. Yards away from the bridge, with the ground trembling beneath his feet, Aiden turned back and looked.

The three chess piece-shaped buildings, along with the rest of the campus, were sinking slowly and steadily underground. The glass panes of the Bishop Building shattered; water and mud were swirling around the buildings, oozing between them.

"What happened?" Flair shouted.

"The greens," Aiden replied. "We never retrieved them! Just keep going!"

Aiden felt they weren't in any immediate danger, as they were far from the campus, however he played it safe and retreated across the bridge, where they watched Restoration College continue its descent into the muddy earth. And then, just as suddenly as the tremors started, they stopped.

"They must have ran out of juice," Flair said. "Granny said crystals lose power. But why did everything sink?"

"The foundation of the whole campus was that giant garden," Aiden explained. "It must've collapsed on top of itself."

It took over an hour for the Restoration College campus to sink completely underground, but the Johnsons weren't aware of it. Everything had happened so fast since they arrived, it felt like time was standing still. While Simone was still testing her legs, Aiden and Flair found a patch of grass to relax upon. Lying on their backs, they stared at the cloudy sky, every now and again, looking at the campus to see if it was still sinking. Only the top of the Bishop Building remained visible.

"So, when you say Dad wanted you to stop the Dominion, do you think this is what he had in mind?"

Aiden chuckled. "I don't think Pops knew what I would do, just that I would figure something out."

"So what are you going to figure out about that?" She nodded to the burlap bag lying on Aiden's chest.

"I don't know," Aiden said. "I'll have to think about it. Maybe take it back to Borneo one day. That's the best place to make sure no one gets it again. Or give it back to Margaret."

Flair looked back to the jumble of mud, dirt and broken buildings. "Aiden, do you think he's gone for good? Mackleford, I mean."

Aiden looked at his shoes, filthy and caked in mud, all the while, envisioning the pale face dipping beneath the water with Mackleford across his shoulders, and the final words he said.

This isn't finished yet, Mr. Johnson.

"The only thing I wanna think about right now is how good Towner Pie would taste. It's the thirty-first. The Reading is tomorrow. Since we both hate my driving, let's see if we can hitch a ride back to the airport and find Nefflin."

"Isn't hitching rides dangerous though?"

Aiden laughed. "I'd love to see someone try and mess with you, sunshine."

Aiden couldn't see it as he was watching a puffy cloud drift by, but Flair was beaming.

Before they knew it, the Falconer 8800 was touching down on the Proctor's Landing runway. Nefflin had let Flair and Simone take turns sitting at the controls of the plane while Aiden slept in the cabin. The memories were more vivid than ever, but they didn't wake him. In fact, Aiden had found a strange peace in them, and allowed his mind to indulge in them. As he explained to Flair, "I need to reacquaint myself with *myself.*"

As the plane taxied towards the small hangar at the back of the airport, Aiden awoke, raising his head, hearing conversation coming from the cockpit.

"You're not coming with us?" Flair said in a surprised voice.

"I'll see ya around," Nefflin said. "If ya need a fly, just give ol' Margie a holler."

"But the Reading, Mr. Nefflin?" Simone said. "You're gonna miss it."

"Ne'er been muchuva bookworm. 'Sides, I've heard that thang dozens of times."

"So where are you going?" Flair asked.

"Got m' cash. Got a plane. Think I'll take this Falconer aroun'. Sucker's better'n my house. An' after what we went through, I'm needin' four weeks in Tahiti, 'nother four in Bora Bora. Got a cupl'a ladies I'd like to catch up with."

Aiden fell back into his seat, imagining spending another eight weeks on a plane. The warm fire of his parents' house sounded more inviting right now...

The Johnsons said goodbye to Marcus Nefflin outside the Proctor's Landing train station and changed out of their muddy clothes before settling in on the East Town Shuttle for the short trip. They were the only people on the shuttle, as it was the first of January, and more than likely the entire town had already convened on the House of Gumm for the Reading.

Forty-five minutes later, the shuttle train rumbled out of the tunnel into the wide, sprawling valley, and a bright afternoon sky beamed through the windows. As the shuttle took the horseshoe shaped curve, sunlight glinted into Flair's face. She shielded her eyes as she looked out the window, smiling. Everything was there: the storybook village, the snow-frosted hills, the crescent moon lake. She rushed over to her brother and sister.

"Yo! Wake up. We're here."

Aiden woke, rubbing his eyes and glancing outside the window.

"Simmy, wake up," he said. "We're back. We're in East Town."

It was as if they'd never left. The gorgeous Christmas decorations were still there, twinkling at them from every direction as Aiden, Flair, and Simone walked the empty streets. Aiden was grateful to the plowmen who had cleared the streets of snow and when they arrived at the corner of Melanie Avenue and Twelfth St, they found it jam packed with vehicles. A chorus of chatter and laughter hung over the front garden of the House of Gumm. The Reading was nearly ready.

Inside, the House of Gumm resembled a festival. Stationed throughout the Grand Room and the Tea Room were booths selling memorabilia: miniature replicas of Grand Gallery artifacts, posters and pictures of East Town, models of the House of Gumm, and hats, tee-shirts, and coffee mugs adorned with *I Love Towner Pie*. An aroma of freshly baked desserts and hot cinnamon tea drifted through the misted glass doors where Harold Mimble and the Majors greeted everyone, handing out programs. Inside the Grand Garden,

Big Tank and his BLD staff served drinks and pie to the masses, pushing carts up and down dozens of rows of chairs.

No one paid the Johnsons any mind: they were just three bodies amongst the multitude. There were more people inside the Grand Garden than it seemed possible to hold. People everywhere and anywhere, chattering, laughing, hugging, and smiling. Some sat along the wading pools, twirling fingers in the water, others on planters, pointing and admiring something in the Garden. The three terraces overlooking the patio teemed with the bright faces of teens and pre-teens, and the chairs were nearly filled. The hubbub was beginning to calm as several prominent East Town residents began taking their seats in the front row.

Margaret's sisters entered, sitting with their families. Harold and Anna Mimble sat next to Elsa Majors, Justin Mimble and his wife, along with Jasper Jones and Cecil Badmore. Big Tank left his cart and hustled to sit with his family behind Brett Morris's family in the second row. Aiden noticed there were six empty chairs to Big Tank's left.

Big Tank tapped Brett's mother in front of him, which prompted the others to turn, look at the empty chairs and glance around the Grand Garden. A murmuring of "Gannares" and "Johnson" erupted from their huddle and Aiden understood. These seats were reserved for the Gannares and Johnson families. Nick and Lydia were nowhere in sight. Apparently the entire Gannares family would be no-shows this year.

An enormous roar of applause broke out. Margaret Gumm, tiny thing that she was, had made her appearance, waddling down the center of the patio, clapping along with them and curtsying to the crowd.

"Thank you!" she proclaimed, waving her hands for quiet, but the crowd roared and cheered all the more. "Thank you all! Welcome back to the House of Gumm and the Reading of the Grand Book of Wisdom!"

The applause had just begun to die when a voice cried out from the third terrace. "Hey Granny, you forgot your book!"

Polite laughter erupted, but then quelled as all eyes fell on Margaret. A buzz of concern circulated through the Grand Garden and Margaret looked uncertainly at her audience.

"Here it is!"

All attention turned towards the misted doors. Aiden held the book high over his head, walking down the center aisle. He grinned at Margaret, whose hand had flown over her mouth, staring in absolute shock.

But before Aiden reached her, Simone jumped in front of him, sprinting at top speed towards Margaret. Margaret gripped the armrest of the stone bench to steady herself. Flair caught up with Aiden, looking self-conscious, fiddling with her hair.

"Why do we have to make an entrance?" Flair said under her breath in Aiden's ear. "My hair is atrocious."

Simone barreled into Margaret for a bear hug, and Flair and Aiden soon followed. Most of the crowd seemed unsure of what was going on, but Harold Mimble and Margaret's sisters stood and applauded.

"You did it!" Margaret whispered in Aiden's ear, clutching Simone tight. "But how? How did you?"

Aiden grinned. "Now's probably not the time," he said, accepting a hug from Margaret. "I'll fill you in later."

He handed her the book and they took seats next to Big Tank and the Russo family and a hush fell over the Grand Garden once again. Margaret sat on the small bench in front of the patio and opened her book.

"Wisdom. The greatest of all gifts. The teller of truths, the keeper of peace, the council of the divine, defender of the innocent, healer of all ills, and the guardian of our souls! Treasure wisdom as you would family, and embrace her like an old friend!"

The Reading went by in an instant, and Aiden was only vaguely aware of what Margaret was said. People around the Garden were quoting their favorite parts along with Margaret, and laughing and applauding at certain others. Flair and Simone seemed to hang on every word, but Aiden's mind was on the three empty chairs to his left, wondering.

The following morning, the campanile's chimes rang in the morning as usual. Six A.M. It was still dark outside.

Flair yawned, scratching her head as she wobbled downstairs and headed for the kitchen, tripping over her long pajama pants, when there was a loud knock at the front door.

She opened the door. It was Margaret, holding a tray of hot chocolate and biscuits in her tiny arms, bearing a large handbag slung over her right shoulder.

"Granny? Good morning. What—"

"Oh my, Flair, help me please! This tray is so heavy."

Flair relieved Margaret of the tray as Aiden and Simone rumbled down the stairs.

"Granny!" Simone squealed, running over and jumping into a hug with her.

"What brings you by, Granny?" Aiden said.

Margaret looked at Aiden, biting her lip.

"Now what?" Aiden asked with a look of apprehension.

"I figured we'd talk because I owe you an apology for everything."

Aiden, Flair and Simone practically stumbled over one another, insisting that she owed them no apology, but Margaret held up her hand until they fell silent.

"I *am* apologizing and it's because I should have known this would happen. I've been around too long, and I can hardly complain about the Youngbloods not listening to us Old Timers when I'm practicing foolishness!"

"Granny, you're being too hard—"

"No, Aiden! Don't make excuses for me! I sent you to Jonas hoping he would help, but not telling him you were coming, keeping you in the dark." She broke off, shaking her head angrily. "Your parents would never have sent you across the world without telling you about our long struggle with the Dominion. It was reckless. And so…"

She opened the handbag, extracting a cumbersome file, thick with papers sticking out at all angles.

"My files. Well, Jonas and mine. When my father disappeared to search for the Purity cure, Jonas and I took the reins of the Guild. These were our best strategies."

"But the Dominion is gone, Granny," Simone said. "Mr. Mackleford is dead."

"Maybe he is," Margaret said with mild skepticism, "but the Dominion is more than Mochtier Mackleford, trust me. And now that you are officially Journeymen—"

"I don't think I want to be a Journeyman," Aiden said, and Flair nodded in agreement.

"Sadly, you may not have that choice," she said, handing the files to Aiden. "Prepare for everything."

Aiden looked at Margaret shrewdly, opening his mouth to ask something, but then stopped, shook his head, and changed directions.

"What have you heard from Gloria?"

"I haven't," Margaret said, and Aiden knew she was being honest. "But don't worry, that girl never stays gone for long. She was very worried about you when she left last week. And speaking of which, are you going to tell me what happened out there?"

For the next hour, the Johnsons ate biscuits, drank cocoa, and explained the whole adventure to a spellbound Margaret. After Simone finished the tale with her animated reenactment of the destruction of Restoration College, complete with sound effects and throwing herself airborne at least a dozen times, Margaret cheerfully applauded and gave each of them a hug.

"Well, your return made quite a stir, as I'm sure you're already aware," she said, slinging her handbag over her shoulder. "I should warn you, however, that a few folks down at the BLD are waiting to hear what happened to you three last week."

Aiden and Flair looked at one another with raised eyebrows, but nodded.

"Not everyone in East Town knows about our business," Margaret said. "And for those that do, not everyone agrees with our methods." She walked towards the front door and laid her hand on the doorknob. "Just be careful who you talk to and what you say."

And on that enigmatic note, Margaret excused herself, but not before reminding them to drop by the House of Gumm, where they each had pile of Christmas presents waiting.

"WOOHOO!" Simone shouted, rushing upstairs. "Let's go! I'm first in the bathroom!"

"And then," Flair said, "let's head back to Brooklyn, okay? I really miss *normal insanity*."

"What's the hurry?" Aiden said. "You have a week left for winter break. I got an extra week from Dr. Lee. We could just chill here at home. Brooklyn can wait."

Flair laughed, grinning from ear to ear.

"What?"

"First you're calling Granny *Granny*, now you're calling East Town *home*? What's gotten into you?"

Aiden smirked and shrugged.

THREE DAYS LATER...

The first morning of the excavation project was as frigid as anyone had remembered. The site had been hit with a blizzard for three days, which had kept the workers at home. On the fourth day, the crew arrived, seeing the site for the first time. There was only one remnant remaining from what was a pre-eminent college campus: the rounded top of a building with large panes of cracked glass, jutting through the center of a mound of snow and dirt.

Hours later, men in hard hats scurried about the site, some carrying tools, some carrying rolls of blueprints. Dump trucks, pile drivers, bulldozers were on the move. It was a busy day.

Amidst this activity, a worker made a discovery that caused him to drop his pickax.

"Jackson, you seen this?"

A skinny man wearing an orange hard hat approached his co-worker, a shovel over his shoulder, staring into a gaping hole in the ground.

"Well, how 'bout that? Another one."

"Another one?"

"Yep." The second man removed his hard hat, scratching his bald scalp. "Fourth one we've found. Ain't it something?"

"Definitely. Whatcha make of it?"

"It's like a...gopher hole," Jackson said. "We had lotsa gophers in my backyard when I was kid."

"A full grown man could fit in there. You think a gopher did that?"

"Dunno what it did it, but I'm telling you, I've seen a million gopher holes in my time, and that there's a gopher hole." Jackson looked at his co-worker, shrugging his shoulders. "Something dug its way from underground."

THE END

Made in the USA
Coppell, TX
14 April 2021

53732608R00213